Christopher Fowler is the award-winning author of more than forty novels – including twelve featuring the detectives Bryant and May and the Peculiar Crimes Unit – and short story collections. The recipient of the coveted CWA 'Dagger in the Library' Award for 2015, his most recent books are the Ballard-esque thriller *The Sand Men* and *Bryant & May – London's Glory*. Other works include screenplays, video games, graphic novels and audio plays. His weekly column 'Invisible Ink' runs in the *Independent on Sunday*. He lives in King's Cross, London, and Barcelona.

Visit www.christopherfowler.co.uk

Praise for Christopher Fowler's Bryant & May mysteries

'Quirky and original . . . the relationship between Bryant and May is done brilliantly'
Mark Billingham

'Imagine the *X-Files* with Holmes and Watson in the place of Mulder and Scully, and the books written by P.G. Wodehouse, and you have some idea of the idiosyncratic and distinctly British flavour of the Bryant & May novels'
Black Static

'What Christopher Fowler does so well is to merge the old values with the new . . . he's giving us two for the price of one'
Lee Child

'Fowler, like his crime-solvers, is deadpan, sly, and always unexpectedly inventive'
Entertainment Weekly

'I love the wit and playfulness of the Bryant & May books'
Ann Cleeves

'Invests the traditions of the Golden Age of detective fiction with a tongue-in-cheek post-modernism'
Evening Standard

'One of the quirkiest and most ingenious pleasures to be found in the genre: atmospheric, sardonically funny and craftily suspenseful'
Barry Forshaw

'Witty, sinuous and darkly comedic storytelling from a Machiavellian jokester'
Guardian

'Atmospheric, hugely beguiling and as filled with tricks and sleights of hand as a magician's sleeve'
Joanne Harris

'Mr Fowler has no trouble convincing readers that London is a place where the occult lives on, the dead might rise, and a detective might absently pluck a kitten out of his pocket. Their very credibility puts quaint old Bryant and May in a class of their own'
The New York Times

'Quirky, touching, profound and utterly original'
Peter James

'Slow burning, adroitly plotted, with a distinct atmosphere . . . goes against the grain of most detective fiction and is the better for it'
Daily Telegraph

'Devilishly clever . . . mordantly funny . . . sometimes heartbreakingly moving'
Val McDermid

'Exciting and thoughtful . . . one of our most unorthodox and entertaining writers'
Sunday Telegraph

'Bryant and May are hilarious. *Grumpy Old Men* does *CSI* with a twist of Dickens!'
Karen Marie Moning

'Witty, charming, intelligent, wonderfully atmospheric and enthusiastically plotted'
The Times

'A proper old-fashioned puzzle. You feel pleased when you spot stuff. This is Golden age detective story-writing'
Kate Mosse

Also by Christopher Fowler

The Bryant & May Novels

FULL DARK HOUSE
THE WATER ROOM
SEVENTY-SEVEN CLOCKS
TEN-SECOND STAIRCASE
WHITE CORRIDOR
THE VICTORIA VANISHES
BRYANT & MAY ON THE LOOSE
BRYANT & MAY OFF THE RAILS
BRYANT & MAY AND THE MEMORY OF BLOOD
BRYANT & MAY AND THE INVISIBLE CODE
BRYANT & MAY – THE BLEEDING HEART
BRYANT & MAY – THE BURNING MAN
BRYANT & MAY – STRANGE TIDE

The Bryant & May short stories

BRYANT & MAY – LONDON'S GLORY

Other Novels

ROOFWORLD
RUNE
RED BRIDE
DARKEST DAY
SPANKY
PSYCHOVILLE
DISTURBIA
SOHO BLACK
CALABASH
BREATHE
HELL TRAIN
PLASTIC
NYCTOPHOBIA
THE SAND MEN

Short Stories

CITY JITTERS
CITY JITTERS TWO
THE BUREAU OF LOST SOULS
SHARPER KNIVES
FLESH WOUNDS
PERSONAL DEMONS
UNCUT
THE DEVIL IN ME
DEMONIZED

Graphic Novel

MENZ NSANA

Memoir

PAPERBOY
FILM FREAK

BRYANT & MAY
The Burning Man

CHRISTOPHER FOWLER

BANTAM BOOKS

LONDON • TORONTO • SYDNEY • AUCKLAND • JOHANNESBURG

TRANSWORLD PUBLISHERS
61–63 Uxbridge Road, London W5 5SA
www.transworldbooks.co.uk

Transworld is part of the Penguin Random House group of companies whose addresses can be found at global.penguinrandomhouse.com

First published in Great Britain in 2015 by Doubleday
an imprint of Transworld Publishers
Bantam edition published 2016

A CIP catalogue record for this book
is available from the British Library.

ISBN 9780857502353

Typeset in 11/13pt Sabon by Kestrel Data, Exeter, Devon.
Printed and bound by Clays Ltd, Bungay, Suffolk.

Penguin Random House is committed to a sustainable future for our business, our readers and our planet. This book is made from Forest Stewardship Council® certified paper.

1 3 5 7 9 10 8 6 4 2

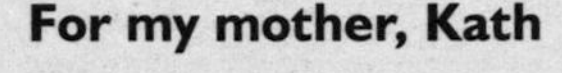

For my mother, Kath

'If you do not want to dwell with evil-livers, do not live in London'

Richard of Devizes, 1177

'I see no reason why gunpowder treason should ever be forgot'

Traditional

ACKNOWLEDGEMENTS

I've always felt that the Bryant & May series was about outsiders who, in their own way, are actually at the freethinking heart of London. We live in a complex city often described as a collection of unique villages, which is probably why so many of its residents behave with the quiddity of innocents seeing off predators.

Among those inside-outsiders are the people who help and inspire me to keep delving further, from Simon Taylor and Kate Miciak, my brilliant editors, to Mandy Little, James Wills, Howard Morhaim and Meg Davis, my perspicacious agents, Kate Samano and Richenda Todd on copy, and PRs Lynsey Dalladay and Sally Wray.

Thanks also to Mike and Lou, who every year head to Lewes for a night of devilry, and helped to provide the idea for this book. The character of Joanna Papis is real – beware of befriending an author!

Thanks go out also to the book clubs, booksellers and readers who have kept this series going from strength to strength; I simply could not do it without you.

For more on the Bryant & May novels, visit
www.christopherfowler.co.uk

Peculiar Crimes Unit
The Old Warehouse
231 Caledonian Road
London N1 9RB

STAFF ROSTER FOR MONDAY 31 OCTOBER

Raymond Land, Unit Chief
Arthur Bryant, Senior Detective
John May, Senior Detective
Janice Longbright, Detective Sergeant
Dan Banbury, Crime Scene Manager/InfoTech
Jack Renfield, Sergeant
Fraternity DuCaine, Detective Constable
Meera Mangeshkar, Detective Constable
Colin Bimsley, Detective Constable
Giles Kershaw, Forensic Pathologist (off-site)
Crippen, staff cat

EXCERPT FROM A SPEECH GIVEN BY MR ARTHUR BRYANT TO THE CITY OF LONDON POLICE CRIME DIRECTORATE AT THE GUILDHALL

'Before I start, can I ask you to look around you at this beautiful building? After eight hundred years it's still the home of the City of London Corporation, the powerhouse at the heart of the world's leading financial centre.

'I search the room and see a great many youthful faces. At my age, everyone is youthful. Some of you look positively prepubescent. So, as the most senior detective at London's Peculiar Crimes Unit, may I be indulged for a moment, and give you a brief history lesson about the city you've been entrusted to look after?

'In Tudor times London was still a box. It was tightly contained by walls on three sides, the fourth being the River Thames. This walled city was stitched into the pattern of its ancient Roman boundaries, and could be entered by only seven gates. London's main road was Cheapside, which ran out to the Shambles in the west and Cornhill in the east.

'It was a city bristling with church spires, the greatest of which was St Paul's, which collapsed after being struck by lightning in 1561. It had two royal palaces, Baynard and Bridewell, built for Henry the Eighth. It had colleges and law courts, bowling alleys and tennis courts, cockpits and theatres. And this is how it would have stayed without the conflagration that transformed it, the Great Fire of 1666.

'The city recovered with incredible speed. Just five years later, over nine thousand new houses and public buildings had been completed. The new middle-class residents wanted a separate residential district and moved west, and so London rolled like treacle across the land, leaving the financiers stuck in the old squared-off section, which became known as the Square Mile, the original City of London. Now most of the walls have gone and fewer than seven thousand people live here, but nearly half a million of us commute to it each day. You have eight hundred and fifty officers taking care of this tiny plot of land. That's a massively disproportionate ratio compared to anywhere else in the country. Why?

'Because the City of London is still what it has always been: a money factory. A 24/7/365 financial dynamo. And that's why most of you aren't strolling the streets with truncheons but working in offices to prevent money laundering, fraud and corruption. There's only a handful of private owners in the Square Mile, and most of them don't even live here. They don't need you looking after them. So, why do you need the Peculiar Crimes Unit?

'Because we perform a unique, invisible service. In many ways, we operate more than half a century behind the rest of you, because that's when our sphere of operations was first decided. We're not constrained by your rules. We use our own judgement. Our task is to prevent public disorder. That includes investigating any serious crimes that take place in public spaces. Because if we don't find fast solutions, the city loses that most quicksilver of all intangibles: confidence. And without the light of confidence we plunge into the darkness of uncertainty, which leads to financial ruin. There's nothing more frightening than watching what people do when they start to lose money.

'Which is why I'm asking you to increase the PCU's funding in this coming year. Because our unit is buying you something which no one else can provide in London: stability and peace of mind in increasingly unpredictable times.'

MEMO FROM RAYMOND LAND TO ALL STAFF

(*See attached.*) Well, we all know how well that speech went down. Like a French kiss at a family reunion. Our budget got slashed by nearly a third. I had no idea Bryant was going to bring out the begging bowl. It's just not done. It didn't help that he forgot the rest of his speech and then sat in the mayor's wife's lap.

Serious crimes in and around the Square Mile are down because the residential population is falling. This might have something to do with the fact that every half-decent flat in the area has been snapped up by war criminals shovelling their loose change into safe havens. Nobody lives here any more. The lights are going off in the Square Mile, so the thinking goes that we can get by on less.

What does this mean to you lot?

It means there'll be cutbacks on our outsourced services, effective immediately. A wage freeze, and no more talk of performance-related bonuses. No more sending your clothes over to forensics to be dry-cleaned, no more running up kebab tabs on stakeouts and no more pawning items from the Evidence Room until payday. It's the end of transport allowances, petty-cash chits and any other salary-enhancing initiatives your crafty little minds can come up with. In fact, I distrust the word 'initiative' altogether; it only leads to trouble. I don't want anyone here thinking for themselves.

But remember this: we are in charge of London.

The Metropolitan Police Service may get to play with helicopters, but they also do all the paperwork and hold all the management meetings, which is why it takes them six hours to log a simple case of abusive texting. The City of London Police fanny about with PowerPoint presentations outlining initiatives that don't work, and get to shift decimal points around sorting out cybercrime with our dopey European cousins. But it's the Peculiar Crimes Unit that prevents panic on the streets. We handle the cases that have the capacity to bring this city down. Never forget that. When it comes to preventing public disorder and stopping our polluted, litter-strewn metropolis from falling apart at the seams, we're on the bloody front line. It's not our public-school twit of a mayor or his cronies who carry the can, it's us. This isn't a job, it's a vocation, and nuns don't get paid so we should count ourselves lucky. I'm sorry, but being underappreciated really gets my goat.

Right, time for a bit of housekeeping:

Halloween is not a pagan festival that entitles you to a day off, despite what Mr Bryant may tell you. It's a retail opportunity created by the Yanks to flog orange plastic buckets to children. You'll have to settle for proper holidays like Boxing Day. If this country had stayed Catholic we'd be taking every other day of the year off like the Frogs, and look at the bloody mess they're in.

Now that we're under City of London jurisdiction may I remind you that we are once more a covert division, which means no more Facebook, Twitter or blogging about how wretched your lives are, no selfies at crime scenes and absolutely no more privately published volumes of candid memoirs. I'm not mentioning any names, but you know who I mean. The less the public know about us, the less stick we'll get. Try not to draw attention to yourselves. When you head off to the pub together in your matching black unit jackets you look like an out-of-shape version of the *Reservoir Dogs* poster, and given the public's current antipathy towards us I'd rather not encourage them to stick burning bags of shit through our letter box again, if you don't mind.

If any of you are wondering why the general public hates us so much at the moment, may I refer you to last week's article in *Hard News*, which appeared under the headline 'Why We Call Them Pigs', in which we were described as 'a textbook example of wasted taxpayers' money'. The tabloid hack behind this hatchet job was transferred to the opinion page from the fashion section, and was upset because we banned her from our press conferences. She had the nerve to describe me as 'vindictive'. Unfortunately it's illegal to slap her in prison without a motive, but if anyone feels like running a check on her vehicle registration we might be able to get her on expired tax and make her life utterly miserable.

The entrance hall's visual-recognition system has been removed after Mr Bryant proved it could be cheated by the addition of a hat. For now it's back to using a secure code. I've taped it on to the wall above the machine.

Our workmen, the two Daves, are staying on after discovering that the first-floor interview room has no central support joists, so make sure you keep fat witnesses away from the middle of the building. They're also trying to open up the basement area, so watch it as you come through the front door, particularly if you've been drinking. Longbright buzzed in the Pizza Hut delivery boy the other night and lost her Napoletana.

The Police Federation's outing to the Museum of London's exhibition 'Living History: Senior Citizens Recall London in the 1950s' will take place on 25 October, although I understand that Mr Bryant will not be coming as he does not yet regard the 1950s as history.

Heaven knows I'm no intellectual but I enjoy an Agatha Christie, and I know some of the 'eggheads' among us attended the British Library's 'Criminal Minds' dinner last week. They want their napkin rings back. I don't care who it was.

The good news is, the city is really quiet at the moment and we can put our feet up for once. Apparently some bloke called Samuel Johnson said something about being tired of London. Well, I couldn't agree with him more; I'm sick to death of it, so I'm going on holiday next week. I'm taking a watercolour course on the Isle of Wight, and if anyone else fancies using up their outstanding leave I suggest you get your request forms in double-quick. There's nothing happening out there. Make the most of it.

1

RIOT!

London. The protracted summer lately over, and the bankers sitting in Threadneedle Street, returned from their villas in Provence and Tuscany. Relentless October weather. As much water in the streets as if the tide had newly swelled from the Thames, and it would not be wonderful to find a whale beached beneath Holborn Viaduct, the traffic parting around it like an ocean current. Umbrellas up in the soft grey drizzle, and insurrection in the air.

Riots everywhere. Riots outside the Bank of England and around St Paul's Cathedral. Protestors swelling on Cheapside and Poultry and Lombard Street. Marchers roaring on Cornhill and Eastcheap and Fenchurch Street. Barricades on Cannon Street and across London Bridge. Police armoured and battened down in black and yellow like phalanxes of tensed wasps. Chants and megaphones and the drone of choppers overhead.

Hurled fire, catapulted bricks, shattering glass and the blast of water hoses. It was as if, after a drowsy, sluggish summer, the streets had undergone spontaneous combustion.

It had taken just one match to ignite this inferno, going by the name of Mr Dexter Cornell. A gentleman first fattened by fine living, then driven to flesh and bone by fear and failure. A partner in the Findersbury Private Bank of Crutched Friars until he bankrupted it. A banker, then, that bogeyman of the early twenty-first century, a Thug of Threadneedle Street, purportedly the very worst of his kind, for he arrogantly gambled with other people's money and lost. And because his board of elderly directors got wind of his dealings they were able to protect themselves, and so Mr Cornell was parting company with the bank to the grudging approval of both sides, taking away a tidy fortune of several millions and leaving behind the acrid stink of insider trading.

At which point the public, in one of its periodic fits of outrage, discovered his misdeeds and took against him, and the City of London erupted. Fingers were pointed in the press, questions were asked in the House, but nothing at all was done, and so the populace abandoned its frog-chorus of complaint and got up off its collective arse to make its feelings known by burning down a few buildings and looting some computer showrooms.

As the banners were hoisted the police arrived, barriers were erected and the kettling began. The incandescent crowds spilled into the roads like champagne from an uncorked bottle, and the TV pundits immediately started their newsroom analyses. And once more, as had happened so many times in the past, the City of London found itself on fire.

He had been walking in the drizzle all evening.

After slipping off the kerb crossing Farringdon Road, it became obvious that he would not be able to walk much further. By the time he arrived at the hostel behind Clerkenwell Green he was hobbling badly, and his ankle was turning black.

Earlier in the week, a rough sleeper he'd spoken to a couple of times before had told him that he might find a short-notice bed here, but as the girl behind the scratched Plexiglas counter shield searched her monitor, he knew he would have no luck. She looked harassed and empathetic, as if she was the one who might end up in a shop doorway tonight, not him. She was wearing a pink plastic Hello Kitty brooch on her sweater.

'You've left it a bit too late, love,' she said, still searching her spreadsheet. The colour was turned up too high on the monitor, bathing her features in an odd shade of mauve, but as she studied the columns, trying to juggle the spaces in her head, he could tell she was genuinely anxious to help him. 'We always fill up earlier at the end of the weekend. There aren't so many shops open on Sundays so people are forced outside more, and they tend to get worn out just wandering around. The last bed went a few minutes ago.'

'Are you sure you've got nothing?' he asked. 'I was told you usually find extra spaces.'

'Was it the one I saw you talking to outside the other night?'

'Yeah. I don't know his name.'

'Well, he's a bit weird. I've seen him hanging around here, looking for someone to talk to. You shouldn't trust him. There's a lot of troubled lads like him about. We used to keep two or three beds spare for busy nights, but Health and Safety stopped us. I'm really sorry.'

'Is there anywhere else around here?'

She sat back from the screen and checked her printed lists. 'Normally I'd say the Barbican or St George's up by Aldgate, but I know they're full tonight because I had to call them earlier.' She was new to the job, he could tell. For a moment he actually thought she was about to get upset. He knew he didn't fit the usual profile. 'Sorry, what are you going to do?' she asked.

'Don't worry, I'll find somewhere to shelter tonight and come back tomorrow.'

'Please do.' She pulled out a drawer and slipped a card under the Plexiglas. 'Ask for me, Karin Scott. I'm part-time but I'll be on tomorrow night. OK?'

'Thanks, Karin.' He didn't volunteer his name.

'Tell you what, if you write down your details I'll try to make sure you get a place tomorrow.' She pushed another card and a Biro under the window.

'I don't like to give out my details.'

'Then how can I save you a bed, love?'

Reluctantly, he scrawled on the back of the card and returned it.

'Is that all?' she said. '"F. Weeks"?'

'Well, I'm not exactly in a position to pick up my emails,' he replied with a touch of bitterness.

'Sorry,' she said again. Judging by the rate at which she kept apologizing, he felt sure she wouldn't last long at the front desk. The first crazy street-lifer who hammered on the counter shield would probably finish her off. 'Is that F for Frank?'

'No,' he said. 'Freddie. Freddie Weeks.' He limped away before she could detain him any longer. Karin was still in that early stage of her job when she thought she could befriend the homeless people she liked and maybe find some way around the rules to help them, but he knew that she would have to raise a barrier against him sooner or later. Getting involved would mean breaking council rules and losing her job.

The streets were wet and deserted. Tomorrow was Halloween, but it would be happening somewhere else, out in the suburbs, where mothers and fathers were preparing to shepherd their children around the neighbourhood in fancy dress, in imitation of the American custom of trick or treat. It seemed unlikely to take place anywhere around here; there were no children.

Clerkenwell was the habitat of the single executive, and no lights showed in the minimalist apartments that had been newly carved from warehouses and factories. There was no one to whom he could turn, and nowhere he could go.

He was tired of walking around the city, tired of being forced to take a few pence wherever he could in order to survive another night. Passing another restaurant window where slender girls sat sipping white wine beneath coppery lampshades, he could no longer remember his old way of life. What was it like to go out for a drink and not check your change all the time? Friends vanished like dogs before thunderstorms the moment things went wrong and you stopped being flush.

Below and to the east lay the city's financial district. The dense cloud base was the colour of bad milk, but something flickered gold closer to the rooftops. Drawn to the brightness, he limped in its direction.

It took him half an hour to reach the source of the light, and what he saw made him forget the pain.

Open fires were glowing and crackling in the middle of the road. A melted yellow 'KEEP LEFT' bollard drooped like a collapsed cake over a traffic island. The front of a Pret A Manger was boarded up, its walls blackened with soot. In the distance he glimpsed protestors in white plastic masks running and yelling between the buildings, then vanishing within the turbulent movement of the shadows. It was as if the threat of a truly anarchic Halloween had finally been realized. Everyone was on the move. Only the lemon-coloured Hi-Vis jackets of the police remained immobile, evenly spaced across the road, a human ring of steel.

Like an avatar in a video game he was forced from one route to another by the warning signs, the metal barriers, the plastic cordons. He knew that after two weeks on the street, rough sleepers developed a frayed grey look that repelled the public and attracted police attention, but there was one more thing he still had to do.

The filigreed canopies of Leadenhall Market were sectioned off by yellow police tape as if marked for demolition, so he cut down to Fenchurch Street, making his way east until he reached the slender avenue called Crutched Friars. Just ahead, beyond the low-slung railway bridge, was the entrance to the bank. Its wide grey marble doorway, stepped and recessed, was carpeted with flattened cardboard cartons. Pulling a black nylon pod from his backpack, he unfolded a thin sleeping bag and prepared to bed down for the night under London's warrior skies.

2

COCKTAIL

Before the day dawned, the air around the Royal Exchange and the Bank of England still held the acid tang of burned varnish, rubber and charcoal, just as it had after the Blitz and the City of London IRA bomb of 1993.

The protestors had been dispersed for now, but the steel police barriers remained in place. The various groups eyed each other from a wary distance. One subset known as Make Capitalism History had attempted to pitch camp in Cannon Street, while members of the official Occupy movement were still amicably negotiating with City of London officers, standing around with cardboard cups of coffee like technicians on a film set. A newer, brasher protest outfit calling itself Break the Banks was attracting a younger membership, thanks to its tactic of planning flash-mob demos via social-networking sites. A smaller, more violent splinter group, Disobey, hung back in the shadows of the buildings. They had been denied official recognition and were now arguing among themselves about the best way to be effective. Unfortunately, they couldn't agree on who was allowed to speak.

The police had adopted a bait-and-switch approach in their determination to keep all of the demonstrators from returning at the same time, but just after first light the main groups started to drift back into the same areas they had filled the night before. To make matters worse it was now officially Halloween, a time when it was understood – at least by civilians – that wild spirits would be tolerated and even encouraged. But there was a danger that mere mafficking would turn to something nastier and less treatable.

Before the rush hour had even started a crowd of several hundred people had formed, and would not be dispersed. Some carried placards bearing photographs of Dexter Cornell, the banker upon whom their hatred had found a focus. The chanting began, and as special-interest groups from around Europe (plus a branch from Canada and another from Venezuela) were disgorged from Bank and Monument tube stations to descend upon the Square Mile, the City of London police wearily realized that they were likely to have another grinding day of disobedience on their hands. Every move they made would be recorded, analysed and denigrated by a hostile press, most of whom could see which way the wind was blowing and were taking the side of the aggrieved public. The police hoped the protests had reached their peripeteia, but the demonstrators expected the same thing from an opposite viewpoint, and had the city's turbulent history on their side. Tonight, they felt sure, the time was right for the forces of anarchy to overwhelm those of law and order.

It was, everyone agreed, a right bloody mess.

Crutched Friars is a short, narrow road capped by a dark railway bridge at one end. It houses a couple of pubs, a coffee shop and a handful of financial institutions, one of which is the Findersbury Private Bank. The bank had been closed over the weekend, so the protestors had not assembled outside it, but as it prepared to open its doors for its final week the mob instinctively made its way over there, on the hunt for Dexter Cornell and his cowardly co-conspirators.

One of the protestors was a fake. He had adopted the name of Flannery, and as he prepared to make his move, he knew that he would have to time it just right.

There were no suspended black eyes that he could see, although there had to be some CCTV globes tucked around somewhere, so he stayed in the shadows beneath the railway bridge on Crutched Friars, smoking nervously until it was time to act. The sky was so grey with cloud that it seemed unlikely to ever get light. Thick black smoke unfurled like funeral ribbons above the roof of the nearest building, and he could hear angry shouting in the distance. Moving anxiously from one foot to the other, he waited for the right moment.

Here came the protestors, pouring into the far end of the street. The police were nowhere to be seen. He darted forward, unzipping his tool bag as he ran. He stayed in the gloom that bordered the edge of the buildings until he reached the entrance of the bank, then lit the bottle and threw it.

The glass smashed, but at first he thought the cocktail had failed to ignite. Reaching the protection of the railway arch once more, he looked back and saw a harsh saffron light pulsing out from the doorway. It grew brighter by the second, and covered the entire entrance by the time the first protestors arrived.

Riot police were pouring in from the Armed Response Vehicles parked in Seething Lane, so he dropped back beneath the railway arch and made his way down to the river, loping through the shadows. The first part of his plan was now complete. It was time to start making arrangements for tomorrow, and the day after. By the end of the week, he felt sure, the whole of the City would be engulfed in flames.

3

PYROPHOBIA

The match sizzled, flared and settled to a soft yellow flame.

It was touched to the branches that had been hacked from the surrounding ash trees, and soon the inferno roared and leaped upwards, orange sparks pulsing into the starry black sky. Behind the spitting, crackling forest a man was caged within its wooded heart. He grew increasingly agitated as he failed to find an exit and was seared by the heat. His cries were lost in the growing thunder of consumed branches. As his clothes burned away, his skin blistered in the conflagration until he was nothing but a blackened carapace . . .

Janice Longbright sat up in bed with a sudden gasp.

It took a moment to remember where she was: at home in her dark apartment, alone. She checked the bedside clock; 4.22 a.m. From behind the insistent sound of rain came the mournful howl of an ambulance. There was no point in trying to get back to sleep now. There was nothing worse than lying awake in the dark. She slipped out of bed and went to the bathroom, mopping her forehead with a tissue.

The nightmares were becoming apocalyptic, unlike anything she had experienced before. She turned and checked her back in the mirror. The old Marilyn Monroe T-shirt she slept in was wet with sweat. Her features looked unnaturally pale. *Dear God,* she thought, *don't tell me it's the menopause. I need a holiday. Vitamin D deficiency. I should get some sun on my face. Fat chance of that happening.* She was broke again; nothing unusual there. This time the dream had been so real that she had to stop herself from checking for burns.

She went to the kitchen and made coffee, then added granary toast, eggs, bacon and – because the Heinz tin was already open – baked beans. She wanted to call Jack Renfield and hear his reassuring voice, but he was spending the night with his daughter and it seemed unfair to intrude upon them. Instead she went online, virtually the only time when she could guarantee a decent broadband speed, and looked up the meaning of her nightmare. The various dictionaries of dream symbolism told her that fire was a sign of destruction, risk, passion, desire, purification, enlightenment, anger and inner transformation, as vague and hopeless as any newspaper astrologer's predictions.

Longbright pushed the keyboard away and headed back to make more coffee, deciding that it had not been a good idea to eat four pieces of cheese on toast while watching footage of the riots just before going to bed.

The detective sergeant was a woman of stoic practicalities, as proportioned and permanent as the grandest public building. She was rarely prone to doubts or misgivings. But on this occasion she phoned someone to get a second opinion.

If Maggie Armitage was surprised to receive a phone call at a little after five on a Monday morning, she didn't sound so. 'You're up with the lark,' she said cheerfully. 'I'm watching a programme about ants. What's going on?'

'It's going to sound really stupid,' said Longbright, already starting to regret having made the call. 'Nightmares. The third one in a row, always the same.' She peered in her mirror, pulling out a knotted curl of bleached hair. 'I know you know something about, well—'

'You can say it,' said Maggie. 'Magic, even if it's largely apotropaic and not the Harry Potter sort.' Maggie Armitage billed herself as a white witch from the Coven of St James the Elder, Kentish Town, a Grand Order Grade Four. 'I *am* qualified, you know. I've got a diploma and everything.'

'Maggie, you know I can't allow myself to believe in that stuff. You're a bit mad, but you're good at reading people.' The two women had known each other for fifteen years, and Maggie had often provided the PCU with advice, even though it was highly unorthodox and inadmissible in court.

'What's your dream about?'

'A burning man,' Janice replied. 'He's trapped in the centre of a vast, terrible fire and I get to watch him go up in flames. But it's as if I'm trapped there with him – like I can see through his eyes and experience his pain.'

'What happens at the end?'

'I'm not sure, but I think he just dies – and I die with him.'

'There's no way out for either of you?'

'None that I can see. I can actually feel the heat scorching my face and arms. I'm overcome with the feeling that we're trapped together, him and me, and then I wake up.'

'Do you have pyrophobia? Fear of being burned alive?'

'No more than anyone else.'

'Well, the obvious answer is that you've recycled images from the day's news into your dreams. Have you been watching footage of the riots?'

'Of course – we all have.'

'You placed yourself inside the scenes. But the man,

well, that suggests something else. How are you getting on with Jack?'

'All right. I'm still uneasy about dating someone I work with.'

'So there's tension,' said Maggie. 'You said it yourself: "I feel trapped." I know fear of commitment is a terrible cliché, but it sounds like the relationship is making you feel claustrophobic. I can get rid of the dreams, mix you a nice calming bedtime drink, something with skullcap and passionflower. I make it for Daphne whenever she's been boxing. I'm letting her stay with me at the moment. It helps with the rent, although I won't let her summon her spirit guide when *Downton Abbey*'s on because he always tells us what's going to happen next.'

'The dream,' prompted Longbright. Maggie had a habit of wandering off the subject.

'Well, I can get rid of the symptom but not the cause, of course. That would be down to you. But it doesn't bode well.'

'What do you mean?'

'You know what you're like when men get too close.'

'No, what am I like?'

'I think you and Jack are going to break up.'

'Jeez – Maggie, I called you for advice.'

'I'm sorry, advice doesn't come with reassurance. Do you love him?'

'I . . . care for him.'

'Hm.' The sound was pregnant with thought. 'Of course, there is another interpretation.'

'What's that?'

There was a small silence on the other end of the line. 'I think you know, my dear.'

Longbright tried to recall what Maggie had told her, and inwardly groaned. 'What, that I'm psychic?'

'Your mother was, and it generally runs in the female line.'

'Maggie, that's what you believe. I don't share your views; you know that. Besides, it would mean I'm foreseeing someone's death, and what am I supposed to do about it?'

'You should know that we're entering a period of terrible turmoil, and it's better to consider the possibility before . . .'

'Before what?'

'Before it's too late to save yourself,' Maggie replied.

So much for the reassurance of phoning a friend. The detective sergeant rang off and buried herself behind the cushions on the couch, waiting for the arrival of dawn and a fresh week's work.

4

CHARCOAL

Like all angry phone calls seeking to apportion blame, it started at the top and worked its way down; the ACPO Commissioner called his Assistant Commissioner, who called the Chief Superintendent of the Serious Crime Directorate, who called Superintendent Darren 'Missing' Link, who summoned the head of the Peculiar Crimes Unit, Raymond Land, to meet with him in front of a burned-out doorway in the Square Mile.

The area surrounding the Findersbury Private Bank had been tented and taped off, sealing it away from prying reporters. Most had moved on, in any case; the action had shifted to St Paul's, where fresh dissent had started on the steps of the cathedral.

Link was an old-school copper from the East End who liked to warn his team that he had come up the hard way and would take every opportunity to practise what he preached. He'd started out in the Special Demonstrations Squad, an undercover unit whose task was to infiltrate and subvert left-wing, anarchist, anti-fascist and environmental-activist groups. His leaving had less to do with the unit's unethical code of behaviour, which had notoriously included exploiting the vulnerable and infiltrating peaceful protest organizations by adopting the identities of dead children, and more to do with the obscene amounts of cash pumped into questionable spying ops. He considered himself to be a deeply moral man.

Link still believed in incarceration, not rehabilitation, and would, in an ideal world, have rounded up all these whining layabout protestors and shipped them out to Afghanistan to serve on the front line. He was a bullet-headed officer in his late forties, with the proportions of a street bollard and cropped brown hair like the bristles on a worn-out broom. His eyes had been chips of ice that could see through brick walls until he was jabbed in the left one by a junkie armed with a broken fence post. The splinter had split his pupil, and although the burst blood vessels had been drained and had healed, he had been left with a strange fractured look, like a damaged toy soldier. He never laughed, joked, smiled or relaxed, and was never fully off duty.

From the moment he met Raymond Land he hated him, for his paunch and his limp handshake, for his weak chin and apologetic face, for the aura of damp appeasement that reminded him of Neville Chamberlain, the prime minister who had failed to halt the Second World War. One look told him that Land was a wishy-washy prevaricator, an apologist, a doormat. And for a copper, he was annoyingly short.

'You took your bloody time getting here,' he said, setting off along the perimeter of the cordon.

'I think there's been some confusion,' Land pointed out, knowing that there was always confusion when it came to the awkward chain of command that ran between the Met, the City and the PCU. 'I thought we only took cases from the City of London public liaison officer, Orion Banks.'

'You would if she was still with us,' said the superintendent, setting a pace that Land had trouble matching. 'Now you're my responsibility.'

'What happened to Miss Banks?' Land was disappointed. He and Banks had been getting on well, even if she did use a lot of media gobbledygook, and he'd rather fancied her, especially now that his divorce was going through.

'She's gone to Channel Four's publicity department, where I imagine her talents will be better served,' said Link. 'If you'd been here a few minutes ago you'd have seen this one.' He nodded his head towards the olive nylon tent covering the bank's blackened entrance. 'They've already scraped him up.'

'Scraped who up?' said Land, trying not to sneeze. The smoke had dissipated, but had left an unpleasant sharpness in the air.

Link held open the tent flap and ushered him in. A more appalling stench assailed Land's nostrils. He had only smelled something like that once before, after a bomb had torn a guardsman apart in Knightsbridge. He allowed his eyes to adjust to the dimness and tried to assess the scene. The mahogany doors of the bank were coated with an ebony craquelure. The windows on either side had cracked with the extreme heat. A thick layer of black ash covered the marble step. Fire paths were capricious. They could obliterate everything within a certain radius but leave parts within the circle completely untouched.

He saw what had been left: a length of corrugated brown cardboard as long as a person but only a few inches wide, scorched along its wavering edge. 'Someone was sleeping rough here,' he said, making out the charred shape of a prone body on the step.

'Well done.' Link headed out, expecting Land to follow. 'A homeless bloke had dossed down for the night and was still curled up in his sleeping bag covered in cardboard sheets when some bastard chucked a Molotov cocktail into the entrance. Petrol everywhere, all over cardboard and rags, and him cocooned inside a nylon tube like a boil-in-the-bag dinner. The only part that didn't melt was the metal zip.'

'It could have been a woman,' said Land, pinching his nose as he mentally measured out the length of the cardboard.

'Unlikely. There's a female shelter a couple of streets over. They keep an eye on girls at risk on the street.'

'You think one of the protestors did this?'

'Of course, who else? He probably didn't realize someone was sleeping there – it was only just getting light – but it's still manslaughter.'

Land's instincts told him different. 'He must have seen the cardboard. Surely he knew someone could be underneath.'

'No, he's just a yob on the lookout for trouble. But we'll get him. There's CCTV up there' – Link flicked a finger at a dome of black plastic embedded in the ceiling above the bank's entrance – 'and over there.' A second unobtrusive lens covered the doorway from the opposite direction.

'So this isn't our case,' said Land, trying to understand why he had been brought here.

'Not technically, but you can give us a hand.' Link wiped black sticky ashes off the sole of his boot. 'We'll track him down, no problem, but we don't have time to ID the victim. My boss reckons that's something you can do.'

'We could take the whole thing over,' Land suggested, knowing that he was pushing his luck. 'We've not got much on at the moment.'

Link shook his head. 'Yeah, nice try; not going to happen, though. Your unit's cock-ups are the stuff of legend around here. I wouldn't trust you to take a banana trifle around to my mum's, but whoever it was who decided to put you under City of London jurisdiction thinks it's better to keep you occupied. Get your forensic lad on it, Dan Banbury: he's a good 'un. Don't give me those ancient mummies you try to pass off as detectives.'

'Arthur Bryant and John May are—'

'I know what they are, and how long they've been around. Our lads reckon they're still working on the Jack the Ripper case.' He snorted at his own lame joke.

'Bryant and May have a higher strike rate than anyone else on the force,' said Land, realizing that he had been pushed into the unenviable position of supporting the very team who so often made his life a living hell.

'Whatever,' said Link dismissively. 'Just make sure they stay a safe distance from my investigation and we'll get along fine. All *you* have to do is identify a man-shaped piece of charcoal and file a few forms, without informing the rest of the fruitcakes you call a unit, OK? You'd better run along now.'

5

PORTAL

The Peculiar Crimes Unit was housed in an awkwardly trapezoidal four-floor Victorian corner building (plus basement and attic) on Caledonian Road, a three-minute walk from King's Cross Station and the international Eurostar terminal. It had been constructed at a time when the neighbourhood had been largely inhabited by anarchists, spiritualists, con men, racketeers, drug-dealers, brothel madams and army deserters: every shade of law-bender, in fact, who needed to get off the street quickly when a copper passed.

There were still a few shady types skulking behind the newly gentrified organic cake shops, but few realized that the unit was even there. From outside it looked less like a police unit and more like a run-down backpackers' hostel. The area was full of cheap accommodation. Occasionally a Chinese student tried to gain entrance, peered through the window and changed his mind.

'Insufferable,' fumed Raymond Land in his first-floor office. 'He only wants you to work on it, Dan, no one else.'

Dan Banbury was, mainly speaking, the crime scene manager of the Peculiar Crimes Unit. 'If he wants an ID

I'll need Giles,' he warned through a mouthful of toast. He'd been forced to do the school run this morning because his wife had a doctor's appointment, and had left his home in Croydon without any breakfast. 'I don't do bodies. We'll have to have a pathologist. And what about—'

'Don't say their names.' Land held up his hand. 'If those two get anywhere near this, you know what will happen. One moment it's a simple case of identification, and the next they'll be hiring Devil-worshippers and trying to uncover some kind of global conspiracy. You know how weird Bryant gets.'

'He gets results,' Banbury reminded him, brushing crumbs from his shirt. 'Does it matter what methods he uses?'

'It does when I have to approve his expenses.' Land slapped the stack of papers on his desk. 'Look at this lot. Two hundred and fifty nicker for the services of an expert on premature burials. One hundred and seventy-five quid for an *occult archivist*, whatever that is. Seven pounds fifty and a hot meal for a bloke who said he could walk through walls – well, at least the price went down after he broke his nose. But it all mounts up, and it makes me look a total fool. I suppose there have been small triumphs,' Land conceded. 'I got Bryant to tidy his desk up and take that disgusting old Tibetan skull of his home. He says he's going to use it as a sandwich container. Anyway, we haven't got the case. We've got a new liaison officer by the name of Darren Link, and he already hates us. We're just being used as an ancillary service, so there's no reason to involve anyone else.'

'All right,' said Banbury, shaking his head as he took the work docket from Land, 'but John and Mr Bryant will find out. They always do.'

'Only if you tell them,' Land all but shouted as his crime scene manager walked away.

'Tell us what?' asked John May, sauntering into the room with his hands in the pockets of his elegant navy-blue Savile Row suit.

'There's a door on this office,' cried Land. 'Would it be asking too much for you to knock first?'

'Frankly, yes. Anyway, there's not a door on your office.' May hiked a thumb back at the bare hinges. The two Daves had taken it off over a week ago, saying something about sanding the bottom because it was catching on the floorboards, but it still hadn't reappeared.

'Then it's a metaphorical door.' Land dropped into his chair. 'Knock before you come in.'

'You want me to mime knocking? Should I also make my own sound effects?' asked May. 'Then what do I do, try the non-existent handle?'

'I'm not going to have a conversation about an invisible door!' shouted Land. 'Just show some bloody respect!'

'Why, what are you up to in here?' May was instantly suspicious. 'Why was Dan coming out with a file under his arm? Have you given him a job you're not briefing us on? Arthur won't be happy about that, you know.'

'It's got nothing to do with either of you. You don't know everything that goes on around here.'

'Yes, we do, because we're the ones who tell you. You know Arthur insists on being in charge.'

Land glanced towards the doorway, fully expecting his nemesis to come wandering in. 'Just get on with your – whatever it is you're doing.'

'That's just it,' said May. 'We're not doing anything. There is nothing to do except paperwork. I thought that woman at the City of London was going to feed us fresh cases.'

'Orion Banks has been replaced,' said Land forlornly.

'Already? That's a shame. I thought she had taken a bit of a shine to you.'

'Mind my grief. Just when my divorce is finally going

through. I wasted the best years of my life with Leanne.' Land looked as if he'd just missed the last bus home. 'I should have dumped her and found someone else while I still had only one chin. Now it's too late.'

'Oh, it's never too late,' said May, catching a glimpse of his handsome profile in the window.

'Well, I don't understand it,' Land said with a sigh. 'You're decades older than me and women can't keep away from you. The effect you have on them is positively creepy.'

'Did someone say we have to knock on a door that isn't there?' asked Meera Mangeshkar, who was passing Land's office and felt like being annoying because she had nothing to do.

'Apparently we have to pretend that it's there,' May explained. 'Think of it as a portal to a mystical sanctum.'

'All due respect, sir, Mr Land's as mystical as a sausage sandwich.'

'Are there sausages?' asked Colin Bimsley, who was passing too.

'There are no sausages, there is no door, now will you all get out?' yelled Land.

'I thought you said there *was* a door,' May concluded.

Welcome to the offices of London's Peculiar Crimes Unit. For the sake of succinctness this account will be trimmed like fat from pork, leaving only the lean facts of the case, but in truth modern British police departments are rather like insurance offices. People stand around and chat, attend unnecessary meetings about performance targets and sit through seminars outlining initiatives that achieve nothing. They argue, drink too much tea and spend hours filling out forms. But in the matter of this inquiry the staff of the PCU won't be doing that. In the space of one week there will be death and destruction for the most mysterious of motives, and it will end in a terrible loss.

All that's missing to start this particular fireball rolling is the detective who always causes the most trouble in any unit investigation: Mr Arthur St John Aloysius Bryant.

6

CURTAIN UP

The spotlight thumped on and the crimson velvet curtains swept open to reveal, downstage centre, what appeared to be a tramp, possibly someone auditioning for *Waiting for Godot*.

The tramp looked around in confusion, spotted the audience, then began to edge his way offstage. Unfortunately he found his exit blocked, and as he was standing in a 1930s art deco lounge beside a woman in a long dress of silvered silk arranging daffodils in a bowl, he was immediately assumed to be some kind of comedy gardener. The more he bumped and shuffled his way around the furniture, the more the audience laughed.

A brilliantined young man in a dinner jacket entered stage right and was astounded to find his place taken by this wizened interloper. However, in keeping with the maxim that The Show Must Go On, he persevered with his cue.

'Don't be so awfully cross with me, Lavinia. You know how you hate wrinkles so. When I saw you outside the casino, standing there in the moonlight, I simply couldn't help myself. You really are the most frightfully lovely creature, you know.' He tried to close in on his mark beside the actress but the tramp was in his way, blinking out at the audience like a befuddled tortoise.

'What the hell is he doing out there?' asked the stage manager in a panicked whisper.

'I'm sorry,' said the unnerved ASM. 'I tried to get him off before the curtain went up.'

'Oh, Roger, if only you hadn't been such a frightful cad,' trilled Lavinia. 'Now there'll always be something utterly ghastly between us.' She eyed the tramp disdainfully as the audience collapsed in laughter and the curtain came down.

'I wasn't going to leave until I had an answer,' Arthur Bryant insisted stubbornly, pulling his coat free of the ASM's hands.

'What are you talking about?' the stage manager asked. 'Who the hell are you?'

'I'm a police officer.' Arthur Bryant handed over what he hoped was his PCU calling card and not an ad for a shoe shop. 'I've been following your stagehand.' He pointed to a ferret-faced young man seated in the corner of the flies, attached to an iron post with a plastic cable tag. 'I tailed him all the way from Piccadilly Circus because of these.' Digging deep into his tweed overcoat he produced two fistfuls of wallets. 'He was dipping tourists. I saw him duck in to the stage door and tried to stop him, but he ran up the steps into the dark.'

'Weren't me, Granddad,' grunted the tethered felon.

Bryant regarded his captive. 'And they say the art of conversation is dead. Well, I'll be on my way, then.'

'Now look here,' said the stage manager, 'you can't just go swanning off like that after ruining our leading lady's opening speech—'

'I'm not swanning off,' Bryant pointed out as he re-knotted his scarf. 'I'm exiting stage left.'

'Is that all you can say?' asked the stage manager, aghast.

'Well, your leading lady could try to sound her aitches,' said Bryant, squinting back at the stage. 'It's Noël Coward. She's meant to be from Westminster, not Wapping. Someone will be along to pick up Mr Chatterbox here shortly. Cheerio.'

At the unit, Arthur Bryant had always been affectionately known as 'the Old Man', even though his partner John May was just three years his junior. Set beside each other, the pair might have been born two decades apart. Bryant had lost his hair in his thirties, and his short, stocky frame seemed to have been predesigned for senior status. He had never lifted anything heavier than a book, and had regarded a flight of stairs as a challenge since his mid-forties. When he spoke it was because his peculiar passions required him to impart information, as he was insensible to the etiquette of small talk. He was a mobile time capsule, insulated from the world by private obsessions. Paradoxically, it was one of the things that made him so valuable to the PCU. In a city that was rapidly forgetting the past, he was an inconvenient reminder of all that had gone before.

Arthur Bryant *remembered*.

'I don't know where to begin,' said John May, shaking his head. 'Even after all these years, your every action remains a mystery to me. You're a detective, you're not meant to behave like some teenaged PC fresh out of Hendon. And why you had to follow him into a theatre of all places—'

'He was a junkie doing some speed-acquisition of tourists' wallets, John. I took one look at him and knew he would test positive for stupidity.' Bryant threw himself down into his old leather armchair. 'Of course I could have alerted a beat copper, but there was less chance of finding one in the area than locating the Nécessaire egg.'

'The what?'

Bryant waved a hand vaguely. 'Oh, one of the eight Fabergé eggs that vanished from the vaults of the Kremlin Armoury. Anyway, I saved some poor spotty rookie from two days of interviews and form-filling. And besides, I'd heard good things about that particular theatrical production. Wrongly, as it turned out.'

'So you cuffed him, then thought you'd have a nose around and got caught by the curtain-up.' May checked his desk and carefully cornered off the few sheets of A4 that he found there. On Bryant's side stood a Himalayan range of screwed-up paper. 'Meanwhile, they're still rioting on our patch, all over the Square Mile, are you even aware of that?'

'Of course I'm aware, but there's nothing I can do about it, is there?'

'On that point I'm afraid you're right,' May agreed. 'Early this morning Raymond was called to a bank in the City by a superintendent called Darren Link. Ring any bells?'

'Oh, yes, ex-Whitechapel mob, fancies himself a real hard nut. To paraphrase J. B. Priestley, what he doesn't know about policing isn't worth knowing, but what he *does* know isn't worth knowing either, because of the bad effect it's had on him. We all used to call him "Missing" Link. He didn't like that much. You know how coppers sniff out weaknesses and play on them. After we went a bit too far with the teasing, he set fire to two of our vehicles in the Whitechapel car pool and disappeared. He surfaced a few weeks later in West End Central, transferred to vice.'

'Not someone to mess with, then.'

'Oh, it's the ones you can't get a handle on who are trouble,' said Bryant, scratching his pug nose as he pondered the matter. 'I can see through Darren Link. He's an evangelist. That's why he joined the force: to clean up the streets. He can't, of course – nobody can truly control people, they're too wilful, and it drives him crazy. I suppose he's not a bad bloke, really. If he called Raymond, it means he can't spare his own men for a clean-up job.'

'It's exactly that, I'm afraid. Raymond wasn't going to tell us but I called him on it. There's a body.'

'Oh?' Bryant's furry little ears perked up. Death was his stimulant of choice.

'A homeless guy was asleep on the steps of one of the banks the protestors attacked.'

'That hasn't made the news, has it?'

'No. I was wondering whose decision it was to keep it out of the press. The BBC is trying hard not to demonize the protestors but I'm betting they weren't given the story.'

'That doesn't make sense,' said Bryant thoughtfully. 'There are usually so many reporters on the ground that you'd think someone would have picked it up. I smell a rat.'

'You don't smell anything,' warned May, sitting up, 'because it's got nothing to do with you. Or with me, for that matter. Dan just has to sign off on the crime scene.'

'Fair enough,' said Bryant with suspicious nonchalance. 'That means he'll ask Giles to ID the cause of death, doesn't it?'

'Very possibly.'

'Hm. I might just pop along and take a look.'

'No, you won't. Raymond will go bananas if you do.'

'Yes, but I have to pass the mortuary later, anyway.'

'You don't. It's not on your way home. Why can't you just go to the pub like normal people?'

'I could just stick my head around the door . . .'

'You know, it wouldn't hurt to let someone else take

the credit,' said May tactfully. 'Leave them alone for a while and let's see what they come up with.'

Bryant enjoyed handling cases that required a bit of showmanship. Identifying the corpse of a rough sleeper accidentally caught in the crossfire between capitalists and rioters was the sort of chore that usually fell to Met officers, and in all likelihood it would never be fully cleared up; wherever there was conflict there would always be innocent victims.

But he thought he might look in anyway. And if he was going, it seemed silly to wait until the end of the day, when Giles had finished and was about to leave, so why not go right now?

7

ABYSS

Bryant headed around the corner to Camley Street, past St Pancras Old Church, one of the most ancient sites of Christian worship in England, to the bizarre Victorian gingerbread house that sat beside it. The squat ivy-covered building was home to the Camley Street Coroner's Office, and as Bryant stumped up the winding path to the front door, he caught a glimpse of Rosa Lysandrou's pale face peering out of a lead-light window at him.

'Thank goodness that was you,' said Bryant cheerfully as the housekeeper opened the door. 'For a horrible moment I thought it was Miss Jessel from *The Turn of the Screw*.'

'I don't know what that means,' said Rosa flatly, 'but I suppose you are being rude as usual.' She stood aside to allow him entrance.

Bryant tentatively extended his walking stick into the hall as if checking for landmines. 'It's a book. And a film. And an opera. Do you enjoy reading?'

'I enjoyed *Fifty Shades of Grey*.'

Bryant quailed at the thought. 'That's not really reading, is it? More like staring at an assortment of words.'

'It is very popular.'

'So is taking photographs of your dinner for Facebook, but that doesn't mean it adds to the total sum of human knowledge.'

'You can't see him,' Rosa pointed out. 'He knows you're not supposed to be here.'

'Who said I came to see him?' Bryant's aqueous-blue eyes were as innocent as a kitten's. 'I find myself inexplicably drawn to you. Every time I imagine you in that shapeless black whatever-it-is you're wearing I get quite—'

'Mr Bryant, will you please stop antagonizing my assistant?' said Giles Kershaw, striding into the hall. Out of his lab coat and tucked into faded jeans, a crisp white shirt and a black waistcoat, he looked like a waiter for a once-fashionable restaurant rather than the guardian of the borough's main mortuary.

'We were just chatting about literature.' Bryant produced a battered but extravagantly beribboned box of chocolates from his overcoat. 'These are for you, Rosa.'

She hesitated before accepting them, perhaps wondering whether they were poisoned, then wrinkled her nose.

'Ah, yes. The cat peed in my pocket, but they should be all right,' Bryant explained. 'They're your favourite, I imagine: hard centres. And you're absolutely correct, of course. We avoid matters of importance and concentrate on the trivial. If we didn't, the burden of life would simply prove too much for us.'

'Spoken', replied Rosa, 'like a man without a god.' She pointedly set the chocolates aside.

'I think I know what you came for,' said Kershaw hastily, flicking back his blond fringe and marching along the hall towards the main autopsy room with Bryant in his wake.

'Oh, I'm not here for anything,' Bryant explained. 'I was just in the neighbourhood.'

'So you didn't know that Dan was here as well?'

'Is he back from the Findersbury Bank already? Well, that's a stroke of luck.'

'I knew you wouldn't be able to stay away,' called Banbury, who was poking through the contents of an opaque green plastic bag on Kershaw's counter. 'There's nothing more to see than this. He's in a terrible state.'

'I've probably seen worse,' said Bryant.

'I tell my students to detach themselves from the fact that this is a human body. If you really start thinking about it, you'll realize that after all your years in the job you've looked at too many corpses, and there's a lot of nightmare potential in that. Just don't—'

'I know – touch anything.' He let Kershaw cut open the bag. 'Well, that's pretty disgusting. His viscera look cooked. How will you get anything out of them?'

'In this job you need to have good visual acuity for pattern recognition. The ability to put together what's been going on. Take a look at that.' Without glancing up, Kershaw brandished a pair of tweezers in the direction of the steel tray further along the counter.

Bryant went over to it and peered in. He saw a small metal rod with blackened ends. 'What is it?'

'An implant,' said Kershaw. 'Probably from his right foot.'

'What kind of implant?' He picked up the rod and sniffed it.

Kershaw took it out of his hands. 'What did I just ask you not to do? It looks like a titanium allogenic graft for segmental lengthening, to replace a part that was damaged. From the upper part of the foot. It's likely he crushed a bone and had it replaced. These things are pretty common, but I thought it would help to narrow down the search field. Then I discovered that the newer models are etched with a unique serial number so that each one is registered to its owner. We'll run a check tonight.'

'Why can't you do it now?'

'The medical database requires search clearance. If that doesn't work out, we'll get him on dental records. If there's time, that is. I'd rather not have to start trawling around the hostels. Link has slapped a limit on our billable hours. He wants this closed as quickly as possible.'

'What about cameras? Don't tell me you can't track his movements?'

'In and out of the street, certainly,' said Banbury, 'but it'll take a while sifting through the hard drives covering the main thoroughfares, unless he went into a shop, somewhere we'd get a close-up.'

'So all this technology we have in the Square Mile is useless,' Bryant harrumphed.

'Not at all. It's just time-consuming. We have another clue as to his ID. In the bottom of the sleeping bag was a plastic wallet. It melted but there were a couple of cards inside, and once we separate them out we might get the remains of a chip from one.'

'If he was sleeping rough, they won't have been credit cards. Are they here?'

'Hang on.' Kershaw carefully shook out a plastic envelope, and a gnarled, blackened lump dropped into his desk tray. Bryant untangled a pair of reading glasses and squinted at it.

'That's a staff card for the Bloomsbury Sustainable Market,' he said without a second's hesitation. 'It's a collective where students stack shelves in return for groceries.'

'I don't see how you can possibly know that,' said Banbury. 'We'd need to get some chromatography on it before—'

'When I was a child,' Bryant interrupted, 'I was very

good at jigsaws. That little mark in the corner . . .' He tapped the blob. '. . . that's the bottom part of a picture. It's the handle of a kitchen whisk – the market's symbol. I'd recognize it anywhere.'

'OK.' Banbury shrugged. 'We'll get on it.'

'What do you think happened?' Kershaw asked.

'Scylla and Charybdis,' said Bryant. 'He got caught napping between them. The riot police arriving on one side, the protestors kettled on the other.'

'It's hard to believe he didn't wake up with all the noise in the next street,' said Kershaw.

'Have you ever spent a day on the streets?' asked Bryant. 'You're on the move all the time. It's incredibly tiring. By the time it gets dark all you want to do is drop down in your tracks and sleep. I doubt this poor devil would have been woken by a bomb going off.'

'Right,' said Kershaw. 'I'll make some calls back at the PCU and we'll get this wrapped up.'

But Bryant showed no signs of budging from the remains of the body. 'It's worse than it ever was,' he muttered. 'Bankers with million-pound bonuses stepping around kids who aren't even guaranteed a place to lay their heads. The poor are worse off now than they were in Victorian times. What's happened to my city?' For a moment he looked as if he was standing at the edge of an unimaginable abyss.

'Come on,' said Banbury gently, taking his boss's arm. 'I'll walk back with you.'

8

MASKS

John May sat back in his chair and thought about the office he had shared for so long with his partner.

It wasn't the same room, of course – that had changed many times since Bryant had accidentally burned down the unit years before – but somehow it always reinvented itself with the same layout, the same esoteric books, the same haphazardly accumulated bric-a-brac. Looking at the empty green leather chair opposite, May suddenly had a change of heart. Bryant had flung caution aside and followed his instincts, heading off to visit St Pancras simply because he could not allow his natural curiosity to be quelled. So, May wondered, why was *he* sitting here content to follow orders? What did that ever gain him?

Grabbing his coat, he left the building and hailed a taxi to Crutched Friars. The least he could do was take a look at the façade of the Findersbury Bank. He did not expect to find anything of value there, but it usually helped to understand the exact geographical layout of the incident scene.

As he walked over the wet tarmac towards the bank's blackened foyer, he saw a pair of firefighters bent over by the entrance examining something in the soot-stains. One stood up at his approach and raised a hand in greeting. 'Hey, John, they've got you on this too, eh?'

'Just an ID job,' said May. 'What have you got there?'

The other officer rose and turned to him. 'Senior Officer Blaize Carter. Good to finally meet you, Mr May. I've heard a lot about your unit.'

May blinked and stared, lost for words.

Carter looked at her colleague wearily, then back at May. 'Go on then, have a laugh. It's not my fault – I was christened with it, OK? My mother actually wanted me to be a concert pianist.'

May decided it was better to let her assume he was taken aback by her name, but he was thinking something else entirely. Carter was slim and tough-looking, with the build of a runner or a gymnast, in her upper forties, her kinked auburn hair tied back, her face free of make-up. There was a world of patience and kindness in her eyes, something he often saw in nurses and firefighters.

'I, um, it's . . . a nice name.' He mentally kicked himself. 'You looked like you'd found something.'

'Yeah, maybe nothing but – here . . .' She stood aside to let him see the base of the entrance. 'The doors have varnished wood surrounds. One side doesn't open. You'd think anyone trying to torch the place would throw missiles here, against the doors, where there was the best chance of setting something alight, but the shards' – she indicated the spot with her boot – 'well, they're all in the opposite corner, so that's your impact spot. Johnnie Walker label, see?'

'That's a concrete step.'

'Exactly. Nothing to burn. Not strictly true. There must have been one thing in the corner: the homeless guy's head. Arsonists often miss their targets but he got pretty close before throwing the bottle. You can see by the force of the impact. So, was he aiming for the bank or the sleeper? Have you got someone doing the site forensics?'

'Yes, my chap's already been,' said May. 'Didn't anyone tell you?'

'*He's* supposed to be in charge, isn't he?' She jerked her thumb back at Link, who was having some kind of argument with a junior officer. 'I don't think he knows what he's doing. Maybe you could get your—'

'Banbury,' said May quickly. 'Dan Banbury.'

'Great, if you could get him to call us direct, maybe we can cut through some of the red tape. At the moment the bank staff are having to use the side entrance. It's not fit for purpose, but they refuse to close so I'd like to get the doors reopened as soon as possible.' She rubbed the tip of her nose with the back of her hand, leaving a smear of soot.

'Of course. How do I—'

'This isn't my jurisdiction,' interrupted Carter. 'I'm based at Euston Road. I guess you know most of the team there.'

'A few, yes.'

'Then now you know me as well.' She turned and knelt once more.

Blaize, thought May as he walked away towards the bridge. *Blaize Carter.*

Superintendent Darren Link held a meeting with the specialist support unit for public order at the CoL's Snow Hill station, one of the three he worked between in the Square Mile. The building had mullioned bay windows set in discoloured Portland stone, and looked like the headquarters of some benevolent Victorian charity. Inside, there was very little charity to be found today. On its first floor, Link was losing his temper.

'You're telling me you can't even round up the ringleaders?' He stared down the support unit with his fractured eye, daring them to argue back.

'Not while they're engaged in legitimate protest,' said one of them, a legal expert named Ayo Onatade. 'They held meetings with us about the prescribed route and the road closures, and we agreed hours and dates up front, all of which they've adhered to.'

'Did you agree which windows they could chuck bricks through? Which cars they could set alight?'

'We've been over this,' said Onatade with weary patience. She was used to bearing the brunt of police wrath. 'The original protest group was joined by unregistered outsiders who were bussed in from other parts of the country.'

'But if the march hadn't been announced in the first place, these thugs wouldn't have come down to join them. How are we supposed to tell them apart?'

'We told you to issue the legitimate campaigners with passes. And you can blame the media for the uproar, not the marchers. There's been a lot of scaremongering coverage. It was intended to be a peaceful demonstration. The press were out on the streets looking for trouble long before the march had even begun.'

Link pulled out the updated fact sheet he'd been handed and read from it. 'Twelve burned-out vehicles, six office buildings set on fire, a "peace camp" which consists of some Glastonbury tents and a lot of cardboard, the Bank of England barricaded, Cannon Street and Mansion House stations still closed down. The Square Mile's becoming unsafe. One hundred and three civilian injuries so far, twenty-one officers injured and one fatality.'

'A fatality?' repeated Onatade, shocked.

'A homeless guy sleeping rough in a doorway, burned to death by one of your peaceful protestors.' He paused to let the news sink in. 'And I hope you haven't got any shares invested right now, because the FTSE's taken a right old hammering this morning.'

'Do you have someone in custody for the death of the homeless guy?' asked Onatade, who was more interested in the personal cost of the protest than in falling stocks.

'We've turned up some blurry CCTV footage of a bloke in trainers, grey tracksuit bottoms, a *V for Vendetta* face mask and a grey hooded sweatshirt. You're welcome to try to identify him – or her,' said Link sarcastically. 'We're pushing to remove the legality of your urban guerrillas to wear masks, effective immediately.'

'You can't do that; it's a human-rights issue,' warned Onatade.

'No, Ayo, it's a criminal issue.' Link had intimidating body language, and used it effectively. 'We can prove our killer wore one, and that means we can stop anyone else from wearing them until we've got someone in custody. I will not allow these events to escalate because people are hiding behind masks. This meeting is over.'

He rose and stalked out of the room, knowing that Onatade would be on her phone challenging the issue's legitimacy within seconds. It had been the tech man over at the Peculiar Crimes Unit, Dan Banbury, who had found the image collected by one of the cameras in Crutched Friars. Even if the shot couldn't be used to identify the bomb-thrower, it had already served its purpose, and would now prevent the anarchists from hiding behind masks.

Unfortunately, the image had a less welcome side effect; it persuaded his bosses to pass the case over to the PCU. While the riots continued, they explained, City of London police would be too engaged to handle it.

Raymond Land studied the headline of the brochure he had been handed outside King's Cross Station at lunchtime. It said: 'DO YOU HAVE WHAT IT TAKES TO BE A LEADER? DISCOVER HOW TO BE MORE EFFECTIVE AND DYNAMIC IN THE WORKPLACE!'

With a heavy heart he tore the pamphlet into pieces and looked around for a bin. He hated visiting the room that Bryant and May shared because he never knew what was likely to happen once he was inside it. Land turned a blind eye to the thriving marijuana plant underneath Bryant's desk, having been provided with many contradictory excuses for its existence, but there was always the problem of where to sit, and what he might find himself sitting in.

Then there were Bryant's fanciful lectures on policing to contend with. Once he started there was no escape, and Land found himself agreeing to the most appalling proposals. He was weak; he knew it and they knew it. His indecisiveness arose from fear, and the only time his fear vanished was when he was really, really angry – as he was now, standing before his detectives.

'I don't believe it,' he complained vociferously. 'I already paid my deposit, I've bought an easel, and now I have to cancel.'

'You can still go to the Isle of Wight,' said Bryant, cheerfully picking the shell off a boiled egg. 'Go on, hop it, you deserve a break. So they've given us the case – once Dan and Giles have nailed their ID it doesn't look like there'll be much more to do. We can manage perfectly well without you here.'

'Thank you, I remember what happened the last time I left you alone,' Land replied. 'You filled my office with Tibetan monks and gave the Bishop of Southwark a black eye. Do you understand how important this case is? The government is going to use it as an excuse to change the civil-liberty laws.'

'I see the problem,' said May. 'Remove the masks and soon you'll be preventing the wearing of burqas.'

'No, it's not that. I'm worried about the publicity. We're not very good at operating as a covert unit. No,' Land decided, 'my conscience won't allow me to go away now. At least I might still be able to get a refund on the caravan.'

'Don't worry about a thing, *vieille saucisse*,' Bryant agreed serenely. 'Dan's about to get his leg-bone reading and the rest of the team will be trawling through footage, tracing his attacker. We'll have this put to bed before you get back to your cold, empty house.'

9

MURDEROUS

As it turned out, Bryant and Longbright nailed the victim an hour before the full official identification came in. Late on Monday afternoon, a member of staff at Bloomsbury's Sustainable Market remembered the lad with the damaged foot who had worked there for five months. Judith Merrill was one of the managers, and as she was shown into the interview room at the PCU, she carefully skirted the hole in the floorboards filled with uprooted plumbing, seating herself behind the rickety desk Longbright had salvaged from the school over the road.

'His name was Freddie Weeks, but everybody called him Lucky,' she said. 'I mean, they meant it sarcastically. He left the store back at the end of June. He was a very private person, didn't make friends easily. I think he had a lot of problems.'

'What kind of problems?' asked Longbright.

'You know, money difficulties, getting chucked out of his flat. He used to miss shifts all the time. He came in with the most terrible hangovers and seemed angry or frustrated or something. He was very moody. I wondered if there were drugs involved. Sorry, I'm not sure if this is very helpful.'

'Do you know if there was anyone close to him, a girlfriend or best friend?' asked Longbright.

Judith thought for a moment and shook her head. 'No. He was a bit of a loner. Don't get me wrong, he was friendly enough but only in a distant way. I think he'd had some trouble in the past. I remember there was something on his employment record but we don't seem to have stored his CV. We're a bit disorganized on that front. Mostly people just fill in the forms we keep in the shop. Maybe he had trouble with the police?'

'Did he have a place to sleep when he was working at the store?'

'He always wore the same clothes, and I have a feeling he was staying on someone's sofa. But I don't think he ever stopped in one place for long. He kept himself very neat and tidy.'

'Do you know what happened to his right foot?'

'He smashed the bone in a skateboarding accident three years ago. He had some kind of operation to replace the damaged part with an implant. He limped a bit and said it bothered him in cold weather.'

It seemed clear to Longbright that the manager had a soft spot for her old employee. She thanked her for coming in and promised to be in touch if she discovered anything of further interest. The Criminal Records Database turned up a couple of minor run-ins for Weeks, one disturbance of the peace, one drunk and disorderly. A few minutes later, Giles Kershaw came back with a match for the serial number on the allogenic implant and confirmed the ID.

'Apparently he was very angry about the accident,' said Kershaw. 'He tried to sue the Euston Square shopping precinct where it happened, without success. He refused therapy.'

Longbright sent a constable to the boy's parents, who lived in Bayswater and had not seen their son in several months. A little later, she made a follow-up call.

'Freddie didn't have much to say to us,' said the father, his voice thickened by anger and grief.

'Did you know he was sleeping rough?' Janice asked. She waited patiently for her answers, knowing it was tough handling questions so quickly after losing a loved one.

'How could we know?' came the indignant reply. 'He hardly ever called.'

'Had you had a disagreement?'

'We'd never had an *agreement*. Freddie wouldn't even use a mobile phone because he said the parts were manufactured in China by people working below minimum wage. I told him, "If you're going to worry about every last thing, you won't be able to eat or clothe yourself," but he was determined to follow his ethical guidelines. Well, this is where his high-minded ethics got him.'

'Do you know the names of anyone he hung out with?'

'No, he had no close friends.'

'Enemies, then. Someone he'd fallen out with.'

'No, he was kind. He didn't make enemies. If you'd known him—'

'Did he have any history of health problems?'

'You mean mental health? No, but he was – what do they call it now? ADD. He could never concentrate on anything for long. Freddie was a very clever boy, too clever for his own good, very highly strung. Always near the top of his class, but he'd get angry over nothing. He got in with the wrong crowd and there was nothing we could do. He was never in trouble at school, he passed all his exams, but he couldn't settle. We tried to lend him money but he wouldn't take it. We both feared for him, but what could we do? You can't tell your children how to live their lives.'

Longbright had heard the story of a good son growing apart from his family and losing his way in the world too many times to count. Everyone agreed it was a tragedy and felt guilty for not having done more, but, all things considered, the outcome had probably been predetermined by the boy's nature.

The case was closed by the end of Monday. Arthur Bryant, who usually took half a day to return a library book, was amazed by the speed of the operation. Having dithered about cancelling his holiday, Raymond Land now found that it was too late to get his deposit back, and decided to head off first thing on Tuesday morning.

At least, that was the plan before John May went to see Anjam Dutta in the new City of London Surveillance Centre, a nondescript black glass stump planted next to the old Billingsgate Fish Market on Lower Thames Street.

The dapper, precise Indian security expert led the way through the dimly lit concrete bunker that ran underneath the building. Here, two dozen operatives monitored feeds from the thousands of cameras placed throughout the Square Mile.

'I'm just tying up loose ends,' May explained as they walked. 'The CoL didn't specifically ask for a sign-off on the CCTV footage but I thought we should at least view it. Last time I came here you seemed to have a lot more staff.'

'The presence of warm bodies isn't really necessary any more,' Dutta explained. 'Motion sensors and face-recognition software track most of the suspicious movement in the area, but sometimes it's a good idea to use a more intuitive identification system. For example, right now, during the riots, we have fresh anti-capitalist support groups arriving from Germany, France, Norway and Canada, with more expected. There are twenty-five individual wards to cover.'

'What happens if anyone moves outside the Square Mile?' asked May. 'Do you lose jurisdiction over them?'

'We liaise with the Met, but we can only step in when the Counter Terrorism Command flags get triggered. And there are anomalies within the zone. For example, it's hard to track what's going on in the Middle and Inner Temple areas.' The City's old legal quarter was a maze of chambers and passageways built on private land, and were largely free of intrusive cameras. 'The idea was to design out terrorism, and to a large extent we've succeeded, but only around the new buildings. Riots are a different matter, though, because they're more spontaneous and unpredictable.'

'I guess in a crowded news week Dexter Cornell might have got away with his insider-trading deal,' said May.

'That's right,' said Dutta, heading for a particular bank of monitors. 'The directors didn't handle that one very well. They should have made sure that Cornell left immediately. Instead, he's still going in to work for the bank's final week, trying to prove a point and tough it out, as are most of the others. Not all of them, though – some are hiding out in their Buckinghamshire mansions. As far as I can tell Cornell has no defence. He got caught tipping off his pals and is still pretending that he didn't. The *Mail* ran a six-page spread on his cars and country houses this morning. No wonder people get upset.'

He pulled out a chair for May, then instructed one of the surveillance operators to run some footage. 'We were monitoring the streets around the main march route and came across this,' said Dutta. 'I thought you'd be interested.'

The sequence was monochrome and without sound. It showed a view of Crutched Friars from a camera mounted beneath the railway bridge. May watched as a figure walked towards the entrance of the bank, where a dark shape lay in the doorway.

'This was taken at five fifty-seven a.m.,' Dutta explained, tracing the figure on the screen with the end of his pen. 'We should have got a clearer shot but the street-light timers are wrongly set. He goes to the entrance, stops, watches for a minute, then walks back to the bridge. Unfortunately he's got his back to us.'

'Looks like our arsonist though,' said May. 'Same clothes, same build. Can you put it up against the later sequence?'

Dutta's operator searched the footage numbers and loaded a second monitor. Now May saw the firebomb-thrower taking the exact same path twenty minutes later. 'That's him all right,' he said. 'He checked out the building to make sure it was the right one. Look at the way he leans forward there, at the entrance.' The screen showed a rectangle of dark pixilations in the doorway. 'There's no way he could have missed Weeks lying against the wall. The guy was right at his feet, sleeping in the doorway. Run it again?'

They watched as the hooded figure swaggered up to the entrance and bent slightly. 'He's checking him out,' said May. 'Damn.'

'What are you thinking?' Dutta asked.

May checked his watch. 'I have to stop the report from being filed. I must get back. Send me a copy of this, will you?'

'Sure. What's next?'

'We launch a murder investigation,' May replied. 'It was a premeditated act. Our arsonist knew Weeks was lying there.'

10

INCENDIARY

The young man stood beneath the red and white awning of the corner store with the tool bag resting at his feet. He watched the workmen digging fat sepia clods of London clay from the hole in the road. The wind was rising. He looked up and saw seagulls dragged and rolled across the sky like sheets of newspaper. After another ten minutes had passed the rain started, becoming so heavy that the workmen climbed out of the hole and took off for Camden's Rio Café, just as he had hoped they would.

The moment they were out of sight, he headed over to the galvanized drum that stood on the flat bed of their truck and disconnected the burner from its cylinder. No one was watching him; he had the street to himself. Coiling the orange rubber pipe around his shoulder, he dragged the grime-coated apparatus towards him. It weighed a ton, but he was strong. His van was parked around the corner, but he also had the canvas tool bag to carry. He couldn't afford to risk making two trips.

Lifting the burner and hooking it into his belt, he raised the bag and tried to prevent the coiled pipe from slipping. When he turned the corner, he saw that there was just one old West Indian woman making her way towards him with loaded shopping bags and eyes downcast.

In one of those coincidences that only ever seem to happen in London, the woman in question was Alma Sorrowbridge, Arthur Bryant's former landlady, who now shared a flat with him in Bloomsbury. She regularly came over to Camden to buy the fresh Caribbean fruits and vegetables she couldn't get near her home, and had no idea that she was walking past a murderer.

He loaded the unmarked van and set off, trying to remember if he'd thought of everything. It was a learning curve; every time he thought he was fully prepared for all eventualities, some surprise came along that threatened to undermine everything. He would have to watch for that in future.

He estimated that the entire process would take one week. After all, if God could make the world in seven days, he could surely unmake London in the same time. The trick, as he saw it, was to keep up his strike rate before the police could figure out what they were dealing with. He had to keep them off balance. He already saw that he had failed to wipe his tracks as thoroughly as he'd thought.

As he crossed the river, heading south to Brixton, he ran over the checklist for the thirtieth time. Once he was satisfied that he had covered everything he needed to do today, he returned to the bigger question, the one people would ask themselves for years to come. Why? *Why would anyone do such terrible things?* Politicians would argue about the lessons that should have been learned, the warning signs ignored, the safety measures not taken. Would things be different? Nobody knew. He wasn't responsible for what might happen in the future. The present, though: that was another matter. The start of the riots provided perfect cover. Revenge could only be enjoyed if the revenger could witness its full effect, and he planned to be there every step of the way.

He parked the van as close as he could to Brixton Market and shifted the gear inside the store. Then he made his second run, to collect the movie posters from a lock-up he had rented in Stockwell. When he returned to the half-empty market, he let himself into the shop and scraped just enough whitewash from the windows to let in decent light, making sure that none of the nearby store owners got a proper look at his face. It took him the rest of the afternoon to clear out the rubbish, install Chinese paper blinds and hang the posters. Then he made the call that would set the next stage in motion.

He knew that there was no going back now. If he made a mistake, every police officer in the city would be looking for him. If he succeeded, he would leave London burning.

In Threadneedle Street, Queen Victoria Street and Cornhill, London was already burning, if somewhat damply. Earlier in the afternoon, sodden crowds had held their vigil for the death of capitalism in Trafalgar Square. They wore smiling Guy Fawkes masks, but represented every age and nationality. After an hour they moved to the Queen Victoria Memorial, their next station on the way to a political Calvary.

The evening march route, a candlelit parade of masked drummers, heading from Mansion House to the other side of the Bank of England, quickly went wrong. Violence broke out as the police tried to move the protestors off the pavements and keep them contained within the planned route. An MP from the Green Party met the leaders and called for calm, but was shouted down and forced to retreat behind the barricades.

A Facebook page promoting the idea of a single amalgamated protest called for all campaigners to 'defend humanity'. It said: '*Remember who your enemies are:*

billionaires who own banks and corporations who corrupt politicians and enslave the people in injustice.' The rhetoric had hardly changed in a century. It was the language of Poland and Latvia, of Jarrow and Aldermaston. The marchers were opposed by an assortment of ragtag groups ranging from UKIP to a pro-capitalist organization of rogue brokers calling itself Capital Offence.

The police feared a concatenation of protest groups, especially when Ayo Onatade succeeded in preventing them from banning face coverings at the rally, after arguing for the right to anonymous protest. For a few minutes the gatherings existed in uneasy symbiosis. Then someone decided it was a good idea to launch fireworks at the police. The rockets and bangers quickly turned to rocks and burning chair legs, and as all leave was cancelled in the capital, members of various press organizations began calling their families to warn them that they would not be coming home tonight. Hot-dog sellers appeared at the key points of the marching route, until the police managed to move them on.

The City's merchants saw that they were likely to lose another day's business tomorrow, and kept their boards up overnight. As the protestors spread out from the epicentre and the crowds thickened, the police closed Leadenhall Market and roads around the Monument. For the first time, the question of closing bridges arose.

From their vantage points in the cocktail bars of the Shard and the Gherkin, the bank directors watched as ominous patches of orange fire appeared in the streets below – a sight that those who knew London's history of blitzes and riots had hoped never to see in their own lifetimes.

11

KING MOB

'Insurrection!' exclaimed Arthur Bryant, rubbing his hands together gleefully as the flames lit up his face. 'Finally!'

'I'll turn it off if you don't stop saying that,' warned May. Raymond Land had installed a plasma TV on the wall of the briefing room, not in the spirit of improving facilities at the PCU, but to get it out of his house so that his wife Leanne couldn't claim it in their divorce settlement. The detectives were watching live BBC coverage of the protestors lobbing petrol bombs at police riot shields.

Bryant had plonked himself on one of the desks and was swinging his legs like a superannuated schoolboy, crunching mint humbugs against his dentures as he watched aerial views of the city fires shot from the newsroom's helicopter. 'Don't you see?' he said. 'King Mob. It's 1780 all over again.'

'I don't have your grasp of British history—' May began forlornly.

'The Gordon Riots,' said Bryant, sticking a match in his pipe.

'The Daves put a smoke detector in here,' May warned.

'Don't worry, I already disconnected it.' He pointed up at the white plastic disc, which appeared to have been shot out. 'The most destructive protest of the eighteenth century, Protestants fighting against the Papists' Act, which had protected Roman Catholics. You have to remember that the world was in a state of unrest. America was fighting the War of Independence. The Frogs were about to invade England. In London, anti-Catholic fever was at its pitch. Ordinary people invaded the streets and tore down entire houses with their bare hands. They smashed all the windows and burned all the furniture within reach.' From the way Bryant's eyes shone, May could have been forgiven for thinking that his partner had been there. 'The inmates of Newgate prison were freed according to a proclamation painted on its gates, by the authority of "His Majesty King Mob". That's why, ever since, the term has denoted an uprising of the masses. And this is most certainly an uprising, wouldn't you agree?' He sucked ferociously on his pipe.

'But this isn't about religion, Arthur. It's orchestrated chaos. And it could just be the start – did you think about that? When any system breaks, people suffer. London isn't alone in this; it's happening all around the globe right now. I don't know how you can eat mints and smoke at the same time.'

'I'm mentholating the tobacco.' Bryant blasted a stream of smoke at the shattered detector as if deliberately to offend it. 'Anyway, this time it's different. As a city we have always rioted against symbols. Our insurrections are brutal but celebratory, intended as signals for change. A banker is let off for insider trading because he cut a deal with his directors – that's corruption, pure and simple, and the facts are easy enough for the average twit in the street to grasp. The act represents a far greater malaise. The public plans a peaceful march, but thanks to rapid communications technology the protest is hijacked by special-interest groups and anarchists. Remember the torching of buildings in Oxford Street a few years ago? This is like that, but on steroids. People are sick of being treated as if they're invisible, fit only to be used up and cast aside like any other exhausted commodity. The uprising is coming from something deep inside us, all of us.' It had always suited Bryant to take a transpontine view on lawbreaking, a thought that wasn't wasted on his partner.

'Funny how upset you got when someone knifed the tyres on your Mini,' May pointed out.

'That's different. One should never confuse legitimate protest with vandalism. There's nothing personal in all of this. Cornell is just the catalyst.'

'What about Freddie Weeks?' May asked. 'A man died, Arthur. Somebody deliberately set fire to him. How does that help to end injustice, burning a homeless man alive?'

'You're right, of course,' Bryant conceded, turning from the television and settling himself in an orange bendy chair situated in close proximity to a fresh pot of tea. For one horrible moment it looked as if he might simultaneously smoke and drink. 'Either the arsonist didn't care who was sleeping in the doorway and went ahead anyway, or he knew Weeks and used the riot as an opportunity to get rid of him. Fire is a cleanser. We can't rely on forensics to explain the culprit's intentions.'

'I wasn't thinking about his attacker,' said May. 'You heard what Weeks's father said. He was a bright kid, a good kid who lost his way. The system failed him. And the anarchists made it worse.'

'They didn't make it worse, they just provided the opportunity,' corrected Bryant. 'Someone used the protest to commit a crime. How are we getting on with the hostels?'

'No record of him on any At Risk registers so far,' said May. 'But we're only doing central London at the moment. Without an account of his movements we can't narrow down the possibilities.'

'What about the footage showing him bedding down at the bank? Can't you follow the cameras back?'

'How?' asked May, exasperated. 'Every reverse step branches off into another set of possibilities. Away from the backstreets are vast crowds of people who all look the same. It's these bloody masks. They're too good at hiding identities, and even if Darren Link still manages to stop everyone from wearing them – which is frankly unlikely – they've already successfully hidden the killer's identity.'

'I saw this thing on the television,' said Bryant, setting aside his pipe to fill two mugs and reach about for the sugar. 'Something about a Los Angeles crime unit, all moody lighting and urgent young people staring at computers, and when they wanted to find someone in a crowd they just zeroed in on one of his ears, analysed it and instantly found a match on the other side of the country. Why can't we do that?'

'It was a TV show,' said May. 'Even if we had the technology it would be an outsourced expense and we'd have to get budget approval first.'

'You see, that's the trouble!' Bryant slapped the table with passion, spilling tea. 'We're in the wrong country. We should be in America. They value free enterprise over there. They have such a refreshingly positive attitude. Our headlines say "More misery on the way". Know what theirs say? "Bring it on, we can handle it". All right, they eat at an absurdly early hour and think jogging's a good idea, but they're stout-hearted and wonderfully unembarrassable. That's just the East Coast; imagine what it's like in the Midwest. We'd get a lot more done if we were allowed to wave guns about.'

'All right, Wyatt Earp,' said May, 'let's concentrate on finding this chap the old-fashioned way.'

*

At nine forty-five on Monday evening Colin Bimsley and Meera Mangeshkar were still out on the street, checking the last of the hostels near the Square Mile. The Transformer was situated off Gray's Inn Road, one of a new generation of hostels catering to the more economically mobile, demanding backpackers. It seemed unlikely that Freddie Weeks had checked in here, but they had drawn a blank at the council-run overnight-stay dives, and were running out of options.

Linda Kzsowolski, the manager, was far from happy about uniformed officers turning up in her tastefully appointed reception area of painted surf and mountain scenes, and quickly ushered them into a tiny side room filled with vending machines and leaflets about faster broadband speeds.

Flipping open her laptop, she checked through the recent stays and failed to turn up Weeks's name. The boy's father had scanned and sent the most recent photograph he had of his son, which showed a slender, short, acne-ridden boy with straggly shoulder-length blond hair and intense blue eyes, aged twenty-three. The picture was two years old, and Weeks's father had confirmed his birth date.

'Wait, he was here a week ago,' said Linda. 'He stayed for three nights. I remember him clearly because on the last night he got into a fight with one of the other lads.'

'Why is there no record?' asked Bimsley.

'Human error, I imagine. We've had trouble with reception staff.'

'Do you know what the fight was about?'

'No, but Jamel, the guy he argued with, is still with us. He just came in.'

'Can we go and talk to him?' asked Mangeshkar.

'I'll bring him down,' said Kzsowolski.

'Of course she doesn't want us wandering around the

corridors,' said Meera while they awaited the manager's return. 'She's worried about what we'd find up there. The testosterone comes off these places like steam. They're little better than knocking shops.'

'I don't know where you get your ideas from,' said Colin, digging out a pound coin and feeding a vending machine for crisps. 'You've got a really puritanical streak, you know that?'

'I can't help it,' said Meera. 'Blame my folks. They're always telling me what to avoid and what not to do.'

'Don't you ever feel like rebelling?'

'Of course I do, all the time. Over the last few days I've felt like being out there with the rioters. A chance to tear it up and start again – who wouldn't want to try that? But then I realize that nothing's going to change.' After the protests and the arrests, the insurance claims and the damage repairs, she felt sure that things would just be the same as before.

'I don't know, it feels different this time,' said Colin, pushing a fistful of crisps into his mouth, then remembering to offer her the pack. 'The presenters on Sky News keep getting all flustered, like they can't believe what's going on. There's a real sense of excitement in the air. Me, I love a good punch-up.'

She watched him brushing oily crumbs from his uniform. 'Were you raised by animals, by any chance?'

'Hey, Romulus and Remus founded a city, so don't knock it.'

'I wasn't thinking about wolves. Baboons, perhaps.'

Kzsowolski reappeared at the door with a fashionably dressed young Arab in his mid-twenties. He wore the Hoxton young-granddad uniform of a trimmed, slender beard, tight cardigan and a narrow-brimmed hat pushed back on the crown of his head. His trousers were too fitted to have useable pockets, so he was forced to stand awkwardly with his mobile in one hand.

'We understand you had a row with this man?' asked Colin, showing him the photograph.

Jamel nodded. 'Yeah, it kind of came out of nowhere. I thought he was going to hit me.'

'What was it about?'

'Phone apps.'

'Apps?'

'I was sitting in the lounge just messing with my phone and I felt someone looking over my shoulder. He asked me what apps I was using, and I told him, and he just went off, shouting and acting all kind of crazy. Linda came along and threatened to throw him out.'

'At first I thought he'd taken something,' added Linda. 'But he didn't have the look, you know? After I warned him he calmed down very quickly, but it gave me a bit of a turn, seeing him blow up like that.'

'Has something happened to him?' Jamel asked.

'I'm afraid he's dead,' said Colin.

'What happened?'

'I can't discuss the details. We need to establish his prior movements.'

Jamel looked aghast. 'It wasn't my fault.'

'Don't worry, nobody's saying it was. Did you have any other contact with him?'

'We spoke a couple of times in the lounge, just casual stuff. He seemed fine then.'

'Did he talk about his plans? Or mention anyone else? Anything you remember that would be useful?'

'No, I don't think so. As I said . . . Wait, something about his girlfriend. Or ex-girlfriend. A girl, anyway. He was waiting for her one evening.'

'A girl. Anything else?'

'I don't think she was British.'

'What makes you think that?'

'I don't know, something about "when she first came here", something like that.'

'Do you remember if anyone turned up to see him?' Meera asked Linda.

'Non-guests can only come into the lobby,' the manager explained. 'They've usually arranged to meet their friends down here, so there's no reason why they would give us their names, or say who they've come to meet.'

After a few more questions Bimsley and Mangeshkar knew they'd gone as far as they could go, and took their leave. 'At least now we know he had a girlfriend,' said Colin as they headed back into the street. 'I've no idea how we track her down.'

'Suppose he met her here and they went somewhere nearby?' Meera began. 'Where are the nearest cheap eats?'

They tried pizza bars, Thai takeaways, pasta cafés, a McDonald's and a Subway. After that they started on the pubs, hitting the Lady Ottoline, the Yorkshire Grey, the Blue Lion, the Calthorpe Arms, the Lamb and the Duke of York, but none of the bar staff recalled seeing Weeks. By the time they had doubled back to the Ship and the Enterprise, last orders were well and truly over and it was starting to rain again.

'We're not going to get anything more tonight,' said Meera. 'Do you need a lift?'

Bimsley hopped on and off the pavement, then stood on one leg for no particular reason. 'Nah, I'm hungry. I think I'll go and get a burger.'

'Why don't you find yourself a girlfriend?' Meera asked.

''Cause I'm still waiting for you,' he replied, as if the answer was obvious.

She touched his arm lightly. 'Please, Colin, don't. Not any more.'

'Why not?'

She hesitated a moment before telling him, and in the gap he felt a chill. 'My parents,' she said. 'I've been meaning to tell you. They've got someone lined up for me.'

Colin couldn't believe what he had just heard. 'I thought they were still trying to get your sister married off?'

'They've sort of given up on that.'

'So who is this bloke?'

'A boy I used to know, Ryan Malhotra. He trained as a doctor and is going into private practice soon. He wasn't seeing anyone serious while he was in med school, because he wanted to concentrate on his career. But now—'

'What? Now you're going to let your parents choose you a husband?'

'Colin – I actually like him. I've known him all my life.'

She felt lousy telling him. Bimsley had the look of a man facing a burglar armed with a broken bottle. 'So he suddenly decides he wants to get married and it suits your folks, and you're just going to do what you're told?'

'It's not like that.'

'Then what is it like? Tough, independent, "I-can-do-it-myself" Meera, who never needs anyone else's help, is going to start having babies to please her mum and dad.'

'That's unfair, Colin. You don't understand the pressure I'm under, and Ryan's a nice guy – he's really nice. You'd like him.'

The fight had gone out of her, Colin thought. Normally she would have instantly punched back.

'No, I wouldn't like him. Why didn't you tell me about this before?' he asked. 'You know how I feel about you, how I've always felt.'

'This isn't about you. We've never been out together. I never said I would. I never, ever led you on, Colin.'

'Yeah, I know. It's not fair of me to put you on the spot. Fine. Well, I hope you'll be very happy with your ambitious doctor. I'm going to do the late-night pubs around here. And I'm off-duty so I'll be drinking.' The rain was falling harder. Turning up his collar, Colin thrust his hands into his jacket pockets and stalked off along the street.

Meera watched him go, then went to collect her Kawasaki.

12

BREAKING FREE

By midnight on Monday the few remaining small fires had been snuffed out by auxiliary units, assisted by the pounding rain, and most of the protestors had disbanded for the night, heading for any shelter they could find. There was talk that the weather had succeeded in clearing the streets where the police had failed. Perhaps that would be the end of it.

But on Tuesday morning, new reports about anarchy in the city quickly infected everyone's mood. The detectives were frustrated by the paucity of leads, Dan Banbury was infuriated by the lack of evidence and Raymond Land was upset about having to cancel his holiday again.

An uneasy truce now held in the roads surrounding the Bank of England and the Findersbury Private Bank. Under advice from Superintendent Darren Link, the police had blocked off further routes with heavy steel barriers. Trains started delivering protestors from all over the country, and even though the authorities had begun checking European arrivals in London, conducting searches whenever flights landed and ferries docked, nothing had been done to stop their arrival from other ports of entry.

Link, who displayed an eschatological attitude about the riots that would have alarmed his bosses had they known, was working with the anti-terrorist squad to identify known activists and lift them off the streets before they had a chance to act. Ideally he would have liked to get each of them in a dark corner for a twenty-minute debrief with a blunt instrument, but senior eyes were watching him.

The weather forecast for Tuesday was at least partially fine, and with Dexter Cornell continuing to goad his adversaries by promising in TV interviews that he would not be intimidated into leaving the bank before he was good and ready, it now seemed likely that further violence would erupt in the next twenty-four hours.

In fact, a bizarre act of violence occurred soon after, but not in a way anyone had imagined, and not in the City's Square Mile.

His muscles were sore and stiffening fast.

He had been working without light for the last two hours, dragging everything he needed up the steep staircase to the roof. The rising dust in the attic triggered his asthma, and he needed to sit quietly on the tiles for a while until he could catch his breath again.

He found he could see more clearly with the skylight propped open. It was never truly dark in the city. The heavy cloud layering the London sky was afflicted with a sickly jaundice that reflected light back. Below, the pitched-glass rooftops of Brixton Market snaked between the buildings, and he could see the traders arriving for the day. He smoked a cigarette, carefully pocketing the stub afterwards.

It was important to make sure that he could effect a fast escape. He knew that it would be tempting to stay and see what happened, but if he took too long they would quickly find a way to cut off his escape route. The old shops that lined the market were terraced, and he had paced out two separate exits across their gutters to fire escapes, back to pavement level. From there he could slip away through the crowds of morning shoppers, beneath the old brick arches on Electric Avenue. The pavements would work in his favour; they were among the most cluttered and impenetrable in London. Now all he had to do was wait for the target to arrive.

He thought about yesterday's death. He'd been sorry to kill the boy but it seemed to him that in any great plan an innocent had to suffer. Sleeping rough was never without attendant risks, but to be burned alive . . . He forced himself to put the thought aside, remembering why Freddie Weeks had had to die. It was better to focus his hatred now and concentrate on humiliating his second victim in the most excruciating manner possible.

Heading back inside the attic, he checked on the camera and the electronic door buzzer, making sure he could take the small equipment with him when he left. Everything else was fingerprint-free and could be dumped. So long as he could travel light and move fast, there was no hope of anyone catching him.

Bryant got the call while he was still at home. After much carphology with the duvet, he tipped his phone out of his pillowcase.

'Morning, Mr Bryant,' said Colin Bimsley. 'I found her.'

'Found who?' asked Bryant. 'Try forming complete sentences.'

'Sorry. The girlfriend.'

'What girlfriend?'

'Weeks had one. She's doing bar work at the Enterprise pub on Red Lion Street, just down in Holborn. She dated Freddie Weeks for a while but it didn't work out between them. I took a statement and gave her my hotline, but I thought you'd want to talk to her. She'll be there at eight thirty this morning. I hope you didn't mind me calling so early.'

'I've been lying here thinking since five,' said Bryant. 'At my age you get more night than day. Where are you? What's that funny noise in the background?'

'I'm at the Shad Thames Boxing Club. When I'm angry, it's best that I hit things before I come to work.'

'Glad to hear it,' replied Bryant, ringing off and heading for the bathroom to see if he could find out what Alma had done with his clean shirt.

The sign above the window showed a bemused polar bear looking up at a four-masted schooner. At 8.37 a.m. Bryant knocked on the door of the Enterprise pub and was admitted into what appeared to be a Victorian hall of emerald ceramic tiles, dark wooden floors and milky pendant globe lamps. The interior had undergone the kind of reverse pimping that had lately taken off in central London, in the realization that traditional pubs were in danger of vanishing altogether. Lagers had been replaced by seasonal beers, plastic signs had been superseded by blackboards and only the presence of roulades and alfalfa sprouts on the snack menus revealed that these were fanciful reimaginings of 1930s boozers, their design ethic influenced by old films and the desire to charge £17.50 for a cube of crusted pork belly.

If the girl had been a craft beer she would have been described as full-bodied and pale with a refined finish. She had ice-blue eyes, a tangle of glossy blonde hair and the kind of happily confident attitude that got her noticed even by London's jaded populace. The faintest trace of an accent suggested that she was Polish.

'I'm Joanna Papis. You must be Mr Bryant.' She shook his hand warmly and ushered him in, guiding him around the pub's vacuum-cleaning equipment. If she was surprised by his age, she hid it well. 'There's a room behind the bar where we can talk without being in the cleaner's way.'

'I understand one of our DCs took a statement from you,' said Bryant, settling himself in the cluttered manager's office. 'But I thought you could tell me a bit more about your friendship with Mr Weeks. We're hoping something in his past will lead us to his killer.'

'I heard Freddie was sofa-surfing for a while, then using hostels,' she said, finding somewhere to perch. 'I feel a bit responsible, you know? I keep wondering whether if I'd stayed with him maybe he'd have got back on an even keel, but it was just too difficult for me.'

'When you say "an even keel", do you mean financially?'

'Yes, but also . . . his behaviour. It wasn't always easy to be around him. We met here in the pub.' She pointed out into the saloon bar. 'Right in that corner. He'd been working in the neighbourhood, in the local market. Before that he'd been employed by an IT company, but it went bust and they had to let him go.'

'From IT to selling spuds – that's a bit of a drop,' said Bryant.

'He couldn't find anything else. He was planning to leave the market because he wasn't happy there, and was looking for another position.' She brushed a blonde strand behind one ear. 'I suppose I only really started seeing him because he was so insistent, and I felt a bit sorry for him. It's not easy having a social life when you work until midnight. I have a day job and I'm working here four nights a week. Freddie used to wait at the bar for me to finish, and usually ended up drinking too much. It wasn't an easy relationship, but he was sweet and I knew he was really trying. But he couldn't find the work he wanted, and his attitude didn't help.'

'In what way?'

'He was very politicized. He felt that all information should be liberated.' She looked out at the TV, which was displaying footage of Julian Assange running a gauntlet of photographers. 'He was a big supporter of that guy. Then he got involved in the Occupy movement. Which would have been fine, but Freddie never knew when to stay quiet. I thought he'd have difficulty finding employment. I paid his rent a couple of times, but eventually I'd had enough of it and broke up with him.' She gave a shrug of apology. 'A couple of weeks later I saw one of the guys he used to come in with, and heard he was sleeping on their floors. I think by that time he'd pretty much run out of options.'

'Given his outspoken views, do you think he made enemies?' asked Bryant.

'I wouldn't have thought so.' She absently touched the neckline of her T-shirt, remembering. 'Freddie was so gentle that it was hard to be angry with him for long. He had a kind of . . . *innocence*. He was thin and had a slight limp, and always looked so downcast. Like the kind of man who would always end up getting hurt. I had a feeling that one day he would suffer some terrible tragedy. I know it sounds selfish, but I didn't want to be around him when it happened. This is my time to build a career and get my life together. We have to make our own futures, and I couldn't understand the choices he made.'

'He was asleep in a doorway when he died, Miss Papis,' Bryant pointed out with a touch of severity. 'He was hardly the engineer of his fate. Some of us need more protection than others. When was the last time you saw him?'

Papis sighed. 'Look, I wasn't perfect, OK? There was never a right time to tell him.'

'Tell him what?' prompted Bryant.

'That I needed to put myself first for a while and that I couldn't see him any more. I'm only working here temporarily while I finish my training in accountancy. I already took an AAT foundation course. I didn't have time to be a mother to him. Freddie was very upset about it. And I probably said things I shouldn't have.'

'When was this?'

'More than six weeks ago. I heard he left his job at the market just after that and started sleeping rough. You don't think it was my fault, do you?'

'I can't absolve you of that,' said Bryant, creaking to his feet. 'When you're out on the street you become an easy target.'

Afterwards, as he walked back up Red Lion Street towards the unit, Bryant felt uneasy. The arsonist had not torched Weeks in an act of mindless cruelty; he'd deliberately launched an attack. Someone who could do that might be capable of doing it again. For all he knew, Weeks's death was a practice run for something much worse.

As he cut through King's Cross Station, he glanced up at the television monitors and saw a blue phalanx of officers being driven back by dozens of hurtling masked figures. The red ribbon running beneath the footage read 'Police cut off by protestors'. Men and women were helping to carry debris, bins, bollards and furniture, laying them across the roads to form a flaming boundary line. By the look of it, the skirmishes had now crossed Ludgate Circus, spreading to the far end of Fleet Street. It meant that the chaos was breaking free of the Square Mile.

Link's men had lost the battle to contain the war. Anything could happen now.

13

FIRE AND SNOW

The young man checked his watch and peered over the filthy parapet of the roof, looking down at the canopy. When Glen Hall suddenly appeared, pausing inside the market entrance to check the directions on his phone, he spotted him at once. Hall always wore expensive dark suits and had a distinctive walk born of easy confidence and a sense of entitlement. You half expected him to stroll with his hands folded behind his back, like the Duke of Edinburgh.

Slipping down from his perch, he dropped back inside the attic. The brazier had been on for hours and was so hot that he could hardly get near it. The tar glowed dully in the cauldron, popping and churning like a miniature volcano. The loudness of the electronic door buzzer made him jump. Hall had found the shop and was pressing the entry button repeatedly. The moment for action had arrived. As he checked the preparations, he realized his hands were shaking. Getting rid of Freddie Weeks had been the trial run. This was where it really started.

*

The shop had no sign, but Glen Hall could see around the paper blinds to the posters on the unlit walls, including a rare one-sheet for the original Japanese release of *Firestarter* and a version of *Indiana Jones and the Temple of Doom* that he had been trying to buy for years. The latter showed Harrison Ford suspended over a pit of lava. Was it a reprint or an original? If it was genuine, did the shop owner have any idea of its real worth? Hell, it was a pop-up gallery in Brixton Market, so probably not. Then again, the way he'd been contacted by the owner suggested that there was something underhand about the whole enterprise. Maybe he was selling stolen goods or copyright-infringing forgeries. When it came to collecting, Hall wasn't averse to bending the rules, but he wasn't about to pay for a fake.

He thumped the buzzer again, but nothing appeared to be happening. Cupping his hands around his eyes, he peered inside and tried to see if there was anyone in the shop. Just then the catch was electronically released and the door popped open by itself.

He stepped inside and looked around. Against the wall was the 1968 poster for *You Only Live Twice,* the quad in which Sean Connery was depicted strolling at a 45-degree angle across the roof of a volcano in a tuxedo. What made the poster so unusual was that Connery had cloven hooves instead of shoes. The artist had read in the script that Bond would scale a sheer wall, but as he hadn't seen the film he'd used his own imagination to work out how the superspy might manage such a feat. His solution made the artwork unique.

Hall could see the price tag from here: £160, an insanely low figure that instantly suggested it was a forgery.

He was starting to feel as if he had been tricked. Why was there no one here? What had he been set up for? God knew there were plenty of people who'd enjoy sending him on a wild-goose chase.

Above Hall, he watched and waited, telling himself to hold on for just a little longer. The heat from the cauldron was starting to sear his bare arms. His thighs were trembling from the strain of steadying it.

Just a little further . . .

Hall was clearly unhappy with the non-appearance of the gallery owner. He stepped closer to the Bond artwork and peered at it, realizing now that it was a cheap photocopy.

He heard a movement overhead, smelled something as pungent as hot liquorice in the air and looked up.

The young man shifted his legs, bracing against the heavy pot, watching through the hole in the ceiling. Just one more step forward and his target would be in place. He had configured the layout of the tiny shop so that his victim would be forced to stand immediately below the hole. Now he slammed all of his weight against the cauldron and swung it over. The bubbling tar lolloped out, decanting more slowly than he'd expected. It dropped into the aluminium funnel he had made for it and fell through the ceiling, down into the shop.

Hall sensed the movement above his head but couldn't see anything at first. He peered up into the hole. What he discerned made no sense: a kind of wide metal tube with something dark and fiery falling out of it.

The heavy liquid hit him with its full weight, searing and sticking, catching him by surprise and hammering him down to the floor. As it made contact with skin and the material of his shirt it burst into flame, exploding in crusted splashes of orange and black, scattering droplets of fire everywhere.

It poured and poured, spattering all over the shop, catching alight wherever it fell. Satisfied with his work, the man above released the white blizzard from the second bucket.

The gallery had no lights on, and at first the paper

blinds stopped any of the early-morning shoppers from looking inside. By the time one of them noticed and stepped forward to see, the fallen tar had already started to cool and harden, sealing Hall to the floor like a king trapped within his own treasure house. The swansdown settled like a sudden snowfall and stuck. The little shop was transformed into an art installation of Icelandic fire as the walls scorched and the paper blinds caught alight, smoke drifting through the fluttering flurry of feathers.

From outside, what people saw made no sense. A fiery maelstrom had been released inside the building. And at the centre of the apocalypse was a fallen golem.

14

BRIMSTONE

Fraternity DuCaine was the first to arrive at the PCU on Tuesday morning, and caught the incoming message. He had been transferred to the North London Met for the last couple of months, and was anxious to get back to the unit where his older brother had died in the line of duty. As soon as he found out what had happened, he called the detectives and set the day's events in motion.

'They don't want us here,' Bryant told his partner, trying to stay upright as their taxi roared into Brixton High Street. 'It's not our jurisdiction. I told them we had a connection to the Freddie Weeks case.'

'We do?' It was news to May. They all leaned as the cab swung a hard right. 'How?'

'Method of death,' answered Bryant cheerfully. 'You took the call, Fraternity – tell John.'

'He was burned alive, Mr May.'

The railway bridge that crosses Brixton Road was just ahead. There was a truck pulling out of a bay in front of Marks & Spencer, and it didn't look as if the taxi was going to brake. 'Hang on, guv,' warned the driver, sashaying into the space. May noticed that he was on the phone, drinking a coffee and possibly scanning the headlines of the *Daily Mirror* at the same time.

'Burned? How common is that in London?' May asked as he alighted. 'I mean outside of house fires?'

'This doesn't look like a house fire,' said Fraternity. 'They're treating it as suspicious.'

'Then why isn't Brixton CID handling it?'

Fraternity pointed to his black face. 'What do you think?'

'Oh.' May got the message. The last thing Brixton wanted to deal with was the murder of a white outsider in a predominantly West Indian community. The area had been gentrified, but a lot of people still suspected that Brixton stood on a racial fault line. With some parts of the press happy to play on the community's worst fears, it was easier for the CID to pass the ball.

They were barely out of the cab before it launched back into the traffic with a screech. The canopied front avenue of the market had been cordoned off, and as the shop owners argued with local officers, Bryant and May, together with DuCaine, slipped between the barriers.

The market had changed out of all recognition since Bryant was last here. Once it had been filled with counters of dazzling fruits, bejewelled fish and forests of vegetables. Now the shops had largely been replaced by hipster cafés serving Brazilian, Spanish, Mexican and Italian food.

'Apparently the corner premises have been empty for a few months,' DuCaine explained as they made their way between the shabby-chic bars. 'The owner rents it out to pop-up stores. A week ago he got a request for a one-week rental, and agreed so long as he was paid cash-in-hand. The next morning he received an envelope containing money. The renter left no name and his address checked out false. He made the call from a chuckaway.'

They were greeted by a local officer who led them to

the corner shop. 'Where's the rest of your team?' asked May, looking around.

'We were told to send them away,' the officer replied.

'By whom?'

'A superintendent over at the City of London, sir.'

'Darren Link,' said Bryant. 'He'll be anxious to stay out of this. A busy market, officers running all over it, press sniffing around, all the things he doesn't want to deal with right now.'

'What about witnesses?'

'We've been told to leave that to you, sir. I don't think even your team has seen something like this before.' The officer ushered them inside the acrid, smoking shop. Curious shoppers tried to peer in but were swiftly moved away.

A figure lay on its back in the centre of the bare-boarded floor, one leg folded under the other. The molten tar had set over his head and shoulders in an accretion of glossy black lava. It had sealed itself to the ground wherever it had splashed. Glen Hall's suit had burned and stuck to him, but with the dying of the fire the liquid had turned to rock, cementing him in place. The room smelled of bitumen, scorched wood, feathers and roasted flesh.

'Good heavens, I thought I'd seen everything,' said May. 'Did the fire just burn itself out?'

Bryant leaned back and studied the walls. 'No air,' he said. 'Look.' The hole in the ceiling had been covered by a metal panel.

May kept to the unscorched edges of the room. The smell was eye-watering. 'Two men dying by fire,' he said. 'What are the odds?'

'Not fire exactly. More like brimstone. It'll take a crowbar to get him off the ground.' Bryant was shocked but there was no disguising the excitement in his blue eyes. 'So, was he scalded or suffocated?' He peered at the ceiling. 'What's up there?'

'No one's been upstairs yet,' the officer replied.

'Well, what if he's still in the attic or out on the roof? Didn't you think to check?'

'We're not allowed upstairs in case of contamination, sir. No forensics.'

The shop door opened and Dan Banbury skirted around the body. 'You've got somebody now,' he said. 'Blimey, that's a bit Dr Phibes, isn't it? Rather a lot of effort. Why not just shoot him in the head?'

'You don't understand the nature of revenge,' said Bryant.

'So you've already decided it's a case of revenge, then?'

'Of course. Our perpetrator would have stayed up there to watch. Will somebody go or do I have to, with my knees?'

Banbury and DuCaine headed up the stairs. DuCaine glanced back, wondering what his boss was thinking. Bryant was standing over the obliterated body, staring hard at its head. 'So we get to ID another victim without a face. Interesting. You must be able to see something,' he called upwards.

'Perhaps you should come up here, Mr Bryant.'

When the elderly detective made it to the top, he found Banbury on his knees examining the iron plate over the hole. 'He left the big stuff behind, but I don't suppose we'll find any prints,' Banbury warned. 'Looks like it was thoroughly planned. He melted the tar in a workman's brazier powered by that gas cylinder over there, so if he was working alone he must be pretty strong.'

'What's that?' Bryant pointed to a white plastic remote lying on the floor.

'Probably the buzzer for the front door,' said Banbury, 'a couple of quid at B&Q. There's no specialist equipment here, but it still took some serious effort to pull off a stunt like this.'

'So what's our best shot at an ID from the evidence?' asked May.

'Do you mean the victim or the perpetrator?'

'Either. Both.'

'For the victim, the suit jacket. If we can get the tar off it he might still have a wallet in there,' said Banbury. 'For the perp, probably the shop surround. The door handle's stiff. He might have touched something to steady himself as he tried to get it open. The poster racks too, if he dressed the place himself. Boot prints; there's a hatch to the roof and a lot of dirt in the roof gullies. He must have passed along them to get out. I can't imagine he came back past his victim. We need to know how he got down.'

'Maybe he didn't get down,' said Bryant. 'How many hiding places are there in a long terrace like this? What's the CCTV situation like?'

'In the market? Virtually non-existent,' said Banbury, who had the sort of brain that stored the location of every camera in London. 'It was meant to have gone in but . . . I don't know, budget cuts, probably.'

'Typical,' said Bryant, 'the whole blasted country's up to its earlobes in government security cameras and he hits one of the few London streets that doesn't have any. Of course, that's probably why he chose the site in the first place. It's not actually a street at all.'

He carefully made his way back down. The stairs were steep and he could no longer fully trust his legs. 'Do we have any idea what this fellow looks like?' he asked his partner, who caught him at the bottom.

May brandished a black Bulgari credit-card holder in plastic-clad hands. '*Voilà*. I got this out from under the tar. Let's have a look.' He removed a laminated driving licence and several cards. 'ID for one Glen David Hall, domiciled in the Onyx – it's one of those new loft buildings on the City Road residential corridor, so he's well out of his territory. Oh, and a business card. A bank, no less. Oh ho. Guess which one?'

'Not the Findersbury?' Bryant's fingers were twitching.

'Keep your grubby hands off. Yes, the very one. And you know what that means.'

Bryant knew all too well. It meant pressure from the CoL to get the case closed within hours. If it had been a young black male lying dead in Brixton, the public perception would be different. 'Drugs and gangs,' ran the popular mantra, 'no smoke without fire, he probably deserved it.' But a wealthy white businessman in a black neighbourhood? It was more about class than race, and therefore at the heart of London's most divisive issue. 'We have to keep the press away,' he said. 'It's taken this area fifty years to shake off prejudice. I'm not going to have the clock turned back now.'

'We don't have much luck with embargoes, but the CoL has clout,' said May. 'I know how much you love dealing with them.'

While Banbury went to work, Bryant slipped out into the covered avenue between the shops and cafés, and stuffed a meditative pipe with Seven Veils Stone Pipe Balkan Ribbon tobacco, which he'd found for sale in an old Mason jar in the Burj Kalifah Shish Shop, halfway up the Edgware Road. As he puffed, the smoke mingling with the scent of *shawarma*s and *albondiga*s from nearby cafés, he decided that it was the murderer's methodology that vexed him most. Who, he wondered, would be so insane as to do something like this? Arsonists enjoyed watching buildings burn. Killing with fire was something new and suggested an aberrant psychology, unless there was a deeper meaning, some other strange purpose.

Bryant's thoughtful attitude was unpopular with many of his more worldly colleagues. For them it was a binary matter: criminals broke the law and got caught; then they acted outraged when they were dropped into a court system that barely acknowledged them. Nothing was black and white in Bryant's world. He saw an infinity of degrees. Urban life was rapidly evolving, reconfiguring social behaviour until it became as unpredictable as climate change. He saw the knock-on effects of bad government, policies corrupted through incompetence and indecision. He saw himself going to the bad at the age of fifteen on the grey litter-strewn streets of Whitechapel, rescued by the kindness of a lone street constable, something that he feared could never happen now. But he also saw the resilience of ordinary people.

In every decade and generation, he thought as the aromatic blue smoke trailed behind his head, *one thing unites us: obstinacy. We're a paradoxical mix of conformity and rebellion, privacy and bravado. We will not do what we are told. That's how it always was. But there's something else going on here today. This man has no fear. When people lose respect, they're capable of anything.*

Drifting in his thoughts, he discovered that he had circled the market and returned to the Brazilian café opposite the burned-out shop. The aproned owner stepped out and came over to him.

'Oi. You can't smoke that thing in here,' he said, pointing to the pipe.

'I'm not *in here,* I'm outside,' said Bryant.

'This is under cover. That thing above us is a canopy. How much longer they gonna be in there anyway?' He pointed at the shop. 'I'm losing business.'

'Probably most of the day, I imagine,' Bryant replied. 'How do you know I'm a cop?'

'You're joking, aren't you? With feet like that? Things are always crazy round here, but 'specially today.' The café owner had actually taken Bryant for a strolling pensioner until the crackle of a radio had given him away. Ruminatively smoking in a ratty tweed coat and mismatched gloves, he certainly didn't look like a policeman.

'Oh. Crazy how?' Bryant asked.

'Crazy crazy,' the Brazilian repeated. 'First some guy running around on the roof, then Metish next door saying there was a body, and police scaring off the customers—'

'You saw someone on the roof?'

'I didn't get a good look, but I see him, sure. That glass ain't safe, he coulda fallen right through.'

'What time was this?'

'This morning, sometime before nine. I was opening up a bit later than usual. My wife's been up with gallstones. They wanted her to have the operation on a Saturday, but she says more patients die in hospitals at the weekend so she wouldn't go, then she changed her mind and now she's gone back to the end of the waiting list.'

'I'm not really interested in your wife's gallstones. Could you identify the man on the roof?'

'No, he was wearing one of them Guy Fawkes masks like you see on the news. Bloke's got no right to go around doing stuff like that.'

'How do you know it was a man?'

'I don't know – he moved like one. He something to do with what's goin' on in there?'

'Maybe,' said Bryant.

'Well, I hope they get these cordons down,' said the owner, carefully straightening the chairs outside his café bar. 'We got a big Halloween party booked in tonight, and I can't afford to cancel.'

'Halloween was last night,' said Bryant.

'For kids, yeah. This one's for the parents.'

'What's your name?' Bryant asked.

'Alejandro Figueroa.'

Bryant peered dubiously at the pastries in the window. 'Is your food any good?'

Figueroa puffed out his chest. 'Best damned empanadas in London.'

'Good. Stick four in a bag for me.'

'What, you gonna pay for 'em?'

'Of course not, and I won't check out your fire certificate, either. I'll be back for them in a minute.' *Halloween,* he thought, tamping out his pipe and heading back into the shuttered shop.

15

GUY FAWKES

'No,' said May on the cab ride back. 'Absolutely not. Don't even think about it.'

'Hear me out,' said Bryant, tearing open his brown paper bag and breaking out the empanadas. 'Samhain is associated with mayhem. This was an act of madness. It wasn't carried out in the heat of the moment with a weapon that readily came to hand; it was a cold-blooded atrocity planned to cause pain. The café owner over the road, Mr Figueroa, saw someone run across the canopy wearing a Guy Fawkes mask. Guy Fawkes Night is just five days away. The two events are so close that they've virtually become fused together.'

'People aren't rioting because of Halloween,' objected May vehemently. 'They're doing it because a banker behaved badly. This cake's got meat in it.'

'Oh, *bankers*.' Bryant spat the word. 'They act badly all the time and the public knows it, and nobody does anything. Halloween has another name – Mischief Night. It started in St John's College, Oxford, during the May Day celebrations of 1790. But when families moved into cities during the Industrial Revolution, the date was changed to November the fourth, the night before Guy Fawkes Night.'

'Why did it change?' May found himself being reluctantly drawn in.

'Because May Day celebrations meant nothing to urban children. But Guy Fawkes: that was a reason to have fun and raise some hell. So they settled on the night before the bonfires were lit.'

'You see what you've done?' cried May, annoyed with himself. 'You've managed to switch my attention away from the case at hand to some pointless piece of forgotten history.'

'Yes, that is what I do,' said Bryant, sucking bits of empanada through his freshly bleached dentures.

'Well, can you kindly not do so. Right now we've more practical concerns. Where did he get the posters from? And the tar? Somebody must have met this guy. And we need to talk to the directors at the Findersbury.'

'It's only been twenty-four hours, John. There's a lot we haven't found yet.' Bryant unglued some stubborn pastry with a digit. 'When I was a nipper, I would spend the whole week building a Guy. He was made of old clothes cadged from parents and neighbours, stuffed with newspapers and topped with a hat and a mask made from pressed grey cardboard – they were sold in all tobacconists' shops. Then I trundled him down to the street corner and collected "a penny for the Guy". I know it sounds Victorian and a bit like begging, but it was fun. Kids have always done such things. On July the twenty-fifth, St James's Day, children used to build little grottoes for the saint and take money from passers-by. It's always about religion.'

'But not Guy Fawkes—'

'Of course it is! Burning the Guy is anti-Catholic. In 1677 Londoners burned an effigy of the Pope filled with live cats.'

'It's all gone now, mate.' The cabbie was taking an interest in their conversation. 'You know why they don't do it no more?' He glanced over his shoulder at them. 'European Parliament. Health and Safety. Political correctness gone mad.' He thought for a moment, adding, 'And them paedophiles.'

'By which I assume you mean that the idea of children taking money from strangers on the street somehow risks turning them into rent boys,' said Bryant, 'a logic which surpasses even my notoriously flimsy mind.'

'No, mate,' said the cabbie, 'it's the God's honest truth.'

'I think you'll find that the truth is somewhat more prosaic,' said Bryant, ever the enemy of misinformation. 'With the retail ascendency of Halloween, children's spending power is used up before Guy Fawkes Night, which falls just five days later. It doesn't help that sometimes Diwali also lands in the same time period.'

'You lot think you know everything,' grumbled the cabbie, turning off his speaker and bringing the conversation to an end.

Bryant hated being stopped in mid-flow. 'Obviously the events are utterly different,' he explained. 'Guido Fawkes was from York. The name was adopted while he was fighting for Catholic Spain against the Protestant Dutch. The night named after him was intended to celebrate the *prevention* of insurrection, but it's become the reverse. Halloween is actually a Christian remembrance of the dead. The term means "Saint's Night". And it has nothing to do with dressing up as a zombie.'

'So perhaps Guy Fawkes Night was on course to die out anyway, at least until the anti-capitalist movement began.' May finished his empanada and balled the paper bag. 'You know that comic book *V for Vendetta*?'

'The last comic I bought was *The Beano*.'

'You missed something special. It was back in the early

eighties. I don't think even the artist and writer realized what they'd done by creating it.'

'The early eighties hasn't come on my radar yet,' said Bryant. 'Far too recent.'

'Well, the book is about a modern-day Guy Fawkes setting out to destroy Parliament. The traditional Guy Fawkes mask was streamlined and became a modern protest symbol. So, although your "penny for the Guy" disappeared, his face re-emerged as the spirit of insurrection, and now it has spread right across the planet.'

'You're telling me that a celebration of rebellion that survived for over four centuries owes its revival to a *comic book*?' said Bryant, amazed.

'It was also a film,' said May.

Bryant was sorting it out in his head. 'Let me see if I've got this right. The protestors wear masks which were created by a studio to sell their film and were probably made somewhere cheap, like Brazil or China. So it's the first worldwide anti-capitalist revolution to be funded by a capitalist franchise.'

'Yes, well, there is that aspect of it,' May agreed. 'There's paradox at the heart of every protest.'

'This is incredibly depressing news.' Bryant shook his head sadly. 'The revolution is not only being televised, it's being licensed.'

'Things have become more complicated since you and I were kids.' May sighed. 'These are conservative times. Everyone's constantly being told to tighten their belts and find work. Our prime minister made another Orwellian speech last month, warning the young that austerity's going to last forever.'

The cabbie, who had either the ability to lip-read or poor soundproofing, clicked his speaker on once more. 'Yeah, he made it in a white bow-tie and waistcoat, standing in front of a golden throne at some bloody business dinner,' he said. 'Now there's riots all over the place and where is he? In Barbados on some kind of fact-finding mission. There's a demonstration going on in Parliament Square.'

'Is it connected with the banking scandal?' Bryant asked, leaning forward.

'No, I mean there's a demonstration going on in Parliament Square so I'm going via Birdcage Walk,' said the driver. 'I don't know why the Queen lives in Victoria; it's a bloody rough neighbourhood.'

'You'd think there would be raging mobs burning down Parliament by now,' Bryant said as they alighted in King's Cross. 'And you wonder why I'm glad that people are at last doing something.'

'But what exactly are they doing?' asked May, swiping their way into the PCU. 'Chucking a few petrol bombs? Burning an innocent kid alive and pouring hot tar on a banker? When you set out to topple a system, you'd better make sure you have something to replace it with. And another thing: what if the connection between Weeks and Hall is just coincidental?'

'Don't be ridiculous. The method links them. That's why we were summoned.'

'No, you and Fraternity made the connection, nobody else. It's what you always do.'

'Then why are they letting us take it on?' asked Bryant.

'Because they obviously don't want the case! A murder in Brixton? If it's fumbled, there'll be attacks from both sides and it'll take down anyone associated with it.'

Bryant girded himself for the climb to the first floor. 'You see, that's the problem,' he told May. 'I'm not as devious-minded as you. I didn't consider the area. In 1873 Vincent van Gogh was living in Brixton, did you know that? One of those odd London facts that seems so unlikely, like Lenin and Marx in Soho, Poe in Stoke Newington or Rimbaud and Verlaine sharing a flat in Camden. Hard to imagine, isn't it? Van Gogh might have painted *Electric Avenue at Dusk*. There's something quite Jamaican about his use of colour. Wouldn't that have been wonderful?'

May felt as if he was going mad. Then he realized, *No, it's not me, it's Arthur.* 'By the way,' he asked, 'where did you go last night?'

'When last night?' Bryant paused halfway up to catch his breath until May gave him a gentle push.

'After you left the unit. I called you and there was no answer.'

'What did you want?'

'To ask you a question, but that's not important. Alma didn't know where you were, either.'

'I wasn't anywhere.'

'You walked home?' May knew that it was no more than a fifteen-minute stroll from the PCU to Bryant's flat, but according to Alma he had not arrived for another two hours.

Bryant carried on up the stairs. 'I remember now, I stopped for a bag of chips.'

'Where exactly?'

'Hang on, let me get to my office and I'll tell you.' Entering the room, he turned the pockets of his overcoat out on to his desk and revealed an old threepenny bit, a pencil with a 1970s troll on top, a conker, a sherbet lemon out of its wrapper, a flick-knife, three pairs of glasses, two hearing-aid batteries, a third-class train ticket for Windsor dated 9 June 1953 and a membership card for the Pentonville Model Battleship Society. 'I must have lost the receipt,' he said, surprised.

'Only there was a report of somebody fitting your exact description sitting on the kerb outside the St Pancras Grand Hotel last night. The doorman called me. When he went back to check, he couldn't find anyone.'

'Well, that was hardly likely to have been me, was it?' said Bryant indignantly.

May meant to ask his partner why he had been planning a trip to Windsor one week after the coronation, but another thought assailed him. The doorman saw them pass the hotel nearly every day, and was unlikely to have made a mistake. Bryant was concealing something.

16

TAR AND FEATHER

On Tuesday afternoon, Giles Kershaw found himself with two scorched corpses in his mortuary. 'We're not a burns unit,' he complained, leading Dan Banbury back to the autopsy room. 'I'm not really equipped to deal with this. Fire examination's a pretty intricate discipline.'

'I know a bit about it,' said Banbury. 'There was a fire officer named Carter at the Weeks site. She's offered to provide us with advice.'

'I think we'll need her,' said Kershaw. 'I've spared you the sight of Mr Hall. A lot of his skin came off with the tar. It had set like concrete.' Even with the extraction fan on and the bodies hidden from sight, the place reeked with the smell of road-surfacing material. As there were only two small high windows at the ends of the room, the overhead LED panels were always illuminated, and their light gave the living a ghastly anaemic pallor.

'It's funny, a bloke like you doing this.' Banbury sniffed, looking around at the laden anatomy station and the scrubbed steel cadaver tables.

'What do you mean?' Kershaw pulled off his hairnet and flicked blond curls out of his eyes.

'Well, you being so posh, friends in high places, shooting grouse, dining on larks' tongues and all that. Seems like an unlikely place for you to have ended up.'

'I always loved biology.' Kershaw shrugged. 'The girlfriend's parents aren't keen, of course. Nor is she, much, especially when I have to meet her from work and she can smell chemicals on me. Did you find any presence of unburned fuels or solvents at the Brixton site?'

'I didn't really know what I was looking for,' Banbury admitted.

'Liquid stains, irregular pooling marks, anything like that?'

'Giles, it was fairly obvious how he died. He was covered in flaming tar. He didn't exactly need a fistful of firelighters chucked on him.' Banbury picked up a steel instrument, realized that it was for hooking something out of cavities and quickly set it down. 'I could see that some of the bitumen had dripped through the floorboards, but I didn't think it could reignite. We should have used hydrocarbon detectors to trace any concentrations of agents used to speed up the fire.'

'What do you mean?' asked Kershaw.

'The shop caught fire again right after the body was removed.'

'No fire officer?'

'No one at the local nick considered it worth dousing the site. It didn't burn for long because the bloke in the café opposite raised the alarm, but the smoke messed up the interior, making our job a lot harder. The tar had already set and the arsonist had cleared out his stuff apart from the heavy equipment in the upper storage area.'

'Surely the main purpose wasn't to commit arson,' said Kershaw. 'It was to kill someone.'

'We don't know that. I mean, it's not exactly a bullet to the head, is it? Standing someone underneath a hole in the ceiling and pouring hot tar on them? It's a bit random.'

'Maybe not as much as you think, old chum.' Kershaw checked the screen on his desk, which listed the contents of the victim's wallet. 'Hall worked in Dexter Cornell's bank. He couldn't be attacked at his office so I guess he had to be lured outside. He lived on the City Road, so he was hardly likely to be caught hanging around any dark alleys. That means the killer knew a bit about his tastes.'

'Good point,' Banbury agreed. 'Collectors will go anywhere. You should see how my lad is with video games. A rare one comes available and he'll travel miles to get his mitts on it quicker.'

'Quite so. You got a good look at the shop, though?'

'Yeah. A single white-painted room with half a dozen posters on hooks. Typically arty and minimalist. Probably took less than half an hour to set up. I'm trying to find out where our killer got the posters from. He didn't leave them behind, but passers-by saw them on the walls. The tar scorched the hardwood floor, it was that hot.'

'I've run prelims,' Kershaw said, 'and it's pretty clear that Mr Hall suffocated. His burns are horrific. The stuff got into his throat and nasal passages. Can you get chromatography on the burned particles?'

'I can put in a request for an outsource budget. I'm not sure we'll find anything more than I already know.'

'Which is?'

'Tar is obtained from organic materials, through what we call destructive distillation.' Banbury picked up a small black chunk and turned it over in his hand. It was one of many that had been removed from the body. 'It's a mixture of hydrocarbons and free carbon. This one is the type used by road-menders. It's a viscous form of petroleum mixed with aggregate particles. We'd have to wait for spectromatic results to be sure. I tested its solubility with carbon disulfide and compared it to standard road-asphalt emulsion, which has a lower boiling point than traditional tar.'

'You can do that at the unit?' Kershaw sounded surprised.

'Mr Bryant's got his old equipment set up on the top floor. Raymond doesn't know it's there, which is just as well as we don't have any safety certificates for it. I reheated a sample of the tar and it got pretty runny, which meant that our man was able to heat it quickly and pour it with relative ease. It was capable of igniting anything with a similarly low burn-point, and stuck like buggery to everything it touched, including Hall's hair and flesh. But I guess it also sealed his nose. I'll send you copies of the splash patterns. In liquid form it's also dense, and turns back into a solid very quickly. I guess once he started pouring it kept on coming down, and knocked the victim to his knees. His attacker was able to direct the flow, and poured it over the whole of his upper body until he was stuck to the boards.'

'That would explain the bruising on the kneecaps,' said Kershaw. 'Which brings us to the topping. Why would his assailant cut open a pillow and scatter its contents into the room afterwards? That's the act of someone who's not in control of their mental faculties.'

'I'd say it was quite the reverse,' said Banbury. 'Your killer was totally in control. He tarred and feathered his victim, and did a bloody good job of it.' He smiled. 'I'm sure Mr Bryant will have a field day with that.'

'A sign of cowardice,' Bryant explained to his partner, slapping down the email he had just laboriously printed out from Kershaw. 'Tarring and feathering started as a uniquely British punishment, an act of humiliation inflicted on betrayers. Look at this.' He clambered behind his desk and dragged down a dust-crusted volume, banging it open. 'Here you go. Tar and feather. Asphalt emulsion. It has a low melting point, just like the pine tar they used to use on victims.'

'I thought it was an exclusively American technique,' said May, batting aside the flying dust.

'No, only in vigilante use,' Bryant explained, 'and much later. Richard the First allowed it as a punishment in his navy as early as 1189, and we think it continued for centuries. Over four hundred years later it was found to be used in Madrid monasteries. There was a nastier version called pitchcapping, which involved pouring boiling tar into a cone-shaped paper cap. The cap was fitted over the victim's head and allowed to cool. Then it was quickly removed, tearing off the skin. That was used by British forces against Irish rebels during the period of the Irish Rebellion back in 1798. Sometimes they shaved the head before tarring and feathering it, or they held a match to the feathers to keep relighting the tar. It's all here.' He tipped up the grubby gold-trimmed volume, entitled *The Origins of British Military and Religious Chastisement*. How Bryant came to have such a book at his fingertips in the office was the sort of thing May knew better than to ask.

'The French and the Irish used it on women they suspected of having sexual relations with the enemy. And more recently it's been used to humiliate drug-dealers. It's a form of punishment that resurfaces every few years, usually in connection with street mobs.'

'Well, we have plenty of street mobs roaming London at the moment,' May pointed out. 'Right now I think we need to concentrate on the practical problems. Let's have a proper briefing session.'

'Good,' said Bryant, rubbing his hands. 'I'll get everyone together.'

'You'd better suggest it to Raymond and let him do it,' May warned. 'You know how he likes to fantasize that he's in control.'

After Banbury had returned from the St Pancras Mortuary, the unit members gathered in the first-floor briefing room for assignments. Armed with tea and a plate of stale biscuits, Bryant seated himself on one of the room's uncomfortable orange bendy chairs, leaving space for Raymond behind the only desk. It was always fun watching Land pretend to know what was going on. As soon as everyone had assembled and settled, the PCU's nominal chief arrived with a fat sheaf of papers which he carried for show, shuffling and re-ordering them with an air of importance before asking his detectives what they thought he should do first.

'Do you want a Jammie Dodger?' Bryant asked as Bimsley sat down.

Colin peered over. 'Have you got any Garibaldis?'

'No, the raisins get under my dentures. I had some Custard Creams in my drawer but Crippen had a wee on the packet. She's been a bit incontinent since she had all those kittens. Pass them around.'

'Right, you lot,' said Land. 'Can somebody tell me what's going on?'

'Shall I start?' May offered, rising to his feet. 'Glen David Hall, a thirty-seven-year-old corporate banker found dead in Unit 72, Brixton Market, this morning. He was discovered by a Mr Metish Kapur, proprietor of the New Delhi Express Diner, the café that diagonally faces the shop. Kapur was opening up when he saw someone inside and thought he'd go over to introduce himself. The site is regularly rented out on short leases. When he entered, the person Kapur saw had gone and Mr Hall was lying in the centre of the room, cemented to the floorboards with burning tar. He was also covered in feathers from a split pillowcase, which we found in the attic above the shop. There were several gawkers, and we're trying to trace them now. Giles Kershaw puts the time of death between eight thirty and nine a.m., so Hall should have been heading from his flat on City Road to his office in Crutched Friars, which means he was well outside his usual commute. Why did he go there? Witnesses say the shop contained rare movie posters.'

'Rare? Somebody say that?'

'Just not the usual images. The idea being that these were valuable originals.'

'Not necessarily real ones,' Bryant threw in.

'Probably not,' May agreed. 'We think it was likely that Hall was lured there on the promise of a sale. He's known to have collected graphic art. We've got his mobile, but there's nothing on it.'

'What about websites?' asked Longbright. 'Suppose he belongs to some kind of a group, I don't know – specialist art galleries – and found this address?'

'The problem is getting a trace,' said May. 'He could have logged in from anywhere under any name. Mr Kapur thinks the unit has been let as a pop-up art gallery before, because he remembers seeing colour on the walls, so we're checking out the previous lessees. By the time we got there we only found a few pinholes, so the attacker must have taken the posters away with him. We're examining the CCTV at Brixton tube station, but it's possible that he had a vehicle in the area. The market is pedestrian-only, so he'd have to have parked in one of the backstreets. He left behind the tar bucket and the pillowcase, no prints, so we need to trace their origins. Also, someone must have seen him moving the gear in, even though the market stores weren't open. This took a fair bit of planning, so while it's reasonable to hope that he left a trail, the likelihood is that he's thought carefully about covering his tracks.'

'Then why don't we go to the other end and start with the victim?' asked Land.

'That's what we're doing,' said Longbright. 'We're

talking to Hall's colleagues and trying to track down his family, but we have to do this under conditions of press secrecy so we need to proceed carefully.'

'Good, we don't want *them* splashed all over the pages of the tabloids again,' said Land, pointing at his detectives.

'I can't help having a following,' said May. 'I'm a grey icon.'

'About the link between Hall and Freddie Weeks,' said Bryant, sniffing his biscuit with suspicion.

'There isn't one,' snapped Land. 'We're getting a crack at this because Brixton doesn't want it.'

'Excuse me, but there is most certainly a link—'

Land raised a firm palm. 'No, one man died during a protest and the other was targeted for some kind of stunt that went wrong, that's all. You always think everything is connected.'

'Everything *is* connected: the riots, the deaths, all of it,' Bryant insisted. 'Like Herodotus, we can't understand the histories of kings without first knowing about the Three Dynasties of the Earth. *The Taming of the Shrew* came from *A Thousand and One Nights*. Columbus's belief in Eden led him to the Orinoco. Christopher Wren led us via the Freemasons to George Washington. And without Dionne Warwick, Cilla Black would never have had a hit.'

'Just once I would like us to get through a case without you dragging in all sorts of irrelevant tosh,' erupted Land. 'Why did you decide to become a copper? All you do is question everything.'

In the silence that followed, Bryant carefully replaced his uneaten biscuit on its plate. Then, as if suddenly remembering where he was, he treated the room's puzzled occupants to a long-range smile of eerie beatitude. 'Do you know, I think . . . I'm going out for a walk.' Having made this proclamation he rose and toddled from the room as everyone stared after him.

'Is he all right?' asked Land, shocked by the absence of an insulting rejoinder, but nobody could give him an answer.

17

JUNGLE

'Where the hell did he go this time?' May demanded as soon as the briefing ended and Land had left the room.

'He's not showing up,' said Banbury, checking the screen of his mobile.

'But that was the whole point of resetting his phone, so that you could track his GPS. We have to keep tabs on Arthur from now on.' He was more fearful than angry. Bryant's otherworldly air had always protected him on the London streets, but to wander about in King's Cross with an aura of innocent confusion was inviting trouble.

'I'm not getting a signal. Maybe he's microwaved it again.' Banbury tapped at his screen. 'I don't understand why you suddenly feel the need to keep tabs on him. He's your partner.'

May ignored the question. 'If the press get any kind of idea that the two investigations are connected, they'll link them to the riots and they'll find a way to him. They know he's our weakest link.'

'When Mr Bryant reappears I'll put another trace on him,' Banbury promised. 'He always wears that disgusting tweed overcoat, doesn't he? I'll stitch it into one of the pockets.'

May went to find Longbright. 'Janice, I want you to come with me. We need to interview as many of Hall's colleagues as we can – every ally and enemy – before they get a chance to collaborate on their statements.'

'Why? You think they're hiding something?'

'With all the media attention Findersbury is getting right now, I imagine they're all on standby for damage limitation. One of his workmates must have seen or heard something. Did you get anything on his family yet?'

Longbright tapped her notepad with a Biro. 'His parents live in New York, no siblings, no obvious personal relationships. There's talk of a "close friend" but no direct ID so far. I can keep going.'

'Get Jack to take over. Let's see what's happening in the Square Mile.'

'I have an online feed open to the site.'

'No, I want to do this the old-fashioned way,' said May. 'We'll go over there. If Arthur's convinced it's all connected and Raymond's sure it's not, I know who I'd put my money on. Although I question the link between Christopher Columbus and Cilla Black.'

Twenty minutes later the pair emerged from Bank station and found that the streaming rain had failed to dampen the enthusiasm of the anti-capitalist marchers. The crowds had grown shockingly. Many of the placard-holders were now sploshing about in yellow slickers printed with a crimson 'Break the Banks' logo. The mood felt different. Gone was the atmosphere of novelty, and in its place a darker determination had dug in.

The drone of helicopters had become a continual underscore to the city's soundscape. Police choppers hung motionless in the clouds like aggressive dragonflies. There was a feeling of pressure building in the air that might at any minute burst out in a storm of temper, bringing real, lasting chaos to the city.

'Darren Link's over at Bishopsgate Police Station,' said May, checking his emails. 'He's holding a meeting with security strategists to see how they can best contain this.'

'He's a hard-liner,' said Longbright, stepping on to the kerb to avoid a group of angry-looking teens. 'He's bound to escalate the situation.'

'The trouble is everyone knows where the central banks are,' said May, turning up his collar as they followed the line of barricades. 'I'm surprised he hasn't cordoned off the Bank of England.'

'What kind of message would that send? Britain's not open for business. You think there's someone coordinating the social-network feeds?'

'You mean some kind of Moriarty at work? I don't see how. The sense of injustice is easy enough to understand. How many more Dexter Cornells are we supposed to put up with? The guy's a liar and a crook, and doesn't care that he got found out. It's a catch-22. Cornell can't be investigated without proof, and there won't be proof without an investigation. At least the prime minister's cancelled Barbados. I bet that hurt.' He looked down at Longbright's patent-leather heels. 'If any trouble kicks off, you won't be able to run in those.'

'Now you're sounding like Jack,' she said. 'Trust me, I can move faster in these than I ever could in flats.'

They made their way to Crutched Friars and found the road barricaded at either end. One of Link's officers eventually allowed them access, and they were buzzed into the Findersbury building. The 1920s exterior of Portland stone proved to be a shell masking a far older suite of dark walnut-panelled offices, but as they ascended from the reception area to one of the meeting rooms on the third floor, they entered a newly constructed cocoon of glass and steel.

The Findersbury Bank had survived for over four hundred years in an architectural patchwork that reflected London's tumultuous times. It had weathered the collapse and disgrace of its rivals, successfully skirting the sub-prime mortgage scandals, only to stumble on a more nebulous threat: suspicion of endemic corruption. Through acres of glass May and Longbright could see staff members hunkered at terminals, never raising their eyes, perhaps in fear of witnessing some fresh hell.

'Siege mentality,' said Longbright, fascinated. 'I wouldn't want to be at one of those desks.'

'You have in the past,' May replied. 'How many times has the PCU been in lockdown?'

'That was always due to external forces, never from within. We've always been able to trust one another.' She held out her hand as a figure approached. 'Mr Burnham, I'm Detective Sergeant Janice Longbright and this is Senior Detective John May. Is there somewhere we can talk?'

At first glance James Burnham fitted the ideal image of a young captain of industry, tanned and well groomed, but there were shadowed hollows in his eyes and early flecks of grey in his hair. As he shook their hands, May noticed the sore, bitten quicks around his nails. Ushering them into a pallid meeting room, he made sure the door was tightly closed behind him before speaking.

'I shouldn't be seeing you in here at all,' he said anxiously, his Manhattan inflection overlaid with received pronunciation, the tone of a high-level English education. 'As you can imagine, we're in crisis-management mode, trying to save what's left of this place. Mr Cornell seems to have gone into hiding. He tried to get into the building for a meeting this morning and some protestors jumped on his vehicle and threw red paint over the windscreen. The police stood by and watched. The city's becoming dangerous. This kind of thing wouldn't happen in New York.'

'Why did he have to come in at all, given the situation outside?' asked Longbright.

Burnham turned to her. 'The bank's going into receivership and the recovery specialists are looking for a buyer. He needs to be here. But you want to know about Glen Hall, is that right? Can you tell me what he's supposed to have done?'

'No one's spoken to you yet?'

'No, but the last thing we need right now is another scandal. What are we looking at?'

May did not like the way in which Burnham had assumed control of the interview. 'He was found dead early this morning. The circumstances were unusual.'

'Oh, Christ.' Burnham pulled out a chair and sat down with the delicacy of a man lowering himself on to broken glass. 'What the hell happened?'

'We're not able to release details until the forensic examination has been concluded,' May explained. 'I can tell you that he was murdered.'

'*Oh, Christ—*'

'The press has received no information about the case, and we plan to keep them out of it for as long as possible. What we need from you are the details of Mr Hall's personal life and business activities.'

Burnham looked like a man at the end of a rope as the stool was about to be kicked away. 'Hell, what can I say?'

'Whatever comes to mind.'

'I'm not the right man to ask about his personal situation, but I can tell you what he was like to work with. A lot of people come into a place like this full of bullshit and big ideas, and never manage to close a deal. That wasn't Hall. He was strictly old school, a real wolf. There's a story about a New York corporate M-and-A guy who arrived to check out the facilities of a private London bank – this was back in 1985, the year before the abolition of fixed commission charges and the switch to screen-based trading. He walked into the bank and looked around, and none of the managers were there to greet him. He asked where everyone was and the counter clerk told him he'd arrived on the wrong day. It was August twelfth – the Glorious Twelfth – the start of the grouse-shooting season. The financier smiled and knew he could take the place apart. That sums up the old world of British private banks. Not any more. Remember "Greed Is Good"? Well, greed is back, and Hall was damned good at it.'

'So he didn't let feelings get in the way?'

'Never. He was an iceman; nothing touched him.'

'Do you think he made enemies?' asked May.

Burnham pressed his long fingers flat on the table, then thought better of it. 'This is private opinion, right?'

'Off the record.'

'Hall's area of expertise was in nurturing start-ups, creaming off profit and dumping them when they failed to perform. You can't pull the plug on companies and not make enemies. And don't ask me to give you a list, because that would be physically impossible. We'd only have records of the companies to whom he'd already made loans – he was dealing with dozens of others in different stages of development.'

'Would he have kept details of those somewhere?'

'Yeah.' Burnham tapped his forehead. 'In here.'

'Did he seem stressed at work lately? Did he mention any clients in particular?'

'Not that I know of. If he had problems, he kept them to himself.'

'He was found in a shop selling rare movie posters. Do you have any idea why he would have gone there?'

'I heard he collected them, the rarer the better. In this business it's better to put your money into art that you're sure will rise in value.'

'How do you do that?'

'Basic economics. You don't buy fashionable artists, because they fall from grace when they try to monetize their work and start overproducing. Exclusivity counts; you need to invest in something with a finite supply. Glen told me that old British movie posters were printed in strictly limited runs, which keeps their value climbing. He loved the damned things, couldn't get enough of them.'

'And you know nothing of his life outside of work?' May asked.

'I don't think he had such a thing. Part of the trade-off when you rise to the top here is surrendering your privacy. This is a career with a built-in shelf life. Theoretically, there's plenty of time to create family ties later.'

'What do you mean, theoretically?'

'The dropout rate is high due to stress-related illnesses. And after a few years of fat bonuses there's a tendency to assume you're invincible. That's when miscalculations occur.'

'You mean like Dexter Cornell?'

Burnham gave a bitter little laugh. 'Let's just say he really picked the wrong day to bury bad news.'

'What do you mean?'

'You're joking, right? With stories about bankers' record bonuses all over the broadsheets?'

'Do you think Cornell—'

'Cornell's not your concern,' said Burnham. 'Whatever I think of him should be of no relevance to you. When the music stops here I aim to be one of the guys who still has a seat.'

'Did Cornell and Hall know each other?' May persisted, checking his notes.

'Of course. They were two of a kind.'

'So they got on well?'

'They hated each other's guts. When you're the alpha male you don't make friends with the troop's new lieutenant. You want to keep the whole jungle for yourself.'

'Do you know where Mr Cornell has gone?'

'No, nobody does. I don't suppose we'll see anything of him until all this blows over.'

'Do you think it will?' May asked. 'What's going on out there – it's getting bigger every day.'

'Yeah, right,' said Burnham dismissively. 'What are they going to do? I mean, really? You heard any ideas other than Break the Banks? No, because they don't have any.'

'Is there anyone here who was close to Mr Hall?'

'There was an accountant. They spent a lot of time together.'

'Can we talk to him?'

'He doesn't work in the building, and I have no contact details.'

'We'll need to take Mr Hall's hard drive with us,' said Longbright.

Burnham's affability vanished. 'That won't be possible. There'll be a lot of sensitive information on it that has nothing to do with you guys.'

'We're not interested in the bank's business,' said May. 'We need to find your employee's murderer before he decides to do it again.' He looked Burnham in the eye. 'Tell me something I don't understand. How can you still respect the chair? It looks to me like the directors of this company sold you out. What makes you so loyal?'

'Loyalty is the most important commodity they bought from us,' Burnham replied.

'I think we need to talk to Cornell.' May peered out cautiously as they left the building for the wild city pavements.

'But if he's not directly connected to the case—'

'He's the one who started all of this.' He pointed up

at a contrail of sooty smoke looping lazily over the rooftops. The sound of helicopters sliced the air.

'You don't think it was Hall who leaked the news about Cornell warning his directors, do you?' Longbright wondered. 'It would give Cornell a reason to take revenge.'

'It crossed my mind,' said May. 'The question is how to get to him. The rich are very good at hiding themselves.'

'Someone must know where he is. Dan will be able to find him. Everyone leaves footprints.'

They turned the corner into Fenchurch Street, where the air was filled with burning specks of paper, a snowstorm of stationery. Longbright looked up into the sky, grabbing at a burning scrap. 'Legal records,' she said, reading. 'Looks like they've broken into one of the banks.' She turned the page around to show him. 'Barclays. I'm surprised they still keep paperwork.'

'People prefer to write on documents. I need to talk to Arthur. Maybe he was right after all.'

'What do you mean?'

'Anarchy in the city.' He raised his hands and turned about in the blizzard. Shreds of paperwork were drifting across the Palladian doorways and windows of the surrounding buildings. From the next street came a massed chorus of rising anger. They stopped and listened, shocked.

The chanting grew until it vibrated the very air. 'The sound of revolution,' said May. 'Who knows where it will end?'

18

ESSENCE OF REBELLION

Arthur Bryant was utterly lost.

Having failed to master the use of Google Maps, he was reduced to consulting the crumpled page of a London *A–Z* that he kept in his overcoat pocket, but he also needed a magnifying glass to read it. He knew these streets like the back of his hand, but had somehow become turned around and could no longer find his way home. Standing beside the pink neon fascia of a Japanese bubble tea shop, he could not have looked more out of place. He had always been proud of his anatopism, but now it had become a liability.

Think, he told himself, *work it out.*

He had passed the old Rising Sun pub in Cloth Fair, and then found himself – with no memory of how he had got there – beneath the baroque glass atrium of Leadenhall Market. It was as if the last half-hour had been wiped clean from his brain. He had come here for a reason, but what on earth was it?

Revolution. The word popped back into his head and glowed there in letters of fire. It ignited other incendiary states: *Sedition. Anarchy. Riot.*

And then he remembered. *Eleanor Hamilton.* Looking about, he found his bearings once more and dug her address from his pocket. The historical novelist wrote rumbustious adventures set in eighteenth-century London, but was also a specialist on the subject of the London Mob, and, as an old friend of Maggie Armitage, was aware of her city's spiritual connections.

Locating the brown-painted door at the edge of the market, he pressed the buzzer and was admitted into a pitch-black hallway barely wider than his shoulders.

'Wait! Sorry! Lights!' called an impossibly refined voice, and suddenly the corridor was flooded with brightness. Eleanor could barely be seen over the balustrade. The novelist was tiny, disarrayed, sparrowlike. 'No lift – can you manage?'

'I think so,' Bryant called back. 'If I'm not there in half an hour, call an ambulance.'

'I've been here forever and haven't the heart to leave,' she explained, ushering the panting detective in and showing him to a sofa. 'You must be gasping. I'll get the kettle on.' Checking that her white hair was still coiled on top of her head like whipped cream, she headed to the hotplate.

The rooms were doll's-house tiny and cluttered with so many ancient books that Bryant instinctively fought the urge to sneeze out dust. 'Everything around here is just *awful* now,' Hamilton told him. 'Even ten years ago it was still bearable, but all my neighbours have gone, and the little pubs and shops have been gutted into offices and something called "luxury loft living" for these revolting bankers you seem to find everywhere.' She shuddered violently. It seemed to Bryant that he knew an abnormal number of ladies who were prone to theatricality. 'The Marxist bookshop is now a flogging estate agency, can you believe it? Utterly sickening. There's nothing left for the struggling artist in this flogging city, thanks to those

Bullingdon Club thugs and their pocket-lining cronies in the flogging financial institutions.' She had a habit of substituting the chastisement in place of its more Anglo-Saxon counterpart, which she found far too ubiquitous and banal on the swaggering, swearing streets of London.

'I'm very well, thank you, Eleanor, and how are you?' said Bryant pointedly.

'Oh. Ah, yes. Sorry. You know how I get. We're supposed to mellow as we get older, aren't we, but I find myself becoming increasingly furious with the way in which things have turned out.' She threw sugar cubes into mugs like a desperate gambler hurling his final dice. 'I hate what I see around me, Arthur. The urban middle class destroyed, the working poor exploited, the vulgar rich elevated to eminence, the underclass demonized, the wasteland of celebrity held in veneration.' She slammed a cupboard door shut. Presumably the neighbours were used to it, or possibly deaf. 'What are we supposed to tell the young? Oh, you've got to pay for your own education now, and you won't get a job at the end of it, and sorry, did we forget to mention that the world is on the brink of total catastrophe?'

'Perhaps you should write an open letter to the next generation.'

'Don't get me started about where that leaves us writers! I was supposed to have a meeting with the BBC yesterday but the department heads are all away on a training course about how to make decisions. My God, if they can't make decisions, why the hell are they in charge of departments? Their consultants get paid flogging fortunes while the writers are paid almost nothing. You know why? Because we originate, and that's the one thing executives don't want. But I ask you, what are they? Nothing more than pipe-layers, emptying the well of our ideas on to the parched soil of their audience demographics. And they've decided we must go because they hate the fact that we own the well.' She swept some loose strands of hair back from the sides of her face and looked around, optimistically hoping to locate the teapot. 'We appear to be out of builders'. I can do you Darjeeling with a dash of Lapsang Souchong. No milk, I'm afraid – our local grocery shop just got turned into a flogging Starbucks.'

Eleanor had a stare that could wither plants and ignite dry objects. Bryant had a great admiration for angry, erudite women, even tiny, slightly mad ones. Rage was nothing without articulation. It was hard to work out how old she was now; her seething passions kept her youthful.

'I was wondering about your take on all this.' He waved his hand vaguely at the smeared window. 'The riots. You're rather in the line of fire here.'

'Bring it on, I say. Flogging well bring it on.' She filled the mugs and hunted for spoons. 'There were more mobs and insurrections during the reign of George the First than in all the reigns since the Norman Conquest. If you felt wronged, you rioted or duelled or fought or printed up your grievances and threw the pages all over the city. You *did* something, damn it. But what have we had in the last thirty years? The miners' strike, a bit of sulky car-overturning during the Thatcher regime—'

'The Poll Tax Riots,' Bryant reminded her, accepting a rather unclean mug and looking for a place to set it down.

'Oh, *those*.' She rolled her eyes. 'Barely more than a day-long hissy fit. This has been brewing for a very long time.' He presumed she wasn't referring to the tea. 'A bunch of Mayfair bully boys deregulate the City and turn us from being the masters of our own destinies into little more than drifting twigs in the gutters of private enterprise. No wonder we all feel so emasculated! And the internet hasn't helped. God forbid you express your beliefs online;

someone will shout "hater" at you, and that's your Socratic discourse brought to a flogging end. No, Arthur, I welcome this, I really do. Let's get back to George the First. The young have had their futures taken from them by stealth. I'm no advocate of public violence, but there has to be some form of civil disobedience. Did you know they're talking about evacuating private residences? Well, why not, if that's what it takes to make the Whitehall mandarins sit up and take notice? The creation of order is a mark of civilization, but what happens when order is allowed to create itself? The big companies dictate the terms and use their lawyers as henchmen.' She shook her head hard enough to bring down a loose curl. 'Poor old George Orwell got it hopelessly wrong, forever worrying about state control when he should have been more afraid of the opposite. The political parties absented themselves and became mere functionaries for the real centre of power: the banks. Do you know why Margaret Flogging Thatcher sited her new financial Xanadu in London's furthest eastern reaches, in Canary Wharf? To send a message to Parliament. To say to them: You are no longer in charge, so up yours. She wanted a new railway line that would service only the financiers and bypass all the poor areas, before even *she* realized that was a step too far.'

'Do you think there's any significance in this happening now? This banker chap, Dexter Cornell, is he just a straw man? It couldn't be connected with Guy Fawkes somehow, could it?'

'Bless you, Arthur, always searching out the universal mantic solution, always happy to drag psychotropism into the argument. I'd have to say no, but the proximity to Guy Fawkes Night did make me wonder. There must be some residual memory of rebellion in the public mind.'

'We have a problem,' said Bryant, hoping to derail Eleanor from her polemic. 'The week has started with two murders which I believe are related. A homeless man was burned alive on the steps of a bank, and a financier died after being tarred and feathered.'

'What makes you think it's the same person behind both cases?' Eleanor asked, not unreasonably.

'Nothing concrete. An assonance of elements. Fire, cruelty, bankruptcy. I don't know. Most homicidal violence is domestic. It happens behind closed doors to partners and children. Part of our remit is to prevent public affright. That's why they gave the case to us. The financier died in a public space, a shop. Neither of these cases has any element of domesticity. There don't seem to be any upset wives, mothers or siblings involved. My team's looking for quarrels within their families, but I have a feeling we won't find anything there.'

'If you think it's someone with an axe to grind, you'll have to find the link between a poor man and a rich one.'

'That's exactly what I'm trying to do, but so far I've come up empty-handed,' Bryant admitted. 'Still, there's something you could do for me.'

'I'll try my best.'

'I presume you're monitoring events in Cheapside and all around the Bank of England?'

'My students and I are filming everything,' she said. 'Someone needs to keep impartial records. The protests aren't dying down; they're spreading exponentially. The groups are learning to work together. Their frustration is born of manufactured powerlessness. No one's advocating the replacement of one system with another; they're not economists. There's no consensual agenda. But it's important for the people to unite and show that they will no longer be taken for granted.'

A light went on behind Bryant's eyes. 'The riots and the murders are linked – one is feeding off the other. Crikey.'

'Nobody says "crikey" any more.' Eleanor leaned back in her tattered armchair. 'And your investigation is far from over. Guy Fawkes Night is Saturday. That's when this riot will come to a head. It's only Tuesday.' She took a sip of her tea and winced. 'It sounds to me as if the person you're searching for is the very essence of rebellion, conducting an ideological war in microcosm. At the very least, you could be looking at four more murders.'

19

BURNING BRIDGES

'What have you been doing?' asked May, exasperated. He had been sitting in his office going through the witness statements again when Bryant wandered in, looking as if he had just climbed out of a wet hedge. In fact, he looked wetter than it was humanly possible for anyone to be. Perhaps he had just climbed out of the canal.

'Do you know, I'm not entirely sure,' Bryant replied. 'It's not something I can quantify with any metaphysical accuracy, as such.' He had always been aware that his thought processes were more those of an academic than a policeman, and as he grew older it became harder than ever to explain them to others.

'Look at the state of you. Get some of those wet clothes off and chuck them on the radiator.'

'Do you always boil a saucepan of sprouts for at least two hours?' Bryant asked.

'What?' said May, thrown. 'No.'

'Good, then you're not my mother.' He struggled out of his overcoat and found that his damp brown sweater had lengthened dramatically.

'What happened to you? You could catch pneumonia.

At least tell me where you're going in future. I'm still your partner.' He had always kept a watchful eye on Arthur, and now it felt more crucial than ever that he should not be left to his own devices. 'There have been a couple of journalists outside asking questions about you,' he warned.

'Really? That's encouraging. I didn't think they left their desks any more. Try tipping a bucket of boiling tar over them.' He gave up trying to squeeze the sweater back into shape and draped it over the windowsill like the pelt of some out-of-condition animal. 'Got anything new?'

'Joanna Papis said she left Freddie Weeks because the relationship was going nowhere and she wanted to get on with her career, yes? Well, it turns out she was working for Glen Hall.'

Bryant's eyes widened. 'In what capacity?'

'She was looking after his personal accounts. Apparently it's a bit of a status thing at Findersbury to have a young lady handling your private finances, a bit like having an English nanny.'

'So there *is* a connection.'

'Just don't say it,' said May.

'My dear chap, I wouldn't be so graceless. Is someone talking to Papis again?' He sneezed explosively.

'It's in hand. What about you?'

'A whiff of a smidgen of a suspicion, nothing more.'

'Of what?'

'That there might be further deaths in or around the Square Mile in the approach to Guy Fawkes Night. Four to be exact.' He unwound his sopping scarf and added it to the hat stand.

'I don't see how that's likely. At this particular moment it's probably the most heavily filmed area in the world. It would take a very determined person to risk so much exposure.'

'Oh, I think we can safely say that someone who's

prepared to tar and feather his victim in the middle of Brixton Market is fairly determined, John. My fear is that he'll attack in a different manner. He'll use fire again, though. Arson's his thing.' He dug out a handkerchief that looked as if it had been used to clean windows and blew his nose. 'The downside of keeping the press in the dark is allowing the killer to think he's getting away with it. And this kind of murder is a drug; next time he'll need a bigger hit. The first time he merely threw a petrol bomb. The second time he planned the death carefully. Now he'll want to get closer. That's what arsonists do. They want to stand close enough to feel the heat of the flames. And what can *we* do – send a warning circular to everyone who works for a bank?'

'Maybe the girl can give us something more on Glen Hall.'

'Fine,' said Bryant, 'by all means talk to her; anything to close the gap.'

'What gap?'

'He's got a head start on us, hasn't he? While we flounder about, he's following some kind of predetermined map. He knows exactly what he's doing, and we can only run behind him.' Bryant went to the window, wiped the dirty pane with his handkerchief and peered down into the street. 'He's out there right now, putting something else in place.'

'Then we're up the creek.'

'Not quite. The Royal Exchange, London's centre of commerce, 1566. The Bank of England, the second oldest central bank in the world, 1694. You don't destroy those institutions overnight, or even in a week.'

'Perhaps not,' said May gloomily, 'unless you have thousands of angry people to help you.'

'What did you say your name was again?' asked the verger of St Mary's Church, Camden Town. He looked sleepy and confused, as if he'd just woken up. The church was in almost total darkness. It was too expensive to keep lighting the place.

'Mick Flannery,' said the young man. 'From Guttridge and Sons. About the leak.'

'You took your time,' said the verger, who had a strong Dublin brogue. 'You were supposed to be here two weeks ago. We've been putting buckets out. The Madonna's started to warp. Where are your ladders?'

'I have to carry out the works inspection first,' he explained. 'You want me to price the job out, don't you? You'll need two estimates for the insurance claim.'

'I suppose so, but you'll have to find your own way up there, I've got my work to do,' the verger warned, although it didn't sound as if he believed the lie himself. He pottered off into the damp gloom, leaving the builder to find his own way to the gallery. Over his head, the warbling of pigeons sounded above the pattering rain.

The verger had disappeared from view. There were just two old ladies in the pews below, with faithful hearts and heads bent in devout prayer, the last of their generation, the end of the congregation. St Mary's was threatened with deconsecration and conversion into luxury apartments, but until the sale got the go-ahead, half-hearted snippets of restoration work continued.

The young man reached the wooden stairs leading to the bell tower, and climbed. He walked around the edges, past the bell no one had rung for years, until he reached the slatted doorway that opened on to the roof. Taking the canvas tool bag from his shoulder, he removed a claw hammer and stepped outside.

It would have been a simple matter to reach down and begin work, if it were not for the fact that the rain was making the verandah slippery. Not for the first time he wondered about the sanity of his actions, but decided he had come too far now to stop. The alternative was a lifetime of spiralling misery and regret.

Dropping to his knees, he examined the great rectangular patches and located the soft metal clips that held them in place. Then, using the end of the claw hammer, he began prising them back. The first section came away in a shower of dirt. As the rain fell harder, he knew it would limit the time he could spend up here before somebody realized what was going on.

The panel fitted exactly into his tool bag. He decided that six would be enough to do the trick.

The old lady was far from pleased. 'I don't know how you can expect me to concentrate on Our Lady's advice with cold water dripping down the back of me neck,' she told the verger.

'Mrs O'Donnell, you know where the problem spots are,' said the verger. 'I've told you before not to attempt communion with the Holy Virgin while sitting under a precipitation; you'll be catching your death.'

'But this is a new one, right near the front.' She pointed an accusing finger at one of the pews. Even from this distance the verger could see rain cascading down into the seats. *Dozens of Catholic churches in this city and barely enough parishioners to fill one of them,* he thought. *What a fecking godless time we live in.* He followed Mrs O'Donnell's finger up to the roof and was shocked to see daylight coming in between the crossbeams. His next realization was far from charitable. 'I don't believe it,' he said, digging out his phone to call the building firm. 'The little bastard's stolen the lead off the roof.'

He had turned the old garage under the arches into a workshop simply by breaking in and changing the lock, and had installed the bench and equipment from his father's shed. This was revenge on a budget; he was completely broke. Worse, he owed everyone money. But he would not be turned from his path now. He had no home, no cash, no job, no friends, no future. Once you've decided to burn your remaining bridges and go to hell, he thought, there's no reason why you shouldn't take everyone else with you.

With tears in his eyes and the fire of righteous anger engorging his heart, he took out the lead slates, picked up the blowtorch and set to work once more.

20

FUGUES

A spiral of acrid smoke hung in the dark morning air like a corpse twisting in oily water. Most of the street fires were out for now, but a branch of Barclays, an insurance company and the offices of Eastcheap Financial Services all bore the blackened scorch marks of the previous night's activities across their stone façades. There was a rhythmic tinkling as street-cleaners swept up broken glass, glittering on the roads like dropped Christmas baubles.

Superintendent Darren Link and his team had made numerous arrests, with accusations ricocheting from both sides about unnecessary force and provocations. The rest of the police stood around like builders waiting to be chosen for a day's labour. Photographers were huddled in doorways, looking as if they were expecting a celebrity to stumble out of a nightclub.

The protestors had come prepared. With khaki flak jackets and backpacks, and their socks tucked into their trousers, they appeared to be planning a moorland ramble rather than confronting capitalists in the city's financial epicentre. The aggression of the previous night had subsided into guarded politeness, but it was clear that everyone was waiting for the next clash to begin.

Bank and Mansion House tube stations had been trellised and nearly all of the surrounding roads were now closed off. Shop fronts had been covered in chipboard slabs, and windows were shuttered. The prime minister had been filmed disembarking from a British Airways flight looking as if he was about to sue his travel agent. A few minutes later he appeared on the BBC promising that the city would remain open for business, but as the Wednesday rush hour began traffic was almost non-existent. The networks were advising employees to work from home, and many had jumped at the chance to cancel their usual commute. Others relished the challenge of tackling a war zone and strode to their offices, daring confrontation. Sirens still sounded distantly, but at least the cacophony of car and office alarms had ceased.

Everyone was wondering how long the truce would hold. Several elderly ladies in matching red knitted scarves were seated by the side of the road on folding chairs, aged campaigners who looked as if they might be waiting for the start of the Lord Mayor's Show.

Jonathan De Vere made his way between the barricades and swore when he saw that Bank station was shut. By some miracle he was able to flag down a taxi, and moments later was fighting off sleep in its back seat as it followed the makeshift detour signs towards Hyde Park. He had been working all night, keeping hackers' hours, as he always did when Lena was away. She was in Amsterdam attending a conference on the restoration of medieval manuscripts, so he put in the extra hours writing presentations. She had insisted on going, even though she was heavily pregnant, so he figured the least he could do was work as hard. Besides, he lived close enough by to get three hours' rest before having to go back and talk to the designers.

At this time of the morning, phalanxes of Filipina women were arriving in Belgravia to clean apartments. De Vere paid the cab and buzzed himself into the building. He stopped in the hallway outside his flat to sniff the air. What was that? It reminded him of something from his childhood: burned iron filings, the autumnal smell of Bonfire Night just after the last of the big rockets had gone off. It was the metallic tang of his grandfather's factory floor, where lathes turned and sparks sprayed across the machinery like Catherine wheels. As a boy he would go with the old man and watch as the workers stepped back in deference. The industry that had brought his family a century of prosperity had finally vanished in 2005, a victim of low Chinese production costs, and his father had retired a broken man, but De Vere still recalled the sights and smells of the engine shed.

Pushing aside the memory, he unlocked the door and entered the maisonette.

'Well, do you know where I can reach him?' asked May, looking at his watch. It was 8.35 a.m. on Wednesday, and Dexter Cornell's Spanish housekeeper had just informed him that her employer had gone away. He covered the phone. 'It sounds like Burnham was right; Cornell's gone into hiding.'

'He's got a bolt-hole in the country,' Bryant mouthed. 'Ask about Oakley Manor House in Burford. It's north-west of Oxford.'

'It sounds like that's where he's gone,' said May as he ended the call. 'The housekeeper wouldn't confirm it, but he packed all the stuff he usually takes when he goes there. He told her not to talk to anyone. She's worried she's going to lose her job. Where did you get that titbit from?'

'My chips,' Bryant explained. 'They were wrapped in

a page from *Grazia* that showed the inside of Cornell's country retreat.'

'I thought he was going to continue coming into the bank.'

'He can,' said Bryant. 'It's a fast commute. We need to get a local officer there, preferably someone with a couple of brain cells. Check on Cornell's security arrangements, find out how long he's going to be staying out of town. I imagine he's got a good alarm system but we'd better have them search the grounds. Right now he's the most hated man in the country, which makes him the most obvious target. He got married at Oakley Manor House. He's got a home cinema that seats twenty in the basement, and a lap pool.'

'I never imagined you'd bother reading something like *Grazia*,' said May.

'Oh, I don't just pore over the obituaries and the *Police Gazette,* you know. Besides, you need something to read when you're eating a saveloy. I kept the page.' He rifled through his coat and dragged out a ketchup-stained sheet, flattening it with exaggerated delicacy.

'So he's got a woman up there with him?'

'Not sure. He seems to be in the process of a messy divorce. His wife – or ex-wife – is what they used to call "flighty". Tends to party with her set in Gstaad. She's Russian, a bit of a handful by all accounts. Last week when he was trying to play down his profits and keep a low profile, she flew her pals to the Hermitage in Monte Carlo for some kind of gorgons' tea party that set him back thirty thousand pounds. Immaculate bad timing.'

'I say, is this going to be the new you? Up on all the latest gossip?'

'Dear God, no,' said Bryant. 'Meera told me that bit. Her mother's been making her read bridal magazines and whatnot. I think she has plans for her daughter. I read it because you have to know your enemy.'

'You're not allowed to have enemies, Arthur. As a state employee you're required to remain non-partisan.'

'I'm speaking to you in private, John, not writing a report. I wonder if the Findersbury directors paid Cornell a kickback for the information. I suppose not, as he was meant to deliver the deal.'

'You know they're pleading innocence.'

'To misquote Mandy Rice-Davies: They would, wouldn't they? And now Cornell's hiding away in a country house just like Julian Assange did in Ellingham Hall. I imagine he feels just as embattled. I need to talk to him.'

'You have no right, Arthur. It's outside of your jurisdiction, unless you can prove that he's directly involved in the investigation.'

Bryant leaned forward, rippling his fingers as if trying to hypnotize May. 'Come on, aren't you the least bit curious?'

'Only within the confines of my job.'

'And that's the difference between you and me,' Bryant said. 'You just want to catch the fish, and I want to study the ocean.' With this he rose and strolled out of the room.

'What the hell does that mean?' May shouted after him. He waited until he could no longer hear his partner in the hall, then punched out a number. 'Dr Gillespie, I need you to call Arthur into your office on some pretext. Tell him he needs a blood test or something. Sit him down and talk casually to him.'

'Why?' asked Dr Gillespie, coughing heavily into the phone. 'Your partner is almost impossible to engage in normal conversation.'

'He's behaving weirdly. I mean, even more weirdly than usual.'

'In what way?'

'It's hard to explain. He's sort of – disconnected. He keeps wandering off. I think he's trying to cover something up. You know how crafty he can be.'

Dr Gillespie blew his nose violently. 'I'm sorry, I have a cold. What do you mean, cover what up?'

'He's having bits of downtime, as if he drifts away and comes back – little fugues.'

'Like mini-strokes? Is he forgetting things?'

'No, he's always had an astonishing memory. But he's getting confused. Talking in riddles. And he goes missing.'

'Has this been happening for very long?' Gillespie released another foamy blast into his handkerchief.

'No, it's only started recently.'

'All right, I'll drag him in and sound him out. He's getting on, you know. He shouldn't still be working at his age.'

'His work is what keeps him going,' said May. 'We're on one of our biggest-ever cases. There are lives at stake and I can't afford to put anyone at risk. Will you let me know how it goes?'

'OK, but you may not like my recommendations. Are there any other symptoms I should know about?'

'He's stopped playing his old Gilbert and Sullivan records. What does that suggest?'

'It might not mean anything. Perhaps he's just sick of *The Mikado*.'

May rang off and sat thoughtfully for a few minutes. There was something he could do.

'Janice?' He swung around the door of Longbright's office. 'I don't want to let Arthur out of my sight while he's on this case, but I can't always be with him. Could you partner him when I'm tied up?'

'I should be able to,' said Longbright. 'Everything's covered here so long as nothing else comes in. Fraternity can take over for me.' She looked around her desktop. 'John, you didn't take anything off my desk last night, did you?'

'I'd have told you if I had. Why?'

'It's just . . . I'm missing some of the witness statements. They were here when I left.'

'You might try Raymond.'

'Land's never read a witness statement in his life.'

'About Arthur – can you do it?'

She gave up looking and concentrated on the question. 'Of course. When do you want me to start?'

'As soon as possible. Just find him and tell me where he is. I'm interviewing Freddie Weeks's mother in ten minutes and Arthur's in that strange mood he gets when he's about to wander off.'

'The things I do.' Janice grabbed her PCU jacket and headed out to look for her boss.

21

DISORIENTATION

Someone had been in the flat. De Vere was sure of it.

A heavy Minotti armchair had been pushed back a few inches, leaving a scuff on the newly waxed hardwood floor, and the stack of letters and bills he had opened in the kitchen had been moved. He knew that Lena couldn't have returned early because he had spoken to her late last night, and the only other person with keys was his cleaning lady. He worked with some crazy people, borderline-autistic tech-heads who were likely to turn up at the front door, find no one home and climb through a window. But they couldn't do that here, in an apartment building that had designed out any possibility of illegal entry.

Yet something had been dragged along the hall; there were more black scuff-marks. While he was thinking about what might have happened, he made himself some strong, sweet tea and found that someone had spilled sugar in the kitchen. He walked around in puzzlement, passing the doorway to the second bedroom. The red light on the voicemail button of his house phone was blinking. It was a line hardly anyone used.

'Mister De Vere, is Katya here, I very sorry not come

today but I come to you and get my bag stolen on the bus and it have your keys in. I am so sorry.'

He knew she would never go to the police because she was here illegally, but Katya was a damned good cleaner. Surely she wouldn't have been so dumb as to put his address on her key tag? If she had, it meant there was a chance that someone had used them to get into the flat.

Heading into the study, he checked his laptop and found it in its usual place. He kept little of real value lying around, but the thought that a stranger might have been going through his personal belongings sent a prickle across his back.

Realizing that he hadn't checked the bedroom, he headed there, but found nothing out of place. He drank some more tea, loosened his tie and lay down on the bed fully clothed. If he just closed his eyes for a few minutes . . .

Strong arms dropped over him and crushed the breath from his chest. De Vere tried to raise himself up, but a hand pressed down hard on his throat. Something dark and heavy descended across his vision.

He could no longer move his head. He smelled heat, then felt it coming closer. He wanted to scream but his voice was cut off, and then there was only the searing white-hot pain that blotted out his senses.

It was a good thing he lost consciousness as the mask went over his face.

It was the cleaner who found him. Katya had forgotten that Mr De Vere had given her a second key the year before. After returning home, she had found it among the loose jumble of house keys she kept in a jar under the sink.

When she got back to the flat, she saw that her employer's briefcase had been set down in the hall, so she knew he had returned. She called out to let him know that someone else was there, but got no answer. The kitchen was barely touched – although he had made himself his usual tea – and she was heading down the hall when she saw his trouser-clad legs on the bed. She called his name tentatively, not wishing to disturb him if he was having a nap, but there was something wrong – a single shoe on the carpet – that encouraged her to push the door a little wider.

When she saw the burned bedcover Katya fought the urge to scream. What had he done to his face? There was some kind of metal mask fitted over it. Backing out, she called the police from the house phone, hanging up before they could ask for her name. On her way out she left the keys on the counter, knowing she would never have cause to use them again. He owed her a month's wages which she now knew she would never get.

The call was transferred to Buckingham Palace Road and was then picked up by the City of London, with the result that Fraternity DuCaine caught it on the first bounce. 'Belgravia SOCO's in first,' he told Longbright, 'but we can take over if we're fast.'

'How come?' Janice looked up from her screen, surprised.

'They're not structured to set up a Major Incident Room, and there are circumstances—'

'What do you mean?'

'The SOCO says it sounds like our guy again,' said Fraternity grimly. 'You'd better tell the old man.'

'God, I'm supposed to be looking after him,' said Longbright.

Fraternity raised his eyebrows. 'Since when did he need looking after?'

Arthur Bryant was a medley of contradictions. Despite being a man who took twenty minutes to locate the right cable channel on his TV remote, he could be out of the door and heading to a crime scene in under thirty seconds. It was fairly likely that at any given moment he could set himself on fire, yet he was capable of drawing an admission of guilt from a suspect in minutes, succeeding where everyone else had failed.

Now, in the company of John May, Banbury and DuCaine, he climbed into May's silver BMW and was taken to Belgravia.

Familiar to its residents as the Grosvenor Estate and still largely owned by the Duke of Westminster, Belgravia is one of the wealthiest areas in the world. The Grosvenor family came from Eaton Hall in Cheshire, hence the address of Eaton Square, Belgravia, where the detectives found themselves heading. Many of the classical cream stucco exteriors were just façades now; the grand families had long gone, leaving behind offices and apartments carved into lateral spaces across the properties, so that in reality a considerable part of the square was little more than a grandiose business development. It was best not to get Bryant on that subject.

'Typical of this bloody country as a whole,' he announced from the back seat as they searched for somewhere to park. 'A shining false front of English propriety hiding the usual wormy muck of greed, corruption and duplicity. "Oh," everyone cries, "it's so English!" Isn't it, though.'

'I'm surprised you haven't joined the protestors yet,' said May testily, checking his rear-view mirror.

'I'm not sleeping in a tent at my age, thank you.' Bryant was indignant. 'I paid my dues from "Ban the Bomb" to "Support the Miners". My marching days ended when councils insisted on providing us with Portaloos. What was wrong with having a wee in an alley?'

May enjoyed winding his partner up. 'This square is one of the grandest architectural set pieces in London. So what if there's strip-lighting and chipboard behind it?'

'It's vulgar, that's what.'

'Says the man with the Fablon-and-Formica kitchen.'

'Are they always like this?' DuCaine asked Banbury as they alighted.

The crime scene manager shrugged. 'No, they've mellowed.'

They took the lift to the top floor of the corner building, where a young constable was standing in the hallway by the open door of a flat. The stench of burned fabric stung their nostrils.

'He's in the bedroom at the back,' said one of the emerging firefighters, pointing over his shoulder.

'You'd better go first, Dan,' Bryant suggested. 'I don't want you nagging me about touching stuff.'

The apartment hall was painted in shades of sour cream and granite, and was lined with small brownish modernist paintings, brightened by the inclusion of what looked like an original Paul Klee and a Joan Miró. Beyond them, a smell of burning emanated from the master bedroom.

'Hey, welcome back,' said Senior Fire Officer Blaize Carter, stepping out into the hall. 'It just keeps getting weirder. Come and take a look.'

The corpse was on its back, sprawled on the remains of a king-sized grey bedspread. Its torso and limbs were still intact, but over the victim's head had been fitted a rough-hewn iron mask. It was hinged vertically and shut so that only a few tufts of singed brown hair and the top half of the left ear had survived outside it, stuck to the blackened pillowcase.

'He looks like a Trojan warrior,' remarked Bryant. 'What is that thing?'

'We've got scorch marks around his shoulders,' said Carter. 'It was put in place while it was hot.'

Bryant bent over the mask and sniffed. 'Roasted flesh. Who kills somebody by sticking their head in something like that? How would it even work?'

'How come you're here?' Banbury asked the fire officer.

'CoL knew you'd caught the call,' said Carter, 'and there was a follow-up from a neighbour who smelled burning.'

'Were there any windows open? Did you have to kick the door in?'

'No, the door was shut but not locked. It would have kept any fire contained. These are expensive properties, renovated in the last five or six years, since the new fire regs came in.'

'So plenty of smoke detectors.'

'One in every room.' Carter pointed up at the white box in the ceiling with wires hanging down from it. 'Easy to disable. I met the Belgravia SOCO, who was very happy to leave this to you. It's a bit outside his comfort zone. He reckons the initial call came from the cleaning woman.'

Banbury closed in on the body. 'It looks like the damage is entirely local, centred on the skull.'

'Nothing on his wrists,' said Bryant. 'How did the killer subdue him? Do a fingertip search around here. I want to know if the victim was knocked out, locked in, what kept him from leaving.' He believed in a system he called ABC: *Assume nothing. Believe nobody. Check everything.* 'How long has he been dead?'

'We picked up the call at nine-o-five a.m.,' Carter replied. 'By the time we got here the smoke had dissipated. The bedspread's not flammable, but the mask scorched everything through to the mattress springs. I don't have to tell you this wasn't self-inflicted, do I?'

'I saw a camera in the lobby,' said Banbury. 'Fraternity, could you find out where the feed goes?'

Bryant had already eased himself over the cordon that the Belgravia SOCO had set around the end of the bed, and was going through a work folder that lay on the dressing table. 'You're lucky the flat didn't go up,' he said, examining the papers.

'There was no air exchange because of the closed windows and sealed internal doors,' Carter replied. 'The problem for you is that the heat has sterilized the immediate site.'

'Jonathan De Vere.' Bryant unfolded a letterheaded sheet and attempted to read it. 'Anyone heard of something called CharityMob?'

'It's an app,' said Banbury, on his knees and peering at the base of the burned bedspread.

'What does it do?'

'It gets mobile-phone users to donate their social reach. It's got a very cool interface.'

Bryant gave his partner a blank look. 'I suppose that means something to you?'

'Information,' translated May. 'It's the number of unique people who read an ad that contains social information. To widen your user circle you need to constantly expand your social reach.'

'Nope, sorry, I still have absolutely no idea what you're talking about,' said Bryant, dismissing him. 'There must be something else here. Dan, have you done that weird thing you always do?'

Banbury also had a system of his own. Before the rest of the circus arrived he would get suited up and go in with his notepad, repeatedly asking himself what he was seeing and hearing. Then he would crawl about, following the left-hand wall around the room, noting blood distribution, saliva, fibres, anything lying around. He would check the central-heating timer to help estimate the time of death, note which lights were on, whether there were any open drawers, and whether the toilet seat was up or down. In his time with the detectives he had experienced more than his share of bizarre sights, but this one ranked in the top ten.

'Giles is standing by to look at the body,' he said, studying De Vere's skull mask. 'That thing looks heavy. Some kind of traditional design . . . Could it mean something?'

'I'll need to check,' said Bryant. 'Can you make sure his head survives the transit in one piece? You don't know what damage that thing's done.'

'So how did this work?' asked May. 'He came into the flat, his assailant followed him in or was already here – then what?'

Bryant rose and grimaced, stretching his back. 'De Vere wasn't restrained. He was drugged first.'

'How do you know that?' asked May.

'Because of the kitchen.' He led the way and pointed to the work surface, where some sugar had been spilled from its container. 'The cup's under the bed, on its side. The carpet's very wet so he hadn't finished drinking from it.'

Banbury crouched at eye level. 'Want me to test these granules?'

'If you would be so kind, Dan, and the tea. And take a sample from the hob, will you? There are some black particles beside one of the rings. Let's get a couple more people over here and talk to everyone in the building. Entry signs, escape routes, all tradespeople and residents listed. It's got to be the same bloke, hasn't it? He's playing with fire again.' He collared the hallway constable. 'You. Spotty teenager in a uniform. When's the ambulance coming?'

'It's already round the back, sir.'

'Anyone notice anything?'

'The neighbour saw the cleaning lady heading down the stairs, sir. She didn't raise the alarm because she'd seen her lots of times before. Lady upstairs called about the smell of burning.'

'Was the front door open?'

'The neighbour says not.'

'Nobody ever sees anything in a building like this. He must have had a key.'

'Don't hold your breath for fingerprints but we might get glove marks,' said Banbury. 'I've got some leathers from the Brixton site.'

'You can do that?' DuCaine was surprised.

'People assume leather gloves are untraceable,' said Banbury. 'They're good for gripping, but there's a leather grain present on the surface of the glove. It can be as unique as human skin because leather itself is skin. New pairs are tricky, but I like old ones. They have pores that pick up dirt and grease from different surfaces, so you can get good transfer particles. Unlined gloves get saturated with oil and sweat if they're regularly worn, and that sometimes comes through. I've heard of DNA traces coming right through a glove.'

'Fraternity, unless you spent the whole of your time at Hendon fast asleep you should know all this,' said Bryant. 'Dan, stop getting overexcited. Just remember you've only got one chance. If you seize the wrong things to start with, you'll set us off in the wrong direction. I'll leave you to deal with the site but it seems pretty straightforward.'

'Straightforward! The mask—'

Bryant was a picture of impatience. 'He got hold of the main-door and front-door keys, probably on the same ring, probably from the cleaning lady, let himself in, doctored either the sugar or the cup, then waited it out. He knows his victims, yes? He knows their habits. I'm taking the folder and the briefcase.'

'Let me dust them first.'

'All right, but hurry up.' Bryant knew it wasn't very professional taking evidence away in a Tesco shopping bag, but in the last few days everything had felt like this: chaotic and disjointed.

The shopping bag fell over. He pulled it upright and rose, then suddenly lost his balance.

The building was slowly tilting on its axis, and then

London was moving too, so that everyone and everything was sliding away from him. Outside the kitchen window the buildings sailed past one another like yachts competing in a race. Arthur Bryant dropped the bag and brought his hands up to his face, trying to make sense of what was happening.

Strange room, strange people, sudden silence – for a moment he felt utterly lost. It was as if someone had stirred the world up with a huge wooden spoon and had let it settle back in a completely different order. He no longer recognized the view from the windows, the cream and grey walls, the hunched figure examining the carpet by the bed, the young black officer looking at him in puzzlement.

He was floating, remembering—

For a long time nothing ever changed in London. It was all comfortably familiar, almost annoyingly so. London had been like his mother's cutlery drawer; there was a special place where every piece fitted. The streets you avoided, the streets you loved. The butcher, the baker, the troublemakers . . .

Now nothing was in its place. People had changed. They had become aliens. The unlined, unblinking young were from a remote, inhospitable planet. Crowds of unfamiliar faces came at him, talking to each other in ways he could not comprehend or staring blankly at their phones, wave upon wave passing without a glance as if he had ceased to exist. Friends and colleagues vanished and were replaced by freshly minted strangers, and there was no one left who knew him or cared . . .

Turning around with an increasing sense of panic, he saw May watching him thoughtfully.

'Come on, old pal, get your bearings,' he said gently, extending his arm. 'I'm here. I'll take you back to the PCU.'

And then they were outside. As he stepped back into

the street, Bryant saw that the right sole of his old brown Oxford shoe was detaching itself. Sagging against a wall, he tried to push it back on but it flapped down uselessly, then fell off. He stared at the black rubber fillet lying on the wet pavement, and turned to his partner. 'John,' he said plaintively, 'I'm falling apart.'

'No, you're not.' May picked it up, smiling with gentle concern. 'We can fix this.'

Bryant heard the sounds of the street returning to his ears. And then there were trees and pavements and cars and pigeons, and he saw the classical Greek ornamentation that marked out the square as part of Belgravia, and knew he was near Chelsea in west London and all would be all right again if he just hung on to his partner's arm. But pride would not allow him to do so.

'Are you OK now?' May asked, looking in his eyes.

'I'm fine.' Bryant pulled himself free. 'It was very hot in there, that's all.' He made his way unaided to May's BMW, impatiently waiting for the passenger door to be opened, because he very badly wanted to be back in his office, surrounded by his beloved books.

22

UNMASKED

When they arrived back on the first floor of the PCU Janice Longbright was waiting for them, and she must have been told that something had happened because she was ridiculously over-solicitous and apologetic, bringing tea and biscuits and sitting Arthur down in his armchair as if he was a damned invalid.

'I'm fine,' Bryant grumbled, wrinkling his nose. 'Stop all this fussing. And take the Custard Creams away, Crippen's been on them again. Well, what have you got for me?'

'There's a yard of stuff online about Jon De Vere,' she said, falling back into her work mode, which he much preferred. 'He's a young start-up entrepreneur, a former hedge-fund manager who gave up his job to "give something back", as he put it.' She tapped a nail on her screen. 'Two years ago he became the managing director of an app-development company called Apptly Said and made a fortune from a voice-activated app called CharityMob. Now he's the rising role model for tech-heads all over the world. Unbelievably popular in the online community; a practising Catholic who raises money for disadvantaged kids. Pretty much an all-round decent guy.'

'So, no obvious nemeses? There must be something.'

'It's useful that De Vere uses social media as much as he does – we've got virtually every move he's made in the last couple of years all laid out for us. Based just off Threadneedle Street, married with a child on the way. I've already spoken to his wife, Lena. She's at a conference in Amsterdam. She sounded OK, no tears, steady nerves, wanted to know the details.'

'Did you give them to her?'

'No, because you haven't told me. She's catching the next flight back, should be here just after lunch. She wanted to know if she could stay at the flat in Belgravia, so I had to warn her that it wouldn't be habitable tonight, and then at least not until Dan had finished collating forensics. She didn't seem that bothered – said she'd check herself into the Palmeira Hampton in Cadogan Place.'

'As you do,' said Renfield. 'She's not short of a bob, then.'

'She's shocked but steady, sounds as if she's up for an interview. Maybe it would be a good idea for me to get to her before the loss kicks in.'

'It doesn't make sense,' said Bryant, shaking his head. 'Glen Hall worked for a bank – in these times, you could conceivably understand why someone might hate him. But Freddie Weeks and this chap De Vere sound like martyred innocents. There must be something that connects them, mustn't there? Do we know when De Vere was last seen?'

'The security guard at his office says he was working there all night,' said Longbright. 'It's something he often does when his wife's away. He left his building some time around eight thirty a.m. The day receptionist usually starts then but was running late because of all the tube diversions.'

'All early-morning attacks – why? Crimes usually occur later. Explain what he does again in terminology I can understand, would you?' Bryant looked suspiciously at the packet of Custard Creams that still lurked on the nearby desk.

'He develops phone and tablet applications for charitable causes,' said Longbright, checking the CV on her screen. 'He was a technical whiz-kid, fast-tracked by Google, and – here's the shocking part – he turned them down to go it alone.'

'Forgive me – why is that shocking?'

'Nobody turns Google down. The problem is that De Vere doesn't seem to have any enemies at all. Not so far, anyway. It'll take time to go through everything.'

Jack Renfield turned the screen of his iPad around. The PCU had no budget for technology, so he usually brought his in from home. 'Have you seen this stuff? The guy's a living saint. He marched with Anonymous against the bankers and launched a smoking-gun site aimed at weeding out corrupt traders. Guess who he had a pop at last week? The Findersbury Bank. He also used the CharityMob site to blow the whistle on Dexter Cornell two days before the whole thing kicked off.'

'Wait, you mean De Vere did this *before* Cornell was outed for suspected insider trading?' asked May.

'The piece kind of implies that it has an inside track on financial irregularities. They're promising more updates to come.'

'So we have a connection,' said Bryant, pleased.

'Not really,' Longbright warned. 'Cornell is just the catalyst for the riots—'

'—which resulted in the death of Freddie Weeks.'

'If De Vere was running pieces about Cornell, it's possible he put himself in the line of fire.'

'Enough conjecture.' May rose, clapping his hands. 'Right, let's get started with the rounds. Janice, you can assign teams for interviews.'

'You know how I hate the procedural stuff,' said

Bryant, easing himself upright. 'I think I'll go and see how Giles is getting on.'

'You really don't need to,' May told him. 'Why not take it easy today? We can cover everything.'

Bryant was petulant. 'You sound like you want to get rid of me. I shall "not go gentle into that good night. Old age should burn and rave at close of day."'

'You what?' said Renfield.

'"Rage, rage"!' shouted Bryant, picking up his walking stick and waving it like a pirate cutlass. '"Rage against the dying of the light"!'

'Has he been at the sherry?' Renfield looked nonplussed.

'No,' said May wearily, 'he's been at the Dylan Thomas. Don't worry, I'll take care of him.'

On his way out, Bryant passed Land's office and bellowed 'Knock, knock' through the invisible door. The unit chief had the look of a schoolboy who'd been caught reading a comic under his desk.

'Yes?' he asked warily.

'Can I ask your advice?'

Land very nearly pointed at himself in surprise. 'Yes, of course.'

'I know I can always count on you for an unbiased opinion because you're not really involved in anything important that goes on here.'

While the unit chief was trying to frame a response to this, Bryant continued. 'Hypothetically speaking, suppose there was a situation in which a detective needed to question someone who could cause trouble for his boss?'

'How much trouble?'

Bryant rubbed his nose. 'Oh, a lot.'

'Would this hypothetical detective be able to prove that the person he wished to question had a direct link to his investigation?'

'More of an implication. But as my grannie used to

say, "You can't stand near a Frenchman without getting onions all over you."'

'Then I would tell the detective to stay away from his high-risk client and not do anything that would make his boss want to beat him to death with a claw hammer,' said Land. 'Hypothetically speaking. Where are you going?'

'I believe the detective has decided on a change of plan and is off to do something else.'

Land peered over the top of where his glasses would be if he wore them. 'Does he need someone to come with him?'

'No, he's quite capable of managing, thank you.' Bryant pulled his hat further over his ears and trundled off.

As he walked, he thought about his health. He had no fear of dying, but the idea of being trapped in a hospital bed surrounded by supine old men and harassed caregivers filled him with unutterable horror. If something bad was happening to him, he decided that he would meet it head-on and fight every last inch of the way.

Accordingly, he refused to allow anyone to accompany him and caught a bus to the St Pancras Mortuary. Unfortunately he got on the wrong bus, ended up in Camden and was forced to backtrack, marching through the rain on a loop that took him past the PCU's former headquarters at Mornington Crescent.

The sky was the colour of a bad sprain. Between the hornbeams and hawthorns of Oakley Square and the rain-glazed cobbles of Camden's backstreets, the dark old offices above Mornington Crescent tube station now shone with harsh LED purity. He wondered who was occupying the building and went over to check the front door. A brushed steel plaque had been set in place of the old PCU sign and read 'Data InfoSpace Hub'.

How many years did we sit up there late at night, he thought, *sifting through the cases that no one else wanted to handle? How many vulnerable women did we manage to protect, how many families did we keep together? It was all about preventive policing back then, when the mere sight of a neighbourhood copper would be enough to stop kids from picking on each other or men from knocking their wives about. And after that, all the crazy cases, hunting for the Dagenham Strangler, tracking down the Mile End Maniac and uncovering the identity of the Shepherd's Bush Slasher. What about all the small neighbourhood cases we solved? Did we get any thanks for catching the Shoreditch Counterfeit Coconut Mob or the Chapel Market Cheese Smugglers? All I got out of that was a pound of Wensleydale from a grateful grocer. When I accidentally blew the place up I should have done a better job of it.*

By the time he reached the St Pancras Coroner's Office his overcoat was soaked to the lining again and his head was filled with sorrows. Even Rosa took pity on him.

'You look dead,' she said, pulling him in from the porch. 'Don't drip on the floor. Give me your coat. Now, now.' She waggled her fingers at him. 'This is madness, a man of your age. And your shoes, look at the state.'

For once, Bryant did as he was told. Squelching meekly down the hall in his darned socks, he found Kershaw in his customary position at the dissection table. 'What happened to you?' Giles laughed. 'Did you *actually* fall into the canal this time? You *have* been busy this week, haven't you? Three bodies in three days: what's going on?'

'I was hoping you'd tell me.' Bryant wrung out a glove and stuck it over an Anglepoise.

'Well, you're just in time. I'm about to open the box.' The coroner gently tucked the grey Mylar coverlet more tightly around De Vere's body. 'I'm not sure what we're going to find underneath, but I imagine it's not going to be very nice.'

'I've never seen anything like this,' said Bryant, dragging over a stool. 'What are you going to use?'

'I already tried a bone knife, but I'm afraid it'll need this.' Kershaw hefted something that looked like a sculptor's chisel in his hands. 'I've used one of these on a ribcage but never on a face before. If you start to feel ill, low-level lighting will guide you to an exit.' He inserted the tip of the instrument into the seam of the mask at the edge of the jawline, and began to tap the end lightly with a hammer. He continued for two or three minutes as fragments of burned skin flaked off from beneath the mask on to the steel table. 'What do you know about the attack?'

'Not much yet,' Bryant admitted, fascinated by the operation. 'He'd been at work all night. We think he'd gone home to have a shower and a quick kip before changing his clothes and heading back to the office. We found something in the kitchen – metal flakes on the stove – and a knocked-over cup of tea, possibly drugged.'

'That should have come off by now,' said Kershaw, peering under the lip of the mask.

'I think there's something else holding it in place,' said Bryant.

'You could be right. I have a feeling—' He bent down and shone a penlight beneath the edge. 'Yes, it's spiked on either side, in the cavities just below the cheekbones. I think your attacker probably hammered it into place. Makes you wonder what kind of man could do such a thing.' He wedged his fingers under the mask and gave an experimental tug.

'Would it have to be a man?'

'I don't suppose so, but metalwork? It's not the sort of MO you'd expect from a woman – or anyone, for that matter.' He strained at the mask. 'Sorry about this.' There was a tearing, splintering sound, and one side of the mask came up. Kershaw took a closer look and winced. 'Yup, a pair of short prongs, right into the tops of the gums. The epidermal layer is stuck to the metal. He heated it up and hammered it on while it was red-hot. That'll be what your flakes are in the kitchen. He put the mask over the burner and probably lifted it off with tongs.'

Kershaw raised the other side and carefully removed the mask in its entirety, leaving behind a grinning crimson-faced skull with livid pink gums, very white teeth, and no lips or eyelids.

Bryant examined the mask. 'I found a copy of the design. It's the face of Vulcan, the god of fire. He's usually depicted holding a blacksmith's hammer. I think we can assume that's how our man got the mask into place. He's used to working with metals. We'll have to check out workshops and factories, colleges, garages, anywhere with access to tools. There are markings on the interior. Looks like some kind of pattern.'

'I'll get the skin off and clean it up so you can have a look.'

'I usually expect to unmask the killer, not the victim,' said Bryant. 'Our man is getting closer.'

'What do you mean?'

'This time he had direct contact with his target. He's gained confidence. I wish we had more to go on.'

'What, you mean you don't already have some kind of crackpot theory on this one?' Kershaw examined a scrap of burned flesh in his tweezers.

'Rather unlike me, isn't it?' Bryant admitted. 'We've got no consistencies, no pattern. The victims are a down-and-out, a bank manager and a start-up wizard; two of them are linked by an attractive woman and in all three cases the method of death involves fire. None of it makes any logical sense.'

'It's probably the woman, then,' said Kershaw amiably, setting the mask beside De Vere's skinless skull. 'Females are unknowable to us because their brains are hardwired differently. The connections in your typical male brain run between the front and back of the same hemisphere, whereas in women the connections run laterally between the left and right sides.'

'How do you know that?' Bryant watched in disgust as Kershaw peered up the remains of the corpse's nostrils.

'Diffusion tensor imaging. It's probably why they know us males better than we know ourselves. You don't suppose he's just selecting archetypes to make some kind of a point? You know, homelessness, corruption, reliance on technology?'

'I can't see how. Surely he'd go after bad role models, not Weeks, who had no power and nothing to give, or this chap, who was carrying out charitable works. Hall was in finance but we've turned up nothing untoward on him so far.'

'Here, take a look at this. God, it's heavy. He's a strong lad, your killer. Take your glove off that.' Giles lifted the mask over to his Anglepoise and spotlit its interior.

The lead was still crusted in patches of burned skin, but Bryant could see what he meant. 'It's a mould,' he said, amazed, studying the inverted nose, eyes and jawline. 'A letter M on either cheek. Why on earth would he make a mould and brand it on to De Vere's face?'

'You're not dealing with a rational mind,' said Kershaw, setting the mask aside and covering it. He removed his cap and shook out his blond curls.

'Perhaps not,' said Bryant. 'You know what I think this is? An old English punishment, like the tar-and-feathering. Branding was used until well into the eighteenth century in London. The M stood for "Malefactor".'

23

THE THREE INTERVIEWS

DS Longbright preferred conducting interviews in people's homes, where they were comfortable and more likely to remember details. Consequently she had booked everyone out for the afternoon, sending them off to talk to the friends and relatives of the three victims.

'I can't have you all disappearing,' Raymond Land complained. 'We've a perfectly good interview room on the floor above, apart from the dodgy floor and that bloody moose.'

'It's a stag,' Longbright pointed out. Bryant had been given the stuffed animal by a grateful neighbourhood resident after he had solved the mystery of the King's Cross stag-man, and rather than refuse the gift he had installed it in the offices.

'It's a health hazard. And it's got alopecia,' Land said. 'There's something moving about inside it.'

Land always felt uncomfortable when the rest of the staff were deployed beyond the confines of the building, mainly because it exposed his own uselessness. Longbright usually tried to cheer him up by reminding him that only he could keep higher authorities off their backs, but Land knew she was just being kind. Everyone had been kind to him since Leanne had left him for her Welsh flamenco instructor. Now his home life was as moribund as his career; the neighbours had stopped coming round, the washing machine had died, the matching halves of his socks had all disappeared and he'd finished the last of the emergency freezer meals. There was only some Quorn left, and he wasn't sure what to do with that. He wasn't one of those independent, self-sufficient men who could replace fuses and do his own plumbing. He needed something more than the love of a good, kind woman – he needed a maid.

It didn't help coming to work and finding that he had no faith in the investigation at hand. He certainly didn't agree that these deaths were in any way connected. A tramp fight, a business vendetta and a lone nutcase, or possibly some kind of weird sex game that had gone wrong. Bryant's trouble was that the old man wanted to join up every inexplicable London occurrence into some kind of vast citywide conspiracy. Land knew it was heresy to suggest such a thing, but sometimes deaths just happened, like that MI5 bloke who climbed inside his own sports bag and suffocated. You couldn't explain away the world, so what was the point in trying?

'I mean, what is the point?' he said aloud.

'Mr Bryant doesn't have anywhere else to store it,' said Longbright.

'Fine, whatever, conduct your interviews on the top of the London Eye for all I care, just get that bloody thing out of there.' He stormed back to his office and even slammed the invisible door, much to Longbright's mystification.

They split up into pairs, as was their habit. Bimsley and Mangeshkar caught a tube to Bayswater to meet Freddie Weeks's parents. Renfield and DuCaine made their way to the Findersbury Bank to interview Glen Hall's colleagues. Longbright headed for the Palmeira Hampton to meet with Jonathan De Vere's wife. Bryant and May sequestered themselves in their room, and Raymond Land went online to find a cleaning lady who'd be prepared to tackle six weeks' worth of laundry.

Sue and Gerry Weeks lived in a 1960s maisonette behind Bayswater tube station. If not for its window boxes of struggling geraniums, the concrete block could have been mistaken for an insurance office. Mrs Weeks had further overcome the severity of the façade by hanging valanced nets at every window and brightening the dark rooms by placing glass puppies, china windmills, fragile galleons, cheery mottoes, smiling dolls and happy angels at six-inch intervals on every available surface around the flat. The cumulative effect had almost hospitalized her husband with depression on a number of occasions. Now he had reconciled himself to the fact that he would end his days as a bull in a china shop, and slumped on his puffy sofa with his huge meaty hands folded between his knees, waiting for Colin Bimsley's questions.

'You say he didn't respond well to medication,' said Bimsley, checking his notes. 'Do you remember what he'd been prescribed?'

'Not really.' Mr Weeks shook his head sadly. 'My wife should be back from the shops soon. She'll remember. She remembers everything.' He made it sound like an affliction. 'He stopped taking the stuff because he said it prevented him from thinking clearly, but he never really thought clearly. He could never hold a job down longer than five minutes. He always got into arguments with his bosses.'

'What kind of work was he doing at this point?' asked Meera.

'Mostly shelf-stacking in depots. He worked for a

delivery company in Mile End for a while. When he said he had a girlfriend we thought he might settle down, but she didn't stick around.'

'This would have been Joanna Papis?'

'That's the one. He put a picture of her on Facebook; otherwise we would never have seen her. He didn't like coming home because he was never close to his mother. My wife discovered religion late in life. Joanna looked very nice. I couldn't help wondering what she saw in Freddie.'

'Is that him?' Meera asked, pointing to a small framed photograph on the mantelpiece.

'Yeah, he must have been about eighteen or nineteen when that was taken.'

The photograph showed a boy in a Glastonbury T-shirt, smiling on a sunny day at the coast. Freddie Weeks had a kind, soft face and shoulder-length dark curly hair. He looked happy. Clearly his parents thought enough of him to keep his picture on display.

'When was the last time you spoke to Freddie?'

'I told one of your officers all about this—'

'I'm not the officer you spoke to.'

'But surely—'

'When did you speak to him?'

'Six weeks ago. He called up late one night—'

'What night?'

'Late September, a Sunday I think. He was in tears, sounded as if he'd been drinking. He didn't make much sense but I knew straight away what he was after.'

'Which was?'

'Money.'

'Was he in debt?'

'He needed to pay his rent. I told him he was on the dole, that should have been enough, and that he should get himself housing benefit.'

'So you didn't give him anything?'

'No, of course not.' He made the idea sound ludicrous.

'He was your son.'

'My son! Going on about how my generation had screwed up the world, leaving his lot with nothing but debt. I wanted my son to be a boxer. He'd been named after Freddie Mills.'

'The world light-heavyweight champ? He shot himself at the age of forty-six, didn't he?' At the gym where Bimsley occasionally boxed, there were still a few faded photographs of Freddie Mills.

'He was a hero round here after the war,' Mr Weeks explained, 'a role model for my old man and my uncles. I used to box. I won trophies. My wife makes me keep them in the garage. And my son grew up to be a pacifist, always going on marches.'

'Do you know if he was registered with any pacifist organizations?'

'Probably.' He sighed. 'He moved about a lot so he used this as his mailing address. We were always getting brochures through. One came just last week. Hang on a minute.' Pulling himself free of the sofa's grip, he fished about underneath the television and handed over a pile of letters. Meera caught Colin's eye and held it. The top leaflet showed a young man in a Guy Fawkes mask tapping the watch on his wrist, beneath the headline 'It's Time to Break the Banks'.

'I'm pretty certain that's my lad,' said Mr Weeks, touching the shot. 'That's the watch I bought him for his eighteenth birthday, back when I thought he might turn out all right.'

The burned remnants of the watch were now in the PCU's evidence room, but Bimsley thought that returning them would only make Freddie's father even more upset. He had failed to produce a son in his own image, and that was enough.

*

The bank was under siege for the sixth day. This morning bricks had been thrown through the windows. The ground floor was now boarded up, so the phones had been put on direct lines and the receptionists had been moved upstairs. No public callers were being admitted, so Renfield and DuCaine were forced to enter via a maritime insurance building at the rear of the premises, crossing the Victorian alleyway that linked the two properties. They were admitted by a harassed-looking security guard who showed them up to the third-floor meeting room.

Alice French was a slender Anglo-West Indian woman with silver-painted nails and a tight-fitting grey suit who looked as if she was counting every second she spent away from her computer terminal. Her partner, a handsome German named Gunther Lange, sat beside her, ready to take notes. If it weren't for the steady cutting of helicopter blades outside, the calm, unruffled pair might have succeeded in pretending that it was business as usual in the world of high finance. Renfield noted that they had been briefed with answers; their notepads were already smothered in handwriting.

'You know we have to distance ourselves from anything Mr Hall might have got himself into,' French began, 'so let's see if we can wrap this up quickly.'

'Mr Hall "got himself into" being murdered,' said Renfield. 'We're not interested in the bank's position. Did he have enemies here?'

French glanced at her colleague as if obtaining permission to speak. 'He put together funding packages for start-ups, and he had to pull the plug on some of them when they failed to return, so yes, of course he antagonized people. But in a purely fiscal sense. You can't run any business without making enemies.'

'Who would you regard as an enemy, then?'

'Anyone who impedes progress.'

'Like us?' asked Renfield. 'We're delaying you from your work.'

Lange missed the irony in his voice. 'Yes, like you.'

'I'd like a list of all the enemies you think Mr Hall might have made.'

'That wouldn't be possible,' said French sharply. 'All trading is strictly confidential.'

'Oddly enough, it's not when it comes to the police.' Renfield was growing angrier by the moment. 'We can sequester your files and confiscate your hard drives while we eliminate you from our inquiries. Did he bring his personal life to work?'

'What do you mean?' asked French, as if the concept of a personal life was too alien to appreciate.

'Did he talk about what went on at home?'

'Nothing went on at home, so far as I know,' said French. 'He put in his hours.'

'No steady girlfriend, then?'

'No, of course not. He was gay.'

'All right, boyfriend?'

'Nobody that I know of.'

'So you're telling me that nobody here knew anything about his life outside of work?'

'We don't discuss our personal lives with each other; it's not professional.'

'He was with the bank for how long?'

'Seven years.'

'I'm sorry, but you can't have shared an open-plan office with someone for seven years and not have gleaned a single bloody thing about them.'

'I did hear he had a nice flat,' said Lange. He had a peculiarly strangled voice that operated in a register beyond any listener's normal expectations, which was probably why French did most of the talking. 'But he was never there much. We don't keep EU-regulated hours.'

'What about Dexter Cornell?' asked Renfield. 'Did he—?'

'You know we can't answer questions about him,' interrupted French.

'Let's keep to public knowledge, then,' said Renfield, determined to get some sort of an answer. 'I only know what I've read in the papers. Didn't he have some kind of big hotel deal going on with Chinese property developers based in East Africa? What happened there? Just as a matter of background interest.'

Gunther Lange laid a placatory hand on his colleague's arm. 'You're right, it's public knowledge that the deal collapsed after the Africans turned down the construction of a port,' he said. 'It put us in an exposed position.'

'All documentation has gone to the National Fraud Intelligence Bureau,' said French. 'It's best to ask them if you need any further information.'

'And I think that concludes our conversation,' said Lange. 'We'll be happy to answer any further questions you may have by email.'

'Well, that was like pulling bloody teeth,' said Renfield as they left. 'If Hall had a boyfriend, could you find something out?'

'Why me?' asked DuCaine. 'It's not like being members of a classic-car club, you know. We don't all wave to each other as we pass on the road. I'm no better placed to find out anything about his private life than you are.'

'Yeah, but you could ask around in clubs and that.'

DuCaine raised his eyes to heaven. 'It's not the 1970s. Nobody over twenty-five goes clubbing any more; they're online just like you and me and everyone else.'

'All right,' said Renfield, 'keep your hair on, I just thought I'd ask, that's all.'

Janice Longbright found herself in an expansive Arabic vision of what the designer thought an English drawing room might look like, with polished marble instead of floorboards and a backlit atrium substituted for a plaster ceiling. The Palmeira Hampton was blandly glamorous in the way of all global hotel chains, and therefore not very English or anything specific at all. At least the red velvet armchairs were comfortable, and she remained silent while the waiter finished pouring tea into Lena De Vere's cup, feeling that the interview was going to be more awkward than she had expected.

'First of all, I'm sorry that I had to find you so quickly, but you'll appreciate that time is of the essence. I'd like to offer my sincere—'

Mrs De Vere waved her condolences aside. She was blonde and attractive in a way that would prevent any real personality from showing in her face for a few more years. 'I understand. I suppose it hasn't really sunk in yet, so now's probably a good time to talk. I'm very tired and would rather get this over with as soon as possible.'

'Of course. I have to tell you that at the moment we have no suspects in this case, so I must ask who was closest to your husband, and if he had enemies.'

'Enemies?' Lena gave a sharp little laugh. 'No, he didn't have enemies. He was too busy changing people's lives. I suppose you could say the banks were his enemies, generally speaking; Jonathan prided himself on his anti-capitalist credentials. When he was still at school he tried to take his local building society to court, but he quickly discovered that didn't work. So he looked for ways of doing good through business. Jonathan worked very long hours. He didn't have much time left over to be with friends or family.'

'That couldn't have been easy for you.'

'Let's just say that we weren't first in the receiving line when it came to getting his full attention.' She unconsciously touched her stomach, and Longbright remembered that she was pregnant. Her clothes were tailored so that she barely showed.

'This is a delicate matter, but I have to ask you who you were with in Amsterdam.'

'I was attending a seminar at the Rijksmuseum.'

'So I understand. But who were you with?'

'I wasn't with—'

'Before you answer, you should know that I called your hotel and they had no record of your booking.'

'Oh, God.' Lena De Vere folded and refolded her napkin. 'Do we really have to go through this?'

'I'm afraid so.'

'I was there, but I wasn't staying under my name. My husband is well known to the press and I was thinking about his reputation. You don't expect something like this to happen. I wasn't prepared.'

'Can I ask once again who you were with?'

'A friend of mine. He makes jewellery; he's a metallurgist. If it's possible, I'd like to leave him out of this. Jonathan and I – we've been having difficulties for some time.'

'You mean your relationship.'

She caught Janice's glance at her stomach. 'To save you the awkwardness of asking, the child is not my husband's. Jonathan was on antidepressants, plus being a heavy smoker – he was impotent. We've been . . . privately separate . . . for a while. I do want to keep this out of the press.'

'I'm not in a position to promise that,' said Longbright.

Lena De Vere's face betrayed no emotion. 'I understand,' she said quietly.

'I need you to think carefully about who your husband knew and saw regularly. I'm afraid we'll have to take his laptop, phones and all his passwords. Did he ever have anything to do with the Findersbury Bank?'

'Well, yes, of course.'

'What do you mean?'

'I'm sorry, I thought you knew. Jonathan was brought in by the board to set up a charitable trust for them. He was in the middle of organizing it when that idiot Cornell set the cat among the pigeons.'

'The connection hadn't been made clear to me,' Longbright admitted, surprised. 'What kind of trust?'

'It involves supplying preloaded computers for schoolchildren in India.'

'So your husband dealt with the directors?'

'I believe so. He never told me any details. As far as I know, they were still being hammered out.' Mrs De Vere winced as the baby kicked.

'When are you due?' Longbright asked.

'In about nine weeks. I'm – My husband was a very good man. Things will be – awful without him. It's just that this – right now – the timing, I mean. I don't know what to do first.'

'I can put you in touch with an appropriate support group if you need one.'

'What I'd like is a drink.' She stepped aside from the thought. 'You wouldn't understand.'

'Wouldn't I?'

'If you dig into my past I'm sure you'll turn up enough about me to counterbalance my husband's well-publicized goodness. I suppose I was one of his improvement projects. After you've done some research, perhaps you'll feel that it didn't take as well as the others.'

'It's not my job to judge,' said Longbright gently. 'If you—'

Mrs De Vere looked away to the window. There seemed to be some kind of commotion outside, a shifting crowd pushing one way and another, like a rugby scrum. An arm was raised and there came an explosion of glass. The window of the lounge bar was shattered by a chunk of concrete. The entire room rose to its feet in a single motion. One teacup dropped to a thick rug and rolled in a circle.

'I think you'd better go,' said Longbright, shepherding Mrs De Vere to the lobby even as the waiters mobilized to usher out the guests.

Longbright ran to the entrance and found an angry horde armed with placards that read 'BASH THE RICH'. The cards were printed in the same sans-serif typeface that Jonathan De Vere used for his CharityMob app.

She looked up the street. A great dark sea of protestors had filled the space between the buildings, flooding down from Hyde Park. She called Renfield. 'Jack, what's going on? I'm still in Knightsbridge. There's trouble breaking out here now.'

'There was a rally in Hyde Park,' he told her. 'They tore down the enclosure fences in protest at the heavy police presence, and it looks like all hell's breaking loose. You should get out of there before they lock the stations down.'

'OK, I'm on my way.' As she headed out, she realized that the rioters were almost at the gates of Buckingham Palace. How much longer would it be before the police decided to raise the stakes and turn its newly purchased water cannons on the crowds?

24

SECURE

'He's going to go bananas if he finds out where we've gone,' remarked May.

'Then he won't find out,' Bryant promised. 'This is our stop.'

The Paddington train deposited the detectives at Burford, where they were able to find a taxi that would take them to Oakley Manor House. They passed over a sluggish meandering river and through a pretty street of stone the colour of Shropshire blue cheese. The town lay in a dip fringed with hawthorn, dogwood and poplars, surrounded by damp emerald hills.

'Blimey, this is depressing,' said Bryant, peering from the taxi window with a grimace.

'What are you talking about? It's beautiful. This is the Cotswolds.'

'I know.' Bryant sniffed disapprovingly. 'Coachloads of Chinese tourists creeping around antique shops photographing everything from teapots to toilet seats so that they can make exact reproductions when they get home. But it's all fake to begin with, mocked up for the tourist trade, so they're just getting copies of copies.'

'What a dreadful old cynic you are,' said May. 'This is an area of outstanding natural beauty. You'd be happier if there were a few more pound shops and some gang-related crime, wouldn't you?'

'Oh, there's crime, all right. Everyone's busily peddling the family plate to anyone gullible enough to think they're buying a bit of Ye Olde Englande. And all those charity shops selling dead people's rubbish just to dodge paying taxes. Have you ever seen people in charity shops? It's like watching tropical fish move about. And why is there always a cake stand? Who uses cake stands? Look out there: it's not right to have so many trees. And it smells funny.'

'It's the countryside. What do you expect? Do you want me to chuck some plastic bags out of the window to make you feel more at home?'

Bryant harrumphed and sat back in his seat, looking like a Brueghelian peasant with gout.

It was late afternoon by the time they arrived at the edge of the ash-tree-lined estate, with its grand gardens laid out after the style of Inigo Jones, dotted with statues of Greek deities that could be glimpsed like ghosts palely loitering between the luxuriant hedgerows.

'So this is where his punters' money went,' said Bryant. 'It's not his family home. I looked this gaff up in my country-house bible. Cornell's only had it for about three years. He bought it from a Russian who tried to turn the Regency master bedroom into a pole-dancing parlour.'

'Pull your tie straight and smarten yourself up a bit,' said May. 'I don't want him thinking you've come here to apply for the position of wrinkled old retainer.'

'What do we do now?' Bryant stepped out on to the gravelled path and looked around as the taxi drove off. 'There's no bell.'

'No, but there's *that*.' May pointed up at the black glass hemisphere suspended from the stone newel that divided the steel gates. Even as he spoke, the barriers swung silently back, allowing them on to the drive. At its centre was a vast cherub-bedecked fountain and a pond filled with lurid goldfish.

They were met at the door by a severe young woman in a black business suit. 'Please wait in the library. Mr Cornell will join you shortly,' she said, clearly expecting them to follow her without a word. They found themselves in an ornamentally plastered room of double height, lined with glass bookcases containing the kind of calfskin volumes no one had opened in a century.

'Keep an eye on the door,' said Bryant, pulling out various desk drawers and checking the contents.

'Don't touch anything,' May warned. 'And let me do the talking.'

'What do you think these are?' Arthur raised a handful of blank white swipe cards. 'Does the bank have an electronic key entry system? I can't remember.'

'Yes, it does; now put those back. He's coming.'

Bryant hastily pocketed the cards as their host arrived.

Dexter Cornell was younger than either of them had expected. Indeed, the banker looked to Bryant's aged orbs as if he had been newly displaced from the womb: pink, unlined and balding, with a thin blond thatch that barely bothered to be hair, and the slightly protuberant eyes one usually found in paintings of eighteenth-century duchesses. His handshake, however, proved surprisingly powerful and was clearly driven by thick arm muscles.

'Please, have a seat.' Cornell indicated an awkward arrangement of red leather chairs and a tiny, unstable-looking octagonal table that had been laid for afternoon tea. As a mantelpiece clock pecked out the passing seconds, an elaborate, parodic ritual began involving silverware and slender pairings of white bread and orange salmon. *He's overplaying the English gentleman a bit*, thought Bryant. *Well, it won't wash with me.*

'Quite a nifty little hideaway,' he remarked. 'We thought it would be quicker to come and find you.'

'It's an investment.' Cornell smiled. 'The upkeep is fairly horrific, but one has to keep these grand old homes going.'

'Did you put the security system in yourself?' asked Bryant. May knew that his partner had logged Cornell as a potential suspect. In May's mind there was an element of psychosis in all powerful men, even if it remained dormant.

'The place is empty most of the time, so you can't be too careful,' said Cornell with impatience. 'I assume you didn't come to discuss the house.'

'Indeed not,' said May, taking over. 'I understand that one of my colleagues explained the purpose of our visit. In the wake of the unfortunate events surrounding your departure from the Findersbury Bank, three men have died, so it seems you may be indirectly connected to the tragedies.'

'There's very little connection, from what I've been told,' said Cornell, allowing them to see that he had knowledge of the investigation. 'I fail to see how you reach the conclusion that it involves me.'

'Nevertheless, in order to eliminate you from our inquiries we'll need a detailed breakdown of your movements at the times in question.' May handed him a folded sheet of paper.

Cornell pocketed the page without examining it. 'What if I'm unable to account for any absences?'

'I'm sure a man with your busy work schedule can account for every second of his time,' said May. 'If you could email that back by tomorrow morning?'

'According to my friend Superintendent Darren Link, two of these men might have simply suffered accidents.'

'We don't believe that to be the case, although we have no proof to the contrary,' said Bryant, unfazed by Cornell's pointed reference. 'It may be that an anti-capitalist organization or one of its splinter cells has also placed you in its firing line.'

'Well, am I a potential victim or a suspect?'

'That's not for us to say at the moment.'

Cornell had started to breathe noisily through his nose, as if trying to let steam escape before something blew up. 'So I'm the one being judged here, not the terrorists who are launching attacks on the banking system.'

'The right to legitimate protest is a keystone of the democratic process,' May reminded him mildly. 'The moment it oversteps its guidelines and endangers life it becomes a police matter. Your – situation – with the bank's directors is of no concern to us. You're entitled to protection just as any other citizen would be in circumstances like this.'

'We're approaching a date that's traditionally associated with anarchy,' Bryant pointed out. 'You may need protection.'

'So – what do you expect from me?' Cornell glared at each of them in turn.

'You can start by giving us an assurance that you'll remain here for the rest of the week.'

'You want to put me under house arrest!'

'It would be for your own good.'

'That's not going to happen,' Cornell warned. 'You have no idea of what's at stake right now.'

'I know that your Shanghai deal in East Africa is still going to make you a lot of money even though it collapsed,' said Bryant casually.

'Let me show you something.' Cornell's features set hard in an effort to contain his fury. Rising to indicate that the meeting was terminated, he tapped his phone and summoned two men to the room.

Although they were dressed casually in jeans and black sweatshirts, the pair wore quasi-military badges and were obviously more used to wearing uniforms. Both had ex-army SLR Blackout rifles slung across their chests, and seemed unable to place their broad arms at their sides.

'I have my own private security team on this,' Cornell told the detectives. 'The bank is off-limits to you, do you understand? As is this house. You think you can just wander down here, spy on me and report back? I don't need your protection, although *you* might if you decide to make something out of this. Go back to your care home and stay out of my business. I'll go wherever I damn well please, whenever I please, without your permission. You really have no idea who you're dealing with.'

'You know what puzzles me?' said Bryant, nonchalantly turning to the disgraced CEO. 'It's not a matter of whether or even how you did it. The insider deal, I mean. I keep asking myself how anyone else knew. If you'd all just kept quiet you would have got away with it. Your building has sprung a leak, Cornell. You don't know where it is and you don't know how to stop it. That's why you've run away here.'

Cornell turned to one of his men. 'Get these two a cab back to the station before I really lose my temper. I don't want to see them again.'

The guards escorted the detectives to the front door and shut it firmly behind them. While they waited on the steps for the taxi, Bryant kicked at a boot-scraper until he managed to break it. 'Well, I thought that went quite well,' he said.

'What part of it went well?' asked May, amazed.

'He revealed his true colours. I've a good mind to stamp all over his flowerbeds. I think we should put him on the suspects list just for being unpleasant. The first thing I'm going to do is check out the licences on those weapons. A banker with an armed-response team? That's a new one on me.'

'Why did he get so angry when you mentioned the Shanghai thing?'

'Cornell set up this huge development project with a corporation in Shanghai to co-finance the building of hotels in East Africa, but they pulled out over the construction of a port and because of increased instability in the region,' said Bryant. 'That's the root of the insider deal. But Cornell knows a lot more than he's telling.'

'How do you know that?'

'Because according to Dan, Cornell is still in contact with the Chinese. Dan's tracking a ton of email traffic to and from Oakley Manor House.'

'How is he doing that?' May was fairly certain they didn't have clearance for such an action.

'It's probably best that you don't know. He tried to explain to me about service-provider protocols but I lost the will to live. I'm certain Cornell is double-crossing his own directors.' Bryant swung the handle of his walking stick at a stone and heard it land in the ornamental pond with a satisfying smack.

'You think he told the directors to dump their shares, and he'll then do a private deal with the Chinese?'

'I'd bet my string vest on it.'

'How did he do it? Tell the directors, I mean? Because everyone says they didn't meet or speak to each other.'

'I don't have the details yet, but I know someone who might be able to provide us with an answer.'

'If your contact knows something we don't, I imagine the National Fraud Intelligence Bureau will already have got to him.'

'Not this gentleman,' said Bryant as their taxi drew up. 'He's mentally unstable and living in a secure care home. I think you and I should go and visit him.'

25

FIREPOWER

The Manderfield Healthcare Centre was an anonymous new-build on East Finchley High Road, but one detail differentiated it from other apartment blocks in the area: if you looked carefully, you could see slender steel bars behind each of the windows.

'He's quite harmless,' Bryant said as they waited to be buzzed in at the discreet side entrance. 'He trained as a psychologist but then switched careers, and ended up managing one of the local banks that went down in the Barings collapse. He didn't handle it very well.'

'Why?' asked May, shaking the rain out of his coat. 'What did he do?'

'He burned his branch down. Knotted invoices all over the counters like kindling, doused them in petrol he'd siphoned from his car and set the whole lot on fire. It turned out he had a history of arson. It rather put paid to his hopes of promotion.'

The home had made great efforts to disguise its true identity, but the lingering odour of municipal cabbage gave it away. A nurse led them to the day room in a manner that suggested she might be showing them where they were to live from now on.

'I don't suppose you've got a lighter on you?' asked Henry Steppe, reaching out a hand in greeting but unable to conceal the excited grasp of his curled fingers. Skeletal and stooped, with the overhanging posture of a man too aware of his own awkward height, he looked to be in his early fifties but illness had aged him. His tartan dressing gown had singed patches around the sleeves, and there was an absurdly large bandage over the top of his head, like a child's drawing of a hospital patient. He was lured to an armchair by the wary nurse, who then stood at a discreet distance until she could be sure that no one was going to attack anyone else.

'I'm afraid not, Henry,' replied Bryant.

'But you're a pipe-smoker. Not even a throwaway?'

'You know I can't do that. You're looking . . . What happened to you?'

'Nothing, why?' Steppe seemed puzzled by the question.

'Oh, it's just . . .' Bryant pointed tentatively to Steppe's head.

'Oh, *this*. I don't like Morecambe and Wise.'

'Er, not quite with you there, old sausage.'

'I had a bit of a fight with the common-room television.'

'He put his head inside it while it was on,' piped up the nurse very loudly, as if speaking to an incredibly stupid child. 'We're getting a nice new flat-screen now, aren't we? I'll leave you to talk to your chums, Henry, is that all right?'

'I don't like Morecambe and Wise!' he told the nurse.

'Try to keep him nice and calm,' said the nurse, reproachfully pursing her lips at Steppe before scuttling off.

'Thank suffering Christ she's gone,' said Steppe, glancing back to make sure the coast was clear. 'You have to let them think you're a moron, otherwise they never leave you alone. I was trying to take the inverter board out of the TV and electrocuted myself. I have to carry out my own laptop repairs, so I nick bits from wherever I can. I assume this is concerning Findersbury?'

'How did you know that?' asked May.

'I picked up some intel from your building. You really need to have a word with Raymond Land about his passwords. He used to use *Leanne* for everything, but lately he's switched to *Crippen*. It's a bit sad when you can only come up with the name of a cat that's not even yours.'

'He's getting divorced,' said Bryant. 'We had a rather unpleasant chat with Dexter Cornell this afternoon. Do you think he's guilty of insider trading?'

Steppe pulled his armchair closer. 'The CoL's Fraud Squad won't release interdepartmental information without Home Office sign-offs, and the encryption's too tough for me to crack from here, but I'd swear Cornell tipped off his fellow directors. He knew about the collapse of the Chinese deal because apart from the lawyers, who are effectively operating *sub judice*, he was the sole negotiator of the contract.' Steppe shifted to the edge of his seat, lowering his voice further. 'As far as I can tell, the bad news somehow transmitted itself to three other company directors in a six-hour time period when they were all in the same building. The story is that the three were in a board meeting on the top floor from ten until four without a break. Nobody left the room, the phones were switched off and nobody came in.'

'What, they didn't even go to the bathroom?' asked May.

'There's a loo and a small kitchen directly adjoining the meeting room.'

'How do you know that?'

'Interior renovation plans lodged with the City of London Department of Works,' answered Steppe, as if it was obvious. 'They're all available online: hopeless security. I fear for this country. There's not an MP who gives a damn about technology. Anyway, a cold lunch had already been laid out before they arrived. While this was happening, Cornell was downstairs in a roomful of managers. The NFIB will be looking for surveillance footage of the missing hours, but you can bet that AntiCap will be searching for the same footage.'

'Anticap?' asked May.

'They started as a tech-based splinter cell from Anonymous UK; basically a bunch of hacktivists trying to expose illegal banking practices by breaking open encrypted emails. They've had some small successes in the past, but the Cornell case could be their big one. Hang on.' They all sat back and drank tea while two nurses walked past. Steppe beckoned them forward again. 'I have some documentation in my room but the print's too small for me to read. I don't suppose you could get me a magnifying glass?'

'Nice try, Henry,' said Bryant. 'I assume the meeting room was swept for bugs.'

'According to AntiCap's website, the bureau took the entire place apart and found nothing. The whole building came up clean. But the question of Cornell's guilt doesn't impact on your investigation, surely?'

'We don't know,' admitted May. 'We're at a loss to find motives. How much do you know about the investigation?'

'A lot more than the journalists at *Hard News,*' said Steppe. 'They got their information from me. Don't worry, I made sure it was misleading.'

'The fact that all three of our victims are associated with the bank makes it too much of a coincidence that they should die within days of each other,' said Bryant, 'but we only have circumstantial links. I keep thinking Cornell might be able to supply a solid connection between them.'

'It's a logical assumption,' Steppe agreed. 'I find it intriguing that the deaths all have an element of fire in them.'

'Yes,' said Bryant, 'I thought you'd like that.'

'He's sending a message – nothing very subtle, just that he wants to burn it all down.'

'Burn what down?' asked May.

'All of it! The system. The City. Everything that's failed.'

'Wouldn't someone with this much rage stand out from the crowd?' May wondered. 'Could he function normally? Wouldn't he be easy to spot? Or would he be able to hide his feelings and carry on going to work without anyone becoming suspicious?'

'I don't see how he could be lucid and able to operate within the community. It shouldn't take an expert to recognize the signs.' Steppe leaned forward and rubbed his hands, smiling unctuously. 'If you could just see your way to springing me out of here—'

'—you'd burn down the first bank you set eyes on,' said Bryant. 'I'd rather have you working on the inside, thanks.'

'Well, if you have any further questions, I'm happy to lend a hand.'

'Actually, I do have one.' Bryant reknotted his scarf. 'Why is he obsessed with fire?'

'Simple, Mr Bryant,' said Steppe, rising to see them out. 'Barring the usual eschatological arguments for playing with matches, he likes it for the same reason we all like it. Fire destroys and cleanses. But it also renews. There's only one thing more powerful than a good fire, and that's the man who starts it.'

'Are we all finished now?' warbled the nurse, appearing from her alcove. 'The dinner bell has sounded. Do you want to say goodbye to your lovely friends?'

'Bye-bye, lovely friends,' said Steppe, sounding simple-minded.

'Why does Steppe let them think that he's crazy?' asked May as they walked away.

'He likes it there,' Bryant replied. 'It's a stress-free environment, and the State pays for his room and meals. And it's better that he's locked away.'

'Why?'

'Because he still wants to burn everything down.'

'Come on,' said May, taking his arm. 'I'll drop you home.'

'You're not going to come and tuck me in; I'm not tired yet,' said Bryant petulantly. 'You know I do my best thinking at night.'

'Maybe so, but I've got a dinner date with Blaize Carter,' said May. 'I'm thinking that perhaps it's time to start a little fire of my own.'

They met in La Veneziana, a catastrophic Italian restaurant in King's Cross whose walls were covered with reproductions of Renaissance art that looked as if they had been painted by an angry clown, but it stayed open long after everywhere else had shut and the spaghetti portions were gargantuan, so police officers ate there to stock up on carbohydrates.

'Tell me about fire,' said May, pouring out the remains of the Chianti. 'What happens if you get caught in one?'

'Well, I'm sure you know the basics,' said Senior Fire Officer Blaize Carter. 'It's usually the toxic gases that prove lethal. Carbon monoxide, carbon dioxide, hydrogen cyanide. Hot smoke and flames singe your hair and burn your airways, so you can't breathe. Burning inflicts intense pain because it stimulates the nociceptors, the pain nerves in the skin. And you get a rapid inflammatory response, which boosts sensitivity to pain in the injured tissues and surrounding areas. Something like forty per cent of all victims of fatal home fires are knocked out by fumes before they can even wake up.' She took a sip from her glass. 'So, don't get burned.'

She had changed out of her regulation navy sweater and untied her hair, and although looking like a civilian still didn't make her think like one there was something different in her voice now, a warmer, more playful tone.

'What drew you to it as a career?' May asked.

She shook her head. 'I didn't intend to join the fire service. I hated the idea of working in an office, and was always fairly outdoorsy and athletic. Then when I started training and learned more about the field, it sort of took hold. It's not all going to fires. I visit schools and community centres, talk to people in their own homes. The poorer the neighbourhood, the greater the risk, even now. You should see some of the sweatshops we go to in the East End. How about you?'

'I suppose I could never have been anything else,' said May. 'I met Arthur on my very first day on the job. He instructed me to decode a message made out of butterflies.'

'What did it say?

'"We're out of tea." He said, "You look fairly sturdy. We could do with someone like you." And that was it. We've remained teamed up ever since.'

'So I heard. Your exploits are fairly legendary among your fans.'

'Really? I was beginning to doubt we had any.'

'You worry about him, don't you?'

'How do you know that?'

'I could see you keeping a watchful eye out.' She gave a rueful smile. 'The PCU's a pretty tight unit from what I hear. We're the same. I was called out at two thirty the other morning to get an obese driver out of his car. He'd stalled it just off City Road and had become wedged behind the wheel, so he rang us. He was drunk, of course, and not for the first time by the sound of it, so we cut him free just to teach him a lesson. Virtually sawed the vehicle in half. He wasn't very happy about it. People never understand when you tell them you enjoy being on the streets.'

'That's why we never take promotion,' said May. 'We have seniority but stay hands-on. There aren't many jobs where you can do that.'

'Well, I'm glad I'm finally working with you,' said Blaize, raising her glass. 'That spaghetti vongole was like eating elastic bands covered in grit.'

'I know, it's amazing, isn't it?' May laughed.

'We have a balti house near the station where everything tastes of disinfectant. The lads love it.' She sighed. 'Just once I'd like to go to one of those restaurants you see in the magazines. Somewhere that isn't popular just because it's open after midnight.'

'I'll take you to one,' May promised. 'When we close the case.'

Blaize smiled. 'You have confidence.'

'Trust me, that's all I have,' he said.

26

INSIDER

Bryant was exhausted. His arms and legs started aching an hour before dawn on Thursday morning, the dull grinding pain travelling from deep inside his joints and radiating out to his skin, remaining until he was finally able to dispel his sense of ill-being with a mug of teak-coloured tea and a marmalade-smeared scone.

'You look terrible,' said Alma Sorrowbridge, a woman he still referred to as his landlady even though she no longer owned the property he rented. After hard times had befallen them both, they had ended up sharing a council flat in Bloomsbury, where she allowed Bryant to continue treating her as a combined housemaid, laundress, cook, cleaner and paid companion because she believed that the Lord was working through her to save his soul, although as the years passed she had come to the realization that there was little chance of Bryant's soul or indeed any other part of him being saved unless it was in a jar of formaldehyde at the Hunterian Museum, where his remains would serve as a grim warning to others.

'Most kind of you to say so,' said Bryant, sitting back down on the end of his bed. 'I'm thrilled to have my bathroom mirror's evidence corroborated. And there was me thinking the reflection was faulty.'

'You're not sleeping again, are you?' Alma tidied away his breakfast tray.

'No, I'm not, as it happens. My brain seems to have a mind of its own. Where's my tweed overcoat?'

'At the dry cleaner's. It was in a disgusting state. What was it doing in the freezer?'

'It's an old forensic trick. Putting your clothes in a sub-zero environment kills all the germs.'

'Wouldn't it be easier to wash them?'

'I was saving you the work. What am I supposed to wear today?'

'It's going to be mild out, so you shouldn't need such a thick coat. It would do you good to get some air to your skin.'

'That's *London* air.' Bryant pointed out of the window. 'Have you seen what it does to statues? I'm not exposing myself to that. I'll wear my grandfather's First World War greatcoat today, thank you.'

'People think you're strange, you know that?' said Alma, pausing in the doorway of his bedroom.

'I don't care what people think, and haven't done so since the old king died.'

'I mean the other people in this building.'

Bryant grimaced. 'I hope you're not referring to the man next door, the one in the sleeveless top who walks like he's carrying the back end of a piano.'

'I went in to meet his wife,' Alma said. 'She's very nice.'

'I saw around their front door the other day,' sniffed Bryant. 'A flat-screen telly the size of Rembrandt's *Night Watch* and not a single book in sight. What on earth do they find to talk about?'

'They're mystified by your comings and goings.'

'I'm not entirely happy with their balcony full of washing, bicycles and pizza boxes. I don't suppose they like having a copper next door. I guess he's having to unload his stolen phones somewhere else.'

'He's an honest man, Mr Bryant. He drives a boring machine.'

'Well, he should change his job.'

'No, boring underground tunnels. He works for Crossrail. He's got kids.' Alma gave a little nod of approval to that.

'Yes, I know. I've never seen such ugly children. One of them looks like a lizard eating a potato.'

'Did it ever occur to you that you might find the good in others if you got to know them properly? You're a misanthropist.'

Bryant was outraged. 'I am not, I just don't like people! They're messy and inconsistent and incompetent and never say what they mean, and when you've finally figured out what makes them tick they die on you.'

'Well, I don't understand it,' said Alma. 'You side with those protestors but you can't possibly know how they feel.'

'I understand perfectly how they feel.' Bryant's face took on a higher colour. 'They feel cheated. In my lifetime this country has been transformed from a benign dictatorship to a third-rate democracy, and I ask you, which is less empowering? To be tricked into thinking that you have freedom is worse than being told what to do. When I was young, dissenters were treated with more respect. Now they're even ostracized by their own peer groups. We're raising the retirement age to seventy but at work you're a has-been at forty – what are these people supposed to do? That's why the bank protest groups don't solely consist of kids without careers; there are just as many adults among them who've found themselves thrown on the scrapheap of industry.'

Bryant shivered at the thought. He unwrapped his scarf from the teapot and tied it in a double knot around his scrawny neck. In his grandfather's greatcoat he looked like an old soldier who had been hit by a shrinking ray.

'I don't see how you can be a policeman and think like that,' said Alma. 'You're the ones in authority.'

'But that's precisely my point, don't you see? We're not any more. There's nobody steering the ship of State. We're adrift on the tide of capitalism and heading for the rocks. Where's my hat?' He rose unsteadily and checked his pockets for phones, pens, bits of paper and anything else he might need for a day at the Peculiar Crimes Unit.

'Don't forget your sandwiches,' Alma instructed. 'Salmon and shrimp paste, in your Tibetan skull. Why you can't use a Tupperware box like anyone else is beyond me.'

Bryant set off, leaving the leafy quadrangles of Bloomsbury for the diesel fumes of traffic-choked Euston. The poor air quality of the arterial road always seemed to clear his head. He badly wanted to break the case, and he needed someone to ignore a few rules. After thinking it through carefully, he decided that Fraternity DuCaine was the man for the job. Cometh the hour, cometh the man, and there was something imposing about the young detective constable that might cause the suspicious to sidestep him. Besides, in the wake of his brother's death he was still desperate to prove himself, and the task would show his mettle.

It seemed to Bryant that the law favoured Cornell's protection over that of his own unit, in which case it was time to circumvent the law. He needed all of the devices and documents with which the directors had been sequestered in their fourth-floor boardroom on the fateful day that they and Cornell had shared the same building. Somehow the collapse of the Shanghai deal had transmitted itself to the board, and it must have been sent into the meeting. Therefore, there had to be physical evidence.

'Anything, you name it,' said DuCaine, delighted to be singled out for a special assignment. 'What can I do for you, Mr Bryant?'

'It shouldn't be too difficult for a man of your skills,' said Bryant. 'I want you to break into a bank. It's something I'm sure your brother could have managed with the greatest of ease.'

Thus, having laced the challenge with a measure of sibling rivalry (and a deceased sibling, at that), Bryant presented his plan to DuCaine.

27

PROFILE

The figure turned slowly about, trying to understand where it was, bare feet balanced on narrow sawn-down trunks. It was too dark to see clearly. There were wavering patches of light ahead, divided by the warped branches of trees. Boughs and foliage had become separated somehow, and appeared to be stacked upright in an immense tepee. The smell of sawdust and pine sap filled the air, wet grass and . . . smoke.

Something was flickering sharply through the brush. The heat from below was welcome at first, gently warming the bitter night air, but quickly grew uncomfortably hot.

The branches caught, flames stepping from one to the next in relays of sparks. Cinders coasted through the smoke into the wooden cage, searing eyes and lungs. The man threw himself against the smouldering branches, but they held fast.

Then the flames fanned and flooded beneath his heels, and the fire became an inferno . . .

Longbright let out a yell of fear.

She was wet with icy sweat. The other side of the bed had not been slept in. Jack Renfield had promised to come back when his shift ended; he had taken Late Turn on Wednesday night, so she had given him a front-door key. He must have been too tired to come here. Checking the alarm clock she saw that it was almost time to get up, even though the night was still deep.

She slipped from bed to shower, dressed with damp hair and headed out into the cool dawn in search of an open coffee shop. This was her life, moving alone through empty streets beneath grey and violet skies, seeing only office cleaners, students and the odd luggage-trundling tourist heading for the first flight off the stand. In front of the station, two smiling, infinitely hopeful young men were trying to hand out brochures beside a board that read: 'What Can Jesus Do for You Today?'

Soon the rush hour would bring the eddying tides of the city's workforce here, a million a week through this station alone. It had reached the point where she couldn't bear to be out on the streets of King's Cross at lunch time, as the foot soldiers of industry passed her clutching sandwiches in bags, discussing the minutiae of office politics, reminding each other who had said what in which meeting and who wasn't pulling their weight, their conversations as abstruse and incomprehensible as those of academic theorists.

Longbright was a career officer, and damaged by being so, unable to function properly in the normal world. Like her bosses, she could not stop herself from searching the most casual conversations for behavioural clues. She was bored by banter and failed to remember the things most civilians never forgot: birthdays, anniversaries, the simple give-and-take of social intercourse.

But then she was at work again, extra-strong coffee in hand, and her skills flowed naturally once more, pressed into the service of the day ahead. *Accept your lot, honey,* she told herself. *It could be much worse. You could be happy.*

She thought about calling Maggie Armitage, but decided against it. No more looking for affirmations and explanations; the dreams would fade once she started spending a little more time with Jack, right up until the moment he crowded her and she felt herself backing away again, as she always did in relationships that threatened to become stable and serious. If she thought about it in any depth, she knew she would come to the realization that they had just three or four months ahead without conflict, maybe less. She wondered which of them would retreat first.

To keep her caffeine levels topped up, she brewed strong Yorkshire tea and seated herself at her desk, warming her hands. She was the second member of staff to arrive after Bryant, whose closed door warned her that he was not to be disturbed. She opened the night's emails to see if any answers had come in.

The first that caught her attention was a scrap of CCTV footage that showed a figure in grey Nike sweatpants and a hooded top breaking into a Mercedes saloon, parked in a concrete underground bunker. The time code read 2.57 a.m., with today's date. There was no address, but she recognized the vehicle.

John May came in behind her and helped himself to tea. As usual, he was immaculately dressed, with not a silver hair out of place. Longbright wondered how he always managed to look as if he'd slept in a vacuum pack.

'Good morning, John. Take a look at this.' She tapped at the screen with an elegant nail, freshly painted with Jungle Huntress crimson polish, an original 1950s shade she'd purchased through a friend in Poto-Poto, Brazzaville. 'Someone broke into Jonathan De Vere's car early this morning.'

May leaned over her shoulder. 'Looks like the NCP car park in Saffron Hill. You can see the rate card in the corner.'

'Why would he park all the way over there?'

'The only other one is Aldersgate and that's usually full.'

'Dan was supposed to dust the vehicle for prints yesterday,' said Longbright, 'but he didn't have time. De Vere's wife said something about picking it up, but I guess she didn't get around to it yet.'

'Was anything taken?'

'The cameras don't cover the interior so it's impossible to tell if there was anything on the seats.'

'Is that the best shot of him? It's not much to go on.'

'He's tall, about six two, solidly built. We know he has to be strong. It looks like our man. I could get Dan to try to enhance the shot.'

'Janice, you know as well as I do what happens when you enlarge footage: you get big grainy pixels. It's not like the movies. What else is there?'

'We've got the rest of the interviews back; nobody has a bad word to say about De Vere. Outwardly devoted to his wife, working for the global community, adored by everyone. All very boring.'

'You cynic.'

Janice gave a shrug. 'There's nothing much you can say about good people.'

'Except that this one's dead.'

'Lena De Vere warned me not to dig into her past, so I had a good nose around. Quite a past, it turns out. She hung out with a party crowd, real tabloid fodder. Cautioned for possession, marijuana, cocaine, yadda yadda, all a bit last-century. She was honest because she knew I'd find it if I looked. She's having an affair with a metallurgist and is pregnant with his child. Then there's her husband's connection to the bank—'

'What connection?'

Longbright turned in her seat to face him. 'Did you even bother to read the report I sent you?'

'Sorry, Janice, it must be on my desk.'

'De Vere had been asked to help them set up some kind of children's charity. I don't think he got very far before he died.'

'You think there's a reason for murder there?'

'What, providing free computers for disadvantaged kids? If there is, the world's an even darker place than I thought.'

May sat on the corner of the desk. 'All right, spit it out.'

'What?'

'Something's up. What's wrong?'

Janice rubbed her eye. 'Take no notice of me. I'm not sleeping very well, that's all. Bad dreams.'

'They're part of the job.'

'That's just it. The job. Except it isn't a job, is it? It's a vocation, like being a blacksmith. Sometimes I wonder what the hell I'm doing. Are we still needed? I mean, honestly? In the second decade of the twenty-first century? Since you and Arthur grew up, crime has changed out of all recognition. Don't you think it's possible that—' She stopped, picked up a pen, toyed with it, set it down.

'What?'

'Nothing. Skip it.'

May wagged a finger at her. 'Never start a sentence you're not prepared to complete.'

'Well, what if *we're* the cause?'

'What do you mean?'

'We get the high-profile investigations. Our cases turn up in the press. What if this guy has a grievance that he can't get aired any other way? So he acts crazy and brings his protest to *our* attention.'

'Well, we'll soon find out if you're right,' said May.

'Why?'

'Arthur has a theory. He thinks our man has such a grievance that he wants everyone to share it, and he won't be finished until he's infected the entire population of London, maybe the whole country.'

'They're smashing up Knightsbridge now,' said Longbright. 'The *New York Times* is calling London "a powder-keg city". They've made the Guy Fawkes connection even if our press hasn't.'

May went to find his partner. Bryant was barely visible behind a humungous stack of ancient, dilapidated books that included *An Informal History of Cow-Staining*; *Stipendiary Justice in Nineteenth-Century Wales*; *Unusual Punishments for Sodomy, Vol. 13: Northern Portugal*; *How to Cook Bats*; and *'Take My Wife, Please': Negotiation Techniques in Abduction Cases*. Behind him, the blackboard had been filled with names, dates, arrows, little drawings and random facts circled in red chalk. 'Oh, it's you. What do you want?' he said rudely. 'I'm rather busy.'

'How did you get on with the doctor? I know you were due to look in on him last night.' May asked the question as casually as he could, instantly placing too much emphasis on it.

'He wants me to smoke electric cigarettes. I won't tell you what I told him.'

'Oh. Anything else?'

Bryant slammed his book shut with irritable impatience. 'He gave me a cognitive function examination. Basically a memory test aimed at the terminally confused.'

'Well, how did you score?'

'Low enough for him to treat me to a rodomontade of statistical flummery before packing me off with some rubbishy pills. I need to talk to you about acts of public defamation.' It wasn't the smoothest of deflections, but once Bryant had decided not to talk about something, nothing would turn him. 'London has a long history of communal shaming. Such events used to attract huge crowds. The public acted as witnesses and judges with the complicity of the government, whipping prisoners and pelting them with dead cats and buckets of offal. They jeered and punched those charged with sedition, corruption, extortion and a whole range of other crimes that people are largely allowed to get away with today.'

May's brow furrowed with the effort. 'Where exactly are we going with this?'

'Show some patience. Look.' Bryant held up a grotesque woodcut of a screaming man being pilloried. 'Some unfortunates did die in the stocks, but those punishments were more about causing dishonour than violence. Often the guilty could get themselves off by recanting and apologizing for their actions, or by paying penance. At some point we lost our sense of shame, John. Now, Dexter Cornell lines the pockets of his directors—'

'We don't know that he did.'

'He did, I just don't know *how* yet – and he refuses to repent publicly, thus avoiding the pillory, the stocks, the cart to Tyburn. These days the guilty keep their nerve and lie barefaced to juries. We no longer whip people through the streets. Instead we send them to executive-level open jails for a few months' R and R before they hire PR teams to restore their reputations. Fraud, perjury, perverting the course of justice count as nothing, so what does our killer do? He takes the law into his own hands.'

'Arthur, you cannot take the side of a murderer.'

'I'm just trying to understand his mindset. He destroys all those who have hurt him. But he didn't start out like that. I think there's a pattern. Look.' He rose and thumped his fist on the blackboard, causing a fog of chalk dust to settle over himself. 'Our killer is angered by something Freddie Weeks does. He goes away, stews about the perceived slight, returns and sets fire to the lad. Perhaps he thinks that Weeks will react fast, that he'll leap to his feet to put the flames out, and that will be enough to show him who's boss. Half the murders in London involve issues of respect.'

He thumped the board again. 'Next, he shames Glen Hall by tarring and feathering him, but this also results in a death. The tar gets into Hall's nasal passages and chokes him – Giles has confirmed this.'

Another thump raised more chalk dust. 'Then Jonathan De Vere is branded by a red-hot Vulcan mask, and he also dies. Don't you see? Burning, tarring and feathering, branding, he's *dishonouring* his enemies, and if they don't survive it's their bad luck. The tarring is for betrayal, the branding symbolizes duplicity. The victim has been two-faced, so now he'll be given two faces! He's convinced himself he's giving them what they deserve. There will be others to come. There *must* be others. But the pattern is artless enough to show that there is no pattern. And these acts are actually not very elaborate at all. They're . . . What's that expression you use when you're trying to sound young—'

'Lo-fi.'

'That's it. These acts of revenge are thrown together with the tools at hand. The victims dragged him down somehow, and now he has nothing, so he's resorted to stealing the instruments of their deaths. The verger of St Mary's Church in Camden reported lead being nicked from his roof. Some road-menders in Kentish Town had their tar bucket and burner stolen. These are not very classy acts, John. At least they give us a radius of operation.'

'Then how would his path have crossed with that of a banker and a dot-com millionaire? It doesn't make sense, Arthur. Have you thought that he might just be a mad anti-capitalist taking potshots wherever the opportunity arises?'

'Yes, of course, but it's my job to think beyond that. There are plenty of officers infiltrating the protestors and making lists of contacts, but we have to see things differently.'

'So you've assembled your own psychological profile.'

Bryant rooted around among the papers on his desk. 'It's an unusual one. He started out with a sense of indignity and anger, but now he's enjoying himself. It's a good job he's still being kept out of the press, otherwise he'd be on his way to becoming a martyr. I think we'll find he has a history of arson, but I still lack data.'

'I can run a search for priors, cross-reference with protest histories and see if we get any matches.'

'Matches.' Bryant nodded. 'Very good. What's happening in the Square Mile? I haven't seen the morning papers yet.'

May pulled a copy of *Hard News* from his pocket and threw it on the desk. 'Have a look at that. Some idiot MP from the shires is championing Cornell and his fellow bankers, trying to make a case for them being misunderstood heroes. The effect of that speech has been to send raging lynch mobs heading towards London. By the end of the day almost every part of the country will be represented in the capital. Link tried to close all of the central stations this morning, but I think it's already too late for that. The mob will find a way in.'

'You're right,' agreed Bryant, 'the gates are being forced open. This could be just the start. How do you get the genie of rebellion back in the bottle without breaking it?'

'You realize this no longer falls under our remit,' May pointed out.

Bryant was indignant. 'It's public unrest!'

'Yes, but we're not equipped to deal with a citywide riot. We can't control what's happening.'

'Of course, there's an obvious solution to ending the crisis. They could throw Cornell to the lions.'

'They could, but it's not happening, is it? Why not? He must have something the government needs.'

Bryant tapped his skull. 'Now you're using your head. What could that be?'

'I don't know, money, power . . .' May thought for a moment. 'The Chinese.'

'I think it's the most likely possibility, don't you?'

May rose and studied the blackboard again. A roll of thunder was loud enough to rattle the windows above his desk. 'If that's the case and we try to intervene,' he remarked, 'we'll get crushed flat from all sides.'

'And if we don't, we'd be failing to do our job,' retorted Bryant. 'Either way, we're damned.'

28

ESMERALDA

Raymond Land was gobsmacked. He read the email once more.

After their recent run-ins with the Home Office, he thought he'd seen the last of his old superiors, unless they happened to bump into each other at their Masonic temple. Oskar Kasavian, their vampiric Home Office security supervisor, had been shunted off to some godforsaken, hellish outpost somewhere in what was left of the British Empire, Baffin Island, perhaps, or Cardiff, but Leslie Faraday, the staggeringly incompetent Home Office liaison officer and the ultimate budget overseer of London's specialist police units, had been kicked upstairs so that he now also had many of the City of London's divisions – except the two largest ones, cybercrime and terrorism – on his books.

Land couldn't believe his eyes. How could someone as stupid as Faraday actually get promoted? This was the man who force-fed his children tainted pork on national television to prove that there was nothing wrong with supermarket meat; the man who complained in Parliament about the lack of decent immigration controls while employing a Filipina nanny and a Vietnamese gardener, both of whom he paid in cash because they weren't registered for tax; the man who once caused a riot in Brixton Prison for insisting that 'the brains of black offenders are less developed than ours'. And here he was back again, demanding to know why the unit was interfering in matters which didn't concern them.

This is my lot, Land thought, *writing bad-tempered emails to bosses I don't respect in games of territorial ping-pong. No wife, no life, no hope of promotion, just ticking over until the ever-receding date of my retirement. At least my father got given a clock when he left the service, even if it did break down the moment he got it home.*

Like so many others of his generation, Land was the son of a policeman, and had started out in a time before initiatives and protocols, before 'community support' and 'response' and 'early intervention', before the era of overpaid consultants and unpaid interns, before think tanks and policy exchange and all of the other career-nurturing enterprises that merely placed more layers of paper between a caring copper and a panicked kid waving a knife. He knew in his heart that he should have been like Bryant and May and stuck to his guns, refusing promotion and working out there on the London streets. At least there was still a grimy exhilaration to be found in the resolution of those tragic and often depressingly familiar stories. It was a satisfaction borne from direct contact with life, something he hadn't had in years.

Direct contact.

He went in to see the detectives. The room was so dark that May was blanched by the light from his computer terminal. His nose was almost touching the screen because he was too vain to wear glasses. Bryant had his eyes shut and was listening to some horrible caterwauling woman on his ancient record player. He held up an index finger, indicating that Land should not move until the aria had ended.

'Ivanhoe,' Bryant explained, eyes still closed. 'Gilbert and Sullivan's least successful opera, utterly dreadful.' He removed the disc and dropped it into his wastepaper basket, slotting another in place. 'I'm switching to these. *Ultimate Hard House Anthems.* Did you get your theoretical door fixed yet?'

'Direct contact,' said Land. 'That's what he wants, isn't it? He's not doing a Goldfinger.'

'I'm sorry, Raymondo, but for once I can't see exactly what you're thinking.'

'You know: "Do you expect me to talk?" "No, Mr Bond, I expect you to die." Goldfinger didn't stick around to see 007 get lasered in half, did he? This bloke's right there, chucking petrol bombs, pouring tar, hammering red-hot masks on to people, for God's sake! He's strong, maybe works with his hands. He's taking direct action and making a point. Have you tried the hostels?'

'Yes, but it's almost impossible to narrow down the numbers,' Bryant explained as his stereo speakers bellowed a noise that sounded like a busload of pensioners going into a ravine. 'There's big money to be had in hostels these days. They're not subject to regular planning laws so they're cash cows for councils, and their booking systems are hopelessly porous.'

'Then try foundries, workshops, anywhere people work with their hands. Can you turn that down a bit?'

'We've already done that.' May slapped his hand on a quire of papers. 'Names and addresses. My colleague here likes everything printed out, so if you really want to help us you can wade through them for us.'

'Absolutely. More than happy to. I've got another idea—'

'What's going on?' asked Bryant suspiciously. 'Raymondo, are you actually trying to *help*?'

'Yes, that's the general plan.'

'Wonders will never cease.' Bryant fired his most probing stare at the unit chief. 'What are you up to?'

'I'm fed up with sitting in the other room stringing paper clips together while you two actually get to work things out,' Land admitted.

'If you really want to do something, then I think I have a job for you. Hang on.' Bryant scrawled something on the contents page of *Neuter Your Own Pet* and ripped it out. 'Oh, and you'll need my list of questions. I hope you can read my writing.' He was about to give Land the page, then withheld it. 'Promise me one thing. That you won't question what I'm asking you to do.'

'OK, I promise,' said Land, accepting the grubby page and folding it into his pocket, even as he wondered what he had just committed himself to.

Land looked at the address again and decided that there must have been some kind of mistake. After alighting from the tube at Finsbury Park, he had watched in horror as a man urinated against the window of a bread shop in broad daylight. Following Bryant's directions, Land turned off the main road into some kind of fenced-off truck park where grass struggled up between broken cobbles, making his way between dog turds and iridescent puddles of oily water, towards a row of penumbral railway arches. He found himself standing beneath the one that had been marked on his page, and looked about for signs of life. From the shadows, a bedraggled rat watched him uncertainly.

Bryant had assured him that someone would appear, but all Land could see were petrol drums, leaking ten-litre cans of ghee, piles of wood, shattered yellow house bricks and several sawn-off green lamp-posts knotted together with baling wire, looking like outsized sticks of asparagus. He leaned against the remains of an old blue

Nissan lying on its roof and waited. From somewhere nearby came the sound of a cat having a fit.

The door of the Nissan suddenly opened and caught Land on the backs of his legs. Out crawled what appeared to be a spherical ball of grey rags. A reek of ammonia filled the air. Land looked down in horror as the ball unravelled and stood upright, revealing something that could possibly be a turnip four hundred years past its sell-by date or a very small, very wide woman. 'You're late,' she said. 'Where is he?'

Land looked around, panicked. 'Where is who?'

'Arthur.' The turnip-woman looked around to see what he was looking for. 'He's supposed to be with you.'

'He sent me along by myself.'

'That's cheating.'

'He's a busy man.'

'He's my husband.'

Land was beginning to feel an uncomfortable prickling on the back of his neck that warned him he was out of his depth. 'Who are you?'

'I'm Esmeralda.'

'What do you mean, he's your husband?'

She spelled out the words slowly and loudly, baring blackened teeth. 'Try. To. Follow. What. I'm. Saying. He. Is. My. Husband. I. Married. Him.'

This was all too much for Land, especially as it had now started to rain hard. 'I'm sorry,' he said. 'I was just told to come here and— How could you be married to him?'

'It was a citizen's marriage.' She rubbed one filthy finger over the other in a peculiarly witchlike gesture. 'He doesn't know we're betrothed, obviously. I don't want to make him over-emotionable. But it's legally blinding. Not here, just in an obscure part of the Austro-Hungarian Empire, where the matrimblial laws are very different. That's where I met him, during the reign of the Emperor

Franz Joseph. I was a Hapsburger. With onion rings. Of course, that was before I fell on hard times. Arthur had the most beautiful eyes, like goldfish bowls filled with Toilet Duck. And his teeth were like stars. They came out at night.'

She's a raving loony, realized Land. *Bryant's done it just to wind me up.* He consulted the piece of paper with his detective's questions. 'Mr Bryant told me to ask you about fire mythology.'

'The fire! Yes, the fire! My husband needs me, just as it was foretold! Come with me.' She led the way across the muddied dump to the darkness of the railway arches, where a simulacrum of a room had been laid out under the dripping brickwork.

'Everyone needs a place where the soul can find tranquisity,' announced Esmeralda, bracing herself and issuing a sound like someone gently lowering a toecap on to a set of bagpipes. 'Excuse me. Sprouts.'

Land looked about. There was a lumpy red Axminster rug, an eviscerated brown leather armchair, its stuffing spewing through burst seams, a broken yellow standard lamp with a torch taped around its top, a Primus stove, a kitchen table with three legs and several half-collapsed bookcases packed with mildewed volumes of Hungarian history and back issues of *Vogue*.

'Please remember to wipe your sleet,' said Esmeralda, adopting a comedy-toff voice. 'Ay'd make you a drink but it's the maid's day orf.'

Land made a show of thrashing his shoes clean and waited while his hostess rooted about among the twisted bookshelves. *OK*, he thought, *this is a test. Arthur wants to see if I can come back with something.*

'So, fire, eh?' she called back over a hunched shoulder. 'You know, there are places where fire reveals the future. Oh, yes. The shape of cinders leaping from the hearth foretells births and deaths, or the arrival of an important visitor. And of course the flames themselves transmute into tableaux that only the wise can interpret. Fire-reading was always practised by the oldest woman in our village.'

'What village was that?' Land asked.

'Hampstead Village. The hearth mother protected the fire and prevented it from burning out. The Devil, too. When a fire won't draw, it's because the Devil is nearby. You must never throw bread crusts into the fireplace because it will drag Satan down your chimney. Oh, yes. Fire is resurrection. Think of the phoenix, reborn in flame. Fire is Purgatory. It cleanses and purifies.'

'But fire kills people,' said Land, feeling he should say something that made sense.

'We must all die in order to be reborn. The myth of Osiris, not reborn into normal life but into a higher plane of consciousness. "I shall not decay," says Osiris in *The Book of the Dead*, "I shall not rot, nor putrefy, I shall have my being, I shall live." Osiris the god of the afterlife, with green skin and leaves for hair, from which we gain the English myth of Jack-in-the-Green, the god of natural regeneration.' Esmeralda spun around and rolled her eyes at him meaningfully. Something fell out of her nose. 'Eternal life is the eternal dream, a fever-dream of spermatozoa, the *prima materia* which explodes with the birthing-heat of the universe, the driving force of the world. Oh, yes. But balancing Osiris is his sister Nephthys, the goddess of mourning, of rivers and night and the Fall. Mary Magdalene is Nephthys embodied, a symbol that proves our world has fallen.' She pointed down at the mildewed carpet. 'Before we can rise again we must touch the lowest point, battle our demons, journey through madness. Fire is our only way out of darkness. It is the tool of revolution, the weapon of the rebel cutting the bonds of imperialism, a sword for one who has already fallen.'

'Who *are* you?' asked Land, staying downwind but intrigued nevertheless.

'Who *was* I,' she corrected, dragging down books, glancing inside them and casting them aside. 'I was a scholar, an iconoclast, an academic, an epidemic of torrential genius. With knowledge comes opinion, and opinions are not wanted in the grand halls of knowledge. In short, I was chucked out of Oxford by a bunch of wankers. Oh, yes. For teaching insurrection. Of course I was; it's my specialist subject. Ah, here it is.' She raised a damp-fattened book and cracked it open on what Land assumed was her knee. 'Do you know what distinguishes those who seek to harness the iconoclastic properties of fire? Most revolutionaries are not afraid to die, but the fire-wielder *expects* to perish. Everything must burn. *Everything.* Otherwise there can be no rebirth. This is the pure heart of the cosmic riddle; for goodness and purity to rise, all must first be lost.'

'And that's in there, is it?' asked Land, pointing to the book.

'This?' Esmeralda looked surprised. 'No, I'm deciding what to have for dinner.' She raised the cover so that he could read the title: *Nigella's Favourite Pasta Recipes*. 'Stay if you like; I have a spare plate somewhere. You investigate things, don't you? So do I. I could take you under my wing and show you a few new wrinkles.'

'That's kind of you, but no thanks,' said Land, backing away.

'Never mind. It's been lovely. We must do this again!' called Esmeralda as he retreated. 'Are you married?'

'No,' he replied, thinking about his newly implemented divorce.

'Well, you are now!' she shouted, rubbing her filthy fingers at him, and he stumbled off for the safety of the high street.

29

TRESPASS

It was time, once more, for someone to die.

The mixture wasn't very hard to make. A blend of saltpetre, charcoal and sulphur, one to oxidize, two to provide the propellant. The main problem was its slow decomposition rate, which meant that unless it was placed under pressure, or in some kind of tube or box, it would simply burn out.

It was granulated, but sensitive to changes in the weather, so the timings were hard to predict. He wasn't a scientist but had been able to find everything he needed online, and the instructions were simple. He liked using different methods of dispatch; it kept everyone on their toes.

He had allowed for a mere handful of deaths, nothing in the grand scheme of things. Hell, seven cyclists had been killed in the last two weeks on London's roads, and the world had not stopped turning. But worlds might be transformed by removing the right people.

At the outset of his plan, the riots were simply fortuitous. Now he saw that the deaths could propel events. They could really count for something. So far the press had been silent. Well, he would change all that.

He let himself into the boarding house. The hall was poorly lit and smelled of vegetable stew. The landlady heard him on the stair and popped out of her room as if on a spring, something she did with the regularity of a Bavarian barometer. 'So you're back, Mr Flannery. Because I wondered when you'd be in. I didn't see you yesterday.'

'Well, I was out looking for work, Mrs Demitriou,' he explained.

'Only I did ask for the rent in advance, and there are my other tenants to think of.'

He failed to see how his non-payment of the rent affected anyone else who lived in the house. 'I'm sorry,' he said, 'it's very hard finding a job right now, but I'm hoping something will happen by the weekend.'

'Very well.' She spoke with an air of exhausted patience. 'Only if you can't pay by Sunday, I'm going to have to ask for my keys back. And you know that if I find any damage to the room, you'll have to pay for repair or replacement.'

The old bitch was clearly counting on that. She had seen around the edge of his door and noted the charts and clippings he had pinned up everywhere. Not that she had a hope in hell of finding another lodger to take the room, because there was a palpable smell of damp, the boiler didn't work properly, the sink leaked and there was a great brown stain spreading over the ceiling like a shadow on a smoker's lung.

'Oh, there's a package for you. Mr Demitriou took it in but he can't be the concierge, not with his back. So just this once, then, yes?' She indicated a brown cardboard box on the floor.

'Thank you.' He collected the box, which was surprisingly heavy, and headed for his room.

He had no money left for food now. He raided the

Demitrious' kitchen when they were watching TV and ate out-of-date sandwiches he found in shop bins. There were always plenty to be found behind the takeaways in the Square Mile. He was used to being hungry. It didn't bother him. But the stomach cramps were getting worse, and he knew he needed a stronger antacid. He cursed himself for not searching through Jonathan De Vere's bathroom cabinet properly.

And there was another problem, some kind of police unit that had been appointed to investigate. He'd seen several of them in King's Cross wearing matching black jackets that weren't standard police issue. And there were two men who seemed to be in charge, one in a huge overcoat who looked incredibly old, the other a little younger and smartly suited. There was also an Amazonian woman with dyed blonde hair who resembled some forgotten movie star. They weren't regular Met officers. He couldn't imagine how they had been assigned, or why, but he needed a contingency plan to take care of them. He knew that if he deviated too far from the original idea and started extemporizing, he increased the risk of being caught.

Locking the door behind him, he set the box on the kitchen table and cut it open. Inside was the final item he needed. Everything else was in place.

He had decided against gunpowder because of the problems of placing it under pressure, and settled instead for fulminate of mercury, a primary explosive that was very sensitive to friction and was used mainly for blasting caps. The crazy thing was that they kept it in the science labs of most secondary schools, and it was absurdly easy to get hold of because it wasn't considered part of a terrorist's arsenal. The equipment in the box ensured that he would be able to move it freely. All he had left to do was pack it correctly and prepare its installation.

He caught sight of himself in the spotted mirror above

the sink. He looked unwell. 'It's showtime,' he told the cadaverous face, smiling so hard that he immediately started to cry.

Like Raymond Land, Fraternity DuCaine had also been following Bryant's instructions, waiting in the shadow of the grey iron bridge until the Findersbury Bank opened on Thursday morning.

The Square Mile had become a no-go zone for almost everyone except the protestors and the police. The morning papers had been filled with photographs of jammed motorways and packed trains as residents fled the city. DuCaine was reminded of old photographs of evacuees leaving stations at the start of the Blitz.

Crutched Friars had now been completely sealed off at either end, so that the demonstrators could only get as close as the next street, while the few remaining employees continued to use the side entrance accessed from the alleyway.

The PCU had been denied a warrant for the premises as they had no grounds for conducting a search. Ironically, the request had been refused by one of their own, Darren Link, because the Serious Fraud Squad was conducting its own investigation on the premises, and needed to ensure that there was no contamination of evidence by other teams.

This created a fresh problem for DuCaine, who was planning to gain access by using one of the swipe cards Bryant had filched from Dexter Cornell's house. Banbury had printed DuCaine a fake staff card, but he would have to pass a battery of bank employees and Fraud Squad officers, any one of whom could get him into serious trouble if he was caught. Knowing that DuCaine was a naturally natty dresser, Bryant had suggested that he should pass himself off as a low-level bank employee in a suit and tie, but DuCaine was starting to doubt that the subterfuge would work. Everyone would be watching their colleagues' backs, knowing that someone was leaking information to the press. So far, news of the three murders had been successfully sidelined, but Cornell's life was being autopsied daily in the national headlines.

On the other side of the bridge an argument had broken out. DuCaine went over to see what was happening.

'I can't deliver down there, they won't let me in today,' complained a young Polish man on a bicycle. In his wicker basket stood a stack of lunch packs bearing 'Cheapside Bakery' labels.

'I'll get them in for you,' said DuCaine, flipping out his ID. 'Give me the basket and your jacket. I'll bring them back.'

The delivery man's reluctance faded on sight of the police badge, and he helped DuCaine load up with lunch packs. The brown linen bakery jacket was a bad fit, but he pushed up the sleeves so that it looked passable.

As he could not risk ringing the bell for entrance, DuCaine tried the swipe cards and found that the third one worked. Taking the lunch packs with him, he slipped through the door and into the hall. Inside, the ground floor was in virtual darkness because of the chipboard that had been nailed over the windows.

He passed a pair of harassed-looking assistants on the stairs. For once DuCaine's colour gave him an advantage; in an old-world bank like this it unfortunately appeared that a black man in a service industry uniform was less likely to stand out than one in a suit.

On the second floor, when a secretary came out of her office as he passed and asked him for a sandwich, DuCaine realized he had no idea how much to charge her, so he suggested £2.50.

The secretary peered at the contents of the sandwich box. 'You've dropped your prices,' she said. 'I'll take another one.'

He used the fire stairs to get to the fourth floor. The glass offices on either side of the main corridor were filled with employees anxiously tapping at their terminal keyboards, and if they noticed him they soon looked away again. He found the boardroom – the only room with frosted windows – at the end of the hall, but the door was shut. One of the other swipe cards opened it, but as they were all blank it was tricky keeping them separate.

He let himself inside, heard the door lock behind him and took a look around. The narrowness of the street kept sunlight away, so he was forced to turn on the lights.

Bryant had told him that the Fraud Squad had prevented anything from being removed. Snapping on anti-contaminant gloves, he checked out the huge walnut table, the blotters, pens and old-fashioned ring-bound notebooks, wondering how much he could move them without being noticed. The team would already have photographed everything, if they were efficient. Overhead was the black glass half-globe of a closed circuit camera. Nobody had mentioned this. Perhaps there was footage of the meeting. Perhaps it was recording him right now.

Three places had been used. Bryant had specifically asked him to note their positions. In front of each black leather chair a notebook had been set on the table. They were filled with handwritten tabulations that meant nothing to him, so he photographed them. He checked Bryant's advice again; some of it made no sense, but he needed to prove that he could follow instructions; he was on loan to the unit, but was anxious to secure a permanent place there.

After he had finished searching the boardroom for the list of anomalies Bryant had specified, he went to leave but found a huddle of staffers in the corridor. Worse, he heard a voice he recognized, and saw that Darren Link was coming to join them. Crouching low, he waited, praying that they were not about to come in.

They stopped before the frosted glass for a moment, talking softly, then moved on. He heard the swing door at the end of the corridor swish shut, and started to leave, but the boardroom door refused to open. Searching his pockets, he found that one of the swipe cards was missing. He could see it lying on the floor outside, just visible beyond the edge of the frosted glass.

There was no other way out. *You wanted to be tested,* he told himself, *and you've got your wish.* Walking to the window, he opened the top pane and stuck out his arm, taking a series of shots on his phone. When he checked them, he saw that it might just be possible to lower himself out and make his way across the concrete ledges to the drainpipes. He wasn't thrilled about the idea, but there was no other choice.

He was still deciding what to do when a shape showed through the window between the boardroom and the hall. It bent and rose. Someone had found the dropped card. What if they raised the alarm?

Swearing under his breath, he pulled himself up and swung his lean body outside in a single smooth action, releasing the window catch behind him so that it silently closed. He was now trapped outside the building, and there was nothing he could do but go forward.

The first thing was to get clear of the glass. From the corner of his eye he saw a young woman enter the room, puzzled. She looked about for a moment, and was joined by a colleague. DuCaine was wearing tough-grip rubber-soled boots that clung to the ledges, but his fingertips were barely able to find purchase on the sharp edges of the steel windows, and the frames were slippery with raindrops. The only way to maintain balance was to shift his centre of gravity by pressing his torso flat against the glass. The street was still empty but there were offices opposite, and someone was bound to be alarmed by the sight of a man climbing across a building.

Crushing his eyes shut, he stepped between the windows. His legs were long, his gait wide, but it was still a stretch, and for one nightmarish moment he was unable to curl his fingers around the corner of the window-frame. Worse, the next office had an open window facing away from him. There was no way around it.

'Hey, where's my stuff?' The Polish delivery man was calling up to him. DuCaine glanced down and saw him pointing to the left, along the line of the floor below, where a narrow steel cleaning cradle hung against the brickwork. He knew then that in order to reach the cradle he would have to jump down to it.

The noise was incredible. He landed hard, sending the platform bumping and clanging away from the wall. Lowering himself over the side and extending his body as fully as possible, he was able to drop on to the lid of a recycling bin and take off before anyone could come after him, throwing the delivery guy's jacket back with a cry of gratitude as he went.

He had no idea what the visit had achieved. Mr Bryant had not explained what he was looking for. As he rounded the corner heading for Bank station, hoping it might be open, John May's words came back to him: 'Don't try to understand what Arthur wants – his only concern will be that you did exactly what he asked.'

The station wasn't just shut; it was on fire. An ugly new mood had seized the seething crowds. As DuCaine veered away from them and headed north, he heard what sounded like a gunshot cracking in the cold morning air, as if to announce the start of a new level of violence in the city.

30

FUGUE STATES

'You sent me to see a tramp,' raged Raymond Land, storming indignantly into the detectives' office. 'A deranged, filthy, stinking, barking-mad lady tramp.'

'If I had told you what she was like in advance, you wouldn't have gone,' said Bryant reasonably. 'She was once regarded as one of the finest thinkers of her generation.'

'Well, she's bonkers now. What the hell happened?'

'Pressure. She became somewhat ideologically confused. Her classes on the history and purpose of public insurrection became lessons in activism, and then radicalism. She began to attract attention in the wrong quarters, and was eventually reported and prosecuted under the Prevention of Terrorism Act. After a diagnosis of schizophrenia and her subsequent mental collapse, she disappeared.'

'But *you* managed to find her.'

'I consider it part of my job to ensure that no one is ever truly lost.' For once Bryant's smile, usually so scary, had a glimmer of distant compassion that suddenly made him look much younger.

'She didn't make any sense, but I did what you asked and wrote everything down.' Land handed over his notebook. 'I still can't imagine how you think it will help.'

'No, but I might be able to see something you miss. It's like . . .' He studied the ceiling, trying to find the words. 'Like examining a painting in minute detail. Instead of just looking at the central figures, you try to understand the peripheral oddities, half of which are usually lost in the shadows. They appear so unimportant to the whole, and yet without them the picture has no cohesion. It's like that Degas painting *The Absinthe Drinker*. In the foreground there's a folded newspaper lying between two tables. What's it doing there? The answer is that its sole purpose is to draw in the viewer's sightline and lead the eye to the main character.'

'I haven't the faintest bloody idea what you're babbling about,' growled Land, heading off in disgust. 'The tramp lady touched me. I need a shower.'

'Murder as one of the fine arts,' remarked Bryant innocently, turning to his partner. 'Why does he get so upset?'

'I don't think he's ever read Thomas De Quincey, Arthur,' said May. 'Don't push him; he's having a hard time at the moment. He's got odd socks on today.'

'It's not my fault his wife left him. I've more important things to worry about. There are three dead men out there, and six suspects.'

'Six? How do you work that out?' May was intrigued.

But he received no reply; instead, Bryant creaked out of his chair and wormed his way into his grandfather's greatcoat, all but vanishing in the process.

'Where are you going?' asked May. 'Let me get Janice.'

'No, I don't need a watchdog today,' rejoined Bryant testily. 'I'm going to the British Library. I may be some time.'

And with that he was gone.

*

His preparations were finished. All he had to do now was wait.

Perhaps it would go wrong; things so easily could. But if they did, he would find another way. He had changed his plans before, first setting out to rid the world of Freddie Weeks, then punishing each of the others. Now he was plotting a new course, spreading his rage to the protestors. The one thing that could not be changed was the timetable.

He walked through the tunnel at the Barbican and carried on across London Wall into the financial district, following the hovering helicopters. He could hear chanting and police instructions issued through bullhorns. The noise came from every direction now. The separate protest chapters from around the country had joined together and were spreading out.

He couldn't believe how much the movement had grown, from Mansion House to Aldgate East, reaching as far up as St Mary Axe and down to Monument and Leadenhall Market, then following pockets throughout the city, wherever there was conspicuous, iniquitous wealth. Soon the main mass would break free of the Square Mile's confines and tumble out into Camden Town and down to Southwark, rippling west to Hammersmith and east beyond Whitechapel. Even if it stopped there, hemmed in by the capital's ring roads, the damage would be done: no one would trust the city again for a very long time.

He climbed to the second floor of the deserted glass-and-brushed-steel mall that overlooked Bank station, and watched the human core shifting back and forth like tidal seaweed in a rock pool. The protestors had stopped fighting for territorial space and were learning to move together against a common enemy. For the first time you could feel their united sense of purpose. Change was in the air, as solid and real as the vulgar new buildings developers were erecting along the Thames. The corruption at the Findersbury Bank perfectly summed up how everyone felt: These people would no longer be allowed to behave as if they were above the law.

The danger now was that the government would throw some sop of an amendment to the process of financial disclosure and buy off the angry crowds. He had to make sure that if they tried to do so, their pleas for calm would not be heard. He had to create a louder noise.

Last night, as he had sat at the table in Mrs Demitriou's squalid little rented room, piecing together the contents of the package, he decided that this could be the start of the biggest war in the world. Not a war of religions or ideologies, but of information. Who would get to control the first global system of mass communication?

The computer hackers had a utopian goal. They had got lucky when they uncovered details of corruption in the bankrupt Icelandic banks. After the video footage of a US helicopter attacking unarmed Afghan civilians, the tortured Bradley Manning had emerged from the shadows to join Julian Assange as another damaged, polarizing hero in the struggle for information dominance, not realizing that the moral obligation to tell the truth in a lie-filled information age could be turned against itself. Credit companies had cut off support for WikiLeaks, but the rallying call was heard and the information proved impossible to suppress. The battle had switched tactics as earnest Edward Snowden followed the dictates of his conscience. But the revelations about NSA spying were simply too numerous for people to grasp. They needed something more manageable, and like a gift from the heavens, along had come the Findersbury Bank.

It was impossible to know how deeply the corruption ran. There were rumours all over the Web that the Chinese were colluding with the Bank of England. Who knew what was true any more? The only thing anyone could be sure of was that at the end of the week Findersbury would follow Barings and Lehman Brothers into the dustbin of history. There could be no return to the days of innocence.

He sat back and looked at the tacky little explosive device, pleased with himself, and set about wiping it clean of prints.

Leslie Faraday studied his door nameplate. It was made of grey die-cut aluminium and glued to a wood backing. It read 'ROOM 2718 City of London Special Unit Coordinator L Faraday Esq'. He'd have liked the sign to be a little bigger, with the lettering in a more traditional serif font, but it would do for now. They had even given him back Miss Queally as his assistant – you weren't allowed to say secretary any more – even though all she did was print out his letters and eat chocolate éclairs over her keyboard, dropping choux pastry on everything.

The offices in Love Lane weren't as nice as his old place in Westminster, but he had been allocated a new mesh chair with sprung arms and an inflatable lumbar area. His window faced the blank walls of grey stone office buildings lined with police ARVs queuing for the underground car park, and a rectangular garden with trimmed hedgerows, flowerbeds and benches where he could eat his sandwiches. All in all, he thought he'd be very happy here. He glanced down at his shirt and realized that he could only see as far as the third button. He was transforming into his favourite food, an apotheosis of pork. *I'll join a gym and lose some weight, maybe get a hair weave, look like I mean business.* He sucked in his stomach and tried to see his belt.

He hadn't fully read the job description; they had been so anxious to get rid of him after his superior Oskar Kasavian left that he had simply goggled at the salary hike and signed the contract. Faraday's astonishing ability to fail upwards amazed even the hardiest of career civil servants.

Now, as he scrolled through the divisions covered by his department, he was horrified to discover that the Peculiar Crimes Unit was there once more, like some kind of stubbornly returning verruca, and that he was in charge of their budget. Scrunching away the headache that was building behind his eyes, he patted down his non-existent hair and considered the situation.

Perhaps they had changed. Maybe they had mellowed. Arthur Bryant could have calmed down a little and agreed to take a back seat for once, and John May might have stopped supporting his insane partner's every move.

No, he concluded, looking at the case schedule that showed him they had been put in charge of the Findersbury murder investigation, *they'll be just as nightmarish as they've always been. If they solve the case they'll get covered in glory and I'll be the one who comes away with his foot in a bucket of paste. Unless I do something right now to put a stop to it.*

He depressed the intercom button. 'Miss Queally, would you please come in here? Bring your notepad with you.' It was odd that the press hadn't picked up on the story. It was time they discovered what had been going on.

'Can I have a word with you?' Raymond Land asked Longbright, seating himself opposite her without waiting to be asked. He liked her room; it smelled of perfumed roses, a scent you never found in a regular cop shop. It reminded him of his mother. 'I just had a call from Dr Gillespie.'

'Oh.' Janice pushed aside the tick-box forms that made part of each day so tiresome. 'What did he say?'

'He thinks Bryant is developing an unusual form of Alzheimer's, not one he's seen before. He wants to run some further tests, but of course Bryant doesn't want them. Did you know about this?'

'I guessed that might be the case,' said Longbright. 'Did he say how long it takes to advance?'

'He can't tell. There's no standard rate of progression. It's irregular, and it might have been going on for years, in which case it could be reaching a point where we lose him quite quickly. The question is: How long can he keep on working?'

'You can't take his work away from him, Raymond. Don't you see he has nothing else? He'll drop dead if he's forced to quit. Retire him and you'll kill him.'

Land looked pained. 'Janice, this is the case of our lives. It's all tangled up with this bank thing, and we're in the firing line whatever we do. If we allow him to continue, he could place everyone in danger.'

Longbright rubbed at her tired shoulder, thinking. 'Does John know about this?'

'Not yet. I wanted to talk to you first. I thought you'd be more . . . impartial.'

'Apart from anything else, you'd be killing our only chance of cracking the case. You know we can't do it without Arthur.'

'And we can't do it with him.' Land was determined. 'He's making mistakes, Janice, and that puts us all at risk.'

'He's always made mistakes. He's always been scatty and confused in his thinking. But he gets it right most of the time. John and I are taking turns to accompany him.'

'Yes, but he keeps managing to slip away, doesn't he? Do you know what will happen if anyone finds out that we've been covering up for him?'

'No one must know,' said Longbright firmly. 'You owe him this much. John and I will take full responsibility for him, just until we see the case out.'

'Janice, I don't see how I can—'

'Please,' said Longbright. 'I've never begged you for anything before. We can take care of it, Raymond. Please let us try until the end of the week, at least.'

'All right,' said Land uncertainly. 'But only until the weekend. Then he's off.'

As Land left, Longbright returned to the coroner statements. Death by fire, three times over. Her nightmare was slowly rising into daylight. With each passing day more of the city was aflame, and a killer was somehow finding the opportunity—

Opportunity.

She went next door to talk to May. As soon as she saw his face, she knew he had also received a call from Dr Gillespie. 'Arthur's gone to the British Library,' he told her. 'He can't get into trouble there.'

'What are we going to do?'

'Cover for him, of course. We can't tell the others.'

'I was thinking,' said Longbright. 'He could be right. We keep assuming that whoever is doing this started using the riots as an opportunity to act, but what if it's the other way around now? What if our guy's somehow *causing* the riots?'

'How could one person manage that?'

'By leaking the news about Cornell's insider deal and sparking the first protest, then bolstering it with further deaths.'

'But the press embargo is still in place.'

'The more I think about it, the more sense it makes,' Longbright insisted. 'We need to find out how the news got out about Cornell. Maybe Arthur's not the only one who's been in a fugue state lately. Maybe we all have.'

'Speaking of which,' said May, 'do you have any idea what Arthur's up to?'

'No, I thought you did.'

They both rose together and headed for the chaotic stacks of paper on Bryant's cluttered desk.

31

CALL TO ARMS

The most polluted route in London takes you along the Euston Road, an ashen artery that traverses the city from west to east, palisaded with dismal concrete boxes. And yet, in one of those anomalies so typical of London, there are all sorts of oddities tucked away on it, including several excellent pubs, a couple of scalding Szechuan restaurants and half a dozen excellent if somewhat idiosyncratically organized bookshops, one of which is in the basement of the British Library. It was here that Bryant found Monica Greenwood waiting for him. The wife of a brilliant but disgraced academic, she'd had a hard time coping with her husband's newly acquired criminal status, but had somehow emerged with her dignity intact. She had lightened her hair and tied it up loosely, in the way that certain sexually confident women in their late forties did without a moment's thought. Her face shone as soon as she caught sight of him.

'It's good to see you again, Arthur.' She hugged him warmly but carefully, knowing that he was liable to leave bits of liquorice, cabbage and tobacco stuck to her.

'I took a chance,' said Bryant, doffing his homburg. 'I wasn't sure if you were still here.'

'I'm sorry I haven't been in touch. I tend to get a bit too lost in my work these days.' She smiled a little ruefully. 'Paul's out of prison now but we split up. I suppose you knew that.'

'No, I didn't. I'm sorry.'

'Don't be. We'd reached the end of the road long before his little transgression. What are you working on?'

'That's where I thought you could help me. I remember you were a member of the Conspiracy Club.'

'Oh, *that*.' She walked around a stack of books, replacing the errant titles. 'I gave it up, Arthur. They got a little too wacky even for me. It was around the time they came up with "scientific proof" that Michelle Obama was a man.' Monica had the kind of laugh that made others smile. 'A step too far, I'm afraid. I joined a lot of cranky societies while Paul was in jail. Funnily enough, it helped to keep me sane.'

He indicated the 'Art & Design Section' sign beside her. 'So you're back in paintings now?'

'Sort of. I'm collaborating on a new book about *The Night Watch*. You probably know the theory.'

Bryant rolled his eyes. 'I did, but I've forgotten.'

'Experts argue that Rembrandt filled his painting with symbols and hidden layers of meaning, the so-called "Fifty-one Mysteries". Ostensibly it's a portrait of a Dutch militia company, so who is the ghost figure, why are there five light sources, why is the soldier behind the central characters firing a musket into the middle of the crowd, stuff like that. It's supposed to involve Rembrandt launching an accusation of murder and corruption that led to his own downfall. The painting was certainly altered, but the "conspiracy" looks more and more like a prank perpetuated by artists and film-makers. It's what we find with most conspiracies: they only exist because somebody wants them to.'

'That's what I always suspected, however much I'd like some of them to be true,' Bryant admitted, loosening his scarf.

'We all would,' said Monica, 'because everyone else out there is denying the very things we can see with our own eyes. We live in a world where a Fox News presenter can tell her audience it's been proven that Jesus Christ and Santa Claus were both white, instead of Palestinian and Turkish—'

'—or mythical—'

'—and the chancellor of the exchequer can stand up in the House of Commons and say that the directors of a British bank are entirely above reproach.'

'He did that?'

'This morning. So how do we react? Either we invent a convoluted unifying theory to explain everything we've ever expected – an Illuminatus conspiracy – or we act on our gut instinct and fight back. Which is what they're doing just a couple of miles from here.'

'It sounds like you and I share the same attitude to anarchy,' said Bryant, 'which is good because I have some inside knowledge about the London riots. I think they're traceable back to one person, and I'm trying to find him.'

'Of course you are. We're all trying to find someone to blame.'

'No, I mean I really *am* trying to find him.'

'I don't see how I can help you there.'

Bryant fixed her with a gimlet eye. 'You have a very visual mind, Monica. You know, our unit was founded by freethinkers who decided that all serious crime was basically problem-solving. They hired people like me because I see things differently. That's what I need from you. Here.'

She waited while he trawled through his pockets,

finally handing her a blue plastic memory stick. 'This contains all the photographs I could cull from journalists covering the riots. You'll also find the faces of five men and one woman in a separate file. I want you to search for them in the crowds. The person I'm looking for must have attended some of the demonstrations. I'm afraid it'll be horribly time-consuming.'

'No, I'm fast at facial recognition. Aren't there computer techniques you prefer to use?'

'I asked Dan, our IT chap, and he said it was too expensive. We don't have the software in-house, so we'd have to outsource it.'

'And I'm cheaper.' Monica tucked the flash drive into her bag. 'You've got a nerve. How soon do you need it?'

'Before the fifth, if possible.'

'I'll give it a go, but I can't promise anything.'

'Thank you, Monica. You're a wonderful woman.'

She gave him an old-fashioned look. 'You sent my husband to jail, Arthur.'

'I know. I thought I'd redeem myself by getting you to work for naught but the thanks of a grateful nation.'

She laughed, despite herself. 'You never change, you know that? I'll call you. Presuming you still have a phone that works?'

'After a fashion. Don't worry, I know where to find you. The future of the city may depend on this.'

Monica Greenwood watched as her old friend attempted to leave via the stockroom, then the toilet, before she finally headed him towards the stairs. *I'm glad the future of the city is in such good hands*, she decided.

Janet Ramsey, the editor of *Hard News,* didn't know much about journalism but she had a nose for a good story. A little London girl reunited with her lost puppy was worth ten famines in Africa because it was human interest. People were tired. They didn't want to hear about mass tragedy, and besides, there was always a famine occurring somewhere. It was like these protests, a lot of unemployed troublemakers running around with nothing better to do, and over what? A corruption scandal, as if that was news these days. It was so hard to put a human face on the damned thing. Cornell had been done to death. They needed a new angle.

Her staff knew how she felt, which made it all the more surprising that they decided to hand her the oddly wrapped cardboard package. Inside, Janet found a set of photographs and a card.

She shouted across the open-plan office to her associate editor. 'Miles, do you know anything about this?'

Miles waddled over, eating some kind of chocolate cake, because there was always a birth, marriage or leaving party to be celebrated with empty calories. 'It came in for your eyes only,' he said, wiping his mouth.

Ramsey checked the envelope. 'No stamps. Did someone drop it off?'

'Dunno.'

'Well, can you bloody well find out?'

He leaned over the desk, trying to see. 'Who prints photos any more?'

'Someone who wants to catch my attention, obviously. I wonder how many more of these went out. We might not be first to run with it but we can put a fresh spin on the story. I want this in tomorrow's edition.'

Miles checked the wall clock and shook his head. 'Not going to happen, chief.'

'Yes, it is,' said Janet. 'Jonathan De Vere's been murdered.'

'Christ! Are you sure?'

She held up the photographs. 'You tell me. And there's a note, just in case we're too slow to make the connection. Our old friends at the PCU are handling the investigation.'

'But they're doing that banker, the tar-and-feather guy

who suffocated.' Miles and Janet had been sitting on that story for twenty-four hours at the request of the Fraud Squad and the effort was killing them. 'Which has got to mean—'

'Sometimes I look at you and can actually see your brain working,' said Ramsey. 'They're connecting the deaths.' She knew that if the PCU were involved in cases with locations outside City of London jurisdiction it was because they'd found a causal link. She'd been crossing swords with Bryant and May's unit for the past twelve years, and knew how they operated.

'What do you want to do?' asked Miles.

'Is the piece on Hall still ready to go?'

'Yeah, it's been filed and subbed.'

Ramsey thought through the options. *Hard News* had a killer story on the UK's new saint of IT. De Vere was thought to be untouchable, a saviour of British industry right up there with Richard Branson and James Dyson. He had yet to be knighted, but barring any unforeseen bad press it was only a matter of time.

Well, *Hard News* had the bad press in hand. It turned out that De Vere wasn't quite as gilt-edged as everyone supposed. His pregnant wife was having an affair and his company was about to file for bankruptcy, leaving a string of smashed charities in its wake. They had been building their case against him for the past few days, knowing that an early release might swing public opinion against them, but now it appeared that De Vere had been murdered and the information was being withheld.

'Who sent you that?' Miles asked as he turned over the unmarked brown packet.

'It'll take you thirty seconds to verify,' replied Ramsey. 'I can smell the civil service all over this. Go with "an anonymous source" for now.'

As Miles ran an advance-guard warning that a new front page was going in, Ramsey called her old frenemy

John May for a confirm-or-deny. It was possible that the photographs had been sent to other nationals, but if the sender was using an old-school delivery system, then presumably the Web press didn't have it as their offices were rarely central – and no one else had the secondary story about De Vere's fall from grace.

She studied the envelope, knowing that what she had on her desk was the perfect lead for their new online service. Judging by the photographs, which revealed the damage to De Vere's face in grisly detail, the killer was someone who was used to getting his hands dirty. The homeless boy burned, Hall tarred and feathered, De Vere branded: it looked like one of the protestors was taking direct action. And there it was, her link to Cornell. Resentment, revenge, a call to arms: it was like *Les Misérables,* and it could syndicate worldwide.

'John,' she said as her call was answered, 'I've got the story. Before I run with it, we need to talk.'

32

INSURRECTION

Leicester Square had always been slightly disreputable, from the days of the Alhambra Theatre, where the leading ladies were not those on the stage but the ones plying their trade in the balcony, to the private beer parlours that could be found above, below and behind the square's more salubrious buildings.

After years of gentrification, sanitization and pedestrianization only a few remnants of the square's raffish past were still on their original sites. The Cork & Bottle wine bar was a seventies time warp, the Talk of the Town had reopened as a Chinese casino, and a couple of small walk-up private members' bars struggled on with watered gin and ageing clientele.

In Leicester Place, just a few paces from the neon-lit square, nothing much had changed in decades. Joan Collins was currently appearing in its underground theatre, and the luxuriously shabby Prince Charles Cinema was still running a repertory programme that was likely to pair *The Wizard of Oz* with *Flesh for Frankenstein*. It was as if the last forty years had never happened.

The club was called Insurrection, and had once been part of the undercroft of the Église Notre Dame de France, a beaux arts church built on the old war-damaged site of an older minster, constructed in turn to replace the Panorama, which had opened in 1793 to display a circular view of all London. The club had returned the site to its sensation-seeking root, and was hung about with inverted golden crosses, apocalyptical vistas and images of uprisings.

'Blimey, how did he get over there?' asked DS Jack Renfield. 'And why hasn't he got any trousers on?' The crimson-painted auditorium smelled of fireworks. It had been evacuated but not made safe, so the PCU staff had been warned that they were there under their own cognisance.

The room had been hosed down. One of the bar alcoves was a smouldering, blackened ruin, but the rest of the place was untouched apart from a single patch of soot on the ceiling that might have already been there. The body had been blasted across the recess and lay twisted in an impossible position, one grubby trainer slightly off the ground. The EMTs had been first on the scene and had ascertained that the blast's sole victim was dead, but on instructions from the PCU they had left the corpse *in situ*. The alcove's central unit had been neatly eviscerated, leaving the ones on either side completely undamaged.

'A detonation will do that.' Dan Banbury stepped over a puddle. 'During the Blitz, people were blown out of bathtubs without sustaining injury, and their mantelpiece ornaments ended up a quarter of a mile away. You never know what you're going to get.'

Renfield leaned forward and squinted, trying to see more clearly through the still-thick air. 'He looks like he's in one piece, even though his head's not the right way round. What's that horrible smell?'

'I think his bowels were caught by surprise.'

'Nice.' Renfield wrinkled his broad nose. 'Pity he didn't live. It would have been interesting seeing him use a chair now, what with his legs bending the wrong way.'

'Severed spinal cord, I imagine,' said Banbury. 'Looks like the blast threw him forward and turned him over, twisting his back.'

'No one else injured?'

'Apparently not. It was a very neat job. I'm interested in the seat.'

Shards of metal were embedded in the rear wall with pieces of cream foam rubber hanging from them, like some kind of avant-garde Christmas decoration. Banbury had slipped on his shoe covers and padded over to the twisted remains of the banquette.

The first thing he found when he looked under it was the base of a slender tin box, blackened and warped by the explosion. When he picked out several fragments of a plastic cover, followed by the spring from a tiny clockwork motor, he knew exactly how the blast had occurred. An unstable primary explosive and a primitive ignition system, in this case a mechanical joy buzzer, placed inside a container on a bed of granules, probably nitrocellulose or fulminate of mercury. Pressing down on the lid in the right spot would have depressed the button on the buzzer, which vibrated in the unstable chemical compound, and because the whole thing was tightly encased it packed a hell of a wallop. It was something a really perverse child could have knocked together in less than ten minutes, although the trickiest part would have been getting it into the seat.

He headed back to the other side of the cordons and went upstairs to the entry booth, followed by Renfield.

'Was he alone in the place?' he asked the shocked Goth cashier whose lacquered upright hair made her look even more surprised.

'He was the first one in,' she managed. 'We'd been shut for cleaning. We had a big stag party in here last night and the lavs were bunged up with vomit.'

'I need details of your clean-up crew,' said Banbury. 'Names and contacts of everyone who was allowed inside.'

'I don't think we can get that,' protested the cashier. 'Most of them can't speak English. They come and go. It's a dive bar, not the Bank of England.'

'Did you see anything odd going on last night?' Banbury persisted.

'You mean odder than forty blokes in grass skirts and Viking helmets? I only looked in once, but no, not really.'

'So someone was able to cut open one of the seats without being noticed.'

'Most of the seats have been repaired dozens of times.' She tapped the sign above her head. 'It's called Insurrection. Our customers get boisterous.'

'Do you have credit-card receipts for the entry system?' asked Renfield.

'It's cash only, mostly students.'

'Why did he take that seat?'

'It's where he always sits,' she explained. 'He's the last out and the first in.'

'So you know who he is.'

'Yeah. His name's Frank Leach.'

'What else do you know about him?'

From the look on the cashier's face, you would have thought someone combusted in the club every night. 'Piss artist,' she said. 'Downs a skinful, makes a nuisance of himself with the bar staff, wobbles off to any other place that'll take him.' She indicated the stairs to the street.

A few minutes later, with the victim's identity confirmed and the names of the cleaning crew placed on request, Renfield left Banbury sifting through bits of burned rubber and metal, and headed back to report to Bryant and May.

33

TENSE NERVOUS HEADACHE

Raymond Land was the last to arrive in the unit's common room. Everyone was in their usual places; in that respect they were like schoolchildren, with the troublemakers (Arthur Bryant and Meera Mangeshkar) at the back and the ones with the smart answers (in this case, Dan Banbury and Jack Renfield) at the front.

'I have a lot of coloured chalks here,' said Land, 'and my pointing stick and Bryant's blackboard. We're not leaving this room until it's all scribbled over.'

Colin tried to stifle a laugh and failed. Albert Camus had once said that there was nothing more despicable than respect based on fear, but Land had the opposite problem. His team failed to respect him precisely because he gave them nothing to be afraid of.

'Four deaths,' he said, holding up the correct number of fingers in an effort to drive the point home. 'And no single line of inquiry providing us with a decent lead. We've got nothing. It's like he doesn't exist. What have you lot got to say for yourselves?'

Bryant raised his hand.

'Not you, someone else,' snapped Land, exasperated.

'And who was the bloke who got his trousers blown off in the club?'

'Frank Leach, online loan shark,' Longbright told the room. 'We're trying to find out about that. No friends, no enemies to speak of, but like De Vere, Leach was heavily linked to social-networking sites. There are a lot of threads to sort through. It's going to take a while.'

Land waved his hand at Dan and Jack. 'You two, you were there. Are you sure this . . . incident is connected?'

'I think you should let Mr Bryant speak,' said Renfield loyally.

'There's no question in my mind at all,' said Bryant, shifting his gobstopper. 'There are the repeated motifs, for a start. The use of fire and cheap low-tech equipment. Then there are the masks. Freddie Weeks was covered with cardboard, Glen Hall's face was smothered with tar, Jonathan De Vere had a mask hammered on to his face, and this chap, Leach, was sitting in this alcove.' He held up a photograph that showed a curving red wall painted with naked men and women wearing fox masks. 'It seems obvious to me that the killer is now referencing the masks of the protest movement.'

'I'm interested in forensic evidence, Mr Bryant, not your whimsical conjectures,' said Land.

'That's not so easy,' said Banbury. 'The incendiary element has prevented us from getting much from the victims, so I've been looking at the secondary sites, the floor above the shop where Hall was killed, De Vere's kitchen and the club auditorium.'

'Please spare me threads and fibres,' Land complained. 'How the hell did anyone manage to *plant a bomb* in a *bloody bar seat*?'

'The cleaning team,' suggested May. 'It seems likely one of them was bogus. They're hired piecemeal and given cash by a dodgy company paying below minimum wage, so they're going to be tricky to track down. There's something else you should know: Janet Ramsey was sent a photographic record of the case lifted from our files, together with a list of names. Someone wanted her to know that the deaths were connected, and that we were in charge of the case.'

Land ran a hand over his face. 'Tell me she's not running the story.'

'It wouldn't make any difference now if she killed it. Other packages went out. The Fraud Squad got the BBC and Sky to hold off until they could organize a press conference. Ramsey has turned over the shots to us, but not before she went to press.'

'Can you lift anything from them?'

'They were just screen grabs. It feels like a pretty clumsy attempt to drop us in it – probably someone we've upset recently.'

Land groaned. 'That doesn't narrow it down.'

'I'm afraid it gets worse,' May warned. 'De Vere was about to be accused of financial mismanagement. Oh, and there's a sex scandal thrown in too, so there's something for everyone.'

'This is going to escalate the protests,' said Bryant.

'Am I missing something?' asked Land, bewildered. 'Why would it do that?'

'Because people are going to see how easy it is to wipe out the bad eggs,' answered Bryant. 'If they start taking the law into their own hands, nobody will be able to hold them back. This country successfully maintains the illusion of democracy. We're under more surveillance than any nation in the world except Monaco, and no one ever complains! The tax authorities go after small firms and individuals instead of the worst avoiders. Now people are being told that they'll have to work harder for longer and live worse lives than their parents. What will it take to start a fire that can't be put out? How big does the match have to be?'

'Just whose side are you on, Mr Bryant?' demanded Land, outraged. 'Your job is to uphold the law, not question it. Why is it always the big picture with you? Why can't you just get on with finding a murderer?'

'A society that doesn't question its laws is doomed to fall.' Bryant was furious now, although with one eye screwed up and his false teeth bared he tended to look like Georges Méliès's image of the moon with a rocket stuck in its eye. 'Don't you dare to doubt my loyalty. John and I sacrificed any chance of having a normal life for this unit. Every man and woman here with us is doing the same thing for what they believe is the greater good. But when even the police start thinking that maybe this fellow is on to something, how are civilians going to feel? He's wiped his trail clean, but he hasn't thought of everything. If he's made a mistake we'll find it, but how much time do we have? I said there were six suspects—'

'Wait,' said Land, relishing the chance to use his coloured chalk. 'Go on.'

'To set up each death the killer has to know something about his victim's habits. He knows where they live, what they like, how their schedules work. De Vere's wife is having an affair with a metallurgist. That gives her partner a motive and makes him a possible suspect. Dexter Cornell has single-handedly become the unacceptable face of capitalism. Maybe he wants to take everyone else down with him. Suspect number two. The three boardroom directors who are just seeing their little insider-trading scheme go up in smoke. If it turns out they're connected to any of the victims it makes them suspects three, four and five. And finally there's the smart girlfriend, Joanna Papis – yes, Raymond, a *female* – who joins Freddie Weeks and Hall together, making her a putative sixth.'

'How did that happen?' asked Land. 'Did I miss a meeting?'

'We haven't even begun to eliminate any of the six because we're not geared up to handle an operation of this size, and Darren Link knows it.'

Land was so busy drawing red and blue lines around the names that he almost missed the point. 'Wait – you're saying that Link wants us to *fail*?'

'Of course, because he hates that this unit was founded by leftie liberal academics.'

'Blimey, one of you must have some good news,' groaned Land. 'Anyone?'

'Glen Hall had a male partner,' said Fraternity DuCaine. 'Because Hall was a banker and concerned with privacy at work he never mentioned him to any of his colleagues, but the partner is somewhere in the deep background, and I'm getting to him.'

'OK, anyone else?'

Meera raised her hand. 'Colin and I are working on an angle. This guy likes handling fire. We think there's something in his job history.'

'Maybe he worked in a foundry,' Colin added. 'We're talking to everyone who might have a connection in that field. Arsonists tend to have long histories going right back to when they were children. We're trawling past cases of criminal damage, particularly those that took place during riots.'

'Good,' said Land, 'now we're getting somewhere.'

'There's a key point we keep coming back to,' said May. 'How did the rumour about Cornell's deal break out in the first place? Arthur and I are trying to find the source of the leak.'

'I've been looking into De Vere's funds,' Longbright added, 'and there's something very wrong with his accounting. His bookkeeper resigned and took off for South Africa, and there's a huge hole in De Vere's finances. He was involved in government-backed charities, so he had some very influential colleagues who are going to demand fast answers as the press story unfolds.'

'Whether we like it or not,' said Bryant, 'the papers are going to link the deaths with the riots, and they'll be only too happy to suggest that some kind of citywide apocalypse is imminent. But you know, they may have a point. I think the killer is pulling out the threads that hold London's stability together. So far he hasn't put a foot wrong.'

'Well, thank you for that cheerful summation of the week's events,' said Land. 'I'll just go and gas myself. Or perhaps I'll go up the Gherkin with a machine gun and wipe out all of the protestors.'

'Raymondo, you're sweating,' Bryant pointed out. 'Are you all right?'

'No, I'm bloody not,' growled Land. 'I have a tense nervous headache.'

'I'm a qualified masseur,' said Colin. 'Do you want me to give you a neck rub?'

'Don't come anywhere near me,' Land warned, knowing how many people Bimsley had damaged with his uncoordinated fists.

'D'you know, Leach's death rings a bell.' There was a peculiar wistfulness in Bryant's voice. 'In the late 1960s, John and I chased a suspect through the slums on the Isle of Dogs. We finally trapped him in the Roxy cinema during a screening of *Bullitt*. Just as we thought the case was closed, our murderer gave us the slip through an alley at the rear of the picture house. I thought perhaps he might have come back, except that he'd be around eighty by now. I was upset about missing the film's climax. I finally saw the end of *Bullitt* on telly in the eighties, and I still didn't understand the plot. But then I realized it never really mattered that much who did the murder, so long as you enjoyed being with the main characters.'

Land stared at his senior detective as if he'd just announced that he was joining the Royal Ballet. This little speech was the clearest evidence so far that Bryant was finally going gaga.

'Robert Vaughn is the baddie,' Bimsley told Bryant. 'The chain was off the hotel door because Johnny Ross was expecting him, but he was double-crossed.'

'Corrupt politician, innit,' added Renfield. 'Nothing changes.'

Land rose unsteadily from his seat and looked at the faces surrounding him. Bryant was mentally fading from view, drifting into vagaries and non sequiturs, and the rest of them were *still* listening to him. 'I don't want to know what you all think about the plot of *Bullitt*,' he said hotly. 'I'm doubling shifts and cancelling all leave until this thing is sorted out or we admit defeat and turn it back to the CoL. Now get on with your work before I do something to you with my pointing stick that goes against the laws of physics and common decency.'

Longbright altered the shift roster, and they divided the interviews between them. John May's resemblance to a dashing but possibly disreputable captain of industry qualified him to fit in with the three directors of the Findersbury Bank, Fraternity DuCaine was packed off to find Glen Hall's partner on Renfield's classic-car-club principle, Jack Renfield got Lena De Vere's metallurgist boyfriend, Meera Mangeshkar agreed to talk to Joanna Papis, and it was decided that Longbright's naturally warm demeanour might draw something more useful from Dexter Cornell.

Out of these came some eliminations. May found that all of the bank's directors could account for their time when the murders occurred, which was annoying because he didn't like them at all. They were slick and glib and crafty, with acquisitive minds and eyes like angry marbles, and their qualified, circuitous conversations were designed to mislead as much as any country-house maze. But facts were facts and they were all willing to provide witnesses for the hours in question, so they were reluctantly dismissed.

The metallurgist boyfriend proved a damp squib, too; a single handshake told Renfield that he was barking up the wrong tree, partly because his suspect had immaculately groomed nails, and partly because his arms were like overcooked white asparagus. The man had clearly never lifted anything heavier than a jeweller's screwdriver in his life. Renfield's instincts were confirmed when he discovered that the metallurgist had been abroad for the previous three days.

This, in the main, left Papis and Cornell.

34

THE GIRL AND THE BOY

By nine-thirty on Thursday night, the entire Square Mile was in lockdown. The protestors were unable to leave and everyone else was unable to enter. Then at 10 p.m. the leading story on the BBC concerned Jonathan De Vere's fall from grace, and all hell broke loose.

Within minutes, rioters poured around the closed Bank and Cannon Street stations, with Occupy and Make Capitalism History 2 (splitters' group) joined by protest latecomers Break the Banks and Kill List, a party dedicated to making the lives of the nation's richest tax-avoiders unbearable. More groups coalesced in Trafalgar Square before a hastily arranged gaggle of guest speakers. This event was organized across a dozen social-network platforms and, inspired by fiery rhetoric, headed off along the Strand, catching the police support units entirely by surprise. As the canary-jackets pursued the mob, ARVs arrived to block the bridges, escalating a peaceful protest into a running siege.

By midnight the streets were on fire again. The amber glow from a dozen makeshift bonfires of chairs and billboards gave the city a strange medieval appearance, and the chiaroscuro effect reshaped the older, overlooked buildings, restoring their strange grandeur with splashes of fierce saffron light and deep black shadows. Somebody had set fire to a sofa in the middle of the Aldwych, and so Kingsway was closed, causing further chaos. There was now a violent picket outside the Freemasons' Hall in Great Queen Street; the disruptions had crossed into Covent Garden.

It was a cool night and groups of figures stood warming their hands around burning oil drums, their faces lit by the flickering flames. TV crews filmed from every vantage point, training their cameras on a pale sea of tiny rectangular panels as a thousand mobile phones recorded the event. Covert footage was beamed via satellite to intelligence agencies in Europe and America. Alarming new images were Dropboxed into news agencies for public consumption. Microsites were launched and subgroups were hashtagged, Instagrams and Vine loops were posted, and grinning selfies were taken against the infernal backdrop.

The great golden grasshopper that hung above Sir Thomas Gresham's coat of arms at number 68 Lombard Street became famous once more for being in the background of a thousand photographs. It was an unlikely symbol for a financier, Aesop's sign of laziness, but it was photographed glistening against a roiling wall of brown smoke and yellow flame, and became a new emblem for the troubled times.

On Thursday evening Superintendent Darren Link met with senior officers to formally request a curfew in the Square Mile. This was a radical move that could override tube hours and licensing laws. Although the 2003 Antisocial Behaviour Act had created zones allowing officers to hold and escort home unaccompanied minors whether they were badly behaved or not, they had this ability only between the hours of 9 p.m. and 6 a.m., and the act was compromised by High Court rulings that denied police the power of arrest. At no other time in its long history had the City of London faced a blanket curfew.

Meera Mangeshkar went to look for Joanna Papis at the Enterprise pub, where she was due to start her shift. As she pushed open the door, the smell of hops assailed her.

'Hi,' Papis called, 'come in. You're probably the only person who will today. All of our regulars are getting out of the City while they still can.'

The two women sized up each other with the curiosity of exact opposites. Mangeshkar was short, dark and intense. Papis had the elegance of height and glossy pale hair framing blue-silk eyes. It didn't feel like a fair fight.

'Why did you withhold information from us?' Mangeshkar demanded after the curtest of explanatory introductions. Realizing that warmth was not her strongest suit, she always found it better to attack.

'What do you mean?' Papis rubbed at the back of her neck and dropped down on to a barstool, as if expecting that this moment would come.

'You didn't tell us you knew another of the victims.'

'Your boss came to talk to me about Freddie Weeks,' she explained. 'He never mentioned Glen Hall. I only found out about his death from the press reports.'

'There was an information blackout while we were following leads,' said Mangeshkar. She knew questions were already being asked about the embargo. In a world of instant information, people expected to receive news as it happened.

'So, yeah, it turns out I knew them both.'

'Seems a bit unlikely in a city this big.'

Papis shrugged. 'I meet a lot of people.'

'How did you get to know Mr Hall?'

'His accountant Aaron used to come into the pub. He was dating Glen, but he'd been in trouble with the law for running some kind of anarchist website. He knew Glen was really paranoid about anyone in his office finding out about his record. The bank had high security clearances for its staff and he said they would find ways of firing anyone they didn't trust. Aaron felt it wasn't fair. He asked me what I thought he should do.'

'Aaron . . . What's his last name?'

'Mossman, I think. He was very loud and funny, too much for someone like Glen.'

'Are you still in contact with him?'

'Aaron? No, he's a New Yorker. He went back home. Glen was very cut up about it.'

'So, I want to get this right,' said Mangeshkar. 'You met Freddie Weeks first, then Hall. Did Weeks know Hall?'

'I don't see why he would. They both drank here, that's all.'

'There's a chance you might have met their killer.'

'What, you think I'm at risk? Why would I be? They didn't have anything in common.'

'They did. They had you.'

'Are you saying I'm a suspect?'

'No.' Meera tapped her notepad. 'I just want you to be sure that you've told me anything that might help us to find this person.'

'Are you from London?' Papis asked.

'Born and bred.'

'Then you probably have no idea how strange your pubs are. A millionaire stands next to a homeless guy and they start talking. They don't introduce themselves, or ask each other what they do for a living. They talk about politics or sport or movies or food. In all my time in this country it's been the hardest thing to understand.'

'What do you mean?' Meera asked.

'The British,' Papis replied. 'They'll tell you about everything and anything – except themselves.'

*

'Couvre-feu,' said Bryant, savouring the word. 'Cover-fire. Lights out. A metal shield in the shape of a half-bell, to be placed over an open fire when the curfew bell rang. Well done, Mr Cornell, you've managed to return us to the eleventh century.'

Having been hauled into the King's Cross unit for a formal interview, Dexter Cornell was more defensive than ever. Bryant had decided to conduct the interview himself, and arrived to find him prowling around the edge of the room looking as if he was waiting for his opponent to step into the ring. In one corner perched a small blond boy whose legs were not long enough to let him reach the floor. In the other sat Edgar Digby, a lawyer with whom Bryant had previously crossed swords.

'I want it noted that I'm here of my own volition,' huffed Cornell. 'I wasn't about to drag my family lawyer in for something like this so I had to settle for a jobsworth from Lincoln's Inn. Digby, introduce yourself.'

'Mr Bryant and I have met before,' Digby said. 'My client is prepared to discuss only matters pertaining directly to your investigation. He is not required to answer any questions concerning the financial operations of the Findersbury Private Bank or its employees, or regulations covering the shareholdings of—'

'Shut up, Digby, I want to ask him about the anomalies in his written statement.' Bryant turned to the financier. 'Well, it's a pleasure to meet you again, Mr Cornell, without your henchmen this time, unless you've taken to employing midgets.'

'That's my son,' said Cornell through clenched teeth.

'Oh. He's dressed like an adult so I assumed he was a dwarf.'

'I *am* here,' said the boy. 'I have a name.'

Cornell ignored him. 'What kind of anomalies?'

Bryant switched his trifocals. He had five pairs dating

from different eras, and could partly see through a different focal band in each pair, but as they were all of the same design (tortoiseshell, heavy) he had to cycle through all the pairs before settling on the right ones. As he squinted about like a mole with cataracts, the lawyer rolled his eyes at Cornell, who glared back. 'Right,' Bryant said finally, reshuffling his pages, 'we have fairly accurate timings now . . . Perhaps this isn't for his ears.' He indicated the boy.

'He stays,' said Cornell impatiently. 'For God's sake.'

'The new timings aren't properly covered by your statement. The lad who was sleeping rough on the steps of the bank, Freddie Weeks – we have CCTV footage that places his attacker at the site while you were in or near the building. You don't have adequate camera coverage.'

'We're a private financial institution, not a bus station. Digby, do I have to answer these?'

'Under the present requirements of the City of London, witness statements are by their nature—'

'Oh, shut up. What else have you got there?'

Bryant squinted at the pages again. 'You've been briefed about the bomb that was planted in the Insurrection nightclub early this morning. We know when and how it was placed, and the timings are not covered by your movements. You were apparently on a train.'

'I'm sure there must be some record of me leaving the station.'

'You didn't use a chauffeur.'

'Amazing as it sounds, not many people do any more. Nor do I have an under-butler or a grouse-beater. If you honestly considered me a murder suspect you'd realize it's the one situation where I'd get someone else to do the dirty work. Anything else?'

'I think we can allow one more question,' said Digby, redundantly.

'This is rather more of a problem,' said Bryant.

'Jonathan De Vere died at approximately eight thirty a.m. on Wednesday – yesterday. You haven't given me your whereabouts.'

'I was with Augustine.'

'Who's she?'

'That's me,' said the boy.

'You must get beaten up a lot,' said Bryant.

'He doesn't go to the kind of school where children get "beaten up", as you put it,' Cornell replied.

'Yes, but his classmates must take the piss. Why wasn't he going to school, anyway?'

'Augustine is already eighteen months ahead in his studies. He has an IQ of one hundred and twenty-five. I also have a private tutor on permanent standby. Are we done here?' Cornell was very close to losing his temper again.

'Look at this,' Bryant insisted, pointing at the boy, 'he's got arms like bits of wet string. With a name like that you could at least teach him to box.'

'That's enough,' said Digby, closing his briefcase and rising. 'My client—'

'Your time's up.' Cornell was icily calm. 'I have another meeting to attend.'

'You still haven't said where you were when Jonathan De Vere was murdered.'

'Ask the boy.' Cornell slammed out of the room with the confused Digby in his wake, torn between cautioning Bryant, taking the child or doggedly trailing behind his client. With grim inevitability, the lawyer chose the option that paid his bill.

'Where was your father?' Bryant asked Cornell's son.

'Like I'm just going to tell you,' Augustine replied. 'You'll have to work harder than that.'

'Well, it's just you and me now. Does he often dump you like this?'

'He'll send for me after his meeting,' Augustine said.

'So don't freak, it's not like you have to do anything.'

Bryant had no experience of children and no emotional connection to them, beyond an ability to make them cry simply by removing his dentures. But this one looked like he wouldn't crack easily. 'How long do you think your old man will be?'

'Old man? Look who's talking. An hour. I can amuse myself.' Augustine took out his phone and unlocked a game.

'Would you like me to show you around?'

'Is this a real police station?'

'No.'

'Then no.'

'Can't you go over to the pub for an hour?'

'I'm not old enough.'

'That's a pain. Well, you can't stay in here. The room's booked. You can sit in my office so long as you don't touch anything.'

He led the boy along the corridor. Augustine looked around the door and wrinkled his nose. 'It smells gross.'

'We have an incontinent cat. If you find a packet of Custard Creams, don't eat them. Just go and sit in that armchair and don't move until your father comes back. If you twitch so much as an eyelid I'll have you thrown to the rats in the basement.' He studied the back of the child's head, his long thin neck and arms. He really was very small indeed.

Bryant fled to Longbright's office. 'Janice, what am I supposed to do?' he pleaded. 'This boy of Cornell's. He's just sitting there staring at his phone like a little – robot or something.'

'Cornell said he was sending someone to pick him up,' Longbright explained. 'He'll be fine with you for now.'

'Do you think I should show him my book collection?'

'What, rare tropical foot funguses and murder victims

of the nineteenth century? Probably not. You don't have to do anything. Children amuse themselves.'

'But it's not a safe place for a child.'

'He's not made of glass, Arthur.'

Bryant thought for a second. 'I'm sure Cornell is using his son as an alibi. I need to talk to him, but you know I can't talk to children. I don't understand how they think. He's an alien and I'm a dinosaur.' He headed back to his office to try to solve the conundrum of modern childhood.

35

THE LIST

It was late, and Bryant was tired. The air was cool and misted, the streets wet and striated with yellow reflections. May took his arm and walked him into Bloomsbury.

'Did you ever see that Michael Powell film *A Matter of Life and Death*?' Bryant asked. 'There's a scene in it where David Niven doesn't know if he's dead or alive. He wakes up and there's fog all around him, and he wonders if he's in heaven. Do you know how the director created that effect? He breathed on the camera lens.'

'Not sure I'm with you,' May admitted. 'What's your point?'

'The point is that perhaps you're right: sometimes the answer is much simpler than you think.'

'Come on, then, give me your simple theory.'

'An anarchist, presumably one who's smart enough not to be listed among the members of organizations like Disobey, seeks to destabilize the system. And he does it by choosing random names from a metaphorical hat. He tries to torch a controversial financial institution but fails, accidentally killing Freddie Weeks in the process.

He tars and feathers a banker, but he's not very good at doing that either because the prank goes wrong and Glen Hall dies. Why would he then pick on a supposedly all-round decent chap like De Vere? Because he's met him and something doesn't ring true. De Vere's a bit too much of a white knight, a tad too charming. So our killer digs a little and finds out that De Vere's a hypocrite, a chancer whose charities are about to declare themselves bankrupt. That way he feels justified in picking him off. What we need to do now is find out what he discovered about Mr Leach.'

'You think the fact that Leach was a loan shark had something to do with it?'

'Well, I found out one thing. With the exception of Freddie Weeks, all of the victims were on that linky thing—'

'LinkedIn.'

'And the bookface thing and the tweety thing—'

'Facebook. And Twitter.'

'And De Vere and Leach both visited the Disobey website. Disobey is one of the splinter protest groups that's currently camped outside the Bank of England.'

'You're sure about that?' May asked. 'Where are you getting this from?'

'Dan got a subscription list from Darren Link. And if Weeks and Hall went to the same pub, the others may have as well.'

'When were you going to share this with me?' asked May, irritated.

'After I'd had a pint,' replied Bryant serenely, rubbing his nose with a paper handkerchief.

'What else have you been holding back?'

'I think I know how the news about Cornell's insider trading got out.'

May stopped so suddenly that a couple of Scandinavian tourists ploughed into the back of him. 'You do? How?'

'Well, obviously Cornell would have been very careful at the bank. He deliberately distanced himself from the other directors, sitting with his underlings in an open-plan office. And as I've said, apart from the lawyers he was the only other person who knew that the Chinese weren't going to come to the table. So if it wasn't any of the lawyers, the information had to come directly from Cornell himself.'

'But that makes no sense. Why would he jeopardize his own deal?'

'That's what I intend to find out.' Bryant was examining the contents of his tissue. 'It's funny. At the beginning of the week I thought we were simply identifying a dead homeless kid. Now we've got a global conspiracy.'

May stepped back and took a good look at his partner. 'You're all there today, aren't you? How do you feel?'

Bryant looked straight ahead, buried deep inside what he called his 'summer scarf', his usual implacable self. 'Fine, thank you.'

'You never told me the rest about your visit to Dr Gillespie.'

'Didn't I? I've forgotten all about him, actually. He needs to give up the oily rags. He's on forty a day by my calculations. His lungs must be like the bottom of a sink trap.'

'Well, what else happened?'

'He showed me some ink blots and asked me what they meant. I told him they were a sign that he should switch to a Biro. Then he asked me to name a current television star.'

'Who did you say?'

'Bruce Forsyth. To my knowledge he hasn't been off our screens for the last sixty years, so I couldn't go wrong. We went back and forth like this for a while and I could tell I was having my usual effect on him.'

'He was getting annoyed.'

'The veins were standing out on his forehead. So I told him to cut to the chase and give me a prognosis.'

'What did he say?'

'Alzheimer's. Trust me to get something German. I'm not nuts, which is a relief. It's a physical disease, it just happens to affect the brain.'

'Yes, I know what Alzheimer's is.'

They stopped at the corner before Bryant's street, beside a lamp-post that threw their shadows across the opposite wall like a shadow play.

'I looked it up in a few of my books,' Bryant said. 'Quite fascinating, really. Protein plaque builds up in the structure of the old brain-box, leading to the death of a few cells. Big deal. One in fourteen over the age of sixty-five gets it. We all eat too many carbs. Some also get a shortage of important chemicals, so the nerves no longer transmit messages, and that makes the process much faster.'

'Do you think that's what's happening? Are you scared?'

Bryant blew a raspberry. 'So you end up a few clowns short of a circus. All feathers, not much chicken. I can get by.'

'I'm not stupid, Arthur. I know you.'

Bryant turned his watery blue eyes to May. 'The honest truth?'

'Yes, please.'

'It's a little more complicated than that. It seems I'm developing an unusual form of cognitive impairment.' Ever the showman, he waited for the effect of the announcement to sink in. 'Gillespie thinks my blank moments might be due to mini-strokes, transient ischaemic attacks that are caused by blockages in the blood supply to the brain. It's irreversible and developing fast. I'm definitely becoming confused. I may have been hiding some of it from you. I write it all down, you know, and I have every one of the symptoms. Loss of memory, mood changes, problems with communication and reasoning. I can't remember where I've been, why I've gone somewhere, how to count out change in shops or how to work the TV remote. Although I've never been able to do that. I enter into fugue states and can't remember anything afterwards. Oh, look at you now, all very serious. Are you sure you want to know about this? It's extremely boring.'

'Of course I want to know.'

'Then can you kindly uncrease your face?'

'What do you want to do?'

Bryant caught sight of himself in a window and adjusted his hat to a nattier setting. 'I want to go on, of course. That's what anybody with more than two brain cells wants to do, isn't it?'

'OK. What else do you want?'

Bryant did not need to think about it. 'I want to get good value out of my free travel card, and the rest of my senior-citizen concessions. God knows I've paid my taxes long enough. I want to arrest people and make suspects squirm. I want to protect those who can't look after themselves. I want to be a thorn in the side of the establishment, and a pain in the arse of the status quo. I want to finish *Tristram Shandy* and *Middlemarch*. I want to see if they're able to milk any more films out of *The Lord of the Rings*. I want a mohawk. I want to train as a French pastry chef, a Spanish matador and an Italian opera singer. I want my clothes to wear out before I do. I want to see a decent production of *Measure for Measure*. I want the unconditional love of a beautiful woman and to sit with her on a beach in Thailand. I want my wife back. I want unfeasible cocktails. I want to get a tattoo and hang-glide from the Shard. I want to eat fusion food, whatever that is. I want to live long enough to see the look of smugness wiped off the faces of everyone who works for Google. I can give you a much fuller list if you'd like.'

'No,' said May, 'that's enough to be going on with.' He thought for a moment. 'Is there anything I can do?'

'Yes, you can lend me five thousand pounds.'

'I haven't got five thousand pounds.'

'Then don't ask if there's anything you can do.'

With that, the subject was closed. May waited until Bryant had turned the corner, then walked back to the tube.

36

THE HAMLET TACTIC

Thursday night was not quite over and done with.

Janice Longbright pushed her chair away from the desk and rose, stretching her aching back. 'How can you still be eating?' she asked Jack Renfield, who was chewing a bright-orange chicken leg, taken from a pirate-brand KFC box.

'I need the carbs,' replied Jack. 'I'm a big bloke, I burn off a lot. Ask Colin.'

'Virginia Fried Chicken? What, they just picked the next state over for the name? Chuck us a piece.'

Renfield flipped her a chunk of breast. 'How are you getting on?'

'Frank Leach ran an online company with offices in Whitechapel. Diamond of the East Financial Services. Sound dodgy enough?'

'Diamond of the East? Leach was lending money to the Bangladeshi community?'

'Looks like it. High interest rates, high-risk clients. Right on Whitechapel Road. The screen-cap makes it look like a dump. Leach's the owner, with a couple of flunkeys doing the churn and burn. His site leads to two other businesses, another moneylending dealership with hilarious interest rates and a pawnbroker service.'

'So Hall, De Vere and Leach were all involved in finance.'

'At different levels, yes,' Longbright agreed.

'Diamond of the East. Doesn't sound like much of a target for an anarchist. I'd have thought there were better targets out there. Why not go after employees of the big five banks?'

'You're right, it doesn't make sense.' She spat a piece of bone into a tissue. 'Maybe the victims really are being picked at random.'

'Not according to the Old Man. You're looking very fetching tonight, by the way.'

'Yes?' Longbright looked down at herself. 'I'm not sure what I'd fetch. I mean, I agree about the anarchist angle and I can see why Arthur wants to pursue it. But I've been through the Disobey membership lists, and these people . . . some have genuine grievances, some are troublemakers, some are just weird outsiders. Add communist and fascist infiltrators, police informers and special-interest groups drafted in from other EU countries: it's an incendiary mix. Darren Link's lads keep finding so-called protestors employed to shoot chunks of footage from the front line so that marketing firms can sell them on as viral GIFs to ad agencies; how pathetic is that?' She set aside some chicken gristle and wiped her hands. 'I don't think we've ever had a case like this.'

'What do you mean?'

'We're meant to talk about opportunity, means, motive, yes? And in cases of premeditated murder it's the last one that dominates. But this is murder as opportunism. I ask myself: Would he have acted if there hadn't been a riot? You commit a crime and drop into the raging mob outside your door. Where's the best place for an outsider to hide?'

'Inside a much bigger group of outsiders,' answered

Arthur Bryant. He was leaning against the door jamb, and looked exhausted.

Longbright sat up in surprise. 'Hey, we thought you'd gone home.'

'John saw me back but somehow I got lost on the final stretch. I can't seem to remember where home is.' He shuffled in and took off his hat. 'I know it's in Bloomsbury somewhere. The streets turned themselves around when I wasn't looking.' His words tore at Longbright's heart. He pulled ineffectually at his scarf and coat until she came over to disentangle him. 'I don't know Alma's number, otherwise I would have called her. And anyway, I'm not sure where my phone is. But somehow I remembered the unit. I thought, if I just came back here and sat for a while—'

'Of course,' said Longbright, concerned. 'Why don't you put your feet up? There's some fresh tea in the pot. Do you want me to call John?'

'No, it was bad enough that I made him walk me most of the way home.'

'I'll get you a cab when you're ready,' said Longbright, pouring mugs of tea.

'The Rookery,' said Bryant, looking back at her with gratitude. 'Henry Mayhew. One sugar.'

Renfield caught Janice's eye. 'Sorry, Mr B.?'

'Mayhew catalogued the lives of those who survived outside of London society.' Bryant's eyes had a faraway look. 'The Rookery was in St Giles, an ancient Plantagenet village that started at the corner of Tottenham Court Road, going down to Seven Dials and Covent Garden. It must have been quite nice once, with cottages and garden plots and an old hospital. Then the impoverished French came in, bringing violence in their wake. And pubs like the Bowl and the Angel acted as halfway houses – you know, halfway to execution, where prisoners were given a free final pint of beer.'

Longbright and Renfield sat back and listened. Bryant seemed quite normal when he was able to lose himself in London's history.

'The Angel's still there, of course. Not a bad boozer. And Seven Dials – well, you know how that came about. There were seven roads that made a star, and at their centre sat a single white stone pillar with just six clock faces on top of it, because two of the roads were angled into one. It was torn down when they searched for the buried treasure underneath—'

'Who searched?' asked Janice, sipping her tea. Bryant continued without seeming to hear her.

'There's a new pillar there now, of course. But the Rookery – Mayhew wrote about it, a tangle of narrow streets where all of the outsiders lived. Wretched houses with broken windows patched with rags and paper. Every room let out to several families. A honeycomb of courts and blind alleys, naked children playing in street sewage.' He raised his palms, imagining the scene, his eyes bright. 'A policeman enters and the call goes up across the rooftops, travelling faster than any officer can walk, so that escaped prisoners, thieves and deserters have time to get out.'

He lowered his hands, then cupped them around the hot mug and took a sip. The slogan on the mug read 'Keep Calm and Lock Someone Up'. 'We have traditions about dealing with outsiders that survive to the present day. We lump them all together, the ones who don't fit in. We don't harm them, we're too civilized for that, but we put them where we can keep an eye on them. First they were kept in slums, then on run-down council estates. Then there was Margaret Thatcher's plan to abandon parts of the north and cut off all support for Liverpool. "Managed decline", she called it. We do the same thing now. Oh, we don't keep the dispossessed in a physical place any more; they're in virtual space where they can be monitored electronically. So the State still looks . . . not liberal, exactly, but at least as if it's full of good old-fashioned common sense. While of course the exact opposite is true. London is corrupted. It always has been, always will be. Good cup of cha, this.'

Longbright sat back and studied her boss. His faculties seemed perfect when it came to recalling the events of the distant past, but he couldn't remember where he lived. 'Do you think we should look somewhere else, then? And not bother with the protest groups?'

Bryant seemed diminished once more. 'I didn't say that. He's hiding among them, a modern-day rook, and we have no way of luring him out. No description, no hint of identity, no idea of a motive beyond anger and hatred. But I think it's someone we've met.'

'Why do you say that?' Renfield asked.

'Because he's working to a very specific master plan. One death a day for the period between Halloween and Guy Fawkes Night, from mischief to full-blown insurrection. Any strategist will tell you that when you plan a war campaign you first make sure you know your enemy.'

'Do you have any ideas?' asked Longbright.

'I do, as it happens, but there's a problem,' Bryant admitted. 'I'm going to have to pull the Hamlet Tactic.'

'What's that?'

'Someone will die tomorrow, and the day after that, and we can't stop it. Six deaths, in all probability – then he'll vanish forever, leaving behind chaos and despair. The protestors have yoked themselves to a cause that can't be resolved. There's no available option they can choose. In its present form capitalism doesn't work – well, we can all see that. But it's not a shirt that no longer fits. You can't simply replace it with another off-the-peg design. There will be six visible victims and thousands of invisible ones. You understand, don't you?'

'When you put it like that, yes,' Renfield admitted.

'Therefore – the Hamlet Tactic. The PCU is an accountable body, but I need to take steps that the CoL would never approve of. So I'm going to use my "cognitive impairment" to cover my actions. I may misdirect others, or lie, or simply vanish for short periods. It means that while I'm doing this, none of you can help me.'

'What about John?' asked Longbright.

Bryant sat up with a start. 'No, especially not John. John mustn't know, do you understand? I have to protect him. I have to protect all of you.'

'You're saying that you're going to go rogue without any unit support?' Renfield rubbed at the bridge of his nose. 'How will that work?'

'If I need something I'll call you on your private mobiles.'

Longbright raised a tentative hand. 'How will we know if—'

'If I'm acting strangely for the case or actually going bananas? You won't. That's why it's called the Hamlet Tactic. This is my swan song, Janice. If you don't think you can do this, you have to tell me *now.*'

'We can do it,' said Longbright, looking to Renfield for confirmation.

'Our job is to protect the public from danger,' insisted Bryant. 'This time I have to protect the public from themselves.'

'I don't know how you even start doing that,' said Renfield.

'No, but I do.' Bryant knocked back the remains of his tea. 'Now if you'll kindly inform me where I live, I'll head home and get some sleep. Tomorrow's going to be a big day.'

'OK,' said Longbright. 'I'll call a cab.'

'Are you the only two left here tonight?' Bryant asked.

'Yes, why?' Longbright glanced at Renfield.

'There's something I need you to do before you knock off.'

'What?' asked Renfield.

'It's a boring job,' Bryant warned. 'Colin and Meera usually handle it.'

'Not bin duty,' moaned Longbright, sinking down into her chair with a groan. 'Or worse, data searches.'

Bryant pointed at the computers. 'I can tell you what you're looking for.'

'And there I was feeling all warm and motherly towards you,' complained Longbright.

37

X MARKS THE SPOT

The building that houses the City of London Police Headquarters, on the corner of Love Lane and Wood Street, is so blandly innocuous that it encourages suspicion. Are there currency-laundering Swiss financiers operating behind this blank fascia? Do its tinted windows shield a cabal of disgraced politicians plotting their revenge on Westminster? Is this where deposed dictators and expunged Russian oligarchs plan their secret return to power? Or is there an overweight civil servant wedged behind an absurdly large desk trying to get the plastic wrapper off a bacon sandwich?

'It's very simple; we have no evidence of insider trading on behalf of Mr Cornell,' said Leslie Faraday, searching for a paper knife. 'He seems a bastion of respectability to me. I've always admired anyone who could juggle figures, never my strong point. Cornell knew the bank was sailing close to the wind – apparently their cash flow was rocky for a long time – and he acknowledges he's at least partly to blame. But you can't send someone to jail for incompetence, otherwise we'd all be inside, wouldn't we?' He tore ineffectually at the wrapper, mangling the sandwich in the process. Arthur Bryant gave his partner a weary look. 'So unless you can prove that the news transmitted itself from Mr Cornell to the directors while they were all locked in a meeting room for the day, you have nothing. And that's what I'll have to report back to the Home Office.'

'If I take you there and show you how it was done, and give you the evidence to indict Cornell, would you be prepared to overlook how I came by the information?' asked Bryant, knowing that DuCaine's illicitly shot footage would not be admissible in court.

'That depends. You see, it's not really up to me.' Faraday eyed his mutilated breakfast with the longing of a dog for its lead. 'But I suppose if I had a look at what you've got, I might be able to—' His speech decelerated so suddenly that the detectives could actually watch his thoughts backing up. 'Yes,' he said finally. 'If you can prove that Mr Cornell contacted the directors, we may have a deal.' Bryant had deliberately allowed Faraday to see a way of claiming credit for the arrest.

'Then let's go.' May had the false keenness of a man who had been given no indication of what to expect in the next few minutes. At times like this he felt like an actor, wondering what his motivation was while waiting for words to be placed in his mouth.

They took a car from the CoL pool even though the bank was just a few streets away and Friday morning had dawned dry, a miracle in November.

'What are you up to?' May hissed at his partner as Faraday went off to find a driver.

'I consider myself something of a locked-room buff, as you know,' replied Bryant, speaking as a man who regularly entered his car by rotating a bent pastry fork in the door jamb, 'and it occurred to me that what we had here was a classic locked-room puzzle.'

May thought for a moment, but nothing came. 'Kindly explain.'

'Last week the three directors went up to the fourth-floor boardroom. They remained locked in there from ten a.m. until four p.m. What was so important that these three had to be sequestered in such a fashion for so long? According to Janice, they were planning a staff restructure. The minuted documents they took from the boardroom at the end of the afternoon attest to this. Fraternity noticed a closed-circuit camera in the ceiling and Dan tracked down the footage.' Bryant's eyes narrowed. 'Guess what it shows?'

'How can I guess?'

'*Nothing.* Not a flicker of anything interesting, just three middle-aged businessmen in expensive suits sitting around a table, two on one side, one on the other, talking business and making notes. During the whole time they were in the room, nobody made or received any phone calls, and the door to the hall was never opened. They just talked and wrote. Nobody did anything unusual at all.'

'Where was Cornell during this?'

'On the ground floor at the front of the building, entirely surrounded by other members of staff. He was told about the collapse of the Shanghai deal by his Kenyan law team at eleven fifty-five a.m., and we have that call logged. So I worked on the supposition that between noon and four p.m. Cornell somehow managed to alert the directors to the fact that the deal had gone sour. But how? He wasn't left alone during all that time. He and his team even went to lunch together. Look out, Lardy's back.'

Faraday had returned with a set of keys. 'There's no driver available,' he reported, 'so can one of you drive? I can't, I'm afraid – lost my licence. Some bell-tinkling twerp of a cyclist got himself tangled under my bumper on Wimbledon Common.'

May snatched up the keys before his partner could volunteer his special brand of vehicle operation, which involved mysterious hand signals, acoustic parking, refuting traffic lights, baiting wardens, scraping other vehicles and conducting arguments with pedestrians, signposts, kerbs, lorry drivers and, on one all-too-memorable occasion, a man carrying a crate of frozen ducks.

The logical route to their destination would have been to pass Bank and Monument stations, then Fenchurch Street, but with the police barricades fast becoming a permanent addition to the financial district, they were forced to tack back and forth around London Wall on the only available route left.

May made sure that his partner was sitting beside him. 'Are you certain you know what you're doing?' he whispered. Bryant tapped the side of his snub nose and said nothing.

The entrance to the Findersbury Bank still showed evidence of the petrol-bomb attack, and although a half-hearted attempt had been made to clean the surround, it had since been daubed with skulls and crossbones and splashes of red paint. Instead of a venerable and trusted financial institution, the bank looked like a derelict ghost train. Bryant had told no one but DuCaine that he had stolen Dexter Cornell's swipe cards, so he waited while a young woman met them and arranged admittance.

'Are you honestly suggesting that Cornell got word to the directors through four concrete floors?' asked Faraday, pacing about.

'I thought it was impossible at first,' Bryant answered. 'All those details about the Chinese shares and Kenya and them pulling out of the proposed merger and leaving the stocks exposed and the likelihood of a collapse in the cash flow and heaven knows what else. But then I remembered that the directors knew all this. They had everything they needed to know. The only single piece of information they were missing was: Would the deal happen before the deadline or would it fall through? And as soon as I realized that, it became like the election of the new Pope. Would there be white smoke or black smoke?' He rooted about in his pocket, pulled something sticky off his mobile and thumped out a number. 'Hello, Fraternity, are you ready? Be so kind as to do it now, would you?'

Faraday went over to the window, frowning. 'Are we supposed to see something happen?'

'They never went over to the windows,' May pointed out.

'That's right,' Bryant agreed. 'You can sit down over here and you'll still be able to see. Remember, Cornell knew that the room was covered by CCTV, so he couldn't do anything that would show up on camera or arouse any kind of suspicion.'

Faraday stretched his bulk on tiptoe and examined the glass globe in the ceiling. 'That thing films a 360-degree picture. Are you telling me he sent them a message that couldn't be picked up by a high-definition camera lens? What was it, some kind of audio signal?'

'No,' said Bryant, easing himself into a seat and raising his eyes with a smile. 'Look.'

There on the ceiling was a bright rectangle with a broad X at its centre. 'X as in no entry, not happening, no go,' said Bryant unnecessarily. 'If the deal had been approved, the X would probably have been halved to a single downstroke, a tick for yes. It's funny, you never know what's in a London street. Take the headquarters of the City of London Police in Love Lane. You know what's underneath that building opposite you, Mr Faraday, the tower of St Alban's?'

'I've no idea,' said Faraday distractedly, staring up at the cross.

'There's a white-tiled stable full of horses. Once a

month, London's only remaining farrier comes along and fits the police mounts with new horseshoes. He has a mobile furnace and a portable anvil.' Bryant rose and waved a hand at the view. 'And on the ground floor of *that* building opposite is a venerable old wine bar, scruffy and stuffy, with real-ale casks and barrel tables in a basement. Cornell popped out for a quick lunch on the day in question, just as the sun came overhead and into the street at noon. He went across the road with two of his mates, and angled the upper window pane so that it reflected on to the boardroom ceiling, leaving it in place while he had a sandwich and a glass of wine. I imagine he'd been in there the night before and had stuck two strips of tape on the glass. That's the great thing about city pubs. Nobody ever notices what you do in them. He must have spotted the light on the boardroom ceiling before and it gave him the idea. And the best part was, the CCTV couldn't pick it up because it was mounted into the same surface as the projection.'

'But there's no sunlight out there right now,' objected Faraday.

'You're right, it's too early,' Bryant agreed. 'Which is why my lad is down there shining a torch at the window to replicate the sunlight.'

'All right, you've proved your point,' Faraday conceded, 'but where's the proof?'

'We have a witness,' said Bryant. 'One of the barmaids saw Cornell open the window. She's already given us a statement.'

'It'll never hold up in court,' warned May.

'Maybe not, but it'll pin him down for a while.'

'What do you mean, pin him down?' asked Faraday, his face a picture of apprehension.

'I'd say that right now Cornell is our main suspect.'

'Are you insane?' Faraday exploded. 'He's at the centre of one of the most intense media spotlights ever turned on a human being in this city. How would he ever think that this was a good time to get away with *murder*?'

'If he could pull it off,' said Bryant placidly, 'I'd say it was the perfect time. Look down there. What does that say?' He pointed to the street sign on the wall beside the bank.

'Crutched Friars,' said May. 'I always wondered about the name. Something to do with a monastery?'

'Exactly so. Over there' – he waved his walking stick at the other side of the road – 'was the House of Crutched Friars, the Order of the Holy Cross, founded in 1298. Underneath that building in 1842 they discovered a group of Roman goddesses bearing baskets of fruit, which is why the site became holy.'

'Where are we going with this, Bryant?' begged Faraday impatiently.

The detective was not to be hurried. 'During the dissolution of the monasteries, Cromwell's emissaries caught the Prior of Crutched Friars *in flagrante delicto,* and down came the hammer on that corrupt little brotherhood. The church was turned into a carpenter's yard, and the friars' hall became a glasshouse. In 1575 a suspicious fire broke out and destroyed everything but the stone walls. Many said that it was arson, an act of Catholic revenge after the Marian Persecutions, when Mary Tudor had burned two hundred and eighty-eight Protestants alive.'

'Are you saying *that* was somehow connected with *this*?'

'A religious legacy, perhaps. As soon as I saw that someone had tried to burn down the bank, I thought of the monastery. There's so much about arson that's identifiable now. We can tell how, where and when a fire starts and what flammable substances were used. We can plot its spread, we know what accelerates and retards it. But the one thing fire does is eradicate the culprit. It's a coward's weapon. We're looking for someone bitter and angry, impulsive and cowardly. Or at least, that's what he wants us to think. Because if he was *really* clever, he'd be none of these things.'

Faraday groaned. 'I'm all at sea here. Who are we talking about now?' He looked to May for help, but found none.

'Leslie, I assume even you know about the recent secret reports into the corruption of the criminal justice system,' said Bryant, 'the threatened juries, the collusion of Freemasons, the "Get out of jail free" cards?'

'Scotland Yard is apparently putting its house in order.' Faraday gestured vaguely.

'You can believe anything you want, but I suggest you look a little more carefully into Darren Link's background.'

'Link? He's working under the jurisdiction of the Serious Crime Directorate.'

'Who are themselves under investigation,' said Bryant.

'Why would Link get himself involved in something like this?'

'That's what I intend to find out. The first question I asked myself was the simplest: Who has the most to gain? While the City's financial institutions remain engulfed in chaos, Dexter Cornell can virtually do as he pleases. And who can protect him?'

'Link? *Really?*' Faraday waved away the whole idea. 'Well, I'm afraid it's a bit over my head. The Chinese, the Africans, the government, plots and conspiracies, and now the police – I mean, such cover-ups aren't very likely, are they?'

'There has to be a reason why someone can keep getting away with murder without leaving any clue to his identity,' said Bryant. 'I'm not saying it *is* Cornell, but right now we know he's committed a major felony. And he has one weak spot when it comes to the deaths: His alibis don't hold up. To exclude him, I have to get his son to open up.'

'His *little boy*?' Faraday was aghast.

'Cornell can keep fudging his whereabouts, but I think the boy is closer to him than anyone else. Let him assume I'm chasing alibis. What I really want is insider information. You know, the coming of fire has always been seen as a sign of the Apocalypse. Perhaps everything we hold dear is going to come tumbling down around our ears. Then where will we be, eh? I'll see you later.' And with that Bryant patted his homburg harder down over his ears, rose and slipped out of the boardroom.

'Do you have any idea what he's talking about?' wailed Faraday, watching Bryant leave.

'I think I should go after him,' said May.

'No, I need you here,' warned the epicene liaison officer. 'If all this is true, we're not finished.'

'But—'

May was desperate to stay with his partner. *The crafty devil,* he thought. *He's used the meeting to get away. This isn't an investigation any more; it's an expedition into his mind without a map.*

38

OPHELIA ON THE SHORE

'Janice, have you got a minute?'

Meera stood in Longbright's doorway, waiting to be invited in, which was a first. Usually she just barged about wherever she liked.

'Of course,' said Longbright. 'Grab that stool.'

'Sorry to collar you so early, I just thought I could have a word before things got busy around here again.' She looked sheepish and uncomfortable.

Longbright put down her pen and gave the DC her full attention. 'What's the problem?'

'Your mum was in the force, right?'

'Yes, Gladys worked for Mr Bryant before me. And both her parents were in the Met.'

'So there was never any doubt that you'd join up, too?'

'Oh, there was doubt. But my happiest memories were with her at work, so I tried it and found that I liked the life.'

'And you never regretted the path you chose?'

'Of course I did. I left several times, tried all sorts of other jobs, but none of them was half as rewarding, and I always found myself coming back. Why? Are you thinking of leaving?'

Mangeshkar was not used to unburdening herself, and the words did not come easily. She swung about on the stool, looking for the right phrase. 'It's not me. My folks – they want me to start a family. They don't think this is a healthy environment for me.'

'Are they putting pressure on you?'

'Yeah. Only because they care, but . . . there's someone they're keen for me to marry. I've known him for a long time. He's nice.'

'Do you want to be with him?'

'That's not really the question. It's not about him at all, but me. Whether I want to stay here.'

'And do you?'

'Yes. I'm suited to the life. I know I bitch about it a lot, but it fits with who I am.'

Longbright shrugged. 'Then stay. We're not nuns. It doesn't mean you have to give up everything else. You can have both, you know. Date a doctor – they keep difficult hours. And there are some lovely blokes in the force.'

Meera looked doubtful. 'There are also some real dickheads.'

'This isn't about marriage, it's about the job?'

'I suppose so, yes.'

'Then I can tell you that you have everything it takes to be a great detective.'

'I think you've just answered my question.' Meera smiled and rose.

'Send the next one in on your way out.' Longbright sighed. 'That's what I'm here for.'

He knew she was alone in the ground-floor Bankside apartment because the other two girls had already left, a leggy blonde with the unearned superiority of someone in an inconsequential media job, and a dumpy, frizzed mess of a thing in a plaid woollen skirt and sweater that her mother must have picked out for her.

A ground-floor flat in a three-storey semi-detached house with six bells beside the front door. Obviously he couldn't be buzzed in, so he would either have to wait for someone to come out or try to gain access through the rear. But he couldn't risk waiting.

He had to catch Joanna Papis inside.

He was still deciding what to do when the front door opened and a young Chinese guy came out. He looked like a very conservatively dressed student, the type that would keep to himself and barely notice anyone around him. It was easy to get up the steps and catch the door before it fully closed. Stepping over a scattering of junk mail, he saw that front doors to the two ground-floor flats had been carved from the home's old hallway; the plaster ivy entwined along the edge of the ceiling came to a sudden halt against a diagonal of painted plasterboard. Checking to be sure that he had the right number, he unloaded his tool bag and set to work, knowing that at any moment the door could spring open and she would emerge, ready to leave.

There was no letter box. That was why the mail had been left in the hall. None of the flats had letter boxes. OK, no reason to panic, he'd have to improvise. There was a narrow gap under the door. The bag yielded a roll of silver tape. He needed to keep the washing-up bottle higher than the tubing . . . There was a noise inside, and he knew that she had stepped into her hall. It was too late for anything elaborate. He would have to take a chance.

Shoving the end of the tube into the nozzle of the bottle, he pushed it through the gap and began to squeeze. The stuff was so pungent he was sure she was bound to notice.

Joanna Papis was running late. She shared the flat with two other girls, both of whom also had long hair, so they took ages in the single bathroom. Early on in their relationship a set of rules had been agreed upon. The first was that no one should spend more than twenty minutes in there each morning. That rule had been the first to be broken. Their second – whoever finishes a bottle of milk buys a new one – had resulted in the last few usages of each pint shrinking by ridiculous proportions.

Joanna had overslept and found herself third in line for the shower, and – gross – she had to clear the plughole of hair because Gretchen-the-top-media-PR-guru (a description she used on her LinkedIn page) was too grand ever to bother cleaning up, so by the time Joanna was ready to leave the flat the others had gone and she was already due at Southern Hub, the virtual workspace in Waterloo where she sorted out her clients' accounts. It looked wet out but felt mild, and she had donned her favourite outfit, a white dress lapped in red and purple flowers, even though it was really too summery-looking to be worn in November. The radio DJ was trying to find the most annoying sound ever recorded, so she turned him off and packed her case, then slipped on a jacket and headed out.

In the hall she stopped to check her hair in the mirror, and was caught by the sudden pervasive smell of petrol. There was nothing in the flat that could have caused it. A truck outside, perhaps? Then she heard the trickle, saw the white plastic pipe extended beneath the front door, watched in puzzlement as it withdrew – and suddenly an undammed river of fire poured in, quickly spreading across the hall carpet and up the walls. It all happened so fast that she barely had time to move.

The plastic pipe reappeared at another spot, twisting back and forth under the edge of the door, spraying liquid fire everywhere. A pile of old magazines on the side table ignited, their pages lifting in the updraught, and she realized how dry and dusty everything was, how easy it would be to burn. The fire took hold in seconds, rising up the front door to produce a dense outpouring of oily black smoke. There was no other way out of the flat, and the windows in the lounge and kitchen had toughened glass.

But the flat had one weak spot.

Joanna dropped her bag and ran back to the bathroom, removing her shoe and thumping it against the small square pane until it cracked, the largest parts falling out.

The window was too high to reach. She needed a chair from the kitchen. Returning to the hall she was horrified to see how thick the fumes had become in such a short time. It was already hard to draw breath. She dragged the chair to the bathroom and scrambled up on it, pulling out the last shards of broken glass.

Wriggling through feet first and dropping into the yard at the side of the house, she tore her dress but landed safely. She tried to imagine who could do such a thing as this, and remembered the number she had added to the phone in her jacket pocket. She rang Colin Bimsley.

The DC was nearby, queuing for a sausage roll in a Southwark Street café when he got the call. He'd started the morning with some Xing Yi Quan training in the twenty-four-hour gym, and now realized that he was doomed to be forever interrupted in his pursuit of carbohydrates. It seemed he had only to step inside a greasy spoon to trigger his phone.

He tensed as soon as he saw that the call was from Joanna Papis. The girl didn't sound frightened, just out of breath. 'I guess I should have stayed in contact with you. He's just set fire to my flat.'

'Where are you?'

'In the alleyway at the side, but I can't get out past the front of the house without running into him.'

'Have you seen him?'

'No, not yet, but I know he has to be just inside the main hall.'

'What about the back of the alley? Any way out there?'

'Maybe. I've never tried.'

'Stay on the line, Joanna, I'll get you back-up and then I'll be there as soon as I can.'

'Do you want me to see if I can get a good look at him?'

'Hell, no! You need to get as far away as possible, OK? Go towards the river. I'll find you.'

She slipped the phone back into her jacket and headed down the alley, but the rear gate was locked and it was too high to climb over. She vaguely recalled seeing a key for it in the kitchen, but she couldn't get back in. As she moved towards the front of the house, there was a dull explosion of glass from within the flat.

She knew she would have to take a chance and risk running into him. The main door looked shut, so presumably he was still in the hall. As she ran into the deserted street, she heard the smack of boots on paving stones and knew that he was coming after her.

She needed to surround herself with people. Her best bet was to head for the walkway by Doggett's Coat & Badge, the pub at the base of Blackfriars station, but as soon as she did so she realized her mistake; he could run around it and cut her off. He would guess she'd go for the river; it was the closest thing around here to open ground.

Sure enough, she saw him heading towards her, a figure in sweatpants, a hooded top and a white plastic Guy Fawkes mask. The awful thing was that because of the protestors and the fact that Saturday night was Bonfire Night, nobody thought twice about passing a man disguised as a gunpowder plotter.

He knew he had beaten her. At her back was the deserted tunnel that ran under the road. Going forward, the river walkway narrowed and she would be forced into his open arms.

Or there was Blackfriars station, the only London

station built on a bridge, its new solar-powered roof shining through the rain-mist like the teeth of a saw. She backed up and ran inside, swiping her Oyster card and dashing to the great glass-sided platforms that spanned the brackish Thames. The main part of the rush hour had already ended. The platforms were vast and empty.

It was too exposed here; there were no columns to hide behind. All she could do was keep moving out of the way and pray that Bimsley got to her soon.

Finding any officer support in the area proved to be a joke; police services in the new financial district had been almost entirely withdrawn. Without a bus or cab in sight, the detective constable realized it would be faster to run. He knew his way through some of the back roads, and stayed on Southwark Street, heading towards the river. Parts had changed out of all recognition since he was a nipper, transformed into a canyon of blank-glass office blocks. He no longer knew which cross-streets could be taken as shortcuts. Immense advertising billboards flashed past, consumerist memes that promised blue skies, clean air, fresh starts. At the great blue bridge he swung off and headed across the road, slaloming between the vehicles.

'Can you see him, Joanna?' he asked his mobile.

'Yes, he's just come up on to the platform at Blackfriars station. He's heading towards me.'

'Is there anyone around you?'

'No, no one, I think a train's just been through.'

'Then you have to get off the platform and put a door between him and you. Look around: there must be some kind of access back down to the Thames walkway.' He tried to listen as he skirted the vehicles, but it was hard to hear her above the noise of traffic and the motionless helicopter overhead.

'There's something that looks like the door to the

roof. It doesn't seem to have—' The connection suddenly broke.

Colin swore and speed-dialled back, but his call failed. Pocketing the phone, he ran faster.

Joanna had cut off the call. She was sure she could be heard across the empty platform. A narrow grey steel door had been propped slightly ajar with a packet of cigarettes. Inside was a short, steep staircase rising to the great solar panels that spanned the entire station roof. Somebody working on the station came here to smoke.

The bitter wind snatched her breath away. She found herself on top of the station bridge with only a single low handrail and a slender walkway between herself and the blossoming brown water. The angled panels of the station's energy system were tall enough to hide her. She looked over the side. Far below, the tide was heading out.

Moving as fast as she dared, she reached the centre of the bridge and ducked into the shelter of the great glass cells. She had no way of knowing if he had seen her use the door and followed her up, and could not raise her head for fear of attracting him, so she crouched there, hoping that Bimsley could find her signal from his GPS.

Colin reached the station platform and saw only three commuters – a bad sign. He hadn't passed her on the walkway, so she must have taken another exit. He was about to head back down when he noticed a shadow passing against the glass roof.

He found an access door easily enough, but it was shut from the inside. When he threw his bulk against it, some kind of obstruction grated against the concrete floor. There had to be a matching door on the other platform. Quickly checking in each direction, he dropped down on to the line and ran across the tracks. The matching door was there all right, propped open. It led directly to the roof, but if anyone was up here they had to be standing between the solar panels, and there were hundreds of them stretching like shiny oversized playing cards in either direction, connecting both sides of the river.

Before he could reach the centre of the bridge there was a terrible cry from the south side. He ran towards the sound, but something dark launched from further along the walkway, falling out into the air.

He got himself to the side in time to see the splash, and knew that Papis had been shoved over. Even if she survived the fall, she would not remain alive for long. The water was bitingly cold and the outgoing current flowed several times faster than anyone could possibly swim. Last year he had been called to Waterloo Bridge after two drunk students had dived over the side for a bet on a sunny, calm day when the tide was at a low ebb. Their bodies were eventually found thirteen miles out on one of the lowest reaches of the estuary.

He had no choice; without thinking twice he pulled off his rubberized jacket and threw himself from the side of the roof, aiming for the spot where she had hit the water.

As he dropped under the girders of the bridge, the wind punched through the arches and hammered at his body, twisting him. Colin had two advantages: he knew how to fall, and he had a good idea where the tide would take him. He had studied flow maps of the Thames as part of his training for secondment to the River Police. He had even swum the river once for a bet.

The water was viscous and opaque, instantly blinding him. He knew not to fight against the direction of the flow, but it was essential to break the surface as quickly as possible. As he did so he saw that he was being swept towards Bankside Pier, which meant that she would be, too. The water's turbulence was astonishing. It dragged at his clothes like a living thing. A length of wood as large as a railway sleeper caught his chest, spinning him around. He followed the hazy light from above, righting himself.

The foreshores had been cleared of debris, but the river's deeper central channel held all manner of knife-sharp dangers. He could not lift his body far enough from the grip of the tide to spot Joanna, and was drawn down, beneath the moored barges at Bankside.

It took all of his remaining strength to fight his way back up and strike out for the embankment. He forced his limbs to move until there was mud beneath his boots, then began walking.

There was no sign of anyone else. He knew he had made a judgement based on emotional response, not logic. He should have stayed on the bridge and gone after her attacker.

As he climbed out on to the rock-studded shore, spitting foetid water, he looked across at the pier and saw that something white and red had beached against its lower struts. The flowers of Joanna's dress were pulled back and forth by the treacherous tides. Her head and shoulders were raised above the waterline, but pale hair obscured her features. She lay in a bower of algae, a shattered Ophelia washed up near the banks of the Globe Theatre.

39

GROSS

'Oi, Frodo – I want a word with you.' Bryant was sitting on a tyre swing eating jelly babies, and threw one at Augustine Cornell as he passed.

The boy appeared even smaller in his cap and blue school jacket with yellow piping, like a tiny naval cadet. He picked the candy out of his shirt collar and looked around, spotting the detective. 'What's the problem, Rip Van Tinkle, do you need to find the toilet urgently?'

'No, but I took one of my brown pills earlier so I haven't got long. Where's your old man?'

'Not around. Can you not harsh my style by turning up at school? It's embarrassing.'

'You haven't seen me be embarrassing yet,' Bryant warned, nonchalantly pushing back on the swing.

'Mr Cornell is at an investors' meeting,' said a tall black man in a trim dark suit and a very white starched shirt. 'Can I help you?'

Bryant twisted back and saw the gleaming black Mercedes limo parked outside the school gates. 'You the dogsbody?'

'I'm Bratling, the chauffeur. I'm here to pick up the boy. You're making him late. Didn't anyone ever tell you not to talk to kids outside schools?'

'I don't make a habit of it unless I'm thinking of arresting them.' He flicked open his badge case and waved it under the chauffeur's nose. 'Go on, hop it.'

'I'll be beside the car, Mr Cornell,' said the mindful Bratling, who did not want trouble.

'Your dad's flat is only five minutes up the road. Why do you need a car?' Bryant asked the boy. 'You should get some walking in occasionally; you're already a bit porky.'

'I'm nine,' said Augustine. 'I don't need to start exercising until long after you're dead.'

'Oh, a smart-mouth, eh? I'll cut a deal with you, Mr Big Brain. We'll take a short walk together. Bratling can follow behind us if he wants. And you can answer some questions for me.'

'What do I get out of it?'

'What do you get out of it? Nasty bruising consistent with a fall down the stairs if you give me grief. Spill the beans and I might decide not to lock you up. That's how being in the police works.'

'That's not fair.'

'I know. Fun, isn't it?' He reached out his fingers. 'Here, pull me out of this bloody thing.'

'No, I'm not touching you.'

Bryant remained motionless on the swing with his arm outstretched. Augustine looked around. His friends would be coming out of class any second now. Gritting his teeth, he grabbed Bryant's hand and tugged until the old man was upright. The tyre released him with a rubbery squawk.

Augustine looked horrified. 'Did you just fart?'

'No, you'll know when I do, believe me.' He beckoned to the chauffeur. 'Follow behind us, Bratling, I need to chat to Mr Cornell's son for a few minutes. You can run him home after; God forbid he should use his legs.'

'Why do you have a stick?' Augustine hopped along beside Bryant, who was moving too slowly for him.

'It's for beating children with.'

'How old are you?'

'A hundred and seventy. Give or take a month or two.'

'No, really.'

Bryant sighed irritably. 'I'm old enough to see, with some bitterness, that you will have a life filled with all the wonderful things I never had. Although you probably won't have as much fun.'

'Why not?'

'Because your dad is filthy rich and you're going to a school for the children of deposed dictators. You'll have everything you don't even know you want yet. And nobody should have all that, certainly not at an early age.'

'I haven't got everything I want. I'm not allowed to do loads of stuff other kids can do.'

'Like what?'

'I can't watch TV until I've done my homework.'

'Oh, poor you. How you must have suffered. If you're doing homework, why aren't you carrying any exercise books?'

Augustine gave him a hopeless look. 'What are *exercise books*?'

'Books for your homework.'

'We use online Dropboxes.'

'Oh.'

'You don't know what they are, do you?'

'Do you read any actual books?'

'What, paper ones? No, they're covered in germs. And they're boring.' They turned the corner with the Mercedes crawling behind.

'Of course. I was foolish to ask. What about London?'

'What about it?'

Bryant rolled his eyes heavenwards. 'Dear God, it's like pulling teeth. London: do you like it?'

'Yes, I like M&M's World and the Hard Rock Café.'

'That's not London, idiot child. *That* is London.' He pointed away from the school, across Charterhouse Street to Smithfield Market. 'Do you know what it is?'

'Some crappy old market.'

'It was once a big field of horses, and a cattle market. And there was a huge fair there, the Bartholomew Fair.'

'How long ago?'

'The twelfth century, when I was just a lad. You know what else happened there? Horrible, gruesome, grisly murders.'

For once the boy was stumped for a comeback.

Bryant pointed. 'Right on that very spot you see in front of you – yes, right there – they hanged at least sixty thousand people, some of them your age. They roasted them alive in iron cages, and put them in pots and slowly boiled them, and bored holes through their tongues with red-hot pokers, and attached horses' ropes to their arms and legs and dragged them apart, and stood heavy weights on them to crush their ribs and branded letters into their flesh and cut bits off their ears and slit their noses and nailed them to bits of wood and whipped them, but mostly they hanged them. And sometimes the prisoners' necks didn't break so their relatives paid extra to be allowed to hold on to their legs and *pull* them to death so it was quicker and they wouldn't suffer for so long. And sometimes the prisoners climbed the hanging scaffold in their pyjamas because the hangman was allowed to keep the clothes they died in, and they wanted to cheat him.'

Augustine pulled a face, and suddenly looked like a normal schoolboy. 'That's gross. Why were they hanged?'

'Oh, they'd broken the law,' said Bryant airily.

'How?'

'They might have stolen a handkerchief or a watch, or simply told a policeman a lie.' He let the thought settle. 'So you live with your mum?'

'Yes, but I visit my dad a lot.'

'You must like him.'

'He takes me to football matches and the zoo. I don't like Richard.'

'That's your new stepfather, I assume. You know what you can say to him when he annoys you? "Sod off, Richard, you're not my real dad, I don't have to do anything you say." Try that next time; it always works. Would you help out your real dad if he was in a jam?'

'Yes.'

'You've been staying with him quite a lot, haven't you? This Wednesday, for example.'

'Yes.'

'You're sure about that? How did you get there?'

'Bratling collected me. '

'There was no one else?'

'Just my IT tutor.'

'Maybe I should sit in on your lessons. I could learn how to open files without destroying them.'

'We're writing code.'

'I can write in code. So you were in your dad's flat.'

'Yes.'

'And your dad was there.'

'Yes.'

'He didn't go out the whole time you were there.'

The boy looked at him blankly, clearly struggling.

'Do you know where he went?'

'I'm not supposed to say.'

'All right, how long was he gone?'

'I don't know. I was watching *The Hobbit*.'

'Which part?'

'The second one.'

'The director's cut or the cinema version?'

'Director's cut.'

'Did your father leave before it started?'

'No, just after.'

'When did he come back?'

'Just after Smaug turned gold. He told me not to move while he was out.'

'So, he was gone for well over two hours. And of course you don't know where he went. Or you wouldn't tell me if you did. I respect that.'

'We're here,' announced the boy. Bryant looked up at the apartment building, a repurposed warehouse with a glass-and-steel frame bolted to its original Edwardian façade. 'Very smart,' said Bryant, checking the boy over. 'I'm sure you have a lot of online businesses to run, so I'll leave you now. Lay off the M&M's, try to get some walking in occasionally and maybe we'll see each other again.' He turned to the Mercedes. 'There you go, Bratling, safely home without any police brutality.'

'Wait.' Augustine called back to him. Bryant held up a finger, slowly pointing to himself in theatrical surprise.

'Do you really know a lot of weird stuff about London?'

'Do I—? Is Kim Jong-un having a bad hair day? I know stuff you wouldn't believe.'

The boy scrunched one eye. 'Like what?'

'Oh, ghosts, beheadings, bombings, tortures, mad killers. I could take you to a spot in the East End where they put prisoners in chains and let the river slowly drown them. They say you can still hear the chains rattling at high tide when it gets dark. Obviously if we did something like that we couldn't tell your father, and I'd have to bribe Bratling, but I'm a copper, we know all about bribes. What do you think?'

'OK – deal.'

'Shake.' Bryant spat in his hand and held it out.

Augustine looked disgusted. 'Do I have to?'

'It's that or blood.'

Grimacing, the boy shook the elderly detective's hand.

Got him, thought Bryant.

40

SPARROW WITH A BROKEN WING

Meera Mangeshkar arrived at St Thomas' Hospital on her Kawasaki an hour after the ambulance bearing Colin Bimsley had pulled into the emergency admittance bay. *Why did they have to bring him here of all places?* she thought. *At least the chances of running into him are—*

And by thinking that, she brought down the curse upon herself, because here was Ryan Malhotra, glossy black hair swept back, handsome in his hospital whites, striding down the corridor towards her with a puzzled look on his face.

'Meera, what are you doing here? What are you wearing?'

She glanced down at her black padded PCU jacket and boots. 'Oh, work clothes. I'm on duty. Are you doing the private clinic today?'

'Always on a Friday. It's going crazy on the public wards. There are as many police coming in as rioters.'

'You've just admitted a colleague of mine, Colin Bimsley. I need to find him.'

'Hang on.' He strode over to one of the registrars and exchanged a few words. 'He was one of two admittances.

The other was a female, unconscious; sounds like there's some confusion about her. A witness says they dived off Blackfriars Bridge?'

'That sounds like Colin.'

'Come on, I'll walk with you.' Ryan looked her over. 'It's great to see you, Meera. I thought we were going to get together on Tuesday night.'

'I'm sorry; it was all kicking off at work. Everyone's flat out.'

'That's what I figured. There's another big clash going on right now,' said Malhotra, pointing up at the Sky News footage on the screen they were passing: an overhead shot of the area surrounding the Bank of England. Police were baton-charging an angry crowd amid pockets of dense black smoke. A rolling caption read: 'London under siege: West End to be evacuated until further notice'.

'The mayor wants to bring in a second water cannon, but human-rights activists are trying to have them banned. We're all on standby. I'm surprised there haven't been more casualties. What's this case you're on – the burnings? It's all over the news. Is that why your colleague is in here?'

'I think he was trying to prevent another death.'

'Don't you people have back-up looking after you?'

'We're an independent unit, Ryan. If we call out back-up, we have to pay for it.'

'Meera, I was talking to your mother last night, and she's very worried about you.'

Meera stopped in the middle of the corridor. 'What were you doing talking to my mother?'

'She couldn't get hold of you so she called me. She wants you to switch to an administrative job, get a placement where you don't stand a chance of being hurt.'

'There are no admin jobs at the PCU. Everyone gets out there; that's the way it's structured. Besides, I would hate it.'

'I knew you'd say that, so I tried explaining to her, but she's not happy. I fought for you, I really did. She wants you to visit her.'

'Ryan, I don't want you to be the go-between,' said Meera angrily. 'Whose side are you on?'

He took her hand and patted it. 'I'm not taking sides, sweetie, but you can understand her point of view. After all, if we're going to be married . . . She was asking about the plans.'

'We haven't made any plans.'

'Yes, we have. I agreed with her that the wedding will probably have to take place in Mumbai.'

'What, just to please her crazy family? I've never even been to India, Ryan. I'm an Anglo and all my friends are here. They'd have to pay for their flights; it would make no sense.'

'It will work out cheaper for us, and if we're saving for a house we'll need the money.'

A look of horror crossed Meera's features. 'Wait, wait, who mentioned a *house*? When did we have these conversations?'

'I can't find you half the time; I have to have them with someone. Your mother thinks—'

'Who are you seeing, Ryan, me or my bloody mother? Look, I can't do this right now, OK? I know you mean well but your timing is lousy. I've got a colleague down and there's just too much going on.'

Malhotra smoothed his hair back into place. 'OK, I respect that. But it seems like you never have time to talk about the future. That's why I always end up having to talk to your mother.'

'Why do we have to *talk* about everything? Why can't we just get on with it?' she snapped.

'It's important to discuss our feelings. We need to know what we're getting into.'

'What, you think I'm not good enough for you?'

'No, of course I don't. It's just that you haven't met any of my work colleagues yet and—'

'They have to approve of me?'

Ryan was flustered. 'I didn't mean that at all. It's just that you're hardly ever around and, well . . . sometimes I think you only do what you want to do. And being married, it means sometimes you have to do things you don't like.' He held open the door for her. 'Your friend will be in this ward. I'll call you later, OK, sweetie?'

She ducked off before he could kiss her, thinking, *If he calls me sweetie one more time I'm going to punch him in the face.*

First she checked on Papis, who had received a cocktail of antibiotic inoculations to protect her against the pestilential properties of the Thames water she had swallowed. Joanna was expected to remain asleep for some hours, but was otherwise fine.

Bimsley was curtained off and hooked to monitors at the far end of the public ward. A dark bruise had blossomed across his right cheekbone and jaw. Meera tapped him awake and waited impatiently while he focused on her. He had been sedated into lugubrious slow motion.

'Hey, you.' He raised a hand, careful not to dislodge the drip in his arm.

'Hey. What happened?'

'I failed her, Meera.' His voice dragged. 'Joanna Papis. I gave her our number but she never called. We should have put surveillance on her.'

'You didn't fail her,' she told him. 'She's a bit bashed up and has torn the ligaments in her left wrist, but she's expected to make a full recovery. You did good, you nutter. What happened back there?'

'He poured petrol into her flat. She barely got out in time. I tried to get there.' Colin licked his lips. Meera gave him a sip of water. 'She headed to the bridge and went up on to the roof. There was no way back down, and he got to her. I saw her hit the water and went in after her but the current—' He started coughing.

'Don't try to talk.' She put the beaker back to his lips. 'Let me find out about your status, see if we can't get you moved to UCH.'

He tried to lift himself. 'I've already talked to the paramedics. There's nothing broken but I twisted my spine when I hit the water, so I have to be X-rayed before I can get checked out. I thought she'd drowned, Meera, a beautiful, bright young woman. What the hell is wrong with someone that they would try to do something like that?'

'There's a team at her flat,' Meera told him, 'but it's completely gutted. The fire spread to the second floor and nearly killed a kid. We'll get this guy. We have to.'

'Mr Bryant said there would be more deaths. That means he'll try again tomorrow, on Guy Fawkes Night. The Old Man says if we don't stop him by then he'll have finished whatever he set out to do and will disappear forever.'

'Then maybe we can find him first. Let's get you out of here.'

'What are you doing over this way, anyhow?' he asked. 'It's off your beat.'

'What do you think I'm doing? I came to see you.'

'You could have brought me something to eat.'

'Yeah, like I want to sit here watching you eat a chicken jalfrezi with a spork. How come you were so near the scene?'

'I'd been to the gym. Papis's call came through just as I was trying to get breakfast. Someone has to phone her parents.'

'Janice is doing it,' said Meera, rising. 'I'll go and have a word with the nurse.'

Colin's hand stayed her. 'Hang on here a minute longer.'

'Why?'

'Just because.'

'Look at you. You're a right madman, you know that?'

'I had to do it. You'd have done the same thing.'

Meera grunted. 'I'm not so sure I would have. You know how many people go into the Thames and never come out.'

'I don't understand,' said Colin. 'Why did he pick her?'

'She knew two of the victims,' said Meera.

'Maybe he thought they told her something.'

'If they did, she certainly didn't know what it was. Bryant's gone missing again, by the way.'

'What do you mean?'

'John has been trying to call him but his phone's switched off. His landlady says he left their flat early this morning. There's something strange going on that they're not telling us.'

'Meera, get this thing off me.' Colin plucked at the needle taped in the back of his hand. 'I can't wait around for a sign-off.'

'I can't do that, Colin. Let me get someone. Besides, you'd have to go on the back of my bike.'

'Fine, I get to put my arms around you.' He gave her an innocent look. 'Just so I don't fall off. Obviously.'

'Obviously. You're not a sparrow with a broken wing, OK? I don't feel sorry for you, so don't even try it.' But as she went to find a nurse she caught herself smiling.

41

UNTOUCHABLE

'Why am I always the last to know what's going on around here?' cried Raymond Land, hurtling out from behind his desk to poke his finger at the TV screen. 'Bryant's vanished again, the press are all over the street asking anyone in a uniform why the case hasn't been turned over to the CID, and the CoL are on the phone threatening to put the building into lockdown because they think we're behind the leak. I turn on the news and see one half of London trying to smash open the doors to the Bank of England and the other half panicking because they've just realized there's a serial killer on the loose. Questions are going to be asked in Parliament. People are terrified. I've got heartburn, tinnitus and blurred vision. Why did nobody show up for this morning's briefing?'

'Which question do you want answered first?' asked May.

'Work with me,' Land pleaded.

'We didn't get a chance to bring you up to speed. Joanna Papis was attacked at her home this morning. The press found out. They're already linking it with the deaths.'

'How? Why the devil would they do that?'

'It started with another arson attack. One of the fire-fighters must have spoken to a reporter. Janice will fill you in on the rest. I have to go.'

'Wait, wait, where are *you* off to?'

'I have to do something for Arthur.' John grabbed his overcoat. 'I won't be long.'

'You're in contact with him?' snarled Land. 'This is completely unacceptable. I cannot be expected to run this unit unless I know where you all are.'

'You never did run the unit,' rejoined May, 'it was always us.' *I shouldn't have said that*, he thought as he headed down the stairs.

He found Maggie Armitage anxiously awaiting his arrival in the reception area of the London Library, at the deepest corner of St James's Square. She was so sombrely dressed that for a moment he failed to recognize her. Usually the Grand Order Grade Four-registered white witch wore fabrics that appeared to have been stolen from a particularly lurid 1970s game show. Bryant joked that Maggie was the only object apart from the Great Wall of China that could be seen from space, but today she was dressed entirely in black. May followed her to the members' lounge and they seated themselves in a sequestered nook.

'I know you think I'm a flake,' Maggie began, 'but Arthur asked me to help him. That's why I'm dressed like this, so I don't stand out. I even covered up my tattoo.'

'I didn't know you had one.'

'Oh, yes, the family escutcheon, crossed spears, ducks rampant. It's a long story.'

'He's not supposed to break confidentiality on this,' said May. 'We're in enough trouble as it is.'

'I understand, but I'd have thought that by now you'd know I can be trusted.' She lowered her voice. 'I'm here because there's an original Dead Diary kept in a subsection of the Crace Collection.'

May knew that for decades his partner had kept daily files on those who died in suspicious or unusual circumstances in London.

'Arthur told me he originally got the idea from the volumes stored in the London Library's basement,' Maggie explained. 'He wanted me to find historical precedents, and sent me a set of guidelines.'

'You mean he actually figured out how to send an email?' May was astonished.

'No, of course not,' Maggie said. 'I asked Deirdre to pop over on her scooter. She was in the area visiting her spiritual chiropodist. She gets her bunions smashed up by lifewaves, swears by it. Arthur has a theory about your killer's psychology.'

'Do you know where Arthur is?'

'Oh, around and about,' she replied nebulously. 'There are angels looking after him.'

'I'm worried he's going to join them,' grumbled May. 'I suppose he told you he's not well.'

'Yes, he talked me through the whole thing, but right now he's lucid and he needs to get to the bottom of this while he still can.'

'You don't sound overly worried, Maggie.'

She peered over her bifocals and arched an eyebrow at him. 'I see very little difference between the living and the dead, Mr May. If Arthur passes over, I'll still be able to talk to him. This case of yours. You understand the significance of its occurrence between Samhain and Guy Fawkes Night, I take it.'

'I can see that someone might believe they could hide their crimes in this particular period. You know I don't have much faith in signs and portents, or supernatural conspiracies.'

'But fire and insurgence! Conflagration and rebellion!

This is a man who wants to take his place in history – *Catholic* history.'

'I have to be honest with you, Maggie, I don't know where you're getting this or what you expect to find in here.'

'Arthur has already followed this further than you realize,' she whispered. 'Did you know that Dexter Cornell is one of Kensington's biggest property tycoons, and that he's been illegally selling buildings to the Chinese by getting his lawyers to delist them from preservation orders? Cornell's not his real name. He's originally from Latvia. He was a small-town fire-and-brimstone evangelist who reinvented himself when he arrived here. We think he might be symbolically seeking to send his victims to hell, as others have before him.'

'Apart from the fact that you clearly have no idea how insane you sound, I'm Arthur's partner and *he* should be telling me this, not you.'

'He knows that you wouldn't go along with him.'

'Fine, but searching through the past . . .' He sighed wearily.

'It's a perfectly valid method of investigation,' Maggie insisted.

'I seem to remember that you also believe cats can sing.'

'If you're referring to Admiral Fanshawe, my feline conduit to the netherworld, I've retired him. A fine castrato, but all he ever does is go on about the First World War. I've a new spirit guide now, Fifi Lamour. I've started picking her up on my toaster. The only trouble is that it has to be turned on and she has a tendency to chat, so we get through a lot of bread.'

'Right, that's it.' May rose to leave. 'Good luck finding the spirit of Guy Fawkes, Madame Arcati or whoever it is you're looking for. Meanwhile, in the real world, we'll be sifting through the forensic evidence.'

'Fine, make fun of me,' said Maggie, looking hurt,

'but let me give you some advice, John. Just once, try seeing things from a different point of view. The term "bonfire"? It originated in Scandinavia, specifically Denmark. It marked the celebration of a battle victory, when the bodies of the dead were piled and burned. The fire provided warmth and light for the survivors' party. The word was used to describe any large celebratory fire, but there's another interpretation. The words "Bon Fire" are supposedly taken from Tudor history.'

'Maggie, this is pointless—'

'No, John, listen to me. In 1555, Edmund Bonner was the Bishop of London. Acting on his orders, over three hundred English men and women were burned at the stake for their faith, and because of Bonner's actions we now call them Bon's fires. The Sussex bonfire societies are gathering in the town of Lewes right now, ready for tomorrow night's celebrations. They're preparing to commemorate the burning of seventeen Protestant martyrs by Catholics in the reign of Mary Tudor. Have you checked the religions of those who have died?'

'Wait, you're saying this is about *Catholics and Protestants*?'

'There were a great many reprisals in the years that followed the dissolution of the monasteries,' said Maggie. 'But your murder plot could be more to do with sectarianism than mere anarchy. And it will end in Sussex tomorrow night, at the martyrs' site.'

'Did you tell Arthur this?'

'No, no.' Maggie shook her head so fiercely that her silver earrings jangled. 'He told *me*.'

'Know what I usually love about this job?' said Dan Banbury as he looked around Joanna Papis's fire-damaged flat. 'Crime scenes are never quite what you expect. But what am I supposed to do here?'

Senior Officer Blaize Carter turned on another of the

freestanding LED lights that had been set up in the only unburned part of the hall. The ceiling bulbs had all burst and the main window had split and was blackened with soot. The ceiling was still dripping. 'At least everyone else in the house got out alive. You can thank the Swedes for that.'

'What do you mean?'

'Cleaner design lines,' Carter explained. 'Curtains connect floors to ceilings, but they're out of fashion these days. Everyone wants blinds, and they're usually flame retardant.'

'You think it's the same MO as in De Vere's flat?'

'Yes, but this time he didn't come inside.'

'Why not?'

'Look at the place.' Carter banged the back of her hand on the wall. 'It's a cheap, badly finished conversion. He must have known it would go up in seconds, but it didn't burn as fast as he expected. There was a rubber mat inside the front door which caught most of the ignited fuel and reduced the spread. There's a reason why we don't see many premeditated arson attacks. British houses are too solidly built. I'm not saying they don't catch fire – they do if they're full of clutter and chintz – but it's hard to predict the patterning. It's usually a spontaneous crime.'

'Give me something to take back to the unit,' Banbury pleaded.

'It's going to sound kind of crazy.'

'You don't know the chaps I work for,' said Banbury.

'All right.' Carter folded her arms, regarding the blackened hall. 'My job is to figure out fires, not understand human nature. But when incidents like these are clearly connected, you get a sense of the person behind them. This guy can't bear to look at his victims. He didn't see Freddie Weeks, he covered Hall's face with tar and he masked De Vere. He blew up Frank Leach with a pressure device, and sprayed petrol under the door in here.'

'What does that mean?'

'It means that despite what you may think, your killer's got a conscience. He's after some kind of skewed justice. In his hands, fire *is* justice.'

'That's not just you talking, is it?' said Banbury. Fire officers were practical people who dealt with physical problems. Psychology wasn't their strong point.

'No,' Carter admitted. 'I had a discussion with your Mr Bryant. He called me a little while ago.'

He's like the Wizard of Oz, thought Banbury. *Even when he's not around, he's always behind the curtain working the levers.*

42

RABBLE-ROUSERS

'I came to you because I thought you might know all about sedition,' said Bryant.

'Bloody hell,' said Raymond Kirkpatrick, the ursine, heavy-metal-loving English-language professor who worked at the British Library. 'The only time you ever come and see me is when you want something you could just as easily google.'

'First of all, I don't use the Google,' retorted Bryant indignantly. 'And point B, your brain is filled with the sort of libellous rubbish that never makes it into history books. Either you're happy knowing that the repository of arcana that exists inside that hairy and somewhat unwashed-looking bonce of yours will go to the worms unused, or you'd like to help the police in their inquiries, the police in this case being my good self.' Bryant flashed his pearly false teeth in a rictus of a grin that he wrongly considered endearing.

'It doesn't say much for the science of investigation in the twenty-first century, does it? Come on then, you can buy me a cake and a coffee in the café, if it's not completely clogged up with cadaverous students poncing off the free Wi-Fi.' Kirkpatrick slipcased a pair of rare pornographic incunabula and took off his white cotton gloves. Together they pottered off to find refreshment, two more scruffy eccentrics in a neighbourhood where you could attract a dozen of them just by waving your arms about.

'I can no sooner give you a simple answer about the riots than I could milk a pigeon,' he warned, easing his ample rump on to a frail and spindly café chair. 'I don't understand people. We once had rebellion ingrained within our souls. Until the nineteenth century the only way we had of addressing our grievances was by holding violent protests. Unlike our American cousins, we have no enshrined constitution. Why else would we have set up safe areas in the capital especially for dissenters? We've always considered those in power to be intrinsically corrupt, but were we any better?'

He took a chunk out of a piece of fruit cake, scooped the crumbs out of his beard and flicked them at a passing student. 'You only have to look at the disrespectful language we used for bad behaviour. When a thief married a prostitute it was known as a Westminster wedding, and if you were vice admiral of the Narrow Seas, it meant you were drunk and had slipped under the table to piss in your neighbour's shoes. Hell, we even kept special stones for chucking at the rich called Beggar's Bullets. And the way we treated each other in the streets! We armed ourselves to the teeth and donned home-made body armour before venturing out. And when we did, there was always a chance that someone would present us with a Tower Hill play – that's a kick up the arse and a slap in the face. And in revenge we would 'make a lion of them' by sticking two fingers up their nose and pulling hard.'

'It's funny,' said Bryant, warming his hands around his mug. 'Foreigners think we're so polite. My father said you could tell a working-class Londoner because he smoked by holding his cigarette the wrong way around, with the tip facing in towards the palm so that he didn't get smoke in anyone's eyes. He always doffed his cap to anyone he considered to be a class above him, but thought nothing of giving his wife a clout.'

'Well, we've always been hypocrites,' said Kirkpatrick. 'But that's what being human is all about, isn't it? Holding opposing views in one's head and learning to calibrate them? We happily allowed certain parts of London to become havens of lawlessness. Did you know there were so many whores and thieves in Southwark that in 1181 we allowed it to become an official sanctuary for fugitives? If you stayed put there for a year and a day you got your "thrall", which meant you were safe from prosecution.'

A neatly dressed Japanese student approached them with a laptop cable in his hand, and politely pointed to the wall socket beside their table. 'No, bugger off,' said Kirkpatrick. He leaned forward once more, dangling his pastry fork before Bryant. 'And you know what? While we protected our felons, we accused bankers of devilry. The Devil public house at number 1 Fleet Street, where Ben Jonson used to preside over the Apollo Club, was a moneylender's and is now a bank. That area is technically St Dunstan's, and the sign above its door showed St Dunstan pulling the Devil's nose. During the Gordon riots our forebears stormed the Bank of England with pistols and burned the rich in effigy. We have a centuries-long suspicion of people who make too much money. Why? The French don't; the Yanks don't. *They* call it the American dream.'

'I've always found something appealing about the underdog,' remarked Bryant.

'Look, Arthur, you know me.' Kirkpatrick sat a little closer. 'I keep my head down in the library stacks, jack my headphones and listen to Megadeth, Judas Priest and Black Sabbath. I play songs like "Breaking the Law" and

"Living After Midnight" and agree with their sympathies. We once bred students with fire in their bellies. Now look at them, a bunch of downtrodden sheep chasing their careers. But this new spirit of street rebellion gives me hope. You only have to look back at the twentieth century to see how often ordinary people marched. The suffragettes, the anti-fascists, the Notting Hill, Brixton, Tottenham and Poll Tax riots, the Countryside Alliance march in 2002 – a middle-class movement, for God's sake – and the Stop the War march in 2003, part of the largest demonstration in the planet's history. These were all causes people felt so strongly about that they had to take to the streets.'

'But this one is different,' Bryant pointed out vehemently. 'Cornell isn't being vilified because he got found out, but because he didn't try hard enough to hide what he was doing. We hate dishonesty, but we *really* hate being taken for fools. And as long as the government continues to ignore that fact, the unrest will grow. Why haven't they made an example of him? They can't because they're in his debt. Waving the flag for British business and all that.'

'I suppose when you put it like that . . .' Kirkpatrick agreed.

'I need to let you in on a secret.' Bryant pulled a package from his pocket. He carefully removed two red rubber bands and unwrapped a layer of greaseproof paper.

Kirkpatrick leaned forward with interest. 'What is it?'

Bryant's hazy blue eyes swam up at him. 'This? It's a corned beef and mustard pickle sandwich. Alma makes them for me every morning.' He checked that his dentures were in place and took a great bite. 'I meant about the case. Suppose I told you that I have another theory about Dexter Cornell? Can I trust you not to tell anyone?'

'Who am I going to tell, Arthur? My wife? She's gone mad and only listens to her astrologer. My colleagues?

Most of them aren't aware of anything that's happened since the nineteenth century. And I haven't got any friends because I relax by going to Slipknot concerts. It's not exactly Glyndebourne. You're not supposed to eat your own sandwiches in here.'

'I can do whatever I like. I'm a policeman. The accepted theory is that the rioters discovered what Cornell was doing. But how?'

The professor gave a shrug. 'I don't know. Through a leak at the bank? Someone must have seen or heard something.'

'Cornell went to great lengths to ensure that nobody else in London knew what he was up to. The directors weren't in contact with his investors or their lawyers, all of whom signed NDAs. Cornell sent a covert message to his pals and covered his own tracks. He made damned sure there wasn't going to be a leak. Nevertheless, the news got out. So, I ask you again: *how*?' He stuck a finger around his plate and unbunged corned beef from his teeth.

'For God's sake, just tell me! You obviously think you know the answer.'

'The news could only have come from Cornell himself. Dog in the night-time, yes? And if that's the case, either he leaked it accidentally, which would be virtually impossible to prove, or he did it deliberately because he wanted to cover up something bigger. What could be bigger than anarchy in the streets? How about a series of murders?'

'So you really think it's Cornell—'

'Keep your voice down,' Bryant warned. This was a bit rich, seeing that he was speaking above the whistle of his hearing aid in a tone that was almost loud enough to blow the froth off Kirkpatrick's cappuccino, not to mention gesturing like someone trying to guide a 747 into its stand. 'A diversionary tactic, albeit the grandest one I've ever come across. If you want to hide a death, start a war. But the plan is backfiring on him because he can't control the public element, and each day it's getting more and more out of hand.'

'Then why don't you just issue a warrant for his arrest?'

'It's one thing to prove he's an inside-trader, and another to pin four murders on him.'

'Then what are you going to do?' Kirkpatrick demanded. 'You can't just wait for him to slip up while he gets rid of anyone who takes his fancy. Presumably you're watching him around the clock.'

'I didn't say he was carrying out these acts himself,' said Bryant smugly. 'He could be paying someone else.'

'It can't be difficult to keep tabs on a suspect in this day and age. Phone records, hard drives, all that stuff.'

'We can't access them.'

'Why not?'

'Because a City of London special investigation team has already made the seizures. It's not our job to arrest Cornell for fraud. We can only look at the entirely separate charge of murder. And we can't do that because their superintendent is Darren Link, the man who appointed us on the case to begin with.'

'Then you've been played for a fool, old chap,' said Kirkpatrick. 'Cornell's made sure that the City of London has subpoenaed all of his data for a different reason, which means you can't touch him. Very clever.'

'Don't worry,' said Bryant. 'I'll get him if it turns out to be the last thing I do. I'll do it for someone who, in another age, could have been me. I'll do it for Freddie Weeks.'

43

LOST

When he emerged from the British Library, Bryant found that a light mist had settled across the red brick forecourt.

In front of him was Eduardo Paolozzi's statue of Blake's Newton, the great bronze figure folded over as he mapped the world with compasses, but now it seemed to soften and dissolve in the nimbus of the nearest street lamp. Gingerly plotting his way across the yard and through the library gates, he heard the familiar sounds of Euston Road returning, but a terrible feeling settled over him once more as he failed to recognize where he was.

He could see the softly focused side of a double-decker bus advertising the latest Hollywood film, some kind of action nonsense that managed to look simultaneously violent and childlike, but as it passed and he read the number and the destination board, he could not understand where it was going. What was *High-Bury*?

The awful sense of panic grew. The rush hour was just starting, and if he turned to the right he faced hordes of strange faces looming out of the mist, Chinese tourists with cameras, Indian accountants with neat briefcases,

African ladies with shopping bags, Italian students with backpacks, all hurrying past on their way to – where? What was in that direction? He really had no idea.

Turning 180 degrees in the middle of the pavement and steadying himself with his stick, he watched their backs retreating and found others closing swiftly about him. They were annoyed because he was in the way, but were too polite to say anything.

He was somewhere near the unit, he was sure of that, but none of the shops or any of the street furniture looked familiar. He might have been standing beside a road in Estonia or Lithuania for all he recognized.

Think, you old idiot, he told himself, *you just came out of the British Library, you were with Kirkpatrick, whom you've known since the Mayfair Black Pudding Scandal of 1967. If you don't work this out you'll lose the unit and they'll put you away. You don't want that to happen, do you? What is the name of this street? Where are you?*

He took a step to the left, then another, and found himself on an alien corner, quite unable to cross the road. Frozen to the spot, he realized to his horror that there were tears rolling down his cheeks. A teenaged boy on a bicycle shot past him, bumping him and sending him into the road and on to his knees, directly in front of the oncoming traffic.

'Mr Bryant, you'll get run over if you're not careful!' Alma Sorrowbridge grabbed at his arm and yanked him back on to the pavement. He had never been more grateful to see his landlady. She was buoyed with half a dozen plastic bags full of vegetables, but still managed to hold on to him in the pedestrian tide. 'You look like you've seen a ghost. These roads are terrible. You have to watch out.' She picked up his fallen walking stick and handed it back.

'I got lost,' he told her simply.

She stopped and held his face. He had the vacant eyes of a trout seen through muddy water. She tenderly wiped his cheek. 'You silly old sausage, you're just around the corner from your office. Euston Road, see, St Pancras and King's Cross over there.' She waved a courgette in the general direction of the station. 'Where have you been?'

'I went to the library, but I got all turned around.'

'Do you have to go back to the unit tonight? I think not. You'd better come with me. We're just over the road from here, remember? Number seventeen Albion House, Harrison Street, Bloomsbury. It's your home, Mr Bryant. It's where you live.'

And then the world began to turn once more and he started to remember, so that everything he saw had meaning and memory attached to it, and he knew that the lapse had ended, and he prayed that it would never come back because whatever else happened, losing his place in the world was the thing that terrified him most.

'I can't get hold of him,' said John May. 'He's got his phone switched off, which usually means he's in a museum, a church or a library. No, I take that back. He always seems to leave it on during funerals.'

Longbright laid a hand on his shoulder. 'Then we'll handle this without him,' she said. 'He'll turn up when you least expect it. He always does. Raymond wants to sit in with us anyway.'

Darren Link was demanding a meeting with the unit's senior staff and had just buzzed the street-level intercom, giving Longbright no time to warn the rest of them. The plan was to keep him out of the detectives' office, where he might spot Bryant's marijuana plant, and steer him away from anyone behaving too oddly.

When the superintendent arrived at the top of the stairs, his features, severe at the best of times, had toughened to Welsh slate. 'The lights are out downstairs and there are two men tearing up the floorboards in your entrance hallway,' he said coldly. 'I'm amazed there hasn't been an accident.'

'That's just the Daves,' said Longbright. 'They're trying to open up the basement. We're planning to move the evidence room down there.'

'And there are mangy cats everywhere.'

'I thought we'd taken care of them. There should only be Crippen. Can I get you something to drink?'

Link took off his coat and hung it carefully. 'I'm here on a disciplinary matter. Let's get on with it.' He looked around for somewhere to sit, and shifted Longbright's stack of 1950s *Photoplay* magazines from a chair. His strangely fractured left eye, with its pale blue semicircle of pupil, turned his most casual glance into a stare.

He had met John May before and liked him enough to feel sorry for him, a talented detective who had ended up in a Jurassic-era unit like the PCU, a hangover from the days when coppers wore belted tunics and carried wooden truncheons.

Raymond Land arrived and attempted to shake Link's hand with an air of fake bonhomie, but was rebuffed. 'You didn't give us time to prepare anything,' he said mousefully.

'That was the general idea.' Link took in his surroundings. 'Where's your operations centre?'

'Right here,' said Longbright, all too aware that PCU HQ looked more like a badly run dry cleaner's than a specialist police division. She hoped he wouldn't wonder why there was a black sequined basque hanging from the coat stand, part of the Halloween outfit she had planned before the case had forced her to skip the party.

'Do you understand the term "core competence"?' Link asked them collectively.

'I think we had a conversation about that with your former public liaison officer, Orion Banks,' replied Land.

Link's appearance was as welcome as having an unshackled bear roaming loose in the office.

'Well, you've exceeded it,' said the superintendent. 'We set you one simple task, to run the ID and follow-up on Monday's DBM.'

'Which we did,' said May. 'I emailed you a full report the next day.'

'But you didn't stop there.'

'No, because we didn't think it was death by misadventure, and were awarded the case as it developed.'

'I'll tell you what you did.' Link swivelled his laser eye at each of them in turn. 'You trespassed into the Serious Fraud Squad's territory by going to see Dexter Cornell, and now he's lodged a legal complaint that could affect the outcome of an investigation that's been going on for the past two years.'

'We were following up a connection between Cornell and Freddie Weeks,' said May. 'It was an entirely valid—'

'We'll come back to that. I've been contacted by your unit GP, Dr Marcus Gillespie.'

May's heart sank. Link had been told about Bryant.

'Your partner has been diagnosed with a life-threatening illness, but instead of signing him off on leave you allowed him to continue working the case.' He relented a little. 'I know how close the two of you are. I'd probably be tempted to do the same if it was one of my mates. There've been four deaths in five days. What if any of them could have been prevented?'

'Arthur's been under constant supervision since the diagnosis,' May said. 'Taking him off the team right now would kill him.'

'And not taking him off might kill innocent people. Where is he?'

'He's continuing to make inquiries in accordance with the properly planned procedure of the investigation,' Longbright answered hastily, glancing at May.

'*You* have a planned procedure.' Link stared about at the room again, turning his entire body in the direction of his good eye. 'A properly planned procedure. So you have internal documentation you can show me.'

'We don't keep internal reports, for security reasons,' May told him. 'We prefer to hold face-to-face sessions with staff in the briefing room.'

'Let me tell you what's going to happen here.' Link's speech had the ominous clarity of a warning. 'You're going to close up the investigation immediately. You will make your final report and email it to me before you leave tonight. It's Friday evening. I don't want anyone working in here over the weekend, trying to patch things up so that it looks like you know what you're doing. This is the end of your involvement in this case. You can leave it to the CoL's specialist team and get back to whatever it is you normally do on Monday.' He gathered up his coat. 'And one other thing. I want you to place your partner on disability leave. Now. And get that hole in the corridor covered over before somebody kills themselves.'

His gaze finally fell upon Land, who swallowed nervously. 'I want you to know that I have nothing personally against the members of this unit. I'm aware that you've done some good work for us in the past. But you don't have the facilities to deal with something this serious. And I can't have you putting lives at risk.' His aura of menace grew as he leaned forward. 'Do I make myself quite clear?'

Land held his breath until he heard the main entrance door close, then went to the window to make sure that the superintendent was off the premises. 'At risk!' he snorted, his courage returning. 'Does he have any idea how many lives we've saved over the years?'

'I didn't hear you speaking up for us.' May was disappointed in his chief. What, he wondered, did it take to rouse Land to ire?

'What was I supposed to say? Do you even know where your partner is right now? Or has he wandered off into fairyland again?'

'He's working towards the resolution of this case,' May answered with dogged vehemence. 'Right now there's nothing in the world that matters more to him.'

'It's my fault,' moaned Land weakly. 'I should have seen this day coming. I should have forced him to retire instead of letting things come to a head like this. I should have recognized the signs years ago, when he started growing rhubarb on the roof of the Mornington Crescent office. You have to stop him, John.'

'I'm not sure any of us can now,' said May.

44

ABDUCTED

'What are we going to do?' Longbright asked.

'Call one last briefing,' said May, pushing open the door. 'If we have nothing at the end of it, we do as the man says and close it up.'

As the rest of the staff gathered in the common room, there was none of the usual sixth-form smut and japery that usually accompanied such assemblies. Word had got around about Link's visit, and an air of doom had settled over the unit.

'Do we *have* to do this?' asked Raymond Land as he walked in and found himself confronted by a row of depressed faces. He always tried to be the last to arrive in order to make an impression, but it never worked.

At the front of the room Bryant's freestanding blackboard had sprouted more coloured strings, chalk-lines, pins, clippings, maps, printouts and numbered photographs. He had been rolling it into each first-floor room in turn so that staff members could look for – well, nobody was sure what exactly, but it seemed to make him happier to have it trundling about.

'Mr Bryant thought it would help us to visualize connections,' said Fraternity, whose new horn-rimmed Tom Ford glasses had transformed him into a black Clark Kent.

'We're not on a Swedish cop show,' Land snapped. 'Sticking up a few pictures and drawing lines between them isn't going to help us solve anything.'

'I thought you were in favour of it earlier,' said May.

'I just don't see that it helps.'

'It always helped Arthur when we first started out.' May omitted to mention that his partner also labelled various items of crockery and cutlery from his kitchen, spreading them over the floor with exhortations to remember that all of the apostle spoons were suspects.

'Fine!' barked Land. 'We'll stare at Bryant's mobile scrapbook for a while and have a revelation, then maybe they'll turn us into a TV series with me shouting "Enlarge that image" at a computer instead of sitting alone in my office, filling in forms and fishing teabags out of the pot with the end of a dart. One day the public will twig that police work is as stupefyingly boring as any other job. I don't know why I bother. Go on then, bring us up to date.'

May stood up. 'OK, final recap. On Monday, October the thirty-first, we were brought in to identify a homeless man.' He pointed to a taped photograph of Freddie Weeks taken in a happier time, just after he had won a school running trophy. 'It seemed he had died from burns after being caught in crossfire between police and protestors outside the Findersbury Bank, Crutched Friars, near the Bank of England. However, we were able to revise that opinion after the arsonist was caught on camera checking out the site before he threw a Molotov cocktail. We couldn't identify him because of his Guy Fawkes mask. Yes, Colin, what is it?'

Bimsley lowered his hand. 'Where's Mr Bryant?'

'He's helping us sort something out. He seemed to

know that Link would close the case tonight, and asked me to present his thoughts. I know he's been calling some of you with instructions, and I'll come back to that.'

Land refolded his arms and unleashed a grunt of disapproval.

'On Tuesday morning, Glen Hall, a financial manager at Findersbury and collector of film memorabilia, was found dead in a burned-out shop in Brixton Market. He'd been lured there on the promise of buying a rare poster. He'd been tarred and feathered. All attempts to find out who rented the shop came to nothing.'

May indicated a further tier of photographs. 'On Wednesday, Jonathan De Vere, a businessman who funded IT start-ups, was killed in his Belgravia apartment. Mr Bryant says the M branded on his face was a traditional London punishment, standing for "Malefactor".

'On Thursday, Frank Leach, a loan shark, was killed in a highly localized bomb blast just off Leicester Square. This morning, an ambitious young accountant, Joanna Papis, was attacked in her Bermondsey flat, and nearly died after being pushed from Blackfriars Bridge. Miss Papis isn't able to add anything more to our picture of her attacker, other than to confirm that it's the same suspect in all cases, a strong-armed male wearing a Guy Fawkes mask, grey sweatpants, hoodie and black Nikes.

'So, connections.' He traced the coloured strings that ran between the photographs. 'Papis had met both Weeks and Hall in the pub where she works part-time. We have CCTV footage of her attacker outside her house. The same figure was seen leaving the first two crime scenes. The verger of St Mary's Church, Camden Town, is the only person to have seen him without a mask, but he wasn't able to give us anything usable, as they'd been standing in the church aisle without any lights on. Jack checked the CCTV files from the surrounding area and found very little, but somebody broke into De Vere's car after his death. We can't be certain it was the same person, but if it was and we go by that ID we can confirm that he's around six foot two, mid-thirties, bulked up, Caucasian.'

'I studied the stats and tried to see how else they would fit the victims,' said Longbright. 'Except for Weeks, who was younger, they were all roughly the same age, late twenties to early thirties, and all lived in Central London, although not in the same boroughs. Hall, De Vere and Leach had connections to banks.'

'Leach was a loan shark,' Renfield pointed out. 'Hardly a financial player. And that leaves Joanna Papis, who only knew two of them socially, and Freddie Weeks, who didn't know any of them.'

'Is that it?' asked Land. 'Is that the best you can come up with?'

'One other thing.' Longbright's crimson nail returned to the fourth photograph. 'Frank Leach changed his name when he arrived in London. He was born Jakob Tarnobrzeg, a Polish Jew. When she was eighteen, Joanna Papis got married. It lasted for less than six months, but after the divorce she kept her husband's name. She was born Joanna Smietana.'

'So what?' said Land. 'People change their names all the time.'

'Janice means we haven't looked at the group collectively under their original names,' said Meera.

'I can do that right now,' said Banbury, opening his laptop. 'Weeks. Hall. De Vere. Spell the last two?'

'T-a-r-n-o-b-r-z-e-g. S-m-i-e-t-a-n-a.'

He waited a moment, then shook his head. 'Anything else you can give me?'

'Try Insurrection Club London,' May suggested.

Banbury finished typing and sat back. 'Well, we've got Smietana and Tarnobrzeg, members of something called Riot. Let me check that.'

Everyone waited while Banbury scanned the pages.

'Riot, defunct website – hipster concierge service and nightclub in Shoreditch, now closed . . . Hang on. Oh, you'll like this.' He turned the screen around. 'Who's that?'

The *Evening Standard* headline read: '*The Banker Who Spent £37,000 on Champagne in One Night*'. The photograph showed Dexter Cornell in Riot nightclub, toasting his fellow financiers.

'That's enough of a connection,' said May. 'We're not shutting the case down.'

'We don't have a choice, John,' Land warned. 'You heard what Link said.'

'We're in with a chance. We keep a low profile over the weekend and make the building look as if it's shut by using the back door. And we bring Cornell back in for further questioning.'

'We can't—'

'We can, Raymond.' May was adamant. 'We'll cut a deal with Cornell to keep him quiet, but we have to speak to him.' He turned to the assembly. 'I'll talk to you individually about Arthur's instructions.'

As everyone went off to their offices, Land fussed around them like a chicken under a convoy of military trucks, trying to turn them back.

At 10.37 p.m. Longbright called Cornell's lawyer, Edgar Digby, and found him in a state of extreme distress.

Cornell had just been reported missing.

At 11.05 p.m., May, Renfield and Banbury arrived at Cornell's flat in Moon Street, Islington. Yolanda, the Spanish housekeeper, was sitting in the kitchen, and two local DCs were awaiting further arrivals from the Upper Street nick.

After the usual demarcation wrangle, May took control of the situation. 'Can you tell me what happened?' he asked the distraught housekeeper. 'What did you see?'

'The doorbell rang. It was just after ten, I don't know exactly. Mr Cornell went down to answer the door. He was very angry because Augustine was asleep—'

'Where was the boy?'

'In his room on the floor above. He's supposed to be at his mother's this week but she was called away on business. The poor boy never knows where he's supposed to be; their schedules change all the time. Mr Cornell didn't want him woken up.'

'Did he know who might be calling at that hour?'

'No. He gave me a look, like: "Who is this?" He went down, and I heard someone fall.'

'What, on the floor?'

'No, back against the door. I heard the door hit the wall. You can see the mark. I didn't go down because I'm thinking my job is to protect the boy.'

'You did the right thing.'

Yolanda pressed a hand to her bosom in a theatrical gesture of gratitude. 'I went to the window and saw Mr Cornell being pulled into a van by a man in a mask – you know, like the ones the protestors wear, Guy Fawkes. Mr Cornell looked . . . I don't know, like he was injured. The man sprayed something in his face.'

'I could smell hydrocarbon solvents on the way in,' Banbury said. 'Mace, maybe. I can get a sample from the front door.'

'You say a van,' said May. 'What colour? Did you get a look at the make or the licence plate?'

'I know the make, a white Ford Transit, my brother used to drive one; it had something about the gas board on the side, but I couldn't see the plate.'

'It won't be hard to track,' May told Banbury. 'There are cameras at the top of the road. Where is the boy?'

'One of the officers is sitting with him,' Yolanda said. 'He didn't know anything about it. He only woke up when the police arrived.'

'Dan, stay and give this place the once-over, will you?' May tapped Renfield on the arm. 'Come on, there's nothing we can do here.'

'Think it's our man?' asked Renfield, following him.

'Right now half the country hates Cornell's guts, and over a million of them have passed through the city wearing Guy Fawkes masks,' said May, heading for the door. 'Why wasn't he protected? Where the hell were his bodyguards, just when they were needed?'

45

PAGAN FIRE

Saturday morning loomed into view with the kind of ligneous dampness the city had only intermittently seen since the invention of the motorcar. The newly refurbished outer walls of King's Cross Station were already coated with the verdant velvet of emerald moss, and near its roof buddleia sprang in sturdy clumps, as it had since the terminus first opened in 1852. A frosty mist refused to unveil the passing buses, and barely visible cyclists risked their lives in the traffic at the corner of the Euston Road, where Bryant had become so hopelessly unmoored.

The dank atmosphere seemed to go hand in hand with the evening's planned festivities. Guy Fawkes Night always took place in such grim weather, as if English pleasures were to be endured rather than savoured. Summer was delineated by the sight of men huddled over rain-sodden barbecues, royal processions were surrounded by fields of umbrellas, and at the Lord Mayor's Show the mournful climate blew a raspberry at the pompous dignity of the city's leaders. But Guy Fawkes Night was usually the most inclement of all, and this one looked unlikely to buck the tradition.

Paradoxically, Arthur Bryant awoke in the smudged grey dawn with a perfectly clear head. He knew who and where he was, but not how he had got here. The hours after his meeting with Kirkpatrick were missing, as neatly as if someone had clipped around them and thrown them away.

He opened his bedroom door at his landlady's first knock, making her jump. 'Yes, what do you want?'

'I came to see how you were,' said Alma.

'Do you come bearing toast? Crumpets? Anything remotely edible?'

'I've made you some sandwiches for lunch, and I have orange sultana muffins in the oven.'

'Then kindly bring them with strong tea, scalding, as soon as is humanly possible.' The door slammed shut.

At least he's back to normal, thought Alma, hastily heading for the kitchen.

Bryant had indeed found his rightful place in the world once more, but was angrier than he had ever been in his long, eventful life. Always his own harshest critic, he was appalled by the encroaching failures of his body. Eyesight could be ameliorated, hearing artificially restored, hips replaced and joints scraped. Digestive acid, stomach ulcers, veins, lumps, bumps and blemishes were all easy to deal with, but this stealthy stealing away of time horrified him.

His mental fogs followed no line of reason, appearing and vanishing without will or purpose. If he tried to rationalize the process, noting that the fugue states seemed more precipitous before he slept and after he had eaten, he knew that he was merely attempting to impose a rational pattern over something perniciously unpredictable.

The answer, he decided, was to focus on the case and nothing else, so as soon as he had washed and shaved he called his partner. But before anyone could answer, the bedroom door opened and there May stood, immaculate as ever in his elegant cashmere overcoat and navy silk tie.

'What did Alma tell you?' Bryant asked suspiciously, after listening to his partner's account of the abduction. 'You have a look of supercilious concern about your features.'

'She didn't say anything,' May lied. 'I take it you're feeling all right?'

'If one more person asks me that this morning they'll feel the benefit of my Georgian toasting fork where they least expect it. I'm perfectly fine. About Cornell—'

'Oh, so you know.'

'Amazingly, I'm still following the case. What are the odds of his kidnapper being our killer? It sounds duff to me, turning up at his flat like that, as if one of the protestors has turned copycat.'

'That's what I thought,' May replied, glad that the conversation had moved to safer ground. 'It's not his MO. But that doesn't lessen the danger of the situation.'

'You misunderstand. I said it *sounds* duff, but then I thought more carefully and realized that might be what he'd want us to think. Cornell's a practising Catholic. He's the *coup de grâce*. It also crossed my devious little mind that he might have staged his own abduction to shift the blame elsewhere. Which would explain why his minders were nowhere in sight.'

'Whether he was abducted by the killer, a copycat or himself no longer makes any difference,' said May. 'We don't have control of the investigation. Darren Link has ring-fenced it because there's a legal problem with the CoL's ongoing fraud inquiry.'

'Rubbish,' snapped Bryant. 'He's taking it away because he can't allow us to continue. How would it look if two elderly men, a handful of unemployable obsessives and a team leader who's as effective as a charity-shop tea towel ended up solving such a high-profile case?'

'I'm not *elderly*,' protested May, nettled. 'I'm mature.'

'Like old cheese. I assume we're not going to look for Cornell?'

'No, Link's got his team on that and we don't have the resources. We need to stay on track.'

'He'll strike again tonight,' Bryant predicted. 'With the smell of gunpowder and charcoal in the air, how could he not want to be a part of it?'

'I was hoping you'd feel the same way,' May said. 'Perhaps you'd come with me to the unit.'

Bryant dragged a crumpled Hawaiian shirt from a drawer and assessed its wearability. 'Where else would I be going at this time of the morning? Can I get away with this look?'

Despite himself, May laughed. Bryant flashed a wide white smile, and in its sole appearance before a long day of rain, sunlight finally flooded the room. 'Alma!' he called into the hall, 'stay out of my things while I'm gone or I'll have your church closed down!'

'I guess we're back in business,' said May as he held open the door.

46

HIGH STAKES

'Mr Bryant, you're back.' Colin Bimsley was unable to suppress a smile. The energy in the room palpably rose.

'I haven't been away, you idiot,' said Bryant, rattling out his umbrella and spraying everyone with the run-off. He unwrapped his mummy-bandage scarf and looked about. 'That's a nasty bruise you've got. Did they have to pump your stomach?'

'No, sir, antibiotic jab.'

'A lucky escape. John and I once chased a burglar called Pearly Gates across Chelsea Bridge and he dived off the side to escape us. Died instantly. Not from the water, though. He went through the roof of a passing banana barge.' He looked around. 'There had better be some tea on, and make sure it's not bags: we need the hard stuff today.'

It was frustrating to hear about the search for Dexter Cornell without being able to take part, but there was nothing they could do without access, so the PCU team concentrated on the more mundane business of checking call logs and CCTV footage. But at least now they moved with a spring in their step.

Renfield called a mate of his and was updated about the abduction. The van that was filmed leaving Moon Street, Islington, was lost after it hit a poorly covered patch on the north side of the Balls Pond Road, and turned out to be unregistered. Police were now covering routes all the way to the Midlands and the east coast.

'I could tell them not to bother,' said Bryant, bouncing about in his old armchair in anticipation of refreshment.

'You know where he's heading?' asked May.

'I have a good idea.'

'Do you wish to share it with us?'

'You'll get annoyed if I do.'

'I'll be more annoyed if you don't.'

Bryant blew out his cheeks, thinking. 'All right,' he decided. 'It's one of four places.'

May groaned inaudibly. Then audibly. 'There are no straightforward answers from you, are there?'

'That depends.'

'All right, I'll bite. Why four?'

'He's a pyromaniac.' Bryant lost interest in the subject as Meera set down his tea mug. She goggled at the tropical shirt he had dragged over his long-sleeved vest.

'That's not an explanation.'

'Dear Lord, how much do you need spelled out? *It's Guy Fawkes Night!* There are a hundred and thirty-seven licensed firework displays in the Greater London area spread across the week but only three major events in Central London tonight: Paddington, Southwark and Russell Square. The rest are in places like Crystal Palace and the Royal Gunpowder Mills at Waltham Abbey. He won't go to those because he wants international attention. The three central displays are the largest in London and will all be filmed.'

'You said there were four places.'

'So I did. The fourth is in Lewes, Sussex, and it's the

biggest in the country. There are seven separate bonfire societies there, each preparing to burn Catholics and political figures in effigy tonight. But one is larger than the rest: the Cliffe Society. They own their own fire site and fireworks company. Tonight they'll sing their traditional song, "*Remember, Remember the Fifth of November*". Ahem.'

Pressing one hand to his chest, Bryant sang out in a penetrating off-key baritone:

'A penny loaf to feed the Pope,
A farthing of cheese to choke him!
A pint of beer to rinse it down,
A faggot of sticks to burn him!
Burn him in a tub of tar!
Burn him like a blazing star!
Burn his body from his head!
Then we'll say old Pope is dead!'

His singing voice was appalling. Once May was sure the cacophony had ended, he ungrimaced his face. 'Now that you've proven you couldn't carry a tune in a bin bag, what do you propose we do?'

'What does everybody want to do? Burn Dexter Cornell at the stake. We don't need to worry about the Central London displays.'

'Why not?'

'Because, old fruit, the Guy Fawkes Night event in Lewes is the only one that burns *giant* statues of unpopular public figures. And tonight it's burning the hated Catholic financial fraud Dexter Cornell in effigy, along with Vladimir Putin, Justin Bieber and the French. I already called them and got all the details. Cornell's going to be the centrepiece of the Cliffe Society display.'

'Then why don't we just alert their constabulary?'

'Because we can't trust them to catch our man in the act. I have a much better idea of what we're up against.'

May wasn't so sure. 'If we get it wrong, Cornell will die.'

'I know,' agreed Bryant cheerfully. 'We always work better when the stakes are high.'

'There'll be thousands of people there. I don't see how the two of us can begin to cover it.'

'We won't be alone. Meera, you can book train tickets for all of us. Charge it to the investigation. Raymondo can stay here and mind the store. We'd better leave Fraternity with him, in case we need data access.'

'We have no travel budget, Arthur,' May warned.

'Put it on my credit card. We'll be able to sign off whatever we like after this.' Bryant sounded confident. May studied his partner, puzzled. He seemed calm and free of confusion, utterly sure of himself, like the Bryant of old. And then he realized why: *I've seen that look before. The crafty old devil knows something he hasn't told me.*

'What time do you want to go down?' he said aloud.

'We have to be there by seven. See if there's a fast train. There's something I have to do first.'

'Can I come along?' asked May, thinking it would be better if Bryant remained partnered during the hours beforehand, just in case he had another bout of disorientation.

When Bryant looked back, May felt as if he could see into his soul. 'No,' he said firmly. 'I'll be perfectly fine. There's no risk attached, and it's better if I'm unaccompanied.'

'Can you at least give me an inkling of what you're up to?'

'Don't worry, it's to do with the case.' Bryant smiled enigmatically. 'It's about the canonical five of 1888.'

'Where's he going?' asked Raymond Land as he watched Bryant grab his battered scarecrow-hat and old overcoat from the stand.

'He's going to look for Jack the Ripper,' said May, as if it was the most obvious thing in the world.

47

A TOUR OF THE EAST END

'You,' Bryant said, looking around the room, 'get your coat on. A fine day like this, you should be outside.'

Augustine tore himself away from the plasma screen and lifted off a pair of £300 Sennheiser headphones. 'It's pissing down. Where's my father?'

'He's been called away on business. I won't have language.'

'What the hell are you wearing?'

'I don't know. It was in a drawer.'

'How did you get in, anyway?'

'Are you sure you're nine? You have the suspiciousness of a middle-aged man. Yolanda let me in. Go on, put that ridiculous game down. I'm sure your video-robot-thingies will still be here when you get back.' He looked about and sniffed. 'It would be nice to see a bookcase in here.'

'Books suck, and I can't go out,' said the boy, still getting over the shock of having to abandon his biowarfare attack on an alien planet in order to attend to an ancient trespasser in his playspace.

'You said you wanted to know something about crime in London, so I'm going to show you.'

'No, *you* said. You can't make me do anything; you're not my father.'

'I taught you that line; you can't use it on me.'

'Where *is* my father?'

'He'll be back later. And I can do anything I like because I'm a policeman. I've got a special pass that allows me to break the law.' He flashed his bus pass before the child's eyes and swiftly put it back in his pocket. 'I'm going to be in charge of you for the next couple of hours, so watch your lip. We're going to see something that will give you nightmares for weeks. Put a raincoat on, we're walking to the tube.'

Augustine looked horrified. 'I'm not allowed to go on the *tube*. Bratling says they're full of germs.'

'I'm sorry, I didn't realize you'd been born without an immune system. Bratling's off duty. Germs are good for you; they keep you from getting sick.'

'We're not even supposed to be in London. Have you seen what's going on? People are, like, getting killed and stuff.'

'During the Blitz nearly fifty thousand bombs and millions of incendiaries fell on London. Over sixty thousand people were killed, and for every one who died, another thirty-five were left homeless. People didn't leave then, so why should they leave now?'

'I'm nine,' the boy reminded him. 'I want to see ten.'

'Look, do you want me to show you where some really disgusting things happened or not?'

'Wait, I haven't taken my pill.' Augustine struggled into his Puffa jacket as Bryant headed down the stairs. Yolanda saw him coming and hastily backed into the kitchen.

'What's the pill?' asked Bryant.

'Ritalin. It keeps me calm.'

Bryant was disgusted. 'A boy of your age shouldn't be calm; he should be bouncing off the walls with excitement. Come along.'

'Where are we going?'

'Have you ever heard of Jack the Ripper?'

'Of course. He murdered some people a long time ago. I saw a programme about him.'

'This isn't on television, it's real,' the detective called back behind him as they left. 'I'm going to show you the truth about Jack the Ripper. Don't dawdle. Keep up.'

Bryant and the boy strode off through the rain, dodging the stalled and steaming traffic, fighting through the umbrellas that blossomed at the entrance to Angel station, heading down into the sooty bowels of the tube network.

Augustine had never been permitted to do anything like this. He sensed that somehow the rules of his life had shifted today, that his father was unwilling or unable to stop this strange policeman, and his nudging curiosity now turned into a hunger. He knew he was right to be afraid of Bryant, who was unpredictable, dangerous and quite possibly mad, but there was also a chance that he would share something that had always been missing: an adventure.

Over half of the tube map was off-limits. All of the central stations were shut until further notice. Bryant and the boy transferred from the Northern line (City Branch) south to the Hammersmith & City line, and managed to reach Aldgate East. Then they rose to the puddled pavements and started walking again. Makeshift tents had been pitched on almost every corner. When Bryant had used the Blitz analogy, he hadn't realized just how accurate it was. He paced ahead, dragging the boy through the chaotic throng, barely using his malacca stick, growing younger and more energetic by the minute.

Everywhere it seemed people were gathering in the streets, huddled together or handing out leaflets with singsong chants. Others were working in relays, sandbagging shops and building barricades. A siege mentality had taken hold. London had become a battleground.

He bought Augustine a collapsible umbrella from an Indian stall. 'That thing will last for exactly' – he checked his watch – 'three-quarters of an hour before it falls to bits. Stay close and keep your wits about you. Don't get separated. Let's talk about Jack the Ripper.'

'Have you ever been tested for mental illness?' asked Augustine.

'Funnily enough, yes, and quite recently. First of all, I have to explain something. There was no Jack the Ripper. He didn't exist. Try not to look so surprised; it makes you appear simple. There were only the Whitechapel murders and a man they called Leather Apron, and we will never know who he really was because at the time there was no forensic evidence.'

'What's forensic?'

'Do they teach you nothing at school?' He pulled the boy clear of some running Indian teenagers. 'Forensics is the scientific collection of criminal evidence, and in 1888 there was no such thing. What's more, every bit of information that was gathered about the killer by the police has been examined in minute detail, and there are no more clues left to find, so we can only make guesses. Oh, they've studied the DNA on a shawl that miraculously survived for nearly a hundred and thirty years without once being washed, and have come up with yet another supposed culprit, but nobody will ever really know the truth. Over four years there were eleven murders, but only between three and six of them were committed by the same person, and it's generally agreed that there were five victims by the same hand. We call these the canonical five.' He grabbed the boy's shoulders and physically turned him. 'Stop here. Turn around. Look at these buildings.'

They were now on Hanbury Street near a boarded-up

Cash & Carry store, outside the only surviving properties from that time.

'Across the road,' said Bryant, pointing at rain-sodden brickwork, 'in the back garden of number twenty-nine, a short, fat, ugly, forty-five-year-old woman with two missing teeth was found lying on her back with her throat slashed from left to right and her stomach slit open to the chill night air. Her name was Annie Chapman, and her guts had been pulled out of her abdomen and thrown over her shoulders like a bloody scarf. Parts of her insides were missing, and were never found. And all this happened just a few feet from where you're standing. It was the day after the funeral of the first victim, and the public became terrified.'

Augustine's eyes widened as Bryant talked, dragging him from one spot to the next, gesticulating wildly, painting pictures in the air, now throwing his arms wide, now thrusting his hands at the startled child, bringing alive the awful history of the area.

'The Ten Bells,' said Bryant, pushing open the door of the pub on Commercial Street so that Augustine could see inside. 'It used to be called the Eight Bells, but the nearby church added two more to its chimes, and they could be heard inside the pub. Annie had a drink in here on the night she was brutally slaughtered. How old did you say you were?'

'Nine.'

Bryant thought for a minute. 'Hm. Old enough. Hang on here for a minute. Whatever you do, don't move.' He returned with two glasses of bitter, a pint for himself and a half for the boy. 'When I was nine my father took me for my first beer. I think it's time you had yours.'

Augustine looked uncertainly at the frothy dark glass. Bryant made a sipping motion. 'Go on, try it.'

Augustine tipped the glass to his lips and recoiled sharply, thrusting out his tongue as if it had just been dipped in vinegar. 'That's totally disgusting.'

'Everyone says that at first. You have to keep going, at least until you've drunk half of what's in your glass. Think of it as an initiation test. But hurry up, there's a lot more to see and do. We have to get to the notorious "double event" – two murders on the same dark night. You must imagine these streets without electricity, and only flickering gas lamps, damp and mist and very bad smells.' Bryant's fingers rippled before the boy's face, conjuring up the scene. 'No trees anywhere, just factories and slums, pubs and doss-houses. After that we'll look at the final victim and how she was found without her heart.'

Augustine belched as he downed his beer and followed Bryant's indicating hand like a hypnotized hen. Then they were off again, lolloping through the downpour, over the roads and between the market stalls, the boy intoxicated less by his half of cloudy warm ale than by Bryant's ability to conjure terrible blood-soaked images from the wet grey air. The shouting, mutinous mobs around them only served to return the area to its dark past.

Bryant brought them to a stop beneath a dripping railway arch and seized Augustine's collar. 'So you have seen where the Ripper walked and hunted his victims, if indeed it was just one man,' he said. 'For the truth is, we know nothing at all about him beyond the fact that he was probably left-handed and literate enough to write a letter. All the crazy people who are convinced they know who committed the murders, all the suspects, all the clues from the writing on the wall to the note the Ripper sent the police, they all amount to nothing. And that is why he is remembered, not for what we know but for what we *don't* know, and that is why we are detectives, because we always want to finish the picture. Every case is an unfinished picture, and only we can find the missing pieces. And now I must tell you the most terrible part of the Ripper's secret.'

He pulled the boy closer, Long John Silver to Jim-Lad, Magwitch to Pip. 'The legend of Jack the Ripper has been kept alive all these years,' he whispered. 'There are nearly four thousand books on the subject. The Ripper breathes and walks almost as if he is still flesh and blood, when he should have been allowed to die long, long ago. His victims were desperate, poor women who could not earn enough to find a bed for the night or a hot meal. Their skin was grey and saggy from a diet of potatoes. They tramped the streets for twenty hours a day, in rain and snow and fog. They were beaten up and treated cruelly for doing nothing more than trying to survive in a mean world that didn't care if they lived or died.' He poked Augustine in the chest. 'Once they were like you, lad, young and full of hope for the world, but unlike you they had nothing beyond a few ragged clothes and their failing bodies. And instead of treating them with kindness and respect, men bullied them and stole away their only precious possession, their innocence, and after they were dead the men – and women – still exploited them, displaying photographs of their ruined lives, writing about the Ripper as if he was intelligent, a surgeon, a member of royalty, an artist, as if he was more worthy of attention than his victims. We raise him up in films and books and TV shows, almost as if he was something to admire. But he wasn't, Augustine. He was just another cruel, evil bully only worthy of our revulsion and disgust, because he exploited the weak. And this is true of all terrible crimes; it's the victims who must be respected and honoured, not the murderers, and that is why I do my job, and will continue to do it until the day I die. Do you want some crisps?'

Augustine was crying.

'Oh, come now, it's just a bad story that has lived too long. There's more kindness in the world than harm. I honestly believe that to be true, and so must you. Look around here at all these people. They want to see good things done, not bad.' Bryant scuffed the boy's tears away and stopped outside an Indian restaurant. 'I'd take you for a Ruby Murray but that might be pushing it. Let's just get some poppadoms.'

The rain had stopped. As they trudged back through dirty puddles and litter towards the tube, Augustine crunched his way through a bag of the savoury discs and they talked of other things: his father and mother, his school, his friends and holidays.

'Tell me one thing,' Bryant said as they neared the tube and he knew he was running out of time. 'You told me your father was with you on Wednesday when I'm pretty sure that he wasn't, and I understand that. You love him, and he only asked you one small favour. Most sons would have done the same thing. But why do you think he asked you to do it?'

Augustine waited until he had swallowed the last piece of poppadom, then balled the bag and looked around for a bin.

'It's OK, you can chuck it into the street,' said Bryant. 'Just this time.' With one end of Brick Lane barricaded by burned-out cars, a paper bag wasn't going to make much difference.

'I think he was doing something for work,' said Augustine finally. 'He wasn't doing anything bad.'

'You're sure of that?'

'Yes.'

'Then I believe you. I believe you're a man of your word.'

'He never tells me anything about his job. Except for the trips away. He's always travelling, and he doesn't like it.'

'He tells you about the trips?'

'Only bits and pieces. Like the Russian taxi drivers, how they drive like crazy, stuff like that. And how the Chinese can't play football.'

'They can't? I didn't know that.'

'No,' said the boy matter-of-factly. 'After his last trip he told me the Chinese won't play ball. I told Uncle Vernon and he laughed. He's not my real uncle, he just comes to the flat sometimes.'

'You told Vernon *Harding* that your father said the Chinese won't play ball?'

'Yes. He didn't know that, either.'

Well, thought Bryant, *there you have it. A new name, and a very well-known one at that. The source of the leak. Out of the mouths of babes.*

'Come on,' he said, 'let's get you home before the rain starts again. Everything that has happened today is a secret between us. Deal? Hang on.' He poked about in his pocket and picked the fluff from a Mint Imperial. 'Open wide,' he instructed, flicking the mint into the startled boy's mouth. 'We can't have you reeking of booze when your dad comes home.'

As the boy sucked the sweet there was a sudden clap of thunder. Bryant looked down to find that Augustine was tightly holding his hand. For one flickering moment it crossed his mind that having a son might not have been the worst thing in the world.

48

HEADING SOUTH

He had bought the second-hand hospital trolley online, but had not thought to check its measurements to make sure that it would fit in the back of the van. It did but only at an angle, so he loaded Cornell on to it and held his wrists and ankles at the sides with plastic cable ties, and gagged him with the torn-off sleeve of an old shirt.

He'd worried that the sedative was too strong, but just as he was trying to lift the gurney into the vehicle, Cornell began to wake up. He couldn't move the damned thing with all that weight shifting about, so he was forced to remove the gag and punch the banker in the face until he understood that he had to be quiet. Cornell had been thirsty now and drank his water greedily, not realizing that there were more sleeping pills in it.

It was another twenty minutes before they properly took effect. As soon as Cornell was under, he loaded the trolley into the van, nearly putting his back out by doing so. To take his mind off the job, he thought about what was happening across town.

In the Square Mile the protests had swelled to five times the number of the previous weekend's attendances.

With no more police to draft and only the army as a last resort, the riots were tipping over into full-blown revolution. The City was no longer being described as a powder keg. It had been ignited by the news of the others he had killed.

After it was all over he could disappear, drop back into anonymity and watch the results from the sidelines. The anarchy would bring collapse. And from the ashes of the old order something new would arise.

After Bryant dropped Augustine Cornell back at his father's apartment, he headed to the PCU via a practice in Harley Street, where he visited Wendy Barnestaple, a psychotherapist recommended to him by Maggie Armitage. Barnestaple ran a private clinic on two mornings each week, but had agreed to see the detective on a Saturday at short notice. Seated in a frosted-glass box, her feathery blonde hair contrasting with a no-nonsense grey business suit, she seemed the last person in the world that Maggie would know.

'So, I finally get to meet the famous Arthur Bryant,' she said, offering him a seat in the consulting room. 'I've heard a lot about you from our mutual friend. She's a fascinating case study.'

'You mean you treat her?'

'As an NHS outpatient. I do one day a week at UCH. I suppose you know she had a lot of problems.'

'Give me a confidential diagnosis – one professional to another.'

'Extreme passive-aggressive identity dysfunction, a borderline histrionic stimulus-seeking exhibitionist.'

'She's a very kind woman with a heart of platinum,' said Bryant defensively.

'Well, let's just say that's what *you* see. I read the notes you sent over. You know I have no background in criminology.'

'I just want a gut reaction,' said Bryant. 'You've read my notes on him. What do you think?'

'You're not on the right track.' Barnestaple donned a pair of miniscule reading glasses and studied the email he had sent her the day before. 'This isn't the behaviour of someone who acts with careful deliberation. He's angry at the world but ineffectual, an opportunist who firebombs a bank that's already been receiving media attention. In the process he accidentally kills. He watches the news coverage, feels more empowered, attacks again, this time hoping to earn public points for tarring and feathering a financier, but he chokes his victim to death through sheer ineptitude. His sense of self-esteem becomes exaggerated, and so does his desire to show how cruel he can be. It's not enough to kill the next victim – he brands him, too.'

'Then how does Joanna Papis fit into his plan?'

'She's the odd one out. Perhaps he has personal, sexual reasons for going after her.'

'But you do agree that he'll act again tonight?'

She folded the email with a little too much precision, setting it aside. 'He must, but the target could be somewhere in the City, as near as he can get to the Bank of England. He must be seen by as many cameras as possible. He has a narcissistic personality disorder, a need for admiration. His perceptions are warped. I imagine he's uncomfortable socially, avoids personal responsibility, lacks any empathy for his victims. And there are classic signs of paranoia; he grandly sets out to undermine the status quo but can't look his victims in the eye. He seeks evidence of hidden schemes. He has the unshakeable conviction that he's acting for the right reasons.'

'And after tonight?' asked Bryant. 'Do you think this will be the end of it?'

'Certainly not.' Barnestaple checked her watch. 'His personality won't be changed by what he's done. If anything, his actions will reconfirm his beliefs. He may only just be starting.'

'You have to go,' said Bryant.

'I'm taking my daughter to the country,' she explained. 'It's not safe for her here any more.'

'One last thing,' said Bryant. 'Do you think he created all of this? The riots?'

'I'd say they created him.' The psychotherapist rose and shook his hand. 'I wish you luck. I'm not sure that what's started will be easily stopped.'

It won't stop until someone stops him, Bryant thought as he headed out into Harley Street looking for a cab. There had been a state of discontent about the behaviour of City bankers for the past few years. He was sure that the killer had been waiting for it to turn into something more so that he could use it to cover his actions.

We have to catch him without any more outside help, he decided as a cab splashed towards him. *Whatever happens, it has to end tonight.*

'You're what?' asked Raymond Land again, hardly willing to believe his ears.

'We're all going to the firework display in Lewes tonight,' said Meera. 'Mr Bryant asked me to book train tickets.'

'While you're at it, why don't you book the royal box at Covent Garden Opera House? Or the Bolshoi Ballet?'

'He didn't say anything about the ballet.'

'Well, I suppose we can be grateful for that. What are we all supposed to be doing in Lewes?'

'Not we, sir; he wants you to stay here with Fraternity.'

Land felt the inexplicable chill of not being invited to something he didn't want to do in the first place. 'If you lot are going to get the unit even deeper into trouble, I should at least be there to try to stop you.'

'The idea is that you'll have data access from here and will be able to help us if we get into a situation.'

'Always the bridesmaid.' Land sighed. 'I don't suppose there's any point in me trying to stop you?'

'I've already booked the tickets, sir,' said Meera, marching out of the office.

'Arthur, do you honestly think it's a good idea to come with us?' asked May.

'How can I not?' Bryant was stuffing things he needed into an old leather school satchel. 'I'm bringing my teddy bear. Don't try to stop me.'

'When did I ever?' May said with an air of resignation.

'Cornell told his son that the deal with the Chinese had fallen through,' Bryant explained as they crossed the concourse of Victoria Station. 'He didn't mean to, he just mentioned something in passing. The boy misunderstood and unthinkingly told a man called Vernon Harding.'

'I've not heard of him,' said May. 'Who is he?'

'Harding is a leopard who never changed his spots. He's a government bank adviser who owns several cable channels, but he came from an old-school Fleet Street family. He started out on *Hard News*'s business magazine. He instantly understood what the boy meant when he said his father told him the Chinese wouldn't play ball, and called his old pals in the newsroom. A classic scorpion-and-frog move. It makes me think that the answer's been staring me in the face all along.'

'You mean you know what's behind all this?'

'I have a very strong idea but no proof as yet.' He looked around the concourse. 'Are we all together?'

'Colin's gone to buy Cornish pasties for everyone. It may be a long night.'

'Thanks, I think I'll stick to the coronation chicken

sandwich Alma made for me. Leaving them overnight in my Tibetan skull seems to ripen them. Come along, we don't have long.'

The train was crowded with families and groups of teenagers heading to Lewes. What had once been just another odd English commemoration in a small country town was now a major event in the social calendar for many party-loving Londoners. May led the way, but when he turned around his partner had already wandered off.

'We can't go in there,' objected Bimsley, as Bryant bagged the best seat in first class.

'You've got your ID on you, haven't you?' said Bryant. 'And he could be on the train, couldn't he? So it's police business. See if you can score free teas and biscuits from the buffet car once we get going. Throw your weight about a bit.'

'Do you have anything resembling an actual plan?' asked Renfield, sitting himself beside Longbright as the train pulled out of the station. 'It would be good to know what we're supposed to be doing down there, in a crowd of tens of thousands. What the hell is it all for, anyway?'

'Guy Fawkes tried to blow up the King and Parliament on November the fifth, 1605,' Bryant said. 'You know that much, I assume.'

'Amazing as it sounds, I did go to school.'

'The following year an act was passed proclaiming that the discovery of the Gunpowder Plot should be held in perpetual remembrance, and that the day should be a holiday in thankfulness to God "for the deliverance and detestation of the Papists". Well, in 1679 there's a record of the Pope being carried through the streets of Lewes in effigy and burned in a bonfire. Typically, the whole thing quickly got out of hand after gangs called Bonfire Boys set fire to the local magistrate—'

'You mean the magistrate's court.'

'No, the *magistrate*. So the town formed bonfire societies. Each one has its own costume. The members of the Cliffe dress as smugglers and still burn giant figures in effigy. Ever see that film *The Wicker Man*? It ends with a policeman being burned alive inside a giant pagan figure. Bit of a spoiler there.'

'You think our killer is somehow going to get Dexter Cornell trussed up inside his own effigy so he can burn him alive while the world watches?' scoffed Renfield. 'You're barmy.' Remembering Bryant's current problems, he felt compelled to add 'sir', but the detective didn't take offence.

'He won't be burning Cornell alive, the world will. That's the difference. The public has already spoken. Cornell's the most hated figure in the country. It's a good day to bury bad news.'

'What about the other victims?' Longbright asked. 'Where do they fit in?'

'Most had a connection with doubtful financial practices, but I think they hurt him personally. And he saw a way of taking revenge while furthering his own anarchistic aims.'

'What about the practical elements of this?' Banbury asked. 'Aren't you going to talk to the local constabulary at all?'

'Only at the very last minute,' Bryant said. 'If we do it any earlier they'll have time to check on our authorization, and we can't allow that to happen.'

'We can worry about the form-filling after we've got him in custody,' May agreed.

'All this is supposing that everything goes according to plan.' Banbury sat back in his seat, trying not to let his anxiety show.

'I warned you all at the outset that this could be dangerous,' said Bryant.

'Yes, but I assumed we'd have someone watching our backs,' Banbury countered.

'We'll only have each other,' said May, bringing an end to the conversation as the train raced over the rainswept South Downs towards Sussex.

49

RURAL INFERNO

As they alighted from the train and followed the dense, slow-moving crowds from the station, they could hear the drumrolls and see the flickering red flares of Lewes High Street. Lit by the first of the bonfire parades, the sifting rain appeared to be composed of crimson needles. Even from this distance the noise was incredible, a pulsing beat interspersed with spectacular explosions.

'Blimey, what's that racket?' asked Bimsley, turning his collar up.

'Drummers and kids throwing bangers into the crowd,' said Bryant. 'Every parade has its own style. Most of them carry anti-papist banners and drag portable bonfires with them along the route.'

'So you've done this before?'

'Many times. It can get quite disorienting out there, so stay close. We'll avoid the main parade path and go to the Cliffe bonfire field.'

Bryant knew that the bonfires would take place whether the rain stopped or not. Already, camera crews would be assembling in the fields around the town, getting ready to cover the biggest pyrotechnic display in the country. This year, more crowds than ever were expected. The full list of public figures to be burned in effigy had a distinctly financial tone; it included caricatures of the prime minister, the head of the World Bank and the chairman of the Bank of England.

As they passed the tail end of the parade, May looked back and saw that the torchlit procession extended the full length of the high street, a fiery scarlet ribbon of road that dipped through a valley between low hills. The buildings were awash with crimson firelight. The view that presented itself was apocalyptic; families in scarlet fox masks hammered drums while Zulu warriors marched beneath sputtering flambeaux, their burning carts releasing clouds of glowing firefly cinders, an anti-papal procession that seemed more like a pagan vision of hell on earth.

Banbury downloaded the map of the procession route on to his mobile and led the way through the back gardens of the town, out into the darkened fields. Here the security marshals had yet to admit the crowds, so they were able to gain clear access to the firework site.

'Nobody warned me it was going to be muddy,' Longbright complained, picking her way over the sludgy furrows.

'You're not much of a country girl, are you?' said Renfield. 'You shouldn't have worn heels.'

'I *always* wear heels. And I've been to the country,' Longbright insisted. 'I went to that crime-prevention conference last year.'

'That conference was in Finchley,' said Meera, stamping through the mud in her non-issue army boots.

'It's Zone Four on the tube. Practically the North.'

May returned from talking to one of the yellow-jacketed site marshals. 'He says the effigies are being brought out right now. There's no chance that anyone can get at them or doctor them in any way. They've been locked in a barn since they were towed out here. Are you sure you've got this right?'

'We have to check every one of them.' Bryant panted with the exertion of crossing the field. 'I can't go any further. Colin, can you and Jack get a look inside the Dexter Cornell statue?'

'Sure thing, boss.' Colin led the way towards the distant tarpaulins covering the statue group.

'Are you OK?' May asked.

'I'll be fine once I get my breath back,' gasped Bryant, coughing. 'I wouldn't mind a sit-down, though.'

'Come on, let's get you over to those hay bales.' May took his friend's arm. 'It's drier under the trees. Colin and Jack can handle this. You really don't need to be here.'

'I want to see him caught,' said Bryant doggedly.

'And you will do, tonight.'

'Well . . . I hope so.'

'What's the matter?' May had seen this sudden change of mood before.

Bryant wiped the raindrops from his head. 'I've missed something. If only I was thinking more clearly. My memory comes back after each attack, but there always seems to be a little less of it. I thought of something in the night, but now it's gone.'

'Then we'll just have to do the best we can.'

May tried to see Renfield and Bimsley in the dark, but they had vanished. A fresh squall of drizzle rippled across the field, rattling the overhead branches and prickling the back of his neck.

Bimsley reached the covered statues first. Another of the marshals, a boy no older than sixteen, tried to stop him from passing through the perimeter fence, but backed away on sight of the police badge. Across the great field a train raced along the line of the embankment, its yellow windows passing like the pages of a flick book.

The smallest of the tarpaulin-covered effigies was at

least fifteen feet high. 'You're sure no one's been near these?' Bimsley asked.

'Yes, sir, someone's been with them ever since we used the tractors to get them out here.'

'Hang on.' Renfield handed Bimsley a torch. The beam exposed the grotesquely distorted face of Vladimir Putin dressed like Mars, the god of war, wielding a flaming sword.

'Are these things hollow?'

'They're chicken wire and papier-mâché over a wooden frame,' said the marshal.

'Where's Dexter Cornell?'

'Who?'

'The city banker, the inside-trader.'

'Oh, him. At the back. The really big one. He's been made up to look like the Devil.'

They found their way to Cornell. 'Jack, can you give me a leg-up?' Colin called. Renfield lent a broad shoulder as Bimsley first knelt, then stood on the laughing figure's folded arms, wedging himself between them as if he was climbing a rock face. 'Do these things have any openings?' he shouted down.

'There's a door in the back,' said the marshal. 'In case they don't catch fire properly we load them with special starter packs of fireworks. They don't go in until the last minute.'

Bimsley clambered around, looking for the hatch, and found a four-foot square held shut with loops of wire. Untangling the ties, he wrenched at them until the door came open. The torch beam revealed nothing inside but wooden prop-beams. 'It's empty,' he yelled.

'He must be waiting until it's on the pyre,' said Renfield. 'Hey, kid, how big are these starter packs?'

'They're pretty big.'

'Big enough to hold someone inside them?'

'Yeah, they're the size of coffins.'

'That has to be it,' Renfield said. 'Colin, get down here. We're going to stay with this thing until it burns.'

While he was waiting for the DC to descend, Renfield walked back towards the darkened storage barn. As he reached it, he realized that the vehicle parked in the mud ahead of him was the gas board van that had been seen leaving Moon Street, Islington – the one with Cornell inside.

Back in King's Cross, Fraternity DuCaine found himself sharing an office with a disconsolate Raymond Land.

'What do they honestly think they're going to find in Brighton?' asked Land.

'It's Lewes, a town outside of Brighton,' DuCaine explained. 'That's where they're burning the effigy of Cornell.'

It had been a long time since Land had seriously followed the working details of an investigation, but he made an effort to do so now. He looked back at the images of the four victims, their dates of birth, their CVs and family histories neatly printed on to cards, their connections woven together with lengths of red and blue wool. Surrounding them were the components of their fates, each murder site a grim memento mori of a life cut short. Handwritten on loose pages were other details: the jobs they held; the pubs and clubs they visited; the restaurants they frequented; the families they lost. To these, Bryant had added a still from *The Wicker Man* in which the star was being burned alive.

Land tipped back in his chair, studying the blackboard. '*The Wicker Man,*' he said aloud.

'What about it?' Fraternity did not raise his eyes from his screen.

'It was a tiny British B-movie. Why do people always go on about it?'

'I guess they like it for what it represents,' said

DuCaine distantly. 'Pagan fire. It appeals to the rebel in everyone.'

'What, a copper goes to an island to investigate a murder and gets his fingers burned? The mob out on the streets, you reckon they like stuff like that?'

DuCaine finally set down his pen and looked up. 'You mean specifically *The Wicker Man*?'

'Yeah.'

'It's a key film in the counterculture movement. It's about taking back power from right-wing authority. I suppose it makes a collective, pagan way of life preferable to a fascist Christian police state.'

Land scratched at his jaw. 'Grammar-school boy, are you?'

'Yes, sir.'

'I can tell. You could hardly call the need to investigate a murder fascist.'

'The ending comes as a surprise if you haven't seen it before.'

'Yes, but that's sort of the point. Everyone knows what happens at the end.'

'I don't see what you're getting at.'

'Forget it, I'm going mad.'

'No – go on.'

'It's just . . . they've all gone haring off to Sussex, expecting to find this bloke stuffing Cornell inside his own effigy, yes? Because Bryant's thinking of *The Wicker Man*. Fire, riot, all that stuff. Wouldn't it be truer to this pagan element of surprise to do something else? Surely that's the point. It's all a trick. He makes sure that the police arrive in anticipation of finding a bloke about to be burned alive, and then fools them by doing the opposite. Like the film, but in reverse.'

'So – what?'

'Well, maybe the killer thinks if he sends them off on a wild-goose chase, it leaves him free to do whatever he likes. He's never operated outside of London before. Why would he start now?'

'Tonight's protest march on the Bank of England,' said DuCaine, tapping in a request for details. 'It starts at Cannon Street and ends with a police-sanctioned bonfire right outside the bank at nine tonight. Two hours from now.'

'We'll have to cover it,' said Land. 'See if you can get a couple of them back here in time.'

But there was no mobile reception in the field in Sussex, and nobody answered the call.

50

CAGE OF FIRE

'Sir, we've found the van.' Renfield punched his chest, out of breath. 'It's parked over by the shed where they store the statues. It's unlocked and empty. The engine hasn't been run for several hours. Something's not right.'

May looked about for the others. 'Take Dan back with you to give it the once-over. Janice and Meera just checked out the other bonfire pyres; they're clean.'

'We've been had,' said Bryant. 'He wants us to think that the sacrifice will take place here but it's somewhere else. Can you call out?'

May held his mobile high. 'No connection. Everyone's on their phones. Let's get back to the town centre.'

Bryant had a go. 'Wait, I've got a signal.'

'You? That's impossible. Your phone *never* works.'

Just then, it rang. Raymond Land was calling in. 'Hello! Arthur Bryant here!' Bryant bellowed above the sound of exploding rockets.

'Yes, I know who it is,' said Land. 'You're in the wrong place. They're building a bonfire on the pavement in front of the Bank of England.'

Bryant took this in his stride. 'Can you get it stopped?'

'The City of London police have sanctioned it as a legitimate right of protest. Part of a deal to get the protestors off the streets at midnight.'

'This bonfire, is it already built?' asked Bryant.

'Looks like it. There's live coverage on Sky News. The chief officer of the City of London Special Constabulary is on TV right now praising his negotiators for reaching an agreement.'

'When is it due to be lit?'

'In about an hour and three-quarters,' said Land.

Bryant put a finger in one ear. 'We'll never make it in time. You'll have to get over there by yourselves.'

'Tell him there's no point in rushing,' DuCaine told Land, concerned about Bryant's health. 'Even if they make it to Victoria, they won't be able to get much further. There are no District and Circle or Central lines running into the Square Mile, and the traffic barriers are all up.'

'We're on our way,' said Land. 'Just get back here as quickly as possible.'

May looked up and saw thousands of people coming towards them in a solid wall. 'Damn, they've opened the gates to let the public in. We'll be stuck here for hours if we get caught up in that.'

'The others will have to fend for themselves. You and I have to find a fast train back.' The field was hemmed by a deep water-filled ditch that kept everyone penned. The detectives skirted the edge of the crowd but found their route cut off by the trough.

Bryant was starting to slow down. 'You go ahead, John,' he wheezed, clearly in difficulty. 'I'll catch you up later.'

'No, I'll wait for you. We do this together. We've half an hour until the next train.' He held out his hand.

As they reached the smoke-filled high street once more, May waited for Bryant to catch his breath and they set off towards the station.

Back in London, Raymond Land ended his call to Bryant and turned to DuCaine. 'You and I will have to face Darren Link,' he said. 'He's probably over at the bank right now, getting ready for his final push.'

'No,' said Link, eyeing them from the doorway. 'I'm here. And neither of you are going anywhere.'

Banbury and Renfield climbed inside, under and on top of the gas board van, but found nothing. The rear section was full of empty cardboard boxes and tools. There was no sign that anyone had used it to transport a body.

'If this is the vehicle, it's been cleaned out,' said Banbury. 'I could have sworn it was the same van. What do we do now?'

'Give Colin a hand,' Renfield said. 'He looks like he's stuck.'

Together they helped the spatially challenged DC down from his perch on the statue, just as Meera joined them. 'John and Mr Bryant have gone to try to catch the fast train back,' she said. 'Where's Janice?'

They looked about, but Longbright was nowhere to be found. 'I thought she was with you,' said Banbury. 'When did you last see her?'

'About twenty minutes ago,' Meera replied. They heard the crowds before they saw them, an ants' nest of bodies swarming into the field as the marshals opened the gates. 'We'll never be able to find her in amongst this lot. Anybody got a signal?'

They all checked their phones. 'The network's overloaded,' said Dan. 'There must be fifty thousand people trying to call each other around here.'

'Right, two teams,' decided Renfield. 'Colin and I will take the bonfires, you two get over to the pyrotechnic station and find out if anyone there has seen her.' *If anything happens to her,* Renfield thought, *I'll never forgive myself.*

As he and Colin pushed their way across the treacherously dark field, a blast of warmth pulsed through the air.

The first of the great bonfires had been lit.

Longbright felt something sharp digging into her shoulder blades. She tried to pull herself upright, but was caught on a branch. The noise of the crowd was punctuated by jolting blasts, the shrieks of rockets, the pockety-pop of crackers, the crackle of Roman candles. At first she could see nothing. As her eyes adjusted, she saw her night terrors coalesce.

A cage of branches and sticks, planks, chair legs, floorboards and bric-a-brac, tied in place with rolls of baling wire. In the vertical gaps between the wooden slats that surrounded her she glimpsed distant figures, a treeline, a passing train, fires.

Her wrists were tied with rusty wire around the wooden stave at her back. She tried to understand what had happened. Her head was pounding. She could taste something metallic and medicinal at the back of her throat, and knew at once that she had been drugged with a liquid poured into a rag and closed over her nostrils and mouth. She had felt him pressing against her and thought of Dexter Cornell, someone with powerful upper body strength. She had knocked plenty of big men flat in her time, but this one had surprised her, catching her off-balance in the mud.

I'm inside my nightmare, she thought. *How?* One realization followed another. *He saw us arrive. We played right into his hands.* She pulled at the stave but it was central to the pyre and would not move a centimetre. The wire was cutting into her wrists. Her feet were unbound, so she kicked out as hard as she could. That was when she discovered that he had removed her shoes. The wood at her feet was splintered and sharp. She shouted, but the great cone of wood deadened her cries.

She tried to fight her fear and think logically. She was between fifteen and twenty feet off the ground. When the pyre was lit, the interior space would create an updraught that would allow it to burn fast, but the flames would have to start at the outer edge. She needed it to catch the central pole that held her, so that she could break it at the base. It would mean holding her breath and saving her strength until the very last moment. She was strong. She could see the weakest parts of the bonfire's construction. If she kept her wits about her, she might just be able to tear herself free and escape.

But then she heard a roar go up from the crowd, and glimpsed several men moving in around the pyre with lit torches, and smelled petrol, and heard the soft explosion of flame underneath her, and felt its warmth increasing by the second, and realized they were lighting it from every side at once.

For God's sake, she thought, *somebody find me fast.*

'We don't even know if she's inside one of the bonfires,' said Banbury. 'She could have nipped off for a pee.'

'She was right with us; she would never have gone without saying something,' Meera disagreed. 'She told me she'd been having dreams about being stuck inside one of those things.'

'What, we're going to start basing searches on people's dreams now, are we?'

Meera glared at him. 'Have you got any better ideas about where she might be?'

They caught one of the senior marshals as he was heading towards a bonfire with his team. 'We need you to stop the fires from being lit,' Dan told him. 'Are you in contact with each other?'

'Why, what's the problem? Have you seen how many people we've got out there waiting to see some papists go up in smoke?' The marshal thought they were joking.

'They're going to get more than they bargained for if you don't call the fires off,' Meera snarled. 'One of our officers may be inside one of your statues.'

'This is a joke, right? Who sent you over?'

'You'll have the chance to think about whether it was a joke in a cell if you don't halt them all right now,' said Banbury.

The marshal relayed the message, but all Meera could hear was static. 'Atmospheric conditions,' he said apologetically. 'Two of them are already lit.' He pointed to the glowing pyres across the field.

'Then we'll need your marshals to check every fire as fast as they can,' Banbury yelled. They ran towards the nearest crowd of yellow-jackets and began to round them up.

Bimsley and Renfield tore at the first of the burning stacks and tried to see inside. 'Janice!' Renfield shouted, but there was no answer. 'She could already be suffering from smoke inhalation,' he warned, tearing at the staves.

'She's not in that one, Jack, I can see right through it from here,' Colin shouted. 'The furthest one has to be nearly a quarter of a mile away. We'll never get to it in time.'

'Then I hope to God Meera and Dan are nearer,' yelled Renfield as they ran over the treacherous furrows towards the next flame-engulfed effigy.

One side of the second bonfire was trailing intestines of choking smoke from the old varnished tables and chairs that had been axed and piled on to it. The air was filled with dancing red devils that stuck to their jackets and melted holes in the neoprene of their sleeves. Renfield's eyes were watering so badly that he could barely see. Marshals who had yet to be warned about the search were shouting at him, trying to force him back from the fire's heat radius.

He knew it was too late to break into this one; the flames were roaring within its conical updraught, tornado-whirling, sucking crimson fire into the sky. He threw his arm in the direction of the next bonfire, the largest of the six. At its peak the governor of the Bank of England sat on a golden throne.

Bimsley saw Renfield's signal and veered off towards the pyre, but the churned-up field made it impossible to run. The bonfires had been spaced far apart so that there was no danger of the wind carrying sparks from one to the other before the marshals were ready to ignite them. The muddy ditches made the going hard, and they did not reach the central bonfire until it was just being lit.

Renfield tried to push the marshals away but one of them took a swing at him. Bad idea; Colin came forward and floored him with one well-placed punch. Throwing himself at the unlit side of the stack, Colin started to scramble up it, but the wood kept sliding down beneath his boots.

Renfield was frantically climbing too, clambering over the rough-hewn ladders of broken furniture with surprising agility. He shone his torch through the staves, but could see nothing.

All he could do was continue to climb, but now the flames were spreading out below him, and he could feel the heat on his legs. He knew that a point would come when he would have to abandon his search or risk being trapped on the pyre himself.

As he pressed his face to the slats, he saw something dark moving inside. 'Janice!' he shouted. This time he received a faint response. The detective sergeant's soot-smeared face came into view. 'My God, hang in there.' He shouted down to the marshals: 'Don't just stand there! She's inside!'

Now the fire was spreading swiftly around the circumference of the pyre, igniting the petrol-soaked planks below him, and a deafening roar filled his ears. Renfield could feel his hair singeing as he clawed at the wooden structure, which remained solid and immovable.

51

BAD TIMING

By the time Bryant and May had managed to get across town from Victoria Station to Holborn, the only tube station still open, the protest rally was reaching its climax at the Bank of England. The bonfire was already ablaze, washing the bank's double columns with bloodstained light.

High Holborn was impassable. Most of the street lights had been smashed. The mob was torch-lit and orderly, and there was no way of passing through it. A rhythm of drums, trumpets and reed pipes echoed from the canyon of buildings. The centuries had rolled back to reveal the city at an earlier time. Tracksuits had replaced tunics, but the stoic faces had barely changed.

'Can you feel it?' asked Bryant. 'They know that by the end of the night they'll be in charge. What will happen after that?'

Some running youths slammed into Bryant, lifting him off his feet and spinning him around. May was just able to grab him before he hit the pavement. 'Come on,' he said, 'it's not safe for you here.'

The detectives were owed a stroke of luck, and now

one finally came. May spotted an ARV being loaded by an old friend from Snow Hill nick. He ran over and arranged for them to get a lift inside the perimeter.

'We're too late to do anything,' May said as the ARV pulled up behind a wall of burning debris in Queen Victoria Street. 'We'll never get across the crowds.'

The protestors were hemmed in by makeshift barriers, some of which had been shoved aside and stood across the road like rows of angry teeth. Ahead was a vast ocean of chalk-white Guy Fawkes masks, moving with the instinctive patterns of shoaling fish. Rain swept over the blank-featured mob in great grey drifts. Many of the protestors were carrying sputtering flambeaux in an urban version of the anti-papist parades in Lewes. The banners which read 'NO MORE GANGSTER BANKERS' and 'INSIDERS OUT' had been professionally printed, but now they had been joined by a new ubiquitous slogan: 'TAKE BACK LONDON'.

Police and newsroom helicopters droned overhead, spotlighting the rally for their cameras. Bryant saw a hundred thousand moving bodies outlined against a painterly frieze of fire. The march was no longer the province of anarchists. There were whole families here, children and pensioners. Some had even brought baby buggies. And yet it felt that at any instant the mood might suddenly change, and the streets would run with blood.

In front of the bank's neoclassical façade the mood was uglier. Here rose a great funnel of fire, its flames fleeing up into the sulphurous furnace of the night. Explosions of glass occurred with metronomic precision; the few shop windows that had not been boarded up were being kicked in. Indistinct instructions were being barked through megaphones, adding to the sense of Orwellian oppression.

'I've never seen anything like it,' said Bryant, awed. 'It's truly out of our hands now.'

'It's what you wanted, isn't it?' May asked. 'Anarchy?'

'Not like this, not for the pleasure of the mob. To change things you have to dismantle and rebuild, not wantonly destroy. It looks like a fascist rally.'

'These are our people,' said May sadly. 'This is what we've become.'

Bryant stopped for a moment longer to frame the scene with his hands. 'It's like that painting by William Holman Hunt. *London Bridge on the Night of the Marriage of the Prince and Princess of Wales,* Tennyson's famous "river of fire" brought to life with torches.'

'Of course it is,' said May patiently. 'Come on, let me get you out of here before someone lobs a brick at you.'

As they left, the great bonfire behind them began to fall in on itself, releasing a fresh firestorm into the air, and the mob bellowed its approval.

'As you can see, there's nobody left in the building because we followed your instructions and discontinued the investigation,' said Raymond Land. Unfortunately the unit chief was painfully incapable of telling a lie, and the effect of his statement was the exact opposite of what he had intended. He'd once stolen an ashtray from the Grand Hotel Eastbourne, only to have it fall out of his jumper as he walked through the reception area.

Darren Link gave him a deeply sceptical look. 'Where are they?' he demanded, looking around as if expecting the other members of staff sheepishly to pop their heads out of cupboards.

'They're not here,' replied DuCaine truthfully. 'It's just the two of us. We're in the middle of closing down the investigation and filing reports.'

'Don't lie to me, lad. I'm not one of your Brixton brothers.'

'That's racism—'

'Or one of your boyfriends.'

'—and homophobia.'

Link stuck an index finger in his face. 'Don't get smart me with, sonny. I know you lot are up to something. The whole team's on voicemail – isn't that a bit bloody strange?'

'It's Saturday evening; they're not required to keep their phones on,' said Land. 'They've probably gone ice-skating.' He didn't know where that came from, but thought of high-fiving DuCaine, only he wasn't quite sure how to do it. 'Anyway, why have you come here?' he asked hastily. 'I don't suppose you just happened to be passing.'

'I thought you might be able to shed some light on what happened tonight.' Link was looking at Land's neatly laid-out pen tray with distaste.

'Why? What happened?'

'I guess you've been too busy to see the breaking news. About an hour ago, Dexter Cornell was burned alive in front of thousands of people outside the Bank of England. His killer filmed the whole thing and released the footage on to the internet. It's getting millions of hits. The inmates have finally taken over the madhouse. Your Mr Bryant will be pleased, I imagine. Doesn't he have anarchist affiliations?'

'So you took back the operation and failed to save Cornell,' said Land. 'I don't suppose you caught his abductor, either.'

'This was never your case.' Link's fractured eye glinted wildly. 'We've been monitoring you from the beginning. If you hadn't muddied everything with your half-arsed investigation, we might have stood a chance. He's got what he wanted now – he's taken out the villain and won over the country. Things are going to change around here, starting with this place.' He looked around the walls and up at the damp-stained ceiling, nodding. 'I reckon this'll be a heavy-metal bar and a couple of knocking shops in three months' time. And you'll all be locked away on the Isle of Wight.'

Right now, thought Land, *the Isle of Wight doesn't sound like a bad idea.* 'I hope you'll admit your culpability in all this. If you don't, I'll make sure it goes in my report.'

Link placed his hairy knuckles on Land's desk. Leaning forward on his fists, he suddenly bore an alarming resemblance to his nickname. 'I don't think you want to start playing that game,' he said darkly. 'You might find the unit going up in smoke as well, with you inside it.'

'You're a thug, Link,' replied Land, trying to keep the tremble from his voice. 'You were always a thug, right from our training days. That's why you'll always make a lousy copper, and it's why you'll always get passed over for promotion. Your bosses know it. Go back and look at your own unit. Ask yourselves why you failed to stop all of this. You're all batons and water cannons, locks and keys. Well, I don't believe in incarceration. I don't want to come back in another life.'

For a moment, DuCaine thought that Link was going to lash out and send Raymond Land through the window, but instead he rose to his full height, glared, opened his mouth, closed it and silently left the room.

'I reckon you got to him, sir,' said DuCaine with a smile.

'Thank God for that,' said Land, breathing out. It felt good to stand up against a bully, even though he felt sure he hadn't seen the last of Link.

'Janice, get back as far as you can.' The wood shifted beneath Renfield's weight. He leaned out as much as he dared and slammed down his right boot, cracking several of the bonfire's staves, but nothing gave. He saw why when he looked down; the cords were held together with baling wire. 'Cutters!' he shouted down. 'Somebody chuck me up a pair.'

One of the marshals threw him the tool and he caught it, snapping open the wires, cracking back branches and boards. He could feel the skin on his arms blistering through the sleeves of his jacket. He worked blindly, without thinking, with no thought but a determination to break through. The wood splintered, then gave way. He punched out the staves and grabbed at her.

'So the prince got through the thicket to rescue Sleeping Beauty,' said Longbright as he appeared before her, but there was a shake in her voice. 'My wrists are tied.'

From below came a loud crack, and the pyre lurched alarmingly. There was no time to waste. Renfield forced his way into the crawlspace, dropped to his knees and cut Longbright's hands free. As they climbed out of the bonfire, the flames caught the central updraught and ignited the wooden interior where Longbright had been sitting.

Bimsley and the marshals helped them down and led them away from the fire. Longbright's hair was so badly singed at the front that she looked suddenly androgynous. Her wrists were bloody from the wire. When she tried to talk, she coughed until she had to rest her elbows on her knees and fight for breath. A marshal gave her a bottle of water.

'My dream came true,' she wheezed, looking back at the roaring bonfire as she caught her breath. 'I was the burning man. Maggie Armitage was right.'

Renfield turned her around. 'What the hell happened? How did you put yourself in that situation? If anything had happened to you—'

'I didn't put myself in any situation, Jack. I was walking behind you all and his hands came over my face. It was so dark on the way to the field, nobody could see anyone else.'

'But he knew you were with the unit.'

'We're in matching jackets and badges,' she reminded him. 'It's a bit bloody obvious.'

He held her so tightly that she started coughing again. 'I thought I'd lost you. I want you to do something for me.'

'Can't breathe,' she said. 'Smoke inhalation. What?'

He let her go, but only a little. 'Marry me,' he said.

Janice took a step back and studied him. Their faces were black with soot. 'You've got a really lousy sense of timing,' she said finally. 'I lost my shoes.'

'I'll buy you a thousand pairs,' Renfield said.

'There's something weird about this.'

DuCaine studied the footage again. He and Land were watching the sequence that Sky News had released of Dexter Cornell inside the bonfire. The shots were intercut with police footage taken from the other side of the road. Across the bottom of the screen ran a bright-red caption: 'Caution – some images may cause distress.'

'What do you mean?' asked Land, peering at the footage. 'I need my reading glasses. What am I looking at?'

DuCaine tapped at the screen with a long index finger. 'The internal shots of the bonfire were supposedly taken on the killer's phone. The news centre seems to have censored it for network use, cutting away to long shots of the bonfire. Their cameras are set up on Threadneedle Street, beside the statue of that soldier-dude. But the shots don't match up. Look at this.'

The footage taken from the inside showed Dexter Cornell unconscious against a post, just as Longbright had been tied. 'Check out the planks behind him. They're not touched by the fire. Now look at the cutaway. The flames are all around.' He flicked back and forth between the images.

'So the phone footage is from an earlier point, *before*

the bonfire could fully catch alight,' said Land.

'No.' DuCaine pointed to a corner of the screen. 'The phone's time-coded: 21.43. The long-distance footage was first shown earlier, at 21.41. The fire didn't suddenly die down.'

'I don't see what difference it makes,' said Land, confused.

'He couldn't have arranged for the phone to shoot Cornell if there were flames in the background.'

'Why not?'

'Cornell would have been backlit by the fire. He needed us to see the guy's face, to prove that it was him.'

'He's not in the bonfire,' said Land, awed.

'The footage was shot somewhere else and released live,' said DuCaine, picking up the phone. 'Dexter Cornell could still be alive.'

52

SKYFIRE

There was no time to waste, so Arthur Bryant dawdled. He leaned on his stick in the doorway and looked around at the office he shared with his partner. One side of the room was immaculate, elegant, stylish even, and the other side was like an illegal street market after a police raid. He wondered how he had inherited the old copies of the 1950s naturist magazine *Health & Efficiency,* or why he still used the tip of a meat cleaver to open his letters.

He knew that the Haitian voodoo bowl had been presented to him by a grateful murder witness, and that he couldn't store bananas in it because they went black overnight, but he had no idea what was in the cylindrical glass jar full of cloudy liquid on his windowsill, except that when you gave it a swirl something with eyes lazily drifted around to stare at you. And he remembered that the varnished purple fish holding down his unpaid bills had once sent Longbright to A & E after she jabbed herself on its spikes. Likewise he recalled every detail of the cases outlined in the broken-spined volumes behind his chair. Each was a self-contained human drama that proved, over and again, that there was nothing so mysterious in the cold reaches of space as the turning of the human heart.

Rain was smacking against the windows, classic midnight rain, drizzling and dripping and leaking in through the rotten frames. The room was his home, his head, and he could not leave it behind. And that ergonomic Spanish leather armchair opposite the soil-filled ashtrays that marked the end of his territory needed John May sitting in it, leaning back with his long legs stretched out under the desk, squinting at a page of evidence because he was too vain to wear glasses. No wonder they had never been able to settle with new women in their lives. How could anyone else hope to fit in when the two of them spent so much time in each other's company? At least John, who needed the kindness of female companionship as he needed air, had found peace with a succession of spectacularly unsuitable lady friends.

Bryant had taken a lonelier path, finding companionship at the office, spiritual union in the pages of books, company in libraries and museums, peace in the solitude of crowds. He was as embedded in London as the Piccadilly Line, or the paving stones of Trafalgar Square. Although he was never one to feel sorry for himself, it was sad, not to mention entirely unacceptable, to be ending his career on a failure.

'Penny for your thoughts,' said May, sliding past him. 'What's that awful smell?'

'Goat's cheese,' replied Bryant absently.

'Where is it?' May looked under the desk, hunting the source of the stench.

'It's in a shoe on the radiator. Remember that corpse in the elevator shaft at Marconi House?'

'No.'

'You must do. September 1968. I think I made a mistake in my report.'

'It doesn't begin to explain that thing.' May waved his

hand in the direction of the radiator. 'Can you get it out of here?'

'He'd been down there for a while before we found him. The putrefaction disguised the smell of the *chèvre*. If we'd known he'd been to the cheesemonger on the day he'd died we'd have nailed his assailant.'

'We've got a rather more pressing problem to deal with right now. With Cornell dead, we have no way of catching our killer. Why are you looking into this old stuff anyway?'

'I thought I might try to clear up my unsolved cases.'

'Why, are you going somewhere?'

'I think so, yes.' Bryant snapped out of his funk. 'Does Raymond know we're back? We need to talk to him.' As the Armed Response Vehicle had dropped them off, they had spotted the unit chief's desk light from outside the building. It was 11.59 p.m. Land usually went home at the first available opportunity.

'He must have heard us come in,' said May. 'Let's go and wake him up.'

'Hang on, I have a paper bag somewhere.'

'No, don't frighten him. The last time you did that he tipped a prawn curry into his lap.'

The detectives went to his office. 'Knock, knock,' said Bryant, miming on the door that wasn't there. He found Land and DuCaine hunched over a computer terminal. 'What's going on?'

'Cornell's alive,' said DuCaine.

'What?' Bryant dug out one pair of his trifocals. 'I saw the news flash about his death on John's phone. Are you sure?'

'Positive,' said DuCaine.

'You're going to love this—' Land began.

Bryant waved him aside. 'Not you, the lad.'

DuCaine proceeded to outline his discovery.

'We have to find him and get hold of the others,' said

May. 'Is there anything else in that footage?'

'I've been through the sequence over and over again but there's nothing.' DuCaine's nimble fingers stepped through the frames that showed the banker's blurry form within the bonfire.

'I've always wanted to say this,' said Bryant, leaning on the desk. 'Enlarge that image. Take it up to 360.'

'I have no idea what that actually means,' said DuCaine. 'I can make it a bit bigger.'

'Did you speak to the officers at the site?' asked May. 'What did they find in the bonfire?'

'They can't get in there. It's still too hot, and the council officials won't let them spray water on it because it will make the pavements more slippery, which would contravene health and safety regulations, so they're waiting for the rain to put it out.'

'So they have no footage and no body.'

'Apparently not.'

'He couldn't have set this whole thing up himself, could he?'

'It seems rather unlikely, don't you think? There must be a simpler explanation. This,' said Bryant, thumping the screen. 'It's vaguely familiar. What is it?' He pointed to the image, which showed a dark curve behind the sticks of wood at Cornell's back. May leaned in and stared hard, but remained silent.

'There's another one further over. Look. Fraternity, can you move along a few frames?'

'It doesn't look like anything, Arthur.'

'They're letters. It could be a name on the side of a building. I need my books.' Bryant stumped off to his room.

'What?' said Land. 'He thinks he's seen something the rest of us have missed? He can't even see across the road.'

'He knows London better than anyone,' May reminded them. 'Give him a chance.'

Bryant pulled at the books, causing an avalanche of dust, dinner and dead insects to cascade over his desk. Finally he found the volume he was seeking, volume R–W of the *Derelict London Properties Manual*. Riffling through the pages, he found what he was looking for and released a cry of triumph. Chucking the book under his arm, he headed back to Land's office.

'Skyfire,' he told them. 'I knew I'd seen it before. The S and the R are unique. The sign was hand-painted back in the mid-nineteen thirties. It's a firework factory. They went out of business in 1993. Cornell was never at the Bank of England. The whole thing was a set-up.'

'Why?' Land was bewildered.

'To keep fuelling the bloodlust of the protestors. They think they've won. We have to show them that they haven't. Cornell's in the old Skyfire warehouse behind Metropolitan Wharf at Wapping Wall.'

As Bryant, May, Land and DuCaine set off towards East London, the rolling storm followed above their heads.

53

WIRED

I could have brought Augustine to Wapping, Bryant thought, *at the drop of the Thames and just a spit from Tower Bridge, where Captain Kidd was hanged twice before being chained and left for three tides.*

Nothing remained of this piratical past except an ancient set of oxidized green steps leading to the muddy foreshore. The flooded ginnels and mildewed alleyways of Bryant's childhood, once so dauntingly forbidden and mysterious, had been paved over, filled in and floodlit as London homogenized its riverside in the rush to build bankers' apartments.

The streets were unrecognizable now, colonnaded with blank suburban properties of orange brick. Between them stood a few emasculated warehouses for those seduced by the notion of a loft lifestyle. The wealthy were never there and the rest stayed in. The dead new streets of the Thames shoreline horrified Bryant.

'This is the evidence of what's wrong, right here,' he complained from the back of May's BMW. 'Inequality rising faster than at any other time in history. The government furthering its own corrupt ideological agenda.'

'I'd be happy to argue political theories with you at some time, Arthur,' said May, taking a rainswept corner at twice its safe speed, 'but I'm a little preoccupied right now.'

'I was thinking about Dexter Cornell, actually,' said Bryant. 'I came up with reasons why the others should be targeted, but not him.'

'But you said yourself he's a hate figure,' said DuCaine.

'But why bother to fake his death? Why not just let him die?'

'Well, perhaps—' DuCaine began before Bryant stopped him.

'It was a rhetorical question. I know the answer.' Everyone banged their heads on the car's roof as May cut a corner and went over a kerbstone. Bryant was unperturbed. 'Why not run wild with a gun, like they do in America? I'll tell you why. Because that shows weakness. A massacre is a display of anger, not strength, and either you get caught or you have to kill yourself. This isn't about the pleasure of killing, but justice.'

'Arthur, you know I'm always ready to listen, but right now I'm trying not to miss a turning and send us into the river.'

Bryant sat back and turned to DuCaine. 'You see? He can only do one thing at a time.'

'I know,' said DuCaine. 'Men. Useless.'

Bryant looked out at the racing view. 'It's changed around here since I was a nipper. I remember playing in Crown and Anchor Alley, waiting for my old man while he was cadging in the pubs. If he could have seen what I saw in the City tonight, how he would have hated it.' He leaned forward suddenly. 'There, on the left.'

Although the Skyfire Firework Factory had been closed down, the building had been saved ready for conversion into apartments. A pair of black wrought-iron gates separated the three-floor warehouse from the street.

'It looks empty,' said Land.

'He's not in there,' said Bryant, 'he's somewhere opposite. The sign I saw is still up there on the outside, so he has to be' – he turned around and unsmeared the rear window – 'over in that corner.'

May parked and everyone got out, scanning the buildings.

'There's nothing there,' said Land, 'just trees.'

'Behind them.'

DuCaine was off and running. As the others followed, they saw the low boarded-up warehouse tucked behind the main road, and could tell from here that its upper windows faced the faded factory sign.

'We could have done with having Jack and Colin on board tonight,' said May. 'We have no back-up.'

'You've got me,' said DuCaine, checking the wooden loading bay doors and windows. 'These are locked. What about the back? If I have to kick my way in it's going to tip our hand.'

May tried the handle of the rear door and watched as it swung open. 'That's not good.'

They entered warily. DuCaine had a pencil torch that he shone around the graffiti-stained walls. There was a sound like a falling telephone directory: pigeons scattering in the rafters. They found nothing on the ground floor, just old filing cabinets, binders, broken office chairs and stacks of carpet tiles. The air smelled of lost contracts, printer ink, redundancies.

They took the rear stairs to the floor above. 'It has to be up here,' insisted Bryant. 'That's where you'd see the sign from.'

May pushed open the doors and they entered the area.

'Don't come any further!' Cornell shouted from the middle of the room.

DuCaine's torch beam fell over the banker's bruised face, making him flinch. He was attached to an office chair with white plastic cable ties, still dressed in the T-shirt and grey tracksuit bottoms he'd been wearing when he was abducted. In front of him was a phone on a tripod, powered off, its timer finished. 'Please,' Cornell croaked, 'get back against the wall.'

DuCaine saw the problem: blue and red wires spiralling away from the rear of Cornell's chair, running to a pair of small black-mesh sensors set out on the floorboards in front of him, about ten feet apart.

'Stay there,' Cornell instructed. 'It's an infrared beam. If you break it I'm dead. I've got some kind of explosive taped around my waist. He's gone. He went hours ago. I'm the only one here.'

DuCaine's torchlight picked out the squashed oblong panel strapped to the front of Cornell's shirt, into which the wires were fixed. It looked as if it was made of putty.

Before May or DuCaine could stop him, Bryant donned his trifocals and stepped forward, thumping his walking stick hard on the floor. He leaned his weight on it.

May waved the others back. It was a straight choice now: to take control, or to trust the man who had just been diagnosed as unstable and a danger to others. The man he had known all his adult life.

'Do it, Arthur,' he whispered.

'You know what I used to like playing with most when I was a kid?' Bryant asked Cornell. 'Plasticine. I made whole armies out of that stuff. I seem to remember restaging the Crimean War with a different outcome, carving the cavalry figures with a palette knife. The only trouble was that at some point you had to throw it all away. It was when all the colours started merging into one, a disgusting shade of purple. And the smell. It stayed on your clothes for weeks.'

DuCaine shot an urgent warning glance at May. *Has the old man lost it again?* Bryant took another step forward and raised his stick across the beam, breaking it as everyone shouted and dropped.

'It was the exact colour of the modelling clay stuck to your chest, Mr Cornell.' He turned to the others. 'You can cut him free, Fraternity. There is no bomb. There's nothing more dangerous here than the odd rat.'

As DuCaine pulled out his Swiss army knife and sawed at the cable ties pinning Cornell's arms, May examined the mobile. 'He put the feed online remotely,' he said. 'Right now everyone out there is thinking the anti-banking movement has claimed its biggest victory. We need to get the truth out fast, before they send in the militia and cross a line that changes everything.'

'I'll leave the nuts and bolts to you, shall I?' said Bryant magnanimously. 'I just do the abstract thinking around here.'

Released, Cornell fell forward on to his knees. 'I'll destroy you for this,' he warned, staggering to his feet and massaging his wrists. 'I'll make sure you never work in this city again.'

'So much for gratitude,' said May. 'You shouldn't have dismissed your bodyguards. What was it, a cost-cutting exercise?'

'I didn't dismiss them, *he* did.'

'So you know who he is?'

'You're the detectives,' spat Cornell bitterly. 'You tell me.'

54

A FACE IN THE CROWD

It was three twenty-seven on Sunday morning by the time everyone managed to find their way back to the offices of the PCU, Bryant having insisted on compulsory attendance. The staff members wove their way through the clutter of the common room looking as if they'd been raised from the dead. Out of respect for their bleary state, the lights had been turned down low. Bryant perched himself on a stool, sensing that if he sat in his comfortable armchair he might never get up again.

'I'm sorry,' he began. 'I know you want this to be over but it isn't, and it might never be. But I need to get it off my chest while I still remember everything clearly.'

Bimsley was the first to ask a question. 'Where's Cornell?'

Bryant waved him down. 'I'll get to that in a moment. If I have another one of my attacks right now you'll never have any answers. I made some notes.' He dragged a crumpled sheet of paper from his pocket and flattened it. 'It starts with Monica. I have an old academic friend called Monica Greenwood. She knows a lot about art. I asked her to go through all the images of the riots that were taken by photojournalists. Dan put them on a memory stick for me. I asked her to look for the faces of our suspects. She's a natural at this sort of thing, better than any piece of software that's been devised.'

'Probably not true,' said Banbury. 'There's a very sophisticated face-recognition programme—'

'Shut up, Dan,' said Bryant. 'Monica is what they call a super-recognizer. They only have to see someone once. The second time they spot the same face, they know exactly where they saw it before. Monica remembers faces with such accuracy that her hit rate beats DNA evidence. She discovered her ability quite by accident, and now she's allowed to visit VIIDO.'

'What's that?' asked Bimsley.

'God, I can't remember what it stands for,' Bryant said. 'John?'

'The Visual Images Identification and Detections Office at Charing Cross,' said May obligingly.

'Monica's one of two hundred super-recognizers currently helping the MPS to identify faces in crowds,' Bryant explained. 'And she found an unmasked face for me. Actually, she found dozens of them. Some were troublemakers who were just wading from one police confrontation to another; others were mere bystanders who enjoyed gawking at the riots from a safe distance.' He wet his lips with a sip from his glass. Before the meeting, he had instructed Meera to break out a bottle of Chinese gin that Land had been given by his local takeaway last Christmas.

'So I had Monica's faces, the ones that were common to many of the photographs, but I didn't know what to do with them. Then I watched the TV footage again. The major channels were showing the same loops of film over and over again. I had a rough description of who we were looking for. He was tall, strong, broad-shouldered, early thirties – but then I remembered where that description came from: the shots from Jonathan De Vere's car park, when somebody broke into his Mercedes. We'd only assumed it was the arsonist. But if it was, what was he after? I couldn't make sense of it. Then, tonight, poor old Raymondo here told me that Darren Link said something odd to him: "We've been monitoring you from the beginning." That's when I realized.' He eyed each of them in turn. 'We'd been frustrating Link at every point in the investigation, so he was conducting his own covert reconnaissance. One of his lads went a bit too far looking for evidence, and broke into De Vere's vehicle. Dan has now managed to pull some shots of him leaving the car park. It's definitely one of Link's plods.'

'I don't understand,' said Longbright. 'What did he get from the car?'

'Nothing. You also lost some statements from your desk, didn't you? Link was clumsily trying to gather intelligence. But all he did was put the wrong image in my head. Which is why I didn't spot who we should have been looking for until it was too late. John?' He indicated that May should take the floor.

'We wondered if Weeks, Hall, De Vere, Leach, Papis and Cornell had all met at one point in their lives,' said May. 'We thought if they had all visited the same bars or clubs we might find a pattern. But there was nothing. How could there be no connection at all?'

'You ain't half dragging this out,' Meera complained. 'Do you know what the time is?'

Bimsley raised Land's bottle of Shanghai Blossom-Taste Happy Dry Gin. 'Do you want a drink?' he asked.

She glared at him. 'No. Do you want a smack in the mouth?'

May called for quiet. 'For me, there was one question we hadn't asked ourselves: Why couldn't we find this guy? All these terrible deaths and still no sign of him?

No prints, no forensic track, nothing. During the briefing Raymondo said something important.'

'I did?' said Land, looking surprised.

'He said, "It's as if he doesn't exist." And of course that was the answer. He didn't exist.'

'This is driving me mad,' said Meera, rising. 'Either you tell us—' Everyone forced her back into her seat.

'The TV footage,' said Bryant, taking the reins once more. 'Monica didn't just spot a face, she spotted a physical movement. A man moving through the crowds, short but strong, with a pronounced limp. She spotted Freddie Weeks.'

Colin Bimsley spat an ice cube into his glass.

'One of the few things we knew about our arsonist was that he was comfortable working with metals,' said Bryant. 'It never crossed our minds to ask what Freddie's father, Gerry Weeks, did for a living. He runs die-cutters in a machine shop. He had the boy apprenticed to him for a while, but Freddie hated it. The man we found on the steps of the Findersbury Bank was so badly burned that he was identified by the serial-numbered titanium implant in his foot. Freddie made a duplicate of his own implant. He had a plan, but to carry it out he first had to erase his own identity. He befriended a homeless man of roughly the same size and age, gave him some money and his watch, and asked him to perform a favour: check himself in as Freddie Weeks at the Clerkenwell Green hostel, then sleep on the steps of the Findersbury Bank.

'And that's where he made a mistake. Because although the CCTV camera at Crutched Friars recorded an image of a man sleeping rough, it also picked up Weeks when he went to the entrance the first time, before throwing the Molotov cocktail. And he had to go there to leave the implant rod at the site. Of course, there were risks involved. He had no way of making certain that the body would be sufficiently burned, and there were other variables. But he kept an eye on them, and did a damned good job of covering his tracks. Of course, he had the rioters to help him do that. We still don't know the name of the homeless man who died in his place. Unfortunately, when Weeks "killed" himself he didn't mean it to look like murder, and accidentally became his own suspect, which convinced us to start looking for him.'

'So where is he now?' asked Renfield.

'For that you have to understand Weeks's mindset,' Bryant answered. 'His revenge was personal, and the sense of empowerment it gave him made him realize that he could take revenge for *everyone* out there. He was physically strong, driven and smart. We knew his mother had discovered religion, but never thought to ask her about it. She'd become a Catholic, just like her son. Freddie Weeks suddenly saw how everything might fit a pattern. The Catholic–Protestant conflicts of the past fed directly into his warped world view of turmoil, protest and conflagration. Having kidnapped Cornell and set up the camera to film him, he headed for the coast. And he had one last message for the police: "Follow me and you'll get burned." He nearly killed one of our best officers tonight.'

'If Weeks wanted to fire up the rioters, why did he leave Cornell alive?' Colin asked.

'Because he decided that letting him live would make everyone even angrier.' Bryant stifled a yawn. 'They've been cheated of their revenge.'

'We'll find him now,' said May with certainty. 'Weeks got Cornell to give him his credit card PIN numbers, but Cornell managed to flag them. Never mess with a captain of industry.'

'We haven't caught him yet,' said Meera, unimpressed.

55

TAKING ACTION

Six days later, Freddie Weeks was arrested in southern Spain, having used his old passport to enter the country. He had managed to draw out a little of Cornell's cash, but by this time Karin Scott had identified Michael Flannery, the man Weeks had befriended, thanks to a series of coincidences so fortuitous that they could have constituted an entirely separate, credulity-stretching chapter in Mr Bryant's memoirs. Weeks was finally confronted by a very nervous policeman in a tapas bar in Plaça Reial, Barcelona.

Weeks was returned to London and brought to PCU headquarters for questioning. He was tanned, short and indifferent of feature, with prematurely thinning brown hair. He twisted as he walked, but to make up for the weakness in his foot, his arms were thick and powerful. For the rest of the day he remained slumped half-asleep in the interview room, bored by the formality of the proceedings. He accepted state representation and resented any delay, clearly blunted by the thought of all that lay ahead. When he finally spoke he showed no emotion and expressed little interest in explaining himself. Next to him a plastic pail plinked, steadily filling with rainwater, marking away the hours.

'I knew that without an identity, I could do whatever I wanted,' he said at one point, sprawled in his chair before the detectives.

'And what did you want?' asked May.

'To burn everyone who wrecked my life.'

'According to your parents you were a bright, politically committed pupil at school,' said Bryant.

Weeks gave a derisive grunt. 'Working hard and being clever isn't enough any more, is it? I had ideas. I came up with a money-maker that could give something back to the community. It was called CharityMob. I pitched it to Glen Hall and he took it to Jon De Vere, who liked it so much he stole the concept. I didn't give up. I tried to go it alone, and borrowed from Frank Leach's loan company. But then Leach doubled the interest and I couldn't pay it back. It should have been simple. Do some good; get a reward. Instead I got shafted, like everybody else.'

'What about Joanna Papis?'

Another grunt. 'The moment I needed her most, she dumped me. I lost my future, my flat, my girl, everything. I was broke, I owed money and someone got rich from my idea. Every time I turned on the TV, I saw them: all the other poor bastards who'd been cheated, just like me.'

'You make it sound as if they were all working together.'

'That's what it felt like.'

'So you waited until the time was right, when Dexter Cornell sparked a riot,' said May.

'I don't feel bad about it,' Weeks said. 'Why should I? None of them showed me any kindness. They deserved what they got.'

'But you didn't kill Cornell.'

Weeks shrugged. 'He hadn't done anything bad to me.'

'Neither had Michael Flannery.'

'Don't you know the first rule of revenge? An innocent has to suffer. Besides, Flannery was a loser. At least he proved himself useful to the cause. I did what was right. I took action. I did what everyone should do.'

He said no more after that. The charges were duly filed. For Bryant, there was little satisfaction to be gained from hearing Weeks's confession. His crimes had roots that would remain for years to come. There would be other men like Weeks, and perhaps they would not be stopped. As much as Bryant loved his city, he was ashamed of the way in which it shamelessly encouraged the greed of others, crushing those who found life a struggle. Once, he too had been one of those young men.

John May was as good as his word. He collected Blaize Carter in his silver BMW, which impressed her, and took her to the Szechuan restaurant in the Shard, where they could study the whole of London spread out below them. She had selected an elegant dark outfit for the evening and looked beautiful but slightly awkward, as if she'd been invited to a fancy-dress party.

'So what happens now?' she asked. 'Do you just sit back and wait for another case?'

'I don't know,' he admitted. 'Everyone else is claiming the responsibility for catching Weeks. There'll be a post-mortem, and we'll be blamed for failing to stop him earlier. And now that our bosses know about Arthur's health condition, they'll want him out of the unit as quickly as possible.'

'What are you going to do?'

'Someone has to look after him.' May traced his toothpick across the tablecloth. 'He always goes a bit vague after we close an investigation, but this time he's changed almost overnight. It's as if it used up his last ounce of strength. But I have to be there for him. I can't imagine going on alone. I don't know what I'd do without him.'

'You need your own life as well,' Blaize reminded him.

'That's what anyone I've ever got close to has said. I had a French girlfriend for a while, completely crazy but fun to be with. She hated Arthur, complained about him all the time. She said, "The trouble is, there are three of us in this relationship." Then she left, and he was still there.'

'What if you had to decide?'

'That's a really mean question.'

'But it's one that must be in some people's heads.'

'I've gone too far down this road to change my priorities now, Blaize.'

'That's what I figured,' she said, finishing her glass and catching the eye of the waiter. 'It's been a lovely evening but I have to go. I have an early start in the morning.'

Afterwards, he wondered about the conversation, and whether he had missed a chance that might never come back.

John May thought about a lot of things that night. Now that the drifting cinders of rebellion had burned themselves out, it felt as if deep and lasting change was in the air. The events of the past had a habit of closing off their chapters and filing themselves away with times, dates and brief descriptions, as though they knew they would one day be required by historians.

And what would historians write of the Peculiar Crimes Unit? That it was another eccentric English institution populated by the sort of strange characters who'd worked at Bletchley Park? Would they recall the incendiary history of the unit and its founders, how they'd deciphered the hidden cryptography of London's most elusive mysteries, and how it had involved blowing themselves up in the process? *It really was a hell of a blast,* thought May as he lay in bed, remembering how his partner had managed to detonate staff headquarters and accidentally initiate a new phase in the life of the unit. *Only Arthur could manage to advance all their careers by killing himself at the outset.*

Chuckling to himself, he fell asleep and dreamed of Londons yet to come.

56

INTO THE UNKNOWN

On the Sunday morning that the case was officially closed, the rooftops of King's Cross were erased in a thick grey fog. Having barely slept, the staff members of the PCU arrived to hand over their documents to the City of London Fraud Squad. The investigation had ended up involving Dexter Cornell, who, together with his fellow directors, was eventually indicted on nineteen counts including fraud and conspiracy. A new company was appointed by the minister of state for international development, who promised 'total transparency'.

Once the public realized that the financier had not been burned alive, and was rather more prosaically awaiting charges in a police unit, the crowds milling around the Bank of England started to disperse as if they had reached the end of a noisy but ultimately unsatisfying Coldplay concert. It didn't help that Cornell issued endless statements through his lawyer about how badly he'd been treated. The more the banker tried to blame others for his predicament, the less interested people were in him.

Finally the revolution fizzled. The tents were folded up

and the placards were taken down, and everyone went back to doing the things they felt more comfortable doing: queuing for trains; standing at bus stops; wandering around shopping centres; complaining about the weather; and tutting over the sex lives of politicians.

The city cleaned itself up. The mayor was photographed holding a broom. MPs made impassioned speeches about 'why it must never happen again'. Life went on.

The fog descended like a veil of forgetfulness, covering the windows of the Peculiar Crimes Unit with racing rivulets and softening the contours of the buildings, turning London into a city of pallid ghosts. Traffic slowed and sounds faded until it felt as if everyone had glimpsed the limbo outside and gone back to bed.

The meandering towpath of the Regent's Canal, which curled from King's Cross to Camden Town, tapered away into oblivion at either end, and the sphere of fog enclosed them as they walked.

'You haven't said anything about my offer,' Renfield remarked in the most casual tone he could muster.

Longbright kicked a stone into the still green reflections. A duck answered and took off, the tips of its wings tapping the surface of the water. She wore a baseball cap over her burned scalp. It would be the first and only time she would ever do so.

'I was mortified when Darren Link came in and saw my Halloween outfit on the coat stand,' she said. 'It reminded me of when I was fifteen. My mother let me go to my first Halloween party at a school friend's house, and I worked on my outfit for weeks. I was a bit obsessed with naval heroes at the time, and somehow decided I should go as Sir Francis Drake. I made the whole outfit, working from a painting I'd seen in a book, except that the tunic was designed to completely cover me, leaving the starched ruff at the top with just a bloody stump sticking out, and I carried Drake's severed head, made out of papier-mâché, under my arm. When I got to the house, I realized I'd entirely misunderstood the purpose of a Halloween party. I was the only girl there who wasn't dressed as a sexy witch. That was when I decided I'd be sexier than the rest of them, and stronger too, just like my mum.'

She stopped and turned to Renfield. 'You see, Jack? I'm still like my mum, still in the force. And I know you. You asked me to marry you for the wrong reason. You thought you'd lost me. I'm grateful you came for me, but I'm not going to change. I'm always going to have this job. I'm always going to be a pain in the arse.'

'I didn't ask you to give it all up,' he said, taking her hand, 'just take something safer, where I can keep an eye on you.'

'Can you honestly see me in some MPS admin role?' She tugged her hand free. 'Look at me, Jack! This is who I am. And I love what I do.'

'You love it more than me.' It was a simple statement of fact that he challenged her to deny.

'I'm really sorry.'

'No, I'm sorry, Janice. I should have known better.'

He kissed her lightly on the cheek and took a step away. 'I've sort of enjoyed my time at the unit. It's been like sitting on the set of some really strange horror film, where you watch things going wrong and don't know whether to laugh or beat someone up. But I have to tell you: I'm not like Bryant and May. And I'm not like the rest of you.' He took a deep breath. 'I'm going to transfer back.'

'Jack—'

'We're just different people, Janice.' Renfield shook his head and smiled to himself. 'I know you all used to make fun of me. I wanted to earn your respect.'

'You did,' she said.

'But I shouldn't have had to.'

'It's not like you'll be gone forever. I'll still see you around.'

'I don't think that's such a good idea.'

'Well, you could at least give me a goodbye kiss.'

'Look after yourself, Janice.' He put his hands in his pockets and turned away, walking back up the canal path. His place was taken by a duck.

'Take care, you,' she called, watching him go. She dug out a tissue and blew her nose. 'I don't know what you're looking at,' she told the duck.

The following week, Jack Renfield applied to be transferred from the unit, and returned to his old position as a Metropolitan Police Service desk sergeant.

Back at the unit, one of the Daves scratched his arse with the end of a bradawl. He peered down between the uprooted floorboards, into the great hole they had made in the hallway. 'Stone me,' he said. 'How deep do you reckon that is?'

The other Dave stuck his head up from inside the pit they had created. 'I'm on the top step of the staircase,' he replied. 'I can't see the end of it from here. Bung us a torch.'

The first Dave poked about in his tool bag and handed down a rubberized flashlight.

'Jesus and Mary, you won't believe what's down here,' he shouted up from the darkness. 'You'd better call someone, fast!'

Colin Bimsley stacked the chairs in the common room and cleared away the last of the cups, but overloaded the tray and managed to drop it, smashing the lot and sending shards of china all over the room. 'Don't come in here!' he shouted, throwing out his hands in warning as Meera appeared in the doorway.

When no sarcastic reply came, he glanced up. She

looked as miserable as London in February. 'Are you all right?'

'Yeah,' she said, scuffing at her cheek with the sleeve of her sweater.

'Sure?' Colin set down his dustpan with a clang. 'You should be happy, what with getting married and everything. You'll soon be in Delhi, riding a painted elephant while everyone pelts you with marigolds. Big party, crying rellies, wedding singers, lots of dancing, pat the dog and screw in the light bulb.' He did a Bollywood bop. 'Crazy old mother-in-law, half a dozen nippers, learn to cook dahl, the works.'

'I'm not marrying Ryan.'

'You'll be able to say goodbye to this place—'

'*I'm not marrying him, Colin.* The wedding's off.'

'What are you talking about? It's what you wanted.'

'No, it's what my mother wants.' She threw her coat on to a chair and bent down to help him pick up the broken crockery. 'The two of them have been organizing the whole thing behind my back. He's become a total control freak.'

'They're probably just trying to take the pressure off you. They know how busy you are with the unit—'

'For God's sake, Colin, will you stop being so bloody *nice* for a minute?' Meera all but shouted. 'I'm trying to tell you something. I don't love him.'

'But you grew up together. You've got all these things in common.'

She released a weary sigh. 'It's not enough of a reason to marry him. I can't just do it to please my mum and my sister. I've got to want to be with someone so much that I can't imagine being with anyone else. I grew up with all those stupid romantic Indian movies like *Devdas* and *Veer-Zaara*. All they do is show you what you're never going to have. Ryan's like someone out of one of those films, and it's not what I want. Being with him – it's like being with a bloody Valentine card all the time. Every time he calls me sweetie I just want to punch him in the balls. That can't be love, can it?'

'Not when you put it like that.' Colin winced as he emptied more pieces of china into the bin. 'I'm really sorry, Meera.'

'So I guess you're stuck with me.' She gave a tentative smile.

'I never wanted anything else.' He smiled back. 'I'm dead boring like that. I'm never going to change. I'll always be here.' He spotted another piece under the table and stooped to pick it up. As he rose, she gave him a kiss on the cheek. Her touch was such a surprise that he gripped the fragment, cutting his thumb.

She pulled a tissue from her pocket and wiped away a single scarlet drop of blood. 'I'm sorry, I didn't mean to hurt you.'

His smile became a grin. 'You could never hurt me. I'm like a tree, rooted and solid. I'll keep the rain off you, Meera.'

She put her arms around him. Her head only came up to his chest. They stayed like that for some minutes. Outside the fog thickened, so that the sound of the traffic was completely lost, and all she could hear was the beating of his heart.

Down at the river it was hardly possible to see at all. Waterloo Bridge looked as if it was only half built. The far side had simply vanished. A barge drifted silently underneath, barely causing a ripple. It was loaded with building materials, but it might have been carrying Queen Elizabeth I and her retinue. One expected to hear only oars dipping into mirrored water, but all sound was now so muffled that it seemed as if someone was holding a pillow over the city.

John May walked slowly towards the centre of the

bridge. As he did so, a lone motionless figure slowly came into focus, leaning on the east-facing balustrade. May quickened his pace, gladdened to find his partner waiting. Of course he had been drawn back there, to the Thames, where his wife and brother had both tragically perished.

As he approached, Bryant seemed to sense that someone was coming and turned around to face him. He had a look of utter desolation on his features.

'I don't know why I came here or what I'm doing,' he warned, raising a hand. 'I think I caught the tube but I don't remember anything. I don't know what day it is, or where I am. How could I have caught the tube? I can't even find my pass.'

'You were all right earlier,' said May. 'You were in your office at the unit. I went to a meeting and when I came to look for you, you'd gone.'

'Then why am I here?' Bryant gestured at the river in puzzlement.

'We've always come here to think.'

'But where am I? *Who* am I?'

'You are Arthur Bryant,' replied May. 'And this is Waterloo Bridge.'

'I'm in London.' Bryant's cornflower-blue eyes widened in amazement. He leaned over the balustrade and looked down. A piece of driftwood passed beneath them with a seagull sitting placidly on one end. It flicked itself into the air and lolloped away across the gelid surface of the river.

'How does it feel?' May asked.

'It's hard to describe,' Bryant answered as he watched the bird evaporate into the gloom. 'I've used up the last of my strength. Everything is just falling away. It's like being a lost child. I can't recognize anything. But I'm not frightened any more. It all feels very peaceful.'

'That's because you know a secret now,' said May gently. 'You know that you're unassailable, and you don't have to worry about anything.'

'I wish someone had told me about this earlier.' Bryant smiled. 'The sense of fearlessness. It's very liberating. And once you can see that those closest to you aren't scared either, you can do anything you want. You're not scared, are you?'

'For you? I was earlier, but now I'm not.'

'That's good. You've no reason to be, John. It's like this.' He leaned his walking stick against the balustrade and held out his hands. 'Like gently walking into the fog.' He looked May in the eye. 'I'm not going to come out of the other side this time.'

'You can't know that.' May felt a terrible loss opening inside him.

'This time it feels different.'

'Arthur—'

'You know I'll still be with you. Here, on the bridge,' Bryant said. 'Whenever you come here, you'll be able to find me.'

'Arthur, don't go,' said May. 'We haven't completed our work.'

Even the fog could not hide Bryant's white smile now. 'Nobody ever completes their work,' he said. He felt for his walking stick and picked it up. 'Have I been very annoying? I mean, over the years.'

'Quite annoying, yes,' said May.

'Sorry about that.' He rooted about in his overcoat pocket and produced a creased fold of paper. 'Do you remember when we first met, I got you to translate a code made from butterflies?' He handed May the page. 'See if you're still up to it.'

May took the offering, puzzled.

'Well, I'd like to stay but my bones are getting cold.' Bryant rubbed his bare red hands together and looked out across the water. 'There's someone I have to go and say goodbye to.'

'Who?' asked May.

Bryant pointed to the smudged grey buildings that hemmed the river. 'Why, London, of course.'

He stood there for a moment, looking out at something May could not see. Then he turned and walked slowly away. After just half a dozen paces, he was already hard to make out.

A moment later, there was nothing ahead but the silent fog.

May unfolded the page Bryant had given him. Set across it was a row of red admirals, but the colours were all wrong. It looked like naval code. Admirals, that was the tip-off. Of course. He translated the letters.

W-E-R-E-O-U-T-O-F-T-E-A

It was the page that Bryant had handed him on the day they met, all those years ago. But now there were some more butterflies, rather more shakily drawn, in a separate line below.

G-O-O-D-B-Y-E-O-L-D-F-R-I-E-N-D

'Arthur, what will I do without you?' May called, seized with sudden anguish. 'How will I manage?'

In his heart he knew the answer to his question. Bryant had been right, as usual. They would always have Waterloo Bridge, on the span of the Thames, in the city which had created them.

Bryant & May Will Return

Christopher Fowler's Bryant & May Novels

'Witty, sinuous and darkly comedic storytelling from a Machiavellian jokester'
Guardian

FULL DARK HOUSE
In the Peculiar Crimes Unit's first great case, the detectives Bryant and May are caught up in a bizarre gothic mystery, which begins when a beautiful dancer is found without her feet . . .

THE WATER ROOM
An elderly woman's body is found. Her demise seems to have been peaceful but for the fact that her throat is full of river water . . .

SEVENTY-SEVEN CLOCKS
Strikes and blackouts ravage the country and members of an aristocratic family are being disposed of in various grotesque ways . . . but what have seventy-seven ticking clocks got to do with it?

TEN-SECOND STAIRCASE
A controversial artist is found dead, displayed as part of her own outrageous installations. No suspects, no motive and no evidence – just a witness who swears the killer was a masked highwayman on a black horse . . .

WHITE CORRIDOR

A blizzard sweeps the country, trapping Bryant and May on Dartmoor while back at the Peculiar Crimes Unit HQ in London, one of the team has been found dead. As the snow thickens a deranged killer is on the prowl . . .

THE VICTORIA VANISHES

On the trail of a killer who targets women at London pubs, Bryant and May find themselves on the pub crawl of a lifetime – and come face to face with their own mortality . . .

BRYANT & MAY ON THE LOOSE

A decapitated body is found in a shop freezer. Then a second corpse is found, again minus its head, and Bryant and May are called in to find the missing body parts – and the killer.

BRYANT & MAY OFF THE RAILS

Bryant and May are on the trail of an enigma: a young man with a false identity. All they know is that somehow he escaped from a locked room and murdered one of their best and brightest.

BRYANT & MAY AND THE MEMORY OF BLOOD

The defenestration of an impresario's young son was definitely not the best way to end the play's first night party. And the crime scene itself was most unusual. A locked bedroom. No sign of forced entry. No prints or traces of blood. Just a sinister, life-size puppet of Mr Punch lying on the floor . . .

BRYANT & MAY AND THE INVISIBLE CODE

While playing a game called 'Witch-Hunter', the children curse a woman and she dies. Her death baffles the coroner – and leads Bryant and May into a labyrinth of secret codes, covert loyalties, madness and murder.

BRYANT & MAY – THE BLEEDING HEART

A body rises from a grave and the ravens have been stolen from the Tower of London – each a perfect case for Bryant and May. But what their investigations unearth is even more disturbing than they could ever have imagined.

BRYANT & MAY – THE BURNING MAN

Anarchy threatens London's streets and a murderer with 'incendiary' methods of execution is at work. For Bryant and May it means confronting corruption, punishment, the history of mob rule and the legend of Guy Fawkes.

BRYANT & MAY – LONDON'S GLORY

Beginning with the case of a department store Santa Claus whose gifts can kill, here are eleven curious, compelling and never-before-told cases from the files of Bryant and May and the Peculiar Crimes Unit.

Discover Christopher Fowler's gloriously entertaining memoirs

PAPERBOY

'One of the funniest books I've read in a long time . . . this is the kind of memoir that puts most others to shame'
Time Out

'Anyone who remembers Mivvis, jamboree bags, streets with no cars, Sid James and vast old Odeons will love this Sixties retro-fest'
Independent on Sunday

'The book is fabulous, and I hope it sells forever'
Joanne Harris

'Paper-dry wit, natural charm, brutally funny anecdotes – Fowler's likeable memoir unearths the trail that led the schoolboy to become a writer'
Evening Standard

'Entrancing, funny, deeply moving and wonderfully written. Please read it'
Elizabeth Buchan

'An almost Morrissey-like lament . . . for a sixties childhood'
New Statesman

FILM FREAK

'Gold-plated writing: uproarious, then dark, and surprisingly moving *****'
Mail on Sunday

'An homage to pre-digital cinema, an elegy for a vanishing London . . . a tribute to friendship, gonzo-style. Two thumbs up for this triple billing'
Financial Times

'Charming, funny, perceptive . . . I found myself laughing loudly and lengthily. Above all, though, I was moved'
Daily Mail

'Brisk, chatty . . . trenchantly funny . . . he's so entertaining'
Daily Telegraph

'A master storyteller . . . a beautifully written and often hilarious book'
Sunday Express